D1360647

"If you love a suspenseful story, told with great skill, then you're definitely going to want to read this one."
— Steve Berry, *New York Times* and #1 internationally bestselling author of *The Amber Room* and *The Romanov Prophecy*

"*KGB Banker* is the espionage thriller at its finest. Timely and suspenseful, McCormick and Christmas use their wealth of experience in Eastern Europe to craft a pulse-pounding tale of spies, assassins, and financial corruption ripped straight from today's headlines. Santa Ezeriņa may be the best action heroine in years. A must read, destined to be a bestseller."
— Robert Dugoni, *New York Times* bestselling author of *The Eighth Sister* and *The Last Agent*

"Dark crimes, cool twists, and an even cooler reporter who just can't resist danger."
— Antony Johnston, *New York Times* bestselling writer and creator of *Atomic Blonde*

"*KGB Banker* weaves a complex web of deception and double-dealing. William Burton McCormick's and John Christmas's sterling pairing manages to achieve a delicate balance between financial thriller in the vein of Christopher Reich or Joe Finder and all-out chase novel reminiscent of David Morrell at his best. The notion of an American working at a corruption-riddled Russian bank that's part of a plan to reclaim Soviet hegemony is pure literary magic. Not to be missed."
— Jon Land, *USA Today* bestselling author of the *Murder, She Wrote* and *Caitlin Strong* novels

"A deftly written thriller with an insider's view into Eastern Europe. This book lands a death grip on the reader from the first paragraph that doesn't ease up until the last man has fallen. McCormick and Christmas open doors to the world of international banking and political intrigue, with a cast of characters so real you'll swear you've met them and a setting that comes to life. This just might be the international thriller of the year! A definite must read!"

　　—Chris Goff, author of *Dark Waters* and *Red Sky*

"From exciting start to finish, *KGB Banker* delivers high suspense, thrilling action, and political intrigue in a fascinating tale of financial corruption and Russia's tightening grip on the Baltic republics. Highly recommended."

　　—V.S. Kemanis, award-winning author of *Your Pick: Selected Stories*
　　　and the legal thriller *Seven Shadows*

"*KGB Banker* is a terrific thriller, set in the world of finance, and with fast action and great plot twists."

　　—Sarah Rayne, author of the *Phineas Fox* series

"In *KGB Banker*, McCormick and Christmas have created a timely and extraordinary work of international finance and suspense, steeped in rich settings and even richer characters, clearly one of the most exciting thriller novels I've read this year and leaving me pining for more of this epic saga!"

　　—Ronald S. Barak, author of the bestselling *JK's Code*, fourth in the
　　　Brooks/Lotello thriller series

KGB BANKER

WILLIAM BURTON MCCORMICK JOHN CHRISTMAS

MILFORD
HOUSE

an imprint of Sunbury Press, Inc.
Mechanicsburg, PA USA

MILFORD HOUSE

an imprint of Sunbury Press, Inc.
Mechanicsburg, PA USA

For information about special discounts for bulk purchases, please contact Sunbury Press Orders Dept. at (855) 338-8359 or orders@sunburypress.com.

To request one of our authors for speaking engagements or book signings, please contact Sunbury Press Publicity Dept. at publicity@sunburypress.com.

FIRST MILFORD HOUSE PRESS EDITION: September 2021

Set in Adobe Garamond | Interior design by Crystal Devine | Cover by Lindsey Korytowski | Edited by Lawrence Knorr.

Publisher's Cataloging-in-Publication Data
Names: McCormick, William Burton, author | Christmas, John, author.
Title: KGB banker / William Burton McCormick & John Christmas.
Description: First trade paperback edition. | Mechanicsburg, PA : Milford House Press, 2021.
Summary: What if you returned to the land of your ancestors and they tried to kill you? When Chicago banker Bob Vanags takes a job at ominous Turaida Bank in Latvia, he hopes to learn of his heritage and to fight economic fraud and corruption. But exposing his company's secrets come with a framed murder . . . and the threat of never returning home.
Identifiers: ISBN : 978-1-62006-669-0 (softcover).
Subjects: FICTION / Thrillers / Crime | FICTION / Thrillers / Espionage | FICTION / Mystery & Detective / International Crime & Mystery.

Product of the United States of America
0 1 1 2 3 5 8 13 21 34 55

Continue the Enlightenment!

Inspired by the whistleblowing of John Christmas.

PROLOGUE

Cruel eyes watched the yacht through binoculars. The powerful spyglass lenses picked up every detail as he waited three hours for the ship to move away from the shoreline and for the long dusk of Baltic summer to fade into night. The man behind the binoculars, hard and cold like the four men in the speedboat with him, possessed the patience of Job and a brutality worthy of Ahab himself. There was no anticipation, no excitement in their manner, only a bleak resolve. For tonight's work, they'd earn a year's salary in their homeland and not a man among them hesitated, least of all their leader. It was the way of things in this part of the world. Pity was an emotion of weakness, of youthful naivety long forgotten if it'd ever been felt at all.

Their speedboat, decorated with nets, poles, and battered freezers to appear a casual fishing dinghy, had followed the twenty-meter motor-yacht the entire day, out from Rīga's Andrejosta Marina, traveling north-east along the Latvian coast to the calm waters and sandy shoals of Vecāķi beach. Always remaining at a safe distance. Always farther out to sea than their quarry. The sole occupants of the yacht, a British man and wife, were certainly unaware they were being studied. Their actions proved it. The couple had spent their journey casually drinking on deck, playing cards, sunbathing, and periodically dancing as Robbie Williams's "Swing While You're Winning" album blared over the ship's loudspeakers. They'd twice made love, brief, mechanical affairs that brought laughter even to the dour men of the speedboat. Now a calm settled over the yacht. The wife sat in the bow, a drink in her hand, enjoying the sea breeze and sunset. The man was somewhere at the aft, unobservable at this angle, but surely leering at the nude and semi-nude bodies on the shore, the hundreds of naturists dwindling to a handful as darkness came.

A darkness the watcher and his men welcomed. They were professionals, trained and ready, and the time for action was close at hand.

Let the Britons come out to sea . . .

Taking little notice of a stray fishing boat on the horizon, far kinder eyes observed the elegant yacht riding in the waves just off Vecāķi's shore. Maija Banga, nineteen, sun-browned and nude sat on the white sands, the waters of the gentle surf washing across her bronzed toes. A strand of braided dark hair stretched over her shoulder, and an extensive tattoo of Laima, the Goddess of Luck in Latvian folklore spread across her back. She regarded the middle-aged man at the back of the yacht some fifty meters out with a mixture of curiosity and bemusement. Dressed in the clothes of casual summer wealth, he'd toasted her with the champagne glass in his hand three or four times before she'd finally raised her bottle of Bon Aqua more out of a genial sympathy than anything else. She knew him as a foreigner. No Latvian man would be so forward on a nude beach nor become so excited after such a minimal response.

If not Latvia, from where? A Frenchman would be more subtle. A Russian more stoic. A German . . . well, truly, do Germans flirt? No, this was an Italian or an American. Only they act like boys when they should act like men. Only they fall in love at first sight.

He toasted again. She waved back. Why not?

"Maija, don't lead the fellow on." Gray-bearded Jānis walked up to her along the water's edge, his brown body leathery and wrinkled from decades in the sun. "These strangers in our country . . ."

"His boat flies a Latvian flag, Jānis. And has a Latvian name, *Leesma.*"

"He's a stranger." He spoke firmly. "I know it and you know it."

Yes . . . She laughed to herself. These old-timers were so conservative, the naturists paradoxically most reserved of all. Jānis thought himself king of Vecāķi, blustery patriarch of the whole beach, settling all disputes and giving unwelcome advice to whomever he wished. He reminded Maija of her father. That dampened her mood.

She finished her bottled water. Watched the sea.

The man on the *Leesma* removed his white wide-brimmed sun hat, fanning himself with it as he motioned for her to join him on the ship.

Jānis shook his head. "Little good can come of this, Maija."

As much to spite Jānis as any other reason, she flashed the man on the yacht a smile, then found her bikini thong from among her things, slipped it on, and dove into the warm July waters. Maija covered the distance to the yacht with the long smooth strokes of an experienced swimmer, feeling the swell of the sea as she left the land behind. She reached the ladder hanging at the rear of the ship in less than a minute, gripped its chrome railings firmly and began to pull herself up.

The man at the ladder-top stood mouth agape, his eyes widened.

"Labvakar," she said.

He blinked a few times at the greeting and finally came to life. "Well, hello Luv," he answered in an obvious accent.

British. Well, not so different than American . . .

"Darling," he called to someone unseen. "We've unexpected company!" He helped her into the boat. "Do you speak any English?"

"A little." Maija replied with Latvian understatement. She was nearly fluent.

Close in, under the shade of the aft deck's awning, Maija observed details of the man unseen from shore. The Englishman was about fifty, not unhandsome, but with thinning red hair above a high forehead and the growing belly of midlife. His skin wore the pink of a fresh sunburn, patches of blazing white at the neckline revealing he was not often outdoors. Despite the yacht, Maija could see he was no man of leisure who spent his life on beaches, resorts, and golf courses. Her host still had to be indoors to work for a living.

A woman, trim and attractive, about the same age as the man, came around from the front. She wore oversized sunglasses that covered most her face, yet still left room to convey an expression of annoyance.

Without a word, she slid open a door and went inside the cabin.

The man laughed, a trace of discomfort in it. "Richard Ash." He smothered Maija's hand with his soft, white fingers. "The lady inside is my better half, Mindy. And your name?"

"Maija."

"Pleased to meet you Maija. Come inside, we've the conditioner on."

She followed him into the ship's main cabin, the interior little darker than the exterior with the burning reds and oranges of a Baltic sunset shining through the yacht's expansive windows.

The woman, Mindy, pressed a button on a console near the door. Shades lowered across all but the most forward windows. Interior lights came on.

"That glare was too much," Mindy said. "Richard, may I see you for a moment outside?"

His smile spoke of surrender. "Certainly, my dear. Make yourself at home, Maija."

She thought to protest, to ask their pardon for her apparently troubling appearance on the ship, but her hosts were out the cabin in an instant, the door firmly closed behind. She heard their half-hushed voices arguing. She tried not to listen.

Maija sat down on one of the plush chairs of the interior, felt its rich fabric tickle the bare skin of her back. The *Leesma* was like no ship she'd ever been aboard with long luxurious couches, elegant glass coffee tables, and dark wood paneling on the walls. It felt closer to the posh lobby of some five-star hotel than a ship's cabin. Off the room's center, a thin spiral staircase passed up to the flybridge and down to a lower cabin, where the bedrooms must lie.

She sat patiently while the Ashes talked outside, feeling the boat gently rise and fall in the surf, running her finger across the glass of an aquarium set into the wall behind her chair. A shimmering green-yellow fish followed the path she traced. It had never occurred to Maija to have an aquarium on a boat when the sea flowed under your feet, filled with greater wonders waiting to be discovered. Some people had to contain things, she thought, to control them.

Sad.

She heard the door slide open from the front deck, Richard's whispers seeping in with it:

" . . . product of a little innocent flirting from the beach, dear. I didn't know she'd come aboard." He smiled as he stepped inside, raising his voice. "But she's here now, and more than welcome." Richard crossed the room to the aft corner, unlatching cupboard doors set in the wall. "Would you like a drink, Maija? Let's see what we can find in the wine cabinet."

Mindy sat down on a couch across from Maija. She removed her sunglasses revealing the lines of middle-age circling piercing green eyes.

"How do you know English, Luv?" Mindy asked in a tone more tolerant than friendly.

"I worked as a waitress two summers in Great Yarmouth."

"Yarmouth? I'm surprised you learned a word there." She glanced down at Maija's bare torso. "Were you only a waitress? Or perhaps some sort of dancer?"

The way she said 'dancer' . . . The English and their fear of the human body. "Only a waitress. And then a term of uni at East Anglia."

"Oh, that's better." Mindy nodded approvingly. She lifted a sherry dispenser from a table near the couch, held it high to the light.

"Amontillado, Maija?"

"It looks empty."

"So it is," Mindy said disappointed. "Richard loves the stuff. It's amazing he can pilot the ship." She raised a finger as if to keep it a secret, though he must have heard.

Maija smiled politely, unsure what reaction Mindy wanted. "What brings you both to Latvia? Tourists?"

"We're living here two years come September. Richard is a big fish at a bank in Rīga. This is even their ship."

"Was a big fish," Richard said, leaning over his wife's shoulder to fill her glass with Bacardi. "Gave my notice last week." He handed Maija a glass, emptying the rum bottle into it.

"Yes, was," repeated Mindy. "We'll be moving back to Chelsea it seems."

"You don't like living in Latvia?" asked Maija.

"Latvia's not the problem," he said softly.

"You and your theories," Mindy said. "If you'd kept your mouth shut, you'd still have the job. We're lucky they still let us use the yacht . . ."

Some shadow passed briefly across Richard's face. Then he consciously brightened it. "That rum's the last of the spirits, Maija. And we've little more than crackers to feed you. We're poor hosts indeed." He glanced at his wife. "Let's head over to that barge restaurant moored near Mērsrags, we can invite our young guest."

Mindy shrugged, said nothing.

Richard turned to Maija. "Have you ever eaten at the Paradise on Waves?"

"It's awfully expensive, isn't it?"

"Our treat if you've the time."

Maija had nothing but time. And she knew Jānis would take care of her things on the beach. In fact, she rather liked that he'd have to do so. "Sure, I mean if I'm not a . . . 'what was the English expression?' . . . not a fifth wheel?"

"Third wheel," said Mindy with a laugh. "But since when did a spare tire trouble Richard? He's had one for years." She set her drink on the table, stood. "Well, you can't go into a restaurant like that," Mindy gave into the situation. "Come on, my dear, let's see what we can find you."

Mindy took Maija's hand, and they descended the twisting staircase to the lower cabin, passing through a door into a lavish bedroom with thin windows head-high in the curved walls looking out over the decking outside. The daylight gone, Mindy switched on an overhead lamp, then directed Maija to a wardrobe closet set in the wall. On the inside of the door was full-length mirror, the interior lined with shelves of soft, beautiful things.

"Try on anything you like," said Mindy. "Beach dresses, sarongs . . . We've Birkenstocks that might fit. The bikini tops may be a little loose. A bit of a hodge-podge, but it should work for a floating restaurant."

"You're very kind."

The ships engines roared outside, the cabin floor swaying with their power. A moment later, Richard's voice came through a speaker:

"Mindy, could you come up here a moment, dear? I want another set of eyes as I pull away from the shore."

"Excuse me," said Mindy, walking away briskly.

She paused at the door.

"If Richard's a bit friendly, it's only the alcohol, Maija. It gives him fantasies." Mindy frowned slightly. "I trust you know he's a happily married man."

"Of course."

"Thank you, dear."

Leaving the door open, Mindy disappeared up the stairs.

As the *Leesma* lurched this way and that, pulling away from Vecāķi and out into the Gulf of Rīga, Maija searched for the proper attire. She donned a top that loosely matched her bikini bottom, then slipped on a blue kaftan of the softest cotton. Maija stepped back and examined herself in the mirror.

She was too thin. An ungraceful girl, yet to age into elegance.

Maija looked at the beautiful clothes around her.

It would be nice to have such things. Someday.

She heard the engine of another motorboat outside, the roar lower, thinner as if from a smaller craft. Then shouts in Russian.

And gunfire.

Maija's mind froze, the stimuli flowing in too fast to process.

A clunk. The ship shuddered, like something hard and heavy had hit the *Leesma*'s hull.

More gunshots. Then a woman's shriek in the air, Mindy screaming something, her English too quick and tortured for Maija to understand.

Horrified, unsure what to do, at last Maija's body responded, at last it moved. She placed a knee onto the cushioned bench below the long thin windows, peeking up through the panes.

Black boots walked across the deck. Two pair marching towards the bow. Over the sea rail, from some lower unseen boat, climbed three more men, ski-masked and carrying black, military-looking guns.

A woman's feet in dark shoes met the boots, a second of chaos, struggle, then Mindy was thrown to the deck, her anguished face centimeters from Maija's, separated only by the thin pane of the window. Their eyes met in a moment of shared horror before Mindy was dragged away on her belly somewhere towards the bow.

The boots of the three late-arriving men headed another way. Towards the door to the cabins.

Maija ducked down.

The ship was suddenly too small.

Eyes wide with horror, pulse drumming in her ears, Maija tried to think. Was this piracy? Where was Richard? Where could she hide?

Half-panicked, she fled for the nearest cover. But the numerous shelves wouldn't let her force herself into the wardrobe closet, to shut the door. She abandoned it, sprinting into the toilet. It was the largest toilet she'd ever seen on a ship with a spacious floor and a full shower that could easily fit two.

Maija began to lock the door . . .

Her reason rebelled. If they try the handle, they'll know . . .

Instead, Maija loosened the light bulbs in the ceiling and around the decorated mirror until they all went dark, then crouched down in the shower bed, knees against her chest, pulling the curtain closed and prayed.

She sat curled in the darkness for what must've only been minutes but seemed like hours, thinking of her family, trying to calm herself, to slow her breaths and remain as still and quiet as possible. Heavy footsteps crisscrossed the ceiling above. Often there were shouts in Russian and English, but distance and the thundering of her pulse made them impossible to understand.

She heard men in the lower cabin. She closed her eyes.

Then a new sound plunged Maija into undreamt depths of despair. The yacht's engines roared to life, the whole ship lurching as it quickly changed directions, the floor bouncing, the walls shuddering against the waves as it picked up speed.

Where were we going? Going so quickly?

Her mind reeled. Staying hidden was no longer an option. She was being taken farther from her home every second. Waiting would only make it worse.

She raised herself up against the shower's shuddering wall, reached her feet, and prepared to open the curtain.

The toilet room door opened.

Maija dared not breathe. She pressed her palms out against the shower walls, wedging herself unmoving in the teetering shower stall.

She heard the repeated flicking of a light switch, on-off, on-off, a man muttering.

A voice in Russian called him.

He exited, leaving the door open.

Maija let out a tortured breath. A reprieve. Yet, their voices remained nearby, the conversation so calm and casual, Maija couldn't believe they were real, that this wasn't some nightmare from which she'd mercifully awaken.

And still the boat rocked over the waves, taking her farther and farther from any shore she knew. It was five minutes at least before the engines slowed and the ship returned to a cruising speed in a calm sea. The Russian voices grew momentarily excited, then receded. She heard their footsteps on the stairs as they climbed to the upper cabin.

Summoning all her courage, Maija stepped out of the shower and peeked around the doorway. The room was empty.

Maija knew little about boats, but there had to be another way out of this lower cabin. At the rear of the room were several paneled cabinets and she had the wild idea they might be storage compartments through which she could somehow escape up to the aft deck unseen. But the cabinets were locked. She rattled them fiercely, the sound she prayed camouflaged by the engine noise. But then the engines stopped fully.

The ship slowed to a stop.

There was no other choice. Maija dared to climb the stairs into the main cabin. The room was dark and thankfully empty of men. Though the shades were still down, Maija could see through forward windows that night had fallen completely outside. And what she spied in the lights of the foredeck filled her with horror.

Surrounded by these armed men, Richard and Mindy lay face down on the deck, the heavy chain of *Leesma*'s anchor coiled high between them. He was wounded in the shoulder, dark crimson covering much of his shirt. Whether Richard lay dead or merely unconscious Maija could not tell. Mindy, however, was clearly alive, sobbing uncontrollably, screaming out in anguish.

Both were handcuffed to the anchor chain.

"Please, please," begged Mindy. "I don't want to drown."

"You won't have time to drown, Mrs. Ash," answered the tallest of the invaders in perfect English, a man with cruel, stone-gray eyes. "The pressure will see that you don't."

The man signaled another, somewhere one of them pressed the button, and Maija heard the anchor's splash as it fell into the sea. The great chain rattled across the deck as it uncoiled, loop after loop tumbling over the side until there was nothing left and Richard and Mindy were spirited away in an instant, down into the depths of the Gulf of Rīga forever.

Maija did not remain to see more of this tragedy. Praying the execution kept the men's attention and the clattering of the chain covered her sounds, she threw open the rear door to the aft deck, sprinted over the tiles and dove into the sea. She plunged down, descending as deep as she could before kicking away through the inky depths.

At last, her lungs gave out and she was forced to surface. It was several long seconds, listening to her agonizing hoarse breaths, and feeling the rise and fall of the sea before she dared look back. She'd swum farther than she'd hoped, at least a hundred meters from the yacht.

All was quiet. No voices. No shouts. No calls of alarm.

Had they really failed to see her?

Maija treaded water for several moments considering a course of action. As she did, several men climbed down into the smaller boat adjacent to the yacht. Her blood went cold, yet she could only watch as they untied their craft. The little boat's engines roared, and so too did the heavy motors of the *Leesma*. The ships separated, churning the waters as they sped away.

Maija's stomach twisted in knots as she watched them go, praying they did not turn in her direction. But the distance only grew, expanding until the little boat disappeared into the night. The yacht's lights turned to pinpoints, dimming until they too were out of sight.

It occurred to Maija briefly that if the *Leesma* had left so quickly, with no sound of raising the anchor, that they must have unfastened its chain, and left it in the depths of the sea. That somewhere far below Richard and Mindy would rest undiscovered for eternity. That she now swam over their grave.

But such thoughts were fleeting. Maija had her own survival to think about. She looked to the heavens. Thankfully, it was a clear night. Maija had spent many summers on wilderness retreats with her parents. Being a naturist was more than being nude. She knew the stars and by them which way was east-southeast. East-southeast where there must be land no matter the distance.

Maija shimmied out of the drag of the kaftan and swam for home.

Fully clothed, Jānis Šimkus sat on the weathered beach log waiting for Maija. The small fire he'd made was dying after all these hours, the driftwood he fed it running out, and he had no desire to venture into the forests that fringed the beach to collect more fuel.

At his age he knew himself well. Knew he'd become an angry and irritable old man. He cared about Maija, fretted about the girl every minute. Yet even that emotion made him angry. She was off doing who-knows-what with that foreign man. Maija was a good child, he'd known her and her family for years, but this younger generation had forgotten their morals. It made a man long for Soviet days when there was an order about things.

Jānis watched a mosquito attempt to bite through the thick, sun-toughened skin of his arm. A futile attempt. As futile as waiting here. He flicked the insect away.

Enough of this.

Jānis stood; shouldered Maija's beach bag loaded with her things. Every regular at Vecāķi knew if they lost something, they could always call on him.

Maija would need her bag, keys, mobile soon enough. He only hoped she didn't wake him at some ungodly hour. She'd done it before. So had many others. They all depended on old Jānis.

He kicked sand over the fire until it smothered, then headed back to his old shack lost among the trees.

Yes, he worried for Maija. It was true. She didn't realize what sort of people populated this world. He sighed. Jānis Šimkus was too old to be everyone's chaperone.

Far out at sea, Maija saw the last light go out on the beach. Exhausted, head barely above water, she'd been unable to judge distance. Was it a bonfire? Or merely a small campfire? But now it was gone, and it seemed some of her strength went with it. Her left leg had cramped long ago. She'd fought it off with will and adrenaline, but it locked like a vice, folding up so her calf pressed tightly against the back of her thigh. Now her right quadriceps were knotting, the pain excruciating. Unable to kick with either leg, she floundered with her arms, her lower body dragging her down.

A swell caught Maija in mid-gasp and she swallowed water. She broke through to the surface again, but new waves pushed her down. She willed her legs to move, but they remained unresponsive as the surf punished her, driving Maija deeper. She spun in an undercurrent, unsure for a moment which way was up.

The currents kept her under too long, snaking along through the darkness. Maija thought of her mother as her lungs gave out and new waters flowed into her throat. She did not choke this time but grew strangely calm. Her body stopped resisting, flowing with the tides. It seemed forever.

At last, her bearings returned. Maija could see the surface far above and higher still the eternal stars over everything. It cheered her. The stars would remember.

And Maija Banga, nineteen, with the Goddess of Luck on her back, sank forever beneath the waves four hundred meters off Vecāķi beach.

PART I

1

At 6:15 A.M. in the Chicago suburb of Park Ridge, Bob Vanags's cellphone rang. Several long moments passed before he reached a hand across the mattress to seize the phone on the nightstand.

"Yeah."

"Bob, it's Joel Legg, executive recruiter."

Vanags rolled over on the bed. "Joel, do you know the hour?"

"Your fault, Bob. You never take my calls at work. Desperate times, desperate measures and all that shit."

"You can't send an email?"

"Real headhunters call. Listen, Bob, I've an opportunity for you. A new banking exec position has unexpectedly opened up—in Latvia."

Despite Bob's chronic exhaustion, he couldn't help but perk up at this. Latvia, the little country on the Baltic Sea, from whence Bob's parents came. Almost a mythic place to him. Often talked about but never seen. For most people, a job offer with the words 'in Latvia,' would be a joke.

Not for him. He wanted to see the homeland. "In Latvia, you say?"

"Downtown Rīga. The nation's largest bank, nearly fifteen billion in assets, wants a Westerner to be their face for meetings with major clients, investors, financial regulators, etc. Bring some money in, help rebuild their country. They need a sharp, polished presenter and a real top-flight trustworthy guy. I put 'honesty,' 'banking,' and 'Latvia' together and made you my first call."

This was interesting. He sat up in bed, tried to shake the cobwebs. "How'd you know I'd be interested in Latvia?"

"We keep notes on you guys after every conversation." Bob heard the rustle of papers on the other end. "I've got it underlined right here, May 12th, four years ago: 'Bob Vanags, Latvian-American, would love to work in Rīga for a few years. Banking, finance, real estate. Wife and son onboard with the move.'"

"It's just a son now."

"Sorry. Divorce is a terrible thing."

"No divorce."

"Oh . . . oh, Jesus, Bob . . . doubly sorry. Was it sudden?"

Diagnosed in September, deceased in February. Is that sudden? For pancreatic cancer not particularly. But it certainly felt sudden to him and David.

"Let's keep this to business, Joel." He glanced at the clock. "In fact, I should be going. I've a big meeting today. Call me tonight about nine."

"They want to fill this job quickly, Bob. These are serious people. They don't take 'no' for an answer."

"We'll talk tonight."

"All right. Good luck with your meeting. I hear it'll be a dozy."

"How could you know about the meeting?"

"An executive recruiter talks to fifty people a day, every day in your industry. There's nobody better informed than a headhunter. Nobody. We're like the CIA, KGB, and Microsoft all rolled into one. I say again, 'Good luck' with the meeting. I'm betting you'll be ready to take a job anywhere on the goddamn globe after it's over."

Recruiters . . . "Yeah, thanks. Talk to you tonight." He hung up.

Bob cracked his back, then lifted his reluctant body out of bed. The shower did little to wake him, and as he shaved in the mirror, he examined the man before him. The face staring back was that of a tired but handsome fellow of forty-one, though once the morning lines faded, he could probably pass for thirty. Bob took a lot of pride in those youthful looks. He'd kept a full head of curly blond hair and the athlete's body he'd sculpted while swimming for the University of Michigan. Indeed, he could slip into his old college Speedos without looking too foolish. He often did at the local lap pool.

A shame then to ruin it all with yellow teeth and fingers. Bob sighed. He'd restarted smoking, more fiercely than ever now that he was single again. Even shaved off his moustache when it became too stained. The special toothpaste and strips cleaned the teeth, and the lemon juice and hydrogen peroxide rinse fixed the nails. But he could still feel it eating him up inside.

An athlete who smoked two packs a day? Maybe Babe Ruth, Mickey Mantle or some other damn Yankee. As a Cubs fan, that wasn't right.

In his bathrobe, Bob went into the front room. His seventeen-year-old son, David, remained parked on the couch. Just where Bob had left him when he went to bed.

"You been up all night, David?"

"They were showing the top five spaghetti westerns of all time."

Bob walked into the adjacent kitchen, pulled a half-empty carton of milk from the fridge. "Who was number one? 'Fist Full of Dollars?'"

"'Django.' The original with some white Italian guy." David held up a crushed pack of Marlboros. "I found these in the patio chair cushions."

"Guilty as charged."

"It'll stunt your growth, Dad."

"All the other kids are doing it, Son." A lie. No one else smoked at Illinois Realty Trust, except the janitor and old Mary in accounting. It made Bob feel like a relic from another era.

He poured a glass of milk. "If I took a job in Europe, what would you think about that?"

"Where Spain? France?"

"Latvia."

"Oh . . . , he shrugged. "It'd be okay as long as we can stream the Bears games."

"You don't mind spending your senior year abroad?"

"I don't mind," he said softly.

Bob wished he minded. David should be attached to his classmates. Get out more. Socialize. Fight him about leaving. At his age, Bob was already sexually active. Had David ever kissed a girl? He certainly never had any significant girlfriend that Bob knew of. David could use a woman in his life.

They both could.

"It is a matter of ethics."

The well-dressed man across the desk from Bob blinked, an unwelcome astonishment growing over his wide face.

"You mean you're rejecting the loan, Bob?"

"I'm afraid I am, Mr. McMillan. I can't take the risk for this financial institution."

McMillan's cheeks began to redden as surprise turned to anger. "What risk? I've secured financing here for years. Never missed a payment, never one issue."

"Our decision is final, Mr. McMillan." Bob leaned back in his chair. He always became overly formal when delivering bad news. He knew it made him appear cold. A habit he wished to break.

"We're not required to reveal this Mr. McMillan . . . Patrick . . . ," Bob continued, "but as you've been a client of Illinois Realty Trust for a decade, I feel it's only fair to tell you our reasons. We've discovered assets of yours in Mexico, Asia, Europe. Assets undisclosed in previous loan applications, assets unknown to the IRS. And that's a problem."

McMillan's eyes grew colder. "Everyone at IRT knows about those properties. Your own president spent two weeks at my hacienda in Mazatlán last June."

"Well, now *I* know about them." Bob folded his hands together. "I'm sorry, Patrick. We're done here."

McMillan stood up, "I'll tell you who's done. You at this bank. And, if not, I'll see IRT in court. No one sullies my name."

"That is your choice, of course, Patrick. But in court our findings would become a matter of public record. Are you sure you want that?"

McMillan's jowly face contorted into a hateful rage. Muttering obscenities, he stormed out of the office.

"Have a good day, Patrick," Bob said softly.

A slamming door was the only reply.

Bob sat at his desk, massaging his temples. Sometimes he hated this job. No, in fact he *always* hated this job. He'd listen to Joel Legg tonight. How much worse could Europe be? He'd had enough of LaSalle Street crooks like McMillan.

Sam Whitcomb, a senior vice president and Bob's immediate superior walked in, a perplexed look on his neatly bearded face.

"Patrick McMillan is out in the hall going bat-shit crazy. You rejected the Oak Shores package? What's the deal, Bob? You tryin' to kill us?'"

"McMillan will be in prison this time next year, Sam."

"How do you figure that?"

"Remember the Festerton reception three weeks ago? Well McMillan got hammered and intimated to me he had tens of millions in unreported collateral to use for future loans. Quadruple his declared net worth, he said. Trying to impress me, I guess. Bad move on his part." Bob withdrew a thick Manila folder from his desk drawer, handed it to Sam. "I've a cousin in Minneapolis who is an investigative reporter, so I set him on it."

Sam flipped open the folder.

"Your cousin's name is 'Elvis?'"

"It's a common Latvian first name." Bob leaned forward, elbows on the desk. "Look Sam, the IRS will catch McMillan eventually. Elvis says they're pretty much onto him now. He'll go to jail and the government could collect all his assets. I can't let IRT be any more at risk then we already are."

Sam shook his head. "This report isn't official."

"I trust it."

"Bob . . . McMillan is pals with half the executive board. I'll catch hell for this and when I do, I'm going to pass that hell onto you."

"I'd hope you'd stand by me."

"Not this time. McMillan is too much a player." He tossed the folder down on the desk. "You can't wear the white hat every day, Bob. That's not how the world works. The bosses will override you."

"Just *read* the report. Show it to the Board if you want."

"Yeah, maybe. Go on home for the day, Bob. Spend time with that kid of yours."

"It's the right thing to do, Sam."

"It's the principled thing to do sure. But company politics have little to do with principles."

"I don't see it that way."

"Go home, Bob."

Home . . . "I'm thinking about it, Sam. I really am."

Joel Legg laughed over the phone. "I hear you almost gave old Pat McMillan an aneurism today."

"That's company business, Joel."

"It was all over the Loop by three o'clock. And if it's industry business it's my business."

"No comment."

"See that's what the boys at Turaida Bank in Rīga are going to love about you, Bob. Let's be honest, the reputation of banks in Eastern Europe is a bit suspect. With a sterling fellow like you out front, there will be no doubt what the company really represents. Western investors will flock to Latvia after meeting a charming fellow like you."

Such sugary words. "As long as I can make a difference."

"It checks all the boxes. Get to live in the land of your ancestors, check. Bring in investments, build infrastructure, make Latvia a better place, check, check, check. Work for a company that appreciates honesty, double check. Transparency is Turaida's motto. Perfect scores from every regulatory body."

He heard Joel lick his lips. "And you might even get yourself a pretty young thing over there."

"Save it, Joel." Bob looked down his notepad. Nothing much else to cover. "So, what's the hiring process?"

"They fly you over next week, interview the hell out of you for two days, then I go get you the best package available. Then you tell IRT and their old boy network to kiss your ass and start your life in Europe."

"This a new position?"

"Yeah."

"Well, who was doing the work before?"

A pause. "An English fellow. He left the company."

"You know why he left?"

Another pause. "Well, he didn't really leave. He died. I was trying to spare you the ugly details, Bob, but the guy and his wife were killed in some sort of diving accident."

"Diving accident?"

"They went out on the company yacht alone. The ship was found drifting empty in the Baltic Sea two days after they were due back. Some of the scuba equipment onboard was missing, so the Latvian police figure the couple must have gone diving and something went wrong."

"Terrible."

"Yeah, a good guy. Our affiliate office in London placed him there. You don't scuba dive, do you Bob?"

"Never."

"See, you got nothing to worry about."

"Sure."

Well, it was now or never. The land of his parents beckoned.

"Set the interview date, Joel. Let's get this thing done."

2

Nine days later, Bob Vanags walked through the medieval streets of Rīga's Old Town. A DSLR camera slung over his shoulder, his face shaded by the brim of his Cubs baseball cap. He'd come a day early to absorb the atmosphere of Latvia's capital. To see a slice of life in his family's homeland unrushed before the busy days of interviews starting tomorrow.

Rīga had not disappointed. For reasons he couldn't quite pin down, Bob felt at peace here a mere sixteen hours after arrival, an emotion growing more prevalent since he'd stepped off the plane. Surrounded by thousands of tourists on a sunny day, he instinctively knew he wasn't one of them. They were travelers, for them Rīga was merely a beautiful city on the banks of the Daugava River, a place to appreciate fabulous Art Deco architecture and sample sumptuous food. For Bob, pending a strong interview, this would soon be home.

It had always been home, somehow. And now that he was here, he wasn't risking losing Latvia. With a mixture of curiosity and instinctual preparedness, Bob needed to take a look at Turaida Bank's offices on this off day, to see exactly where the hub of his new life would be. So, there could be no surprises later.

Bob withdrew the crumpled city map from his jeans pocket, tried to discern his location. The Old Town was a charming labyrinth of little brick lanes, snaking this way and that off the occasional plaza or park. One wrong turn sent you into a side-street filled with colorful flower-boxed windows, silent smoking cafes, lively jazz clubs, or a pocket museum dedicated to some important point in Rīga's eight-hundred-year history. He'd made this pleasant mistake a half-dozen times this morning, tarrying too long at each discovery, and now navigated mainly by watching his position relative to the jutting spires of St. Peter's and the Dome cathedrals, the former towering into the sun, the later squarish and massive in shadow. Now he stood almost directly between them.

He studied the map again.

This way. Maybe.

Bob stepped into a narrow alley, the door to an amber shop on one side, the rear entrance to a restaurant on the other, the strings and flutes of Latvian traditional music seeping in through opened windows. Penetrating deeper, he passed under an archway at the alley's end, then out into a much wider street.

There it was.

Bob instantly recognized Turaida's headquarters from the photos on their website. A green and white, neo-classical building dominating the center of a major avenue, stretching at least a block in either direction. He felt a bit foolish, having struggled to find such a large street inside the Old Town. Okay, he *was* still a tourist. For now, at least.

Bob laughed at this and began a leisurely walk around the building to see the landscape. The ground floor contained the wide panel windows one would expect in a bank, through them he could see the service counters and currency exchanges for customers. The three stories above were decorated with office windows, while the roof, flat for the Old Town, held a surprising number of antennae and satellite dishes, their wires crisscrossing the surface down to the highest windows. It gave the impression of an old time, Old World structure jury-rigged for the modern age. All in a charming way.

As he continued to the bank's end, the avenue opened into a thin strip of parkland and he found himself within sight of the long yellow walls of Latvia's parliament building. Despite the proximity to such places of interest, the streets around him were sparsely populated by Old Town standards, even a bit lonely, and when Bob turned back to walk along the bank building's opposite side, the road grew practically deserted. Bob noticed too that on this side several of the windows on Turaida's top floor were heavily barred. He found this odd. Surely, the vault, day safe and all deposit boxes were on the ground floor. Who would climb four stories . . . to get . . . to get what?

Something to ask at the interview. He might even suggest they disguise those bars with some-sort of wrought iron design. Better for the bank's image. They'd appreciate his attention to detail, surely. Western thinking is what they wanted, Western thinking he'd give them.

He continued along the road until a large, gated tunnel opened up in the bank's walls. Through the gate, Bob could see an elegant interior courtyard inhabited by comfortable-looking chairs and tables resting in the shade of a maroon awning. Along one side of the courtyard was a small, covered parking lot.

Being a Sunday, he expected the building to be unoccupied, but to Bob's surprise, a white van was parked just inside the tunnel, a man with a rag washing its hood.

Working on the weekend, poor fellow. But this could be useful. You can tell a lot about an organization by how they treat their low-level employees.

"*Labrīt*," he said, motioning the man towards the gate. Bob's Latvian was embarrassingly basic. He preferred to try English. "Can you help me a moment?"

The man stopped his washing and took a few steps closer. He was tall and lean, with muscular frame straining his worker's overalls. His stare was cold with unblinking stone-gray eyes.

"Can you help me?" Bob repeated.

"Help?" The man replied in a tone that made assistance seem unlikely.

Bob wasn't quite sure if the man didn't speak English or was bemused at the idea of helping a stranger. "I just wanted to know if you like working at the bank." Bob donned a friendly grin. "Yes? At Turaida? They treat you well?"

"Closed. Sunday."

"Yes, I know. At the bank, you work here?"

"Closed."

"I see." Bob considered trying again in the little Latvian he knew, but something in the man's manner said, 'abandon all hope.'

"*Paldies*," he said leaving the gate. "Sorry, to bother you."

The man watched him go.

Bob retreated to an outdoor café across the street. Like much of this avenue it was empty. He ordered a latte, then a pancake and sour cream lunch, waiting patiently, basking in the late August sun. He was generally satisfied with his exploration of the bank's exterior. It'd be a nice place to work. Elegant with that Old-World appeal. So different than the glass boxes of American office buildings.

He removed his camera's lens cap, aimed it at the Turaida Building. Something to show David.

"No, no, no," said his waitress, walking up from the café's interior. "No photos of that building. Please."

Bob lowered the camera. "Why not?" I'm going to work there."

"You work there?"

"I will."

She paused. "Do you have identification? Proof that you work there?"

"For heaven's sake." He pulled out his smartphone, brought up an email from the bank's human resources director with an image of Turaida's triple serpent logo at the top.

"Satisfied?" he asked.

She said nothing. Nodded.

He took his photos.

The lunch came soon afterwards, the portions generous. When Bob tried to pay, she refused. When he left money anyway, the waitress followed him three blocks to give it back.

"We are all friends of Turaida," she said. "Please, don't tell them I troubled you."

3

"Terēze, call me 'Bob'. At last."

The woman at the desk in front of him laughed. "'Bob' does not fit well with the Latvian language. 'Roberts' sounds much better. 'Roberts Vanags, Vice President of International Relations at Turaida Bank Latvia.' Now, that rolls off the tongue. What do you think?"

"Is that an offer? I've another day of interviews, Terēze . . ."

She waved this off. "A formality. I'm the decision maker here, Roberts. As long as you don't punch anyone in the nose tomorrow, the job is yours."

Bob smiled. "I'll do my best to refrain from violence."

"Do so. We've such a peaceful work environment at Turaida."

Terēze Ābele, Turaida's Senior Vice President of the Capital Markets Department, had pleasantly interviewed Bob for half the afternoon. She was a tall, broad-shouldered, almost-suspiciously-buxom redhead in her early fifties who did most of the talking. She spoke little about banking, less about his role at Turaida, mostly about life in Latvia. It was, frankly, the easiest interview he'd ever had.

And the Turaida organization was far more impressive than the headhunter had said. Not only was Turaida Latvia the largest bank in Latvia, but with banks in four other countries—Estonia, Lithuania, Moldova, and Ukraine—the Turaida Group's total assets were north of seventy billion U.S. dollars. A leader in the free states of the former Soviet Union, Turaida employment offered the opportunity to visit amazing cities, experience new cultures, help emerging economies throughout Eastern Europe.

A far cry from arranging tax shelters for criminals like Patrick McMillan in Chicago.

Terēze glanced at an elegant watch on her over-tanned wrist. "Almost three hours exactly. Let's have a cigarette, Roberts."

This he liked. That Latvians assumed you smoked rather than the reverse. No more excuses, no more shame for a cigarette break.

"Of course, Terēze. Where?"

"This way, VP Roberts."

She rose from her desk, straightened any wrinkles in her sky-blue suit-dress, and led him out of her expansive, conservatively styled office. The Capital Markets Department dominated most of the second floor of the Turaida Building, decorated in oak paneling, heavy desks of dark wood, marble columns, and brass everywhere—brass on the stairway railings, on the frames of the diplomas and awards on the walls, and in the assorted classical figurines on the desktops. The people smartly dressed as any LaSalle Street firm, the women's dresses a little higher, the cleavage a little more and both sexes noticeably thinner than Americans. Latvians are a conservative people but at Turaida employees apparently dressed to impress, each person a product selling themselves as a brand. It didn't quite fit Bob's personal Midwestern tastes, but as his main job would be to sell Turaida as a partner to foreign banks and investors, having a staff that presented well would be a boon indeed.

They reached the elevator doors—brass-looking, naturally—and stepped inside.

"The smoking café is one floor up," said Terēze. "Coffee, tea and an assortment of cigarettes, cigars, and pipe tobacco free to all employees."

As she pressed the button for the third floor, Bob noticed the button for the fourth had key access only. He recalled the bars on one side of the building.

"What's on the fourth floor?" he asked as the elevator doors closed.

"The offices of Turaida's president, Baiba Lāce, though she's never here. And two foreign investors. They too are usually absent. We call it the 'ghost floor.' Always empty."

"I saw bars on a couple of the windows."

Terēze nodded. "We've a few holding pens up there. The Latvian police are notorious for being late when called for an emergency, Roberts. If our security catches some criminal—a thug with a gun holding up the tellers downstairs or some white-collar embezzler on the floors above—we need to have a place to keep them until the authorities arrive. Why not the 'ghost floor' where there'll be less of a disturbance?"

The doors opened. She held them ajar, letting Bob exit first. "Fortunately, in my fourteen years at Turaida we've never needed those cells, Roberts. Not once."

"Nice to know."

The third floor, dominated by local mortgages and administrative operations, was less richly decorated than the second or the lobby. Cubicles and movable-partition walls in gray or maroon stretched out before them under a lower ceiling. No brass or marble to be found, instead potted plants were the accessory of choice, sitting at every corner, giving the whole scene a needed shot of greenery. The staff was generally younger here, even thinner, though nearly as well-dressed as their second-floor colleagues. Fashion-model-looking people with fine features and sharp Baltic cheekbones passed to and fro in front of Bob as Terēze directed him to a ceiling-high glass partition at the very end. They walked into a room of billowing smoke, coffee tables, and low, plush chairs. At one end of the sparsely populated room was an opening to a small, neo-classical balcony, nearby a cart displaying an impressive range of tobacco products, as well as teas, chocolates, and bags of coffee beans. The uniformed elderly woman standing behind looked barely awake.

"What would you like, Roberts?" Asked Terēze, walking to the cart.

"No worries. I've some Marlboros in my suit pocket."

"Nonsense. Anna, an Insignia for me and Louixs for the gentleman."

The woman went to one of several glass-paneled humidors in the corners, returning with a cigarette for Terēze and a cigar for him. She handed them out, then lit the ends with a silver lighter emblazoned with the Turaida coat-of-arms.

Bob and Terēze took seats in the room's center, puffing away silently for a few minutes.

This was the life . . .

Something twinkled in Terēze's eyes and he found she was watching him carefully, sizing him up. Finally, she said: "So, Roberts, I have done most of the talking this afternoon. Tell me. Why do you *really* want to come to Latvia? It's not the money, surely there is more in America. It can't be the title; what use are those? The women? You are handsome. You'd never be lonely anywhere unless you wished to be. It isn't just to research your ancestors, Roberts. You could do that on a week's vacation. Or over the internet. So, why live here?"

"The weather," he said jokingly.

"As good as the weather is in summer, we pay for it with hellish winters."

"It's Chicago all over again," Bob answered with a smile. "You want the truth, Terēze?"

"Some women like to be lied to. I'm not one of them."

"I wish to be my father's eyes."

"I don't understand. What do you mean?"

"Do you have time for a story?"

"You have until my cigarette is finished, Vice President Roberts."

"Deal." He took a last puff of his cigar. "In 1959, at seventeen, my father left Rīga to attend university in East Berlin. It was difficult to get an appointment outside of the Soviet Union, even in the Eastern Bloc, but the East Germans were desperate for future scientists after the brain drain of the previous years and my father had perfect marks. When he arrived in East Berlin, my father could see things were changing between the two sides, that should he wish to go West it would only become more difficult. With no warning to our family back in Latvia, he boarded a train to Rostock. At that time, many East Berlin train routes still passed through West Berlin to leave the city, even those bound for East Germany. It was the last residue of a united Germany. So, when his car passed briefly through West Berlin, he made his peace with God and jumped off."

"A most dangerous action."

"Yes. He landed in a field. A dirty open lot on the edge of the city. As he lay there, recovering only for the briefest moment, a car one or two behind passed with *transportpolizei* on it. They saw him, they had pistols and rifles ready. They might have shot him there in the dirt easily. The laws allowed it. He never saw a train move so slowly. But he believed in the humanity of the men holding guns, that they would not murder him for such a simple action as jumping off a train. And the *TraPos* didn't fire, Terēze. They shouted, they cursed, but they didn't fire. It was a great lesson, a lesson he passed onto me about the spirit of mankind. I've never forgotten it. My father safely entered West Berlin. A year later, maybe a little more, they finished the *Berliner Außenring* and moved the train routes. His escape would have become impossible."

Bob took another puff of his Louixs. "In Germany, my father met my mother. She was Latvian too. Her family had escaped to the West before the end of the war. Eventually my parents immigrated to Michigan where I was born."

"My father's family back in Rīga paid for his sins. He never saw them again. The Soviets deported his parents to Vorkutlag above the Arctic Circle. My grandfather did not survive to return. My grandmother remarried and died in 1987. She's buried near Daugavpils."

"The guilt over their fates crushed my father. Even when Latvia regained independence, he did not visit this country. Time has abated his pain a little, but now he's old, too ill to travel. I must see Latvia for him, Terēze. I must be his eyes; can you understand that?"

She looked at him curiously for a long time. Then: "I do. Now let me show you what my eyes see."

Terēze put out her cigarette, rose, and bid him do the same. To Bob's surprise, she took his hand and directed him out to the tiny balcony. The two of them could barely fit, standing shoulder-to-shoulder, looking out over Rīga's Old Town.

"I come here twice every working day to see this view freshly, Roberts," she said. "I like to count the changes. The Old Town around us is incredibly beautiful but moored to the past. And here—see the parliament building, the *Saeima* and there the Latvian president's offices? A government striving at democracy, imperfect, but doing its best during impossible times. How can we help them?" She pointed. "Look beyond the Old Town, Roberts. Do you see the buildings going up in the center? The development of all sorts? Those are funded by Turaida. Every day, I see them advance, little-by-little making Latvia better. Stronger. Fully equal to Europe. As it should be. In a year's time you won't recognize this view, Roberts. And through you, your father will see wonders undreamt in 1959. Any sacrifice is worth that."

Her cellphone rang. Terēze spoke briefly to someone on the other end, then said:

"Your limo to the ethnographic museum is here, Roberts." Something sparkled in her eyes. "What if we change the plans a bit?"

"If we need more interview time the museum can wait, of course."

"You misunderstand me, Roberts. We'll have the driver take you to Daugavpils so you can visit your grandmother's grave. Do you have the address of where she's buried?"

"I do. But Daugavpils is so far away. I can't ask you to spend the petrol."

"No place is far away in Latvia. We are not so big as America." She laughed. "I'll have the driver pick up the company photographer along the way, so you can take professional-quality pictures at the gravesite. For your father. Family is most important in our culture."

He never imagined he'd have time to go out to the gravesite on this first visit . . . "If you're sure it's no trouble."

"The driver will wait as long as you need and have you back in Rīga early enough that you'll be well-rested for tomorrow's interviews." She walked him back through the third floor to the elevator. "I don't want you grumpy and punching people in the noses remember?"

"Okay."

"I've someone to chat with on this level, Roberts. The driver is waiting for you in the lobby. Have a safe trip to Daugavpils. If I don't see you in the office tomorrow, then we'll meet for dinner that evening. *Atā.*"

"*Atā!*" Bob said, stepping into the elevator. "And thanks again, Terēze. I'm grateful."

"It is nothing."

The doors closed.

Taking a limousine all the way out to Daugavpils. And at IRT he couldn't even get Sam Whitcomb to comp him for an "El" train ticket.

The doors opened on the second floor. A dark haired, ruggedly handsome man of about thirty stepped in.

"*Labdien,*" said Bob.

The man looked at him, smirked. Then said in clear English: "By your accent, you must be the American chasing the veep position?"

"Latvian-American actually."

"How's it going? Terēze treating you well?" He asked with more than a little hostility in his tone.

"Couldn't ask for better."

The man looked at Bob darkly. "I've got one word of advice for you."

"What's that?"

"Run."

The doors opened and the man walked out into the lobby. Bob tried to follow up with him, but his limousine driver stepped in the way.

"Hello! I am Alberts! You are Roberts Vanags? We go to Daugavpils?" he said in broken but very enthusiastic English. "Now we go? Long drive, yes?"

"One moment." Bob walked over to the girl at the lobby desk. "Excuse me. Who was that man? The man who just got off the elevator with me?" He watched the fellow march through the main doors and disappear into the busy streets of the Old Town.

"That's Ēriks Helmanis," said the lobby clerk. "He's our assistant director of international relations. Do you want me to buzz him back?"

Assistant director of international relations . . .

Someone in line for the same job as he was. Probably bitter they're trying to give the vice-presidency to an outsider . . . Such tactics were most unwelcome. If Bob *did* become Ēriks Helmanis's boss, he'd have a stern heart-to-heart with him the first day.

"No, Miss. Thank you." He turned to the limousine driver. "Let's go Alberts."

Late the next evening, Bob Vanags dined with Terēze Ābele and her family at the rooftop restaurant *1221* in the Old Town, the mammoth tower of the nearby Dome Cathedral a truly impressive backdrop for their meal. A slight breeze had relieved a little of the late summer heat, making for a pleasant environment for discussion. Despite the presence of Terēze's family in many ways the conversation still felt one-on-one. Terēze's husband, Markuss, a smiling bear of a man in a wide-collared suit jacket, spoke no English and her son, Stefens, a young fellow a year or two older than Bob's own son, was more interested in flirting with the waitress than chatting with his mother's latest business associate.

By the time the sea bass was finished, and the wine glasses refilled, he'd learned many interesting things about his future employer. That Terēze was a quarter Azerbaijani on her mother's side, that she held an MBA from Columbia and had worked during the '90s in New York and Texas for various banks and financial consulting firms, including two years for the doomed Enron Financial Corporation (though Terēze claimed she was long gone before any scandal). That she loved Hillary Clinton, though she thought Bill a "weak man troubled by lust."

After cigarettes together at the roof's railing, he and Terēze returned to the table to find her husband had grown bored of looking at Bob's graveyard pictures from Daugavpils and instead offered to show his own photos on his iPad. He swiped through dozens of digital pictures. The family had a luxurious house on the Majori beach; another, older son, now off studying at Moscow State University; Arabian horse stables at Bauska near the Lithuanian border; a Maltese puppy named Porziņģis.

An office party picture appeared on screen, Bob's elevator 'adviser' Ēriks Helmanis right next to Terēze pouring her a glass of champagne.

You've got the job, don't blow it Bob . . . A complaint about Helmanis would only show him unable to handle his own issues.

A few more swipes. There was the exterior of the Turaida Building. Bob guessed *someone* could take photos of it.

"I tried to take almost this same picture."

"And you were prevented?" asked Terēze, leaning over her husband's shoulder.

"Initially. At a café near the offices."

"Oh," she said, appearing almost relieved. "Turaida owns all the buildings on the perimeter of the main offices, Roberts. We encourage our tenants to thwart picture-taking."

"Why?"

"To prevent enemies from finding weakness. You'll note we only show the offices from certain angles on the website or company literature. The first principle of Turaida is 'transparency,' but 'security' is a close second. Very close."

"'Enemies?' Like thieves or robbers?'"

"Yes, like them."

With all the tourists in the Old Town Bob thought that'd be simply impossible to police.

Terēze's husband said something in Latvian too complex for Bob to follow. The couple bantered back and forth for a few minutes, Markuss laughing heartily at the end. He then resumed swiping.

They soon came to Terēze lounging sexily on the deck of some fabulously looking ship. She looked good for her age in the itsy-est bikini Bob had recently seen. In the next picture she wore even less.

Bob felt himself blushing. He looked over to Stefens, but their son had long abandoned the table for the waitress station.

The husband smiled at Bob, a proud look on his face. "Eh? Eh, Roberts . . . ?" he said in some universal language. "Eh?"

"Another picture," said Terēze in a tone of light censure.

A swipe to the next. A landscape shot of the whole ship, a luxurious yacht cruising near some forested island. "Leesma" written on the bow.

"Is that the ship Richard Ash was on when he died?" asked Bob.

Terēze did not hesitate in her response.

"Yes. Tragic."

"What happened? If you don't mind me asking?"

"No, of course not." She whispered something to her husband, and he closed down the iPad. Then Terēze moved to a seat at the table near Bob. "The latest theory is they drowned while scuba diving. The *Leesma*'s anchor somehow became dislodged. It was missing when the ship was found. The police believe it may have come loose while Richard and his wife were underwater, and the yacht drifted out of their swimming range by the time they surfaced. There are terrible currents in the Gulf of Rīga. If a ship is not secured it can be carried away in minutes. They would be separated quickly." She sighed. "Richard and Mindy Ash must have floundered until their strength gave out. Poor people."

"I'm sorry for your tragedy."

Terēze's husband began to sniffle.

"Yes, it has devastated the office," she continued. "Richard was very well-liked. There were several of the younger ladies on the third floor who had grown quite attached to him. This I can say with certainty. And Mindy . . . she and I attended a spa together only last May. So sad."

Terēze took a glass of wine, massaged her husband's shoulder with her free hand. "But, without sounding cold, I think it was a bit of their own fault if I may be honest, Roberts. You should always have a dive master with you and leave someone on the boat for just these sorts of problems. Turaida offers both as a perk when an executive takes out the *Leesma*. Markuss and I never go out without one. The master is the fellow who took those pictures."

Stefens tried to revisit the table, but Terēze directed him away with a flick of her wrist. She watched him go before returning her gaze back to Bob.

"Richard wanted to be alone with Mindy, to be romantic, Roberts. And to pilot the yacht himself unfortunately."

Her green eyes welled up.

"And now they are no more."

4

Terēze Ābele personally drove Roberts Vanags to the airport the next morning, wishing him a safe trip and assuring the candidate he'd have a formal offer by the time he landed in Chicago. When his plane was safely in the air, she returned to the Old Town, driving through the tunnel in the Turaida Building to park her Mercedes in her spot within the inner courtyard. Ignoring her office for the moment, she took the elevator to the fourth floor, walked down the east hall past the eternally empty offices of the president and the foreign investors to a metal door at the end. Terēze was immediately buzzed into a small room with computers on the tables, heavy bars on the windows.

The room's sole occupant, a stern, bald man of about thirty-five sat behind a desk cluttered with electronics, his blue eyes intensely examining Arabic writing on his computer screen. He did not look up at his visitor when he said:

"Good morning, Terēze. What was your assessment of the applicant yesterday?"

"High. Any partnering bank, client, or policing agency will see nothing but an honest, earnest, and trustworthy man in Roberts Vanags. He thinks he's Latvian but is a 'Captain America' type through and through. Pending anything startling from your department, I want to hire him."

The man looked up at her at last, sat back in his chair. "I wish you'd give us another week before extending an offer. There are branches of his family not fully investigated. It's hard to track them down in the United States. They anglicize their names often. He could have connections to the American government, CIA, media . . ."

"I need a Westerner *today*, Kārlis. Richard Ash's accident was most poorly timed."

Something glimmered in Kārlis's eyes. Something like pride. "Fate, Terēze, has its own agenda."

"And what is the Scorpion's agenda?"

"Whatever he tells me it is. Don't ask questions Terēze, we need to maintain your plausible deniability. It's better for you, better for us."

"I wonder." She watched him close the window with Arabic writing, an assortment of windows popping up behind in English, Latvian, Russian, French, German, Polish, Lithuanian, Romanian. Others she didn't even recognize.

"We can always withdraw the offer to Roberts Vanags if you find anything damning, Kārlis. Give me your report."

"I don't like your tone, Terēze."

"And I don't like delays. I've a bank department to run. Proceed."

"You act as if you want the bank to succeed, Terēze?'"

"Proceed."

With a sigh of resolution, Kārlis maximized one of the English-language windows on his screen.

"Roberts Vanags's academic records at the University of Michigan were exceptional as they were for his master's degree at Northwestern near Chicago. His work record is equally outstanding. A few remarks about a lack of tact early in his career, but consistent praise for Vanags's presentation skills and dedication in recent years. He's advanced quicker than his peers, Terēze. Most importantly, he's renowned for bringing up ethical issues with his superiors which means if there are any potential problems, he'll let us know first."

"Good."

Kārlis maximized another window, this one in Latvian. "Here in Rīga our people found nothing amiss in his behavior. No trips to casinos or gentlemen's clubs. He rejected the escort we sent to his room." Kārlis sneered at this. "Could mean he's moral, could mean he's a homosexual. Either way, nothing anyone could use against Roberts or us at the moment. He spent most his free time in the Old Town visiting art galleries and cigar taverns . . . he's quite a smoker this one. We collected hairs from his hotel shower drain, had them tested." He switched to yet another window. "Tobacco only, nothing stronger."

"Any points of concern?"

Kārlis shrugged, massaged the stubble on the back of his shaved head. "He visited the Occupation Museum twice which might indicate an anti-Soviet political bend. And then there was this phone call with his son . . ."

He pressed a button on his desk. Roberts's voice played over the room's speakers. ". . . have you been doing while I've been gone, David? No wild parties, I hope."

"Dad," said a younger voice clearly annoyed. "I'm sitting here alone drinking soda, watching 'Godzilla vs. Megalon' on the SciFi channel."

"Fast Times at Maine South High, eh?" Roberts sounded almost disappointed.

"I don't get that, Dad."

"No, I guess you wouldn't."

Kārlis stopped the playback. "We're investigating to see if this 'Godzilla vs. Megalon' is a code for something but think it likely harmless."

"Anything else?"

"You wanted a thorough job, Terēze. Investigations take time."

"And what of the boy?"

"The son, Dāvids, has been relatively sedentary. One trip to a local swimming pool where he worked a shift as a lifeguard, regular visits to quick food restaurants. He is apparently studying for a boating license and attended a class at a marina on Monday. He also spent three hours last night at a store for comic book magazines but bought nothing. Other than that, Dāvids remained at home. The private detective we hired is on retainer another week. We'll get more."

Kārlis tapped a few keys on his keyboard. "There was one bit of good news. On a blog from 2012, the now-deceased wife, Maria, mentions their son was named after Dāvids Osis, the Latvian politician. Apparently, he was something of a hero to Roberts Vanags."

"If I'd known, I could have introduced them during the interview process."

"Well, it could have benefits later on."

Kārlis reached down and lifted a television monitor from the messy floor beneath his desk, shoved it onto a shelf nearby with a hefty crunch. "That's it for my report. Now, that you've had a chance to assess my work, we should assess yours."

"What do you mean?"

"There's trouble again in your department, Terēze." He hit a button. A black-and-white image appeared on the television monitor. Roberts Vanags was standing inside the elevator, pleasantly staring forward. A door opened and Ēriks Helmanis, Terēze's Assistant Director of International Relations, stepped in.

"Let me get the sound," said Kārlis, fiddling with some switches on his desk. He was late feeding the audio, but when the voices broke in over the speakers it was enough to turn Terēze's blood cold.

"I've got one word of advice for you."

"What's that?"

"Run."

Kārlis paused the playback. "You really can't mind your store, can you Terēze?"

"I'll fire him immediately." She rushed to the door but Kārlis wouldn't buzz her out.

"Let me go."

"No, no," he said. "I talked to Moscow last night. The Scorpion wants Ēriks to stay."

"How can he stay after that?"

"Oh, it gets worse. Ēriks is calling newspapers again."

"Again?"

"He was too close to Richard Ash, Terēze. We should have seen this. Fortunately, Turaida still has a man on every newspaper board in the country to block the stories." Kārlis switched off the monitor. "Every board but one. You ever heard of the *Baltic Beacon?*"

"No," she said tersely.

"It's a combination gossip rag and tourist pamphlet. It's junk, never been worth the money to keep someone there. Problem is they've one reporter who has broken criminal stories. A few big ones. A woman named Santa Ezeriņa. Ēriks has been calling her to set up a meeting."

"What's he told her?"

"Nothing so far. Probably. I think Ēriks suspects we are monitoring his calls, his texts, his emails. We've just managed to get a feed into Santa Ezeriņa's email accounts last week. Her phone is still secure. For the moment."

"Kārlis, I can't let Ēriks have another minute alone with Roberts Vanags. He'll corrupt him completely and we'll have to start again."

"Moscow is aware of that, Terēze. The Scorpion has given me two options. A lenient option and a harsh one. Which I choose depends on the subject's actions."

Kārlis hit a button, releasing the door.

"Stay calm and do nothing, Terēze. Stop asking questions. I assure you one way or another, the Ēriks Helmanis problem will be solved by the day Roberts Vanags arrives for work."

He returned his eyes to the computer screen. "Now leave me to important matters."

5

"I tell you, Dad, someone was spying on this house the whole time you were gone."

Bob Vanags sighed, leaning back against the inside of the bedroom door-frame. "David, I've just come off a transatlantic flight. One delayed three hours in Frankfurt. I'm exhausted. We can talk about your weird theories later."

David pointed out the window towards the shady streets and well-kept lawns of Park Ridge suburbia. "There was a maroon coupe parked up and down the block the last three days. A guy sittin' in it all hours."

"David . . ."

"And that coupe was on the highway when I went to the marina on Lake Michigan. And sittin' outside the Penguin Grill last night when I stopped by for a burger."

"Why didn't you mention this on the phone, then?"

"I . . . I wasn't absolutely sure until I saw him at the restaurant." David shrugged. "It was same the coupe, Dad. Same guy inside."

"See, you *weren't* sure. We all make mistakes." Bob stepped fully inside the bedroom. "I'm takin' a nap."

"At three in the afternoon?"

"Night, David."

He closed the bedroom door.

"Parents . . ." David muttered.

An hour later, David Vanags pulled his father's Nissan Pathfinder up to the curb where his best, and truly only, friend Steve Cooper stood. Steve, dressed as always in black jeans and a Japanese anime t-shirt, spat out a few sunflower seeds, opened the door and sat his scrawny body down inside. He immediately wrinkled his nose.

"Your car reeks of smoke, Dave."

"It's my dad. Three packs a day."

"Jesus." Steve shut the door. "Get some air freshener."

"Open the window then."

"Might mess up the hair. The ladies, you know, Dave. The ladies."

"What ladies?"

"They're out there. Somewhere." Steve shrugged, smiled. "How'd your dad's interview go?"

"Fine, I guess." David pulled away from the curb, accelerating up the road. "They made him an offer."

"You're really going to live in Latvia?"

"Looks like it." David glanced over at his friend. "Dad needs something like this to get him going since Mom died. It'll be good for him maybe. I know my grandparents want Dad to be more 'Latvian.'"

"You'll probably develop an accent."

"I can sacrifice a bit for Dad. Shit, if it keeps him out of therapy."

"Good one."

"Who's joking?"

"Oh."

Steve was silent for a few minutes. The car moved from the summer green of the residential area to the glass storefronts and brick buildings of the old Cumberland retail area.

As the buildings zoomed by, David turned up the music.

Some old junk from his dad's U2's albums—the later ones nobody cared about—blared through the speakers. Bono whining on about the world as usual.

Steve turned it down again. "It sucks, you missing our last year and all."

"Won't be so bad. Ten, eleven months over there, then back here for college. Kind of like taking a semester abroad early."

"The Euro-trash babes will be waiting."

"Aren't those only in France?"

"No, the whole continent, I think." Steve's eyes widened, imagining.

"Well, I'll be damned."

"Seriously, they're all over the place."

"No . . ." David stared into the rearview mirror. "That guy in the coupe behind us . . . He's been following me the whole week."

Steve turned around in his seat to look. "Really? The dude in the hat?"

"Yeah."

The coupe was three or four cars back in the next lane but clearly the same one David had seen these past few days.

"Try and get a license number, Steve."

"It's too congested right now."

David slowed, pulled up along the curb to the front of a used mattress store. He left the engine running.

"Let's see what he does, Steven."

"Don't call me 'Steven.'"

"Shhh . . ."

The coupe pulled into the near lane and then over into the strip of parking spaces a few storefronts back. The driver backed his car into a narrow alley between two stores.

David knew that alley. It was right next to the Kirby Forever Comics Shop and it was a dead end.

"No, you can't hide there shit-head."

"What are you doing, Dave?" asked Steve.

"Gimme a minute."

Waiting until there were no cars on the road between them, David threw the Nissan in reverse and floored the accelerator. Their car flew backwards up the road, crashed over the curb to the front of the alley, blocking the exit, trapping the coupe inside.

"Dave?! Are you outta your mind!?"

"He's not gettin' away from me this time." David slammed the Nissan into park, pressed down the break, and climbed out.

The coupe's driver hammered the horn to no avail.

"Get out!" shouted David over the blaring of the horn.

The man inside did so. He was six foot five at least, dressed in a fraying Sears suit, a size too small. His black fedora shaded the snub-nosed face of weathered, vicious-looking man. The sort of dangerous old coot who could easily take younger men apart regardless of his years. A veteran of a thousand street wars.

"What the Hell are you doing?" shouted the man. "Move this car!"

David pooled his courage. "Why've you been chasing me the past couple days?"

"Chasing you? You're crazy, Kid." He threw down his hat. "Move this car or I'll call the cops."

"You been stalking my house too. What's the deal?"

"I'm getting pissed now." He brushed back his suit jacket to reveal a pair of steel knuckles hanging at his belt. "Haul your car and your ass out of here before I get rough."

David took a few steps back, pulled out his cellphone. Hoped the guy couldn't see the tremble in his hand.

"Maybe, *I'll* be the one to call the cops, you old prick."

"Well, somebody better call them, Sonny. Cause there's gonna be a crime."

"I can't believe Steve called the cops, Dad. I had the situation well in hand. Coward."

Dying cigarette between his lips, a very tired Bob Vanags drove his son home from the police station three hours later.

"Seems to me that Steve was the only one involved thinking sensibly. I've never been more disappointed in you, David. Never." He threw a weary glance over at this son. "You're lucky the police only gave you 'reckless driving' in the end."

David snorted. "It won't matter. We'll be in Latvia by the time of the hearing. Guess we can plead "No contest" or a get a lawyer."

"No. You broke the law, David. You'll have your day in court to stand accountable. A good lesson for you. Our family doesn't run from their mistakes. We face them."

"Dad . . ."

"Don't roll your eyes at me, fellah." Bob shook his head, put out the cigarette in the tray. "You can join me in Rīga after the hearing. The house won't have sold yet. We'll get Cousin Elvis to come down and stay with you. Make sure you show up for court."

"I'm an adult, Dad."

"You showed today you aren't."

David *did* roll his eyes this time. "You know you'll probably have to pay him to babysit me."

"Cousin Elvis can use the money."

"Please stop saying 'Cousin Elvis,' Dad. It makes you sound like a redneck."

Against his will, Bob, smiled.

"Sorry."

"The guy *was* a detective, you know, Dad," said David, sensing the slightest thaw in his father. "Told the police himself, you heard him." David adjusted his seat back. He wanted to sleep. But he wanted to be right more.

"You think it was a coincidence that the man I thought was following me turned out to be a private eye? What are the chances?"

"I didn't say you were wrong. Just wrong in how you handled it."

"Too bad he didn't give up his client. I mean who could it be, Dad?"

The car turned silent for a long time. Not a word was said all down Courtland Avenue.

Then:

"There was a fellah named Patrick McMillan, a local land developer, David. Shady guy. Petty. He accused me of sullying his name not long ago. This could be him trying to get some dirt on us, retribution or something"

"You think this McMillan guy really has a vendetta against you?"

"Don't know. Could be." He reached out and put a hand on David's shoulder. "No worries. We'll be in Latvia soon enough. Out of harm's way."

6

There are still spots in Rīga where payphones may be found. Ēriks Helmanis waited patiently, fearfully, until three A.M. on a stormy September night to find his. It remained their best hope. For himself. For his country. For much of the world.

He descended rain-slicked steps into a dimly lit subterranean passage. Like most former Soviet cities, Rīga's largest avenues are crossed via underground pedestrian tunnels. The mammoth intersection of *Raiņa bulvāris*, *Satekles iela*, and *Gogoļa iela* formed a double "Y" with eight entrances into the maze of passageways beneath. At this hour, on a Tuesday, with the terrible storm in the air, they were all but empty. Ēriks's footsteps echoed off the lonely concrete walls as he quickly walked to the heart of the labyrinth where three battered payphones hung on the wall. He slipped a phone card into the nearest, a card he'd bought anonymously at a kiosk far from his *Teika* neighborhood home, then punched in a number he'd memorized long ago.

Several seconds passed before the connection went through, then far too slowly it rang . . . rang . . . rang . . .

Come on. Where was she?

No answer. The journalist's voicemail came on.

"You've failed to reach Santa Ezeriņa. Leave a message and I'll consider calling you back. Don't take it personally if I don't. Bye," it said in Latvian, the message repeating in English, Russian, and Italian.

Ēriks's nervous panting was eclipsed by the crash of thunder far out in the Gulf of Rīga. He dared not leave a message and hung up.

He pulled the phone card out, slipped it back in and called again. More ringing . . .

Someone else entered the tunnel. A vagrant taking shelter from the storm. Drunk or high from the heroin sold on nearby *Avotu iela*, he stumbled to the wall ten meters from Ēriks, collapsed at its base. Soft, half-conscious moans rose up from the body, a twitch in his leg hinting at longtime nerve damage.

"Yeah?" said a tired woman's voice on the phone. "Who is this?"

"Ms. Ezeriņa!?" shouted Ēriks, surprised and elated at an answer. "It's your anonymous source from . . ." He lowered his words to a whisper, ". . . from Turaida. Turaida Bank in the Old Town."

"Oh, you again . . . 'Anonymous,' it's a quarter past three . . ."

"I need to meet you, Ms. Ezeriņa. Urgently."

"You've said that before, 'Anon'. I'm hanging up . . ."

"No! Ms. Ezeriņa, please! I'll show this time. I promise."

The voice hesitated. "All right, meet me at the *Baltic Beacon* offices, ten tomorrow morning. I'll have my editor there too."

"Tonight! Alone. At the Brīvības Monument. There are guards there twenty-four hours. We'll be safer."

She sighed. "If I'm getting out of bed at this hour in this weather, 'Anon,' you've gotta give me something special. Show it's worth my while."

He gritted his teeth, glanced again at the vagrant on the ground. "Turaida Bank plans to steal billions of euros from the Latvian government, Ms. Ezeriņa, and through it billions more from America, Britain, the world at large."

She whistled. "Congratulations, 'Anon,' you've finally become a source. You have proof of any of this?"

"I can get it. And there's more, much more. I'm only scratching the surface. I think they mean to topple governments."

"A bank?"

"Yes."

"You mind telling me who you are within the Turaida structure that you know these things?"

"Not now. Not over the phone. At the Brīvības Monument in fifteen minutes."

"Okay, 'Anon,' you better be there. Don't flake out on me again. I get a dozen calls from nutcases a day."

"I'll come. I swear."

Ēriks hung up the phone. The Brīvības Monument was less than five minutes' walk, but as always, he feared being followed. Instead, he'd take one of the taxis sitting all night at the train station nearby, circle the city center a few times before being dropped off at the monument. It was the prudent thing to do.

And prudence had kept Ēriks alive this long.

He took the passage towards the train station. As he was about to turn the corner to the stairs, he heard heavy Russian voices around the bend. Russian was by no means rare in Rīga. A third of the city spoke it as their native language. But something of the harshness in the voices at this hour gave him pause. He turned, hurried down an alternate tunnel, and took its stairs to the surface.

On the top step, bathed in the after-hours lights of the great Finnish department store behind, stood a man. A husky, unmoving silhouette of a man, apparently uncaring of the torrential downpour around him. A man who shook his head "no" as Ēriks began to climb the steps closer.

Ēriks retreated into the tunnels, his pace quickening.

Paranoia, Ēriks, only unjustifiable paranoia. . . .

He passed through the passage with the phones. The vagrant was gone.

Ēriks broke into a run.

Paranoid or not, he'd skip the taxi. Instead, he'd sprint, sprint as fast as he could along wide public *Raiņa bulvāris* to the Brīvības Monument and the safety of its military guards. He'd be there in two minutes.

Prudence, prudence. . . .

He reached the stairs leading up to *Raiņa bulvāris*. At the top was another man. This one descended a few steps as Ēriks arrived, the metallic gleam of a pistol rising from under his black rain jacket . . .

Ēriks was tackled from behind, crashing onto the steps, splitting his lip on the hard, wet concrete. He fought, kicked, turned himself around on the stairs, but his attacker—the vagrant—was the stronger man, shoving Ēriks back, holding him down. The other man was upon him too, pressing the pistol's muzzle against his temple. Then the cloth in the vagrant's hand reached Ēriks's face, covering his mouth and nose. He screamed, but they smothered him. His eyes and nostrils burned from the fumes, the strength abandoning Ēriks's limbs instantaneously. That vagrant held the cloth forever in place, a vice grip over Ēriks's face, punches to his stomach by both men forcing him to breathe. The vapors scalded his throat and lungs. Losing consciousness, he collapsed limply over the concrete steps, as the cold rainwater ran down his collar. Dizzy, fading, the last thing Ēriks saw was the grayness of his assassin's eyes before the world dissolved into blackness . . .

Umbrella in hand Santa Ezeriņa walked the five blocks from her *Lāčplēša iela* apartment towards the Brīvības Monument. Sleepy, without makeup, her frizzled hair pulled back in a loose ponytail, she was sure she looked much older than her twenty-seven years. Men often called her beautiful, but the hideous reflection in the rain puddles and storefront windows refuted those sentiments at this hour, made them laughable indeed.

She stepped off the curb, crossing cobble stoned *Tērbatas* and felt the flowing rain waters flood over her sneakers, soaking her feet and ankles. This journalist's life was wearing on her, the days long, the pay little even by Latvian standards. And the calls at any hour from the strangest of people. Her newspaper, the *Baltic Beacon*, was such an odd mixture of scandal sheet and tourist-trap puff piece that the ludicrous would-be interviewees might seem humorous if they weren't so sad. Yesterday, the call from a man out in the eastern province of Latgale, claiming a monster swam in the lake by his home, the chap clearly reaching for the "Loch Ness" effect to benefit his failing bed and breakfast. Then, later the same day, the woman who'd seen a member of Swedish royalty bathing in a Cēsis spa with his mistress, she had photos to prove it available for two hundred euros each. The sample, of course, was a photoshopped fake, too obvious even for the slimy editors of the *Beacon* to run.

Now, this anonymous guy claiming Turaida Bank was going to take down the world. He'd skipped out on two previous meetings. She had to be crazy to take his call again. But Santa had no lover to keep her in bed, so what did a little walk in the rain hurt . . . ?

She turned onto *Brīvības*, the monument directly ahead of her on the edge of the Old Town. A testimonial to Latvia's dogged persistence to exist, the "Freedom Monument" as it would be called in English, was a thirty-meter column and base topped by the greenish copper figure of Liberty, depicted as a woman holding high three stars for the traditional regions of Latvia: Latgale, Vidzeme, and Kurzeme. Built at the time of Latvia's first independence during the 1930s, it had survived the Nazi invasion and the forty-six years of the second Soviet occupation. Now it was a hallowed place, where American presidents and Middle Eastern kings placed wreaths in remembrance and every Latvian politician who wanted attention made speeches.

At the monument's base stood two uniformed soldiers, relentlessly stoic, unblinking, un-distractible, Latvia's little version of the Buckingham Palace guards. On the margins in the small plaza about the column were more subtle yet active protectors: Military police with walkie-talkies, conventional cops holding umbrellas and leaning against their bicycles, tired from circling for hours. Pro-Putin thugs had been vandalizing Rīga recently, stirring up the Russian minority, and the monument's security had been expanded to around the clock. No one, at least no one who considered themselves an ethnic Latvian, wanted the country's most important symbol damaged.

With the storm unabating all the benches on the plaza's margins were soaked, so Santa found an out of the way spot and simply stood and waited.

As she did so, she used an app on her iPhone to reverse lookup the number of her anonymous caller. It revealed the location to be a payphone somewhere on *Gogoļa iela*.

Payphones were so rare these days, where had she seen one on *Gogoļa?* She searched her memory but could think of nowhere. The well-trafficked intersection with *Raiņa bulvāris* and *Satekles iela* would be the most obvious place. Maybe in the underground pedestrian tunnels?

Yes, there was a bank of phones there . . .

When the time for their meeting had come and passed, Santa was livid. A third time he'd failed to show. What was the old Ian Fleming expression? 'Twice is coincidence, three times enemy action.' She left the monument plaza, marching up *Raiņa bulvāris* in the direction of the great intersection and its tunnels.

She felt a fool for being tricked again but she'd craved a lead into Turaida, had wanted a source into that enigma for years. Turaida had been the second privatized bank in Latvia, after the now-defunct Parex Bank, established more than two decades ago in 1995. To the world, as far as Santa knew, Turaida had a sterling reputation. The Big Four auditors, major ratings agencies, and financial regulators always gave it perfect marks. The bank had steadily advanced itself westward, getting its sticky fingers into the business world from here to Madrid without incident, indeed usually with international acclaim.

Yet, in Latvia, Turaida had a different reputation. It was the 'mob' bank, known mostly for the horrific cautionary tales of those who crossed it. In the poor parts of Rīga, where Santa had spent much of her girlhood, Turaida was a boogeyman of sorts. Late with the rent? The landlord might threaten to sell the flat to Turaida and let them collect the money with *their* methods. You'll never be late again.

And strange things were always happening to those associated with Turaida. Like that yacht of theirs found drifting empty this summer . . .

No one ever talked from Turaida. No one. It was like a cult. Breaking it could be a ticket away from the *Beacon* to a proper newspaper, an international newspaper. And it had made Santa desperate, gullible enough to fall prey to pranksters like this guy.

She hurried up the boulevard feeling additionally idiotic for wasting her time at half past three trying to find a payphone where a sociopathic liar might *once* have been. As she went, Santa passed the strip of Bastejkalna Park on her right dominated by a winding little river, the great neoclassical Latvian National Opera House on its far bank. On her left, across the road, stood many buildings of the University of Latvia, as well as several darkened tourist pubs. All very beautiful. But whether you wanted art, education or a drink, no one was out in this weather.

In fact, the only soul in sight ahead was a rain-drenched man helping his near-comatose drunken friend up into the rear of a white bread van. He had to tug and push to get the body inside. Good to know bread deliverymen partied so hard before making their early morning rounds. The van doors shut, and the vehicle swerved away at a wild, dangerous rate, nearly running Santa down on the pavement as it careened off into the night.

Inebriated bread truck drivers. Another reason to keep off the roads at this hour.

Santa reached the stairs leading down from *Raiņa bulvāris* into the crossing tunnels. The individual steps were flooded, pooling rainwater. On one step, near the bottom, Santa thought she glimpsed a strain of red. But as she descended, each footfall overloaded the steps' pool, sending water cascading down. By the time Santa reached the bottom the crimson was washed away.

If it had ever been there at all.

7

On a stormy Thursday afternoon in Rīga's Pokrov Cemetery nearly three thousand mourners gathered for the funeral of Turaida employee Ēriks Helmanis. The deceased's parents spoke first, followed by a wheelchair-bound aunt and then a powerfully voiced Lutheran minister, each successive eulogy engendering anguished moans and occasional tearful laughter from those seated nearest the speaking platform and gravesite. Every few minutes the winds briefly relented allowing the hundreds taking shelter beneath the boughs of swaying birch trees to react, to applaud or cry, but mostly the multitude sat silent unable to hear over the tempest. The inclement weather gave the proceedings an ominous, Biblical feel; a dark-cornered brooding landscape worthy of Renaissance oil paintings locked away in museums.

A most moving scene. Though it would be *more* moving to Bob Vanags if he understood what the eulogists were saying. Seated near enough to hear, forty-five minutes into the service he'd followed little of it, his knowledge of Latvian wholly inadequate to the task. Terēze, sitting with her husband in the row ahead of him, had occasionally leaned back and whispered translations but she'd grown tired of the effort in recent minutes and left Bob on his own. He couldn't quite blame her.

A great "welcome to Latvia," Bob thought. Fourth day on the job and he was spending most of it in a cemetery. No one ever died during his time at IRT at least. Mark one up for Chicago.

He was bored and felt guilty for the boredom. And the remorse ran deeper still. Ēriks Helmanis had committed suicide, hanging himself in his *Teika* apartment last week. Several Rīga newspapers, even the English language ones, had printed the deceased's lengthy suicide note blaming his fate on drug addiction, a domineering father and numerous failed romances. Yet, it was that single word "run" spoken by Helmanis to Bob in the Turaida elevator during his interview that haunted him. Bob had taken Helmanis's warning as a political tactic, a stratagem from a desperate rival after a job. Instead, it was the voice of a deeply damaged man crumbling under the weight of reality. Psychologists might call it the classic "cry for help." Once Bob learned of the death, he told Terēze what Helmanis had said. She agreed such words were not uncommon from the deceased, that Helmanis had uttered similar things to her and to many Turaida employees and clients. She felt, through inaction, we were all a little culpable in his demise. To prevent a repeat of this tragedy, Terēze was recommending regular psychological evaluations for all employees. Mental health was paramount to Turaida. The more we know, she said, the less we have to worry.

Bob couldn't really disagree with her. Those long Baltic winters were coming where the suicide rate skyrocketed. Of course, this suicide was in September. A bit early . . .

A twisting gust of wind rustled hats, umbrellas and mourners' veils throughout the crowd. Bob reached down and pinned the little place card on the seat of the chair next to him preventing it once again from blowing away. The fifth or sixth time he'd done so today. An excessively organized ceremony at the behest of the Turaida Bank itself, each invited attendee was given an assigned seat marked with such a card. The rain-shriveled one on the empty chair next to him read:

AGNESE AVENA

International Development Bank

He didn't know who Agnese Avena was or where she'd been throughout the service, but Bob was well-acquainted with her organization. The International Development Bank, or IDB, was a global financial institution based in Frankfurt that specialized in using investment to create new market economies in nations where the previous economic systems had collapsed or never fully functioned in the first place. They'd been established in '92 to help rebuild Eastern Europe after the Soviet Union's demise but now were aiding nations on every inhabited continent. They'd been a good friend to Latvia in the early days of Independence. The Turaida Group often shared initiatives with them to make sure needed monies went to the right places. Ēriks Helmanis had worked closely with IDB. As he would too.

Despite IDB's German headquarters, "Agnese Avena" was a Latvian name. She might be someone to meet. But so far not a glimpse of her.

A light applause through the winds broke Bob's musing. The minister was descending from the podium, a new speaker rising to take his place.

He sighed. Why had Terēze forced him to come here? Bob checked his watch, disappointed that there was yet another eulogist. Until he saw him.

Dāvids Osis!

Was it possible?

Yes . . . Bob recognized the tall, exceedingly lank, white-bearded man who stepped up onto the platform. *The* Dāvids Osis. Iconic Member of Latvian Parliament; friend of NATO; champion of the EU; purveyor of democracy; an idol of Bob's father and longtime hero to Bob himself. Hell, Bob even named his own son after Dāvids Osis.

Bob sat there amazed. He'd hoped to meet Osis sometime during his employment in Latvia. But to see him speak during his first week, at the funeral of a Turaida employee no less, was an unimagined surprise. Osis was truly one of the nation's few living legends. He'd been the most visible and arguably most popular member of Latvia's Independence movement in the '80s and early '90s. After the murder of fourteen civilians by the Gorbachev regime at the television tower of "brother-city" Vilnius in January 1991, Dāvids Osis had chained himself to Rīga's own TV tower in solidarity, rallying hundreds of protesters and practically daring the KGB to assassinate him on live international television. They didn't. Less than a week later on the "Day of Barricades" he'd shown even greater bravery when 700,000 people, one-third of Latvia's population, assembled in Rīga's Cathedral Square to build defenses against the Soviet Army. As Russian tanks rolled nearer and enemy helicopters flew over the crowd dropping leaflets that said "Disperse or Face Execution" Dāvids Osis had stood on the barricades, megaphone in hand, shouting out for Soviet soldiers to ignore orders to shoot, to lay down their weapons and join international humanity. It was an image of Osis captured on televisions and magazine covers around the world. For a brief moment he might have been more famous than the country he defended. And a framed photograph of the moment hung in the Vanags household ever since.

Things moved fast after the "Barricades." By August of '91 Latvia was independent. Osis spent most the intervening decades serving in the *Saeima*. Despite numerous urgings to serve as Latvia's president by public and political parties alike, Osis refused, saying he had no taste for the "autocratic" executive branch and could do more good in the parliament. When the Pope visited Latvia, he met first with Dāvids Osis. As did Prince William, Lyndsey Graham, Sylvester Stallone, and Angelina Jolie. He was unanimously considered one of the ten greatest men in the country's history.

What had Ēriks Helmanis ever done to deserve a eulogist like Osis?

Bob found himself jealous of a dead man.

As the speech started, he hoped Terēze would offer a few translations. But she didn't say another word. Bob found this disappointing. Other eulogists she translated without request, but his new boss left him unaided for the one speaker he really wanted to hear.

Bob cupped his ears and through the gusting winds tried to listen, to remember all the Latvian he'd learned at those American Latvian Association youth camps in Michigan as teenager. It did him little good. He heard the "Helmanis" name frequently, "Latvia" occasionally, recognized a few words that might be translated "altruism" or "philanthropy." There must be more to it than that. The crowd was responding positively, even those too far away to hear applauding after every utterance. Like a master politician Osis was turning something as sad as a suicide funeral into a rousing event of hope.

What genius . . .

It was not long, however, into this speech of growing cheers that Bob heard a dissenting emotion. A sobbing woman, clearly unaffected by the uplifting oratory, moved her way along the back of the chairs. Dressed in proper funeral black, she was a statuesque blonde of about thirty, who might have been exceedingly attractive under other circumstances, but her eyes were now blood-red and puffy with tears, her makeup running down over cheeks and chin. A heart-breaking figure anyone with an ounce of soul would want to instinctively console, soothe, tell lies that everything would be all right. Clearly half-blinded by the tears, as she stumbled along chivalrous people stood to assist her, gently passing the grief-stricken woman hand-to-hand down the line. When it was Bob's turn he rose, hand out to take hers, but to his surprise she sat down in the empty chair next to his.

Was this . . .

"Roberts," said Terēze leaning over the back of her chair, "this is Agnese Avena, a good friend of Ēriks's."

Something in the way she said "good" implied more than friendship. Maybe this was one of the "failed romances" mentioned in the suicide note. Bob marveled. To lose a beauty like this, well, you might just feel you've nothing to live for . . .

"How do you do?" Bob asked, immediately embarrassed by his choice of an old-fashioned, Midwestern American-sounding greeting.

She nodded, continued to sob, face red with anguish.

He withdrew a handkerchief from his coat pocket. "Here, take this."

"Thank you," she said softly.

"I'm Roberts."

"I heard Terēze the first time."

"Oh," Bob laughed. "Of course."

She looked up from the handkerchief. Behind the tears, the red and swelling, he could see she had the most beautiful violet irises. He felt a jolt of attraction that startled him. *"Colpo di fulmine"* as the Italians say.

Those eyes turned colder.

Bob regretted laughing. There was a long pause as any pretense of conversation crumbled away. He returned his attention to the eulogy. Dāvids Osis was wrapping up, his voice escalating to a harrowing crescendo. Bob caught a few references to mythic figures, the hero Lāčplēsis, the folk goddesses Laima and Kārta, then something happened that he'd never seen at a funeral—a standing ovation for the eulogist. As Osis left the stage, exchanging heartfelt embraces with the Helmanis family, the crowd rose to their feet almost in unison, the thunderous applause drowning out strains of real thunder in the skies above. Not a soul lingered even a moment in their seats.

Except Agnese Avena. She remained in her chair, face in hands, weeping over the loss of Ēriks.

In that instant Bob felt ashamed of his attraction for her. It seemed predatory, perverse. Sick. Wishing to right this emotional wrong, he took his seat, placed a consoling hand over her shoulder. Agnese said nothing but let him keep it there.

He listened to her cry as thousands clapped.

8

As the Helmanis funeral ended, Bob offered to walk Agnese Avena to her car. She was still so inconsolable, he had to help her from the chair, and they found themselves with interlocked arms as they walked through the still-substantial crowd of the park-like cemetery. Bob said little, avoiding bringing up the deceased or even asking her role at IDB. With the expanding storm, he couldn't even chat pleasantly about the weather.

For her part, the tears had slowed slightly but Agnese seemed unwilling or unable to discuss anything other than the route to her automobile. What sort of mind, personality or views lay behind those tears remained a mystery.

He was curious why no one approached wishing her greetings, condolences or anything else. If she'd been a part of Ēriks 's life in the past or at the time of his death, Bob thought *someone* here should know her. Even when they'd passed the Helmanis family, Agnese didn't wish to go over and the family's casual glances at the two of them seemed to elicit no strong reactions or even recognition.

Maybe Terēze was mistaken. Maybe Ēriks and Agnese were only casual friends through shared projects between Turaida and IDB. Maybe she was just one of those emotional people who bawled continuously at funerals.

He tired of these musings. The parking lot in sight, Bob would politely bid Agnese goodbye and go back to his own worries. He had a life to set up in Latvia.

These immediate plans changed, however, when Bob spied the tall, slim figure of Dāvids Osis standing alone near the cemetery entrance. In the next instant, he found himself reflexively tugging Agnese along towards the politician.

"M.P. Osis," said Bob, unlocking himself from Agnese to shake the great man's hand. "I've admired you for years. And I immensely enjoyed your speech today."

He replied in Latvian.

"But I don't speak the language."

Osis smiled, said in heavily accented English: "Then you didn't enjoy my speech so much as you enjoyed the effect of my speech."

"Some things are universal, M.P. Osis. They require no interpreters."

He nodded, shifted his weight to his good leg, the other having been injured against the Soviets all those years ago. It was a famous stance, one Osis used when sizing up political opponents on the *Saeima* floor. As he was sizing up Bob this very moment.

"You have me at a disadvantage, sir," he said.

"Oh, yes, it's Roberts—Bob—Vanags. Vice president of International Relations at Turaida." He gestured towards Agnese. "And this is . . ."

"Agnese Avena, Director of Small to Medium-sized Enterprise Lending for the International Development Bank," said Osis. "I know her and the good work she does well, Roberts. I gave her a parliamentary medal for her outstanding contributions to the greater good only last autumn."

"Two autumns ago, Dāvids," corrected Agnese with a rare smile.

"Two? Oh, I am getting senile. Time to put me out to pasture."

To Bob's surprise Agense laughed. The hoarse, half-rasp of one who's been crying, but a laugh nonetheless. "Where would Latvia be without her favorite son, Dāvids?"

"I agree," said Bob, happily marginalized. "You're the most important one here."

Osis looked bemused. "I respectfully disagree, Roberts. You're a banker—a businessman. If we want to grow Latvia's economy to where it must go by 2025, every honest businessman is worth a hundred old politicians."

"But not an *honest* old politician, Dāvids."

"If we're going to talk about fantasies, Agnese, we should consider unicorns, fairy godmothers and the Zalktis snake too. You know that."

She chuckled again, the laugh cleaner this time. Bob watched this gorgeous blonde who'd been on his arm only moments ago. The woman he'd thought a fragile overwhelmed mourner had transformed into a national medal recipient before his eyes, one who spoke on equal footing with Dāvids Osis.

Marvelous. He'd have to get used to how the sexes related in Latvia. It was a very matriarchal society.

Agnese took his arm again.

Bob was considering whether to bring up the framed photograph in his father's house or the naming of his own son, when another woman entered their sphere of conversation. A thin brunette in her mid-to-late twenties, she

was as fine-featured as Agnese, but without tearful-redness in her eyes or a
spot of makeup on her face. Bob found her clothing wholly inappropriate for
a funeral: red denim jeans and a black t-shirt with "MORE ISSUES THAN
VOGUE" written down the front in white lettering.

Ignoring all others, the stranger's attention remained locked on Osis, barking out some quick question in Latvian that Bob had no prayer of deciphering.
There was a flash of sternness in the M.P.'s face before the politician's composure returned and he gave a practiced smile. His answer, when it passed from
his bearded lips, was calm, measured, elegant sounding. It could pass for poetry.

The stranger asked another question. Osis's façade came slower this time,
the smile slightly forced, the answer bordering on terse.

Bob thought he heard "Helmanis" among the Latvian words.

"Who is she?" he asked Agnese.

"A funeral crasher. Some sort of journalist . . ."

Osis turned his back on the stranger, eyes to them. "The paparazzi invading
a private service, friends. Is there anything more gauche? They've no respect for
the families." He motioned for someone in the crowd to come closer.

The journalist zeroed in on Bob. Queried something in Latvian.

Bob made no attempt to understand. "I'm sorry I speak little Latvian. I've
only begun working in Rīga this week."

She replied in perfect, accent-less English. "You work for Turaida?"

"Yes."

"And what do you think of attending a funeral your first week?"

He glanced at Agnese, Osis, before answering. "Tragic. I didn't know the
deceased but by all accounts, he was a good man. Look at the turn out . . ."

"It's staged, don't you think?"

"Staged?

"Do you think a banker's funeral should be *Triumph of the Will*? Or May
Day on Red Square?" said the journalist. "Every time someone dies at Turaida,
it's a big event. They turn it into a photo opportunity, a press release for their
latest martyr to Latvia's bright future."

"Latvia *has* a bright future."

She snorted. "Oh? Can I quote you on that? What's your name and title at
Turaida?"

Bob looked to the others. Osis had disappeared into the crowd seeking
someone, while Agnese spat out a few cruel-sounding Latvian words. The
stranger ignored her.

He returned his eyes to the journalist. "Miss, I'm not really sure I wish to continue this conversation."

"And what of the rumors that Ēriks Helmanis's suicide was coerced? That bruises were found on the body, face, and wrists? That he struggled against the hanging? That the note was forged? Do you believe it? Do you have a comment?"

"I've never heard any such rumors."

The stranger smiled. "Of course not. Not in Turaida circles. Not with her on your arm. Break out." She reached into a small purple purse at her shoulder. "I've a card here if you want to talk."

"I don't want it."

"You will."

He reluctantly slipped the card into his pocket, if only to help end this meeting. "Isn't this a private service? You really should be going."

"At least give me your name. I might want to call you."

"No."

Four husky men in suits arrived that could only be security. Agnese gestured towards the stranger. Ignoring the journalist's warnings, one of the men seized her arm, tugging her towards him. She spun him around, forcing the man to the ground in a clear display of combat training. The others descended upon the intruder immediately, two dragging her back, holding her down as the third man delivered a cold, straight jab to her jaw that horrified Bob and elicited a gasp from Agnese. The stranger went limp in their arms as the men dragged her away, out of the cemetery and into the parking lot beyond. The one who had been on the ground, brushed at the wet grass stains on his suit, then picked up the intruder's purse, and followed his comrades.

Despite his distaste for the paparazzi invading a funeral service, Bob stood revolted by the violence he'd seen. As he stepped away from Agnese to find Terēze or anyone to report it to, Dāvids Osis returned.

"Did security arrive, Roberts?"

"They pummeled that reporter and dragged her off across the parking lot."

His eyes widened. "Did she resist?"

"Well, yes. But they may have broken her jaw."

"Disgusting. I'll have their licenses."

"Are they cemetery employees or government agents?"

"Neither. Turaida contracted out security for the funeral." A frown grew across his ancient, experienced face. "Some of these contractors don't share the ideals of their clients. Or our nation. We are trying, Roberts, yet even after nearly thirty years, there are still some residues from totalitarian times." Osis put a hand on Bob's shoulder. "Let me make sure things don't grow worse than they already are. Those thugs will listen to me."

"I'll go with you."

"Do me a favor, Roberts. You stay. Show a softer side for our country. I think your lady needs you."

"Agnese? Oh, she's not my lady."

"She was close to Ēriks. Women need a man at times like this. We are all gentlemen here."

The stranger didn't remain stunned long. Beyond the sight of Bob Vanags and Dāvids Osis, the security men dragged the kicking, cursing journalist over the gravelly ground of the parking lot before depositing her harshly onto the grass of a deserted playground on the other side. Three stood over her, while the fourth sat on a swing, rummaging through her purse. He slipped her cellphone into his coat pocket, then withdrew her driver's license and a rain-proof plastic container of business cards.

He nodded. Satisfied.

"You know who we are. We know who you are," the man pocketed the license and cards, picked at the grass stain on his knee. "In a day, we'll have the address, description, bank account numbers, and criminal record of every friend, colleague, and family member you have. Understand me? Santa Ezeriņa, *journalist*? There is no shelter."

Her reply was to send a grunting kick out at the nearest man. They widened their circle around her.

"You work for us now," said the man on the swing. He withdrew a money clip thick with bills from his pocket, deposited it into her purse. Dropped the purse onto the ground. "We're a generous client. This is what? Thirty times what the *Baltic Beacon* pays? Write a glorious piece about the funeral. Maybe something on the suicidal tendencies of young bankers." He exited the swing, motioned his men over. "Anything more and we'll talk again."

The men walked back through the parking lot towards the cemetery. They passed Dāvids Osis without a word. The politician's eyes widened as he saw the journalist on the ground. Latvia's great man hurried over to Santa Ezeriņa.

She glanced up at him. Sighed. "Don't use that 'assessing stance' bullshit with me. I've always hated that."

"Should I call you an ambulance?"

Santa rubbed her jaw, winced. "No. A taxi. I'm minus a phone it seems."

His next question was slow in coming. "Did they hurt you?" Dāvids offered her a hand.

She took it, rose to her feet. "I reject the premise, M.P. Osis. A better question would be did I hurt them?"

He frowned. "Well, did you?"

"Not sufficiently." She picked up her purse, looked down at all the money inside. "Now, I might not get the chance. For a while."

9

In the shadows of an early morning bedroom, Bob Vanags said:

"How long have you had this foot fetish, Agnese?"

"At least since sixteen, Bob. Come up here."

He gave one last sensual kiss to Agnese's toes, waited patiently for her laughter to subside, then crawled up the mattress, sliding his nude body over hers, and hesitating only to languish kisses on the softness of her stomach and breasts. Moist with sweat, the paleness of her bosom reflected the early morning sun through his apartment windows. The sight, the taste, the touch aroused him yet again. He would be lost here, forever. He knew it.

"What are you doing?" she giggled.

"To you? Well, a gentleman shouldn't really describe it."

"To me, I know." She pulled him up, face to face, gave him a passionate kiss. Agnese let it linger for what seemed like eons.

"I mean doing in Latvia?" she asked, her words breathy.

"I work at Turaida." He bit her earlobe, draped kisses across the nape of her neck.

"Tell me a better lie. A better . . ." her voice dropped away as he entered her and their rocking drove the words away, replaced with soft moans and growing gasps. They made love once more on the bare mattress, the sheets long ago thrown to the floor in passion. Aching, sunrise sex, their bodies exhausted from a night of coupling, more painful but no less pleasurable than the first time. Those twelve hours since the funeral seemed so long ago and innocent.

When the sex was over, Bob collapsed on the mattress. Agnese lit up a cigarette. To his own amusement he didn't want one, hadn't all night. First time in years.

"Well?" she asked when the ash of her cigarette had grown long and brittle.

"Well, what?"

She reached down and tapped the ash clean into a wineglass on the bare wooden floor. "Every time I ask, 'Why are you here?' you kiss me instead of answering."

He smiled. "Isn't that the best answer?"

Her expression disagreed.

Bob shrugged. "You don't believe me about Turaida?" He rolled onto his side, facing her, head propped up by one hand. He smiled warmly. "Okay, CIA all the way, every day, baby."

"No 'baby.' I'm not a woman for such names."

"What do other lovers call you?"

"Agnese."

She pulled her cigarettes from the nightstand and finding them empty, stole a Marlboro from his pack, lit up again. "You can't be CIA."

"Who says so?"

"Men called 'Bob' don't work for the CIA. They all have names like Trevor or Sebastian. Bourne or Oswald."

"Lee Harvey Oswald worked for the CIA?"

"Everyone outside of America knows this."

He smiled internally. What other outlandish theories did she have? If an educated, successful, international woman like Agnese believed such things, what might the average Latvian think? No wonder some spouted ridiculous stories about Turaida . . . He thought of that reporter and her theories about Ēriks Helmanis. All examples of the national predilection towards conspiracy . . .

"Bankers have simple names like 'Bob,' 'Toby,' 'John,'" she continued.

"Toby?" He rubbed her shoulder. "Then you've answered your own question. I'm no hero. Just a banker named 'Bob.'"

"It is not as exciting."

"Blame my parents. They considered Siegfrieds."

She rolled onto her side away from him, pressed her lower back and buttocks against his body. He wanted her again.

"A Siegfrieds would never kiss my toes."

"Lucky you then." He threw an arm over her shoulders, peppered the back of her neck with soft kisses.

"Maybe you are both a banker and a spy. A spy for Turaida."

"Turaida doesn't have spies."

She glanced over her shoulder at him with dreaming violet eyes, the pupils wide and open after a night of sex.

"All banks have spies, Bob."

He snorted slightly. She didn't like the reaction. He tried to atone by caressing the curve of her thigh. Such perfect smooth hips . . .

She looked at him, waiting . . .

Bob let the silence linger, listened to the growing din as Rīga began to stir outside. He didn't want this to end.

"When do you go back to Frankfurt?" he asked.

She rubbed her temple lightly, as if the question were an unwelcome dose of reality. "A week. I've a meeting next Monday in the Turaida offices. Probably with you."

Only a week . . .

"Where do you stay in Rīga?"

"With my brother." Her face reddened at this, but the change was no afterglow. "I was supposed to stay with Ēriks." She shuddered, suddenly cold, pulling herself away from him. "I shouldn't be here."

He feared this sudden turn of emotions "It's all right." The words as inadequate as the gentle rub he gave her shoulder.

"No, it isn't." Her voice was harsh, a tone of censure. "In his note, he said he loved me. Ēriks never said he loved me."

"The note found at his apartment?"

"I should have said I loved him." Her voice cracked. "I didn't love Ēriks, but what would it have hurt to say it? He might be alive if more people said they loved him."

"Agnese . . ."

"Now, I can never . . ." She shoved him back with her hand, her nails scratching him. "And I'm here with *you*."

The blow startled him. Where was the woman, he'd made love to a half-dozen times tonight? She was again the despondent mourner from the funeral.

He fumbled for something to say.

"You need some tea."

Agnese collected a pillow from the floor, sobbed into it, shook her head "no."

"A shower then?"

She said nothing.

"A shower?" he repeated.

She finally nodded, said through the pillow's body. "You first."

It felt wrong to leave her, but worse to argue.

"Okay," he said, and reluctantly pulled himself from the bed. "I won't be a minute."

The shower water wasn't particularly warm, but Bob paid it little mind. His body ached pleasantly everywhere, a burn running down through his stomach, thighs, and buttocks, the muscles unused to strenuous lovemaking. No matter how many hours you spend in the gym or pool, there was no workout like extended sex.

But these sensations were pushed back to the margins of his perceptions. Bob anguished over Agnese. Last night, she'd assured him when things had turned romantic in the Old Town bar that he wasn't taking advantage of her emotional state, repeated that this is what she wanted now.

It'd been a test of ethics. A test he'd forgotten he was playing. A test he'd failed.

He ripped open a shampoo packet left over from his move-in and lathered his scalp, almost punishing himself with the vigor which he applied it. As Bob did so, his wedding ring scratched slightly along his hairline. He lowered his hand, looked at the band on his finger.

The things he'd done with this on. Another mistake tonight. Or the same mistake really, just viewed from another angle. Maria would want him to move on. She'd told him so in the last days of her sickness. Yet here he'd been caressing another woman's body while wearing a ring given by his true love before the altar, by the mother of his son.

This was not a good night for his conscience.

Bob slipped off the ring and set it in the soap dish. Such an easy motion physically, yet nearly impossible emotionally.

The shower was turning even cooler. Wanting to save a few minutes of heated water for Agnese, Bob washed his hair clean and stepped out of the shower. He quickly toweled himself off, then returned to the bedroom.

"Okay, you're turn . . ."

She was gone.

Agnese Avena stepped into the elevator outside Roberts Vanags's apartment and pressed the button for the ground floor. When the doors closed, she breathed a sigh of regret and observed her disheveled reflection in the gold-tinted mirrors of the elevator's interior. Her hair was just passable, and the blackness of her dress hid most of the creases created by a night bundled on the floor, but Agnese's face told the true story. A tale of funeral tears, too much wine and a sleepless night filled with dark thoughts occasionally broken by ecstasy. She'd desired sex initially to push aside the pain but as she'd approached her first climax with Roberts the guilt had brought her to tears even as she'd bitten her bottom lip in pleasure. She was fairly certain Roberts hadn't noticed the tears. But they were as real as any shed at the memorial.

In their twelve months together, Ēriks had never made her orgasm though he'd tried and tried. The doctors couldn't explain it. Now on the night of his funeral it was happening with another man. Somehow that release, that most human pleasure after a year unsatisfied made her feel worst of all. Ēriks had committed suicide. What was she doing? The words she called herself as she'd laid curled on that American's mattress were obscene indeed.

The elevator doors opened, and she walked briskly through the lobby out to the timeless cobblestone street of *Teātra iela*. Nearby taxis with tourist rates waited on paved *Kungu iela*. Her car far from here, she'd pay that fare for a speedy exit from the Old Town. Agnese hailed a cab and climbed inside.

She lay down on the backseat of the taxi, head resting on her hands. If she'd stayed, if she'd waited for Roberts to come out of that shower, there would be no resistance. She'd have called in sick and spent a remorseful day on a mattress, hips in the air, engaged in relentless lovemaking.

And who wants that?

She did. Again.

Agnese felt the taxi vibrate as they accelerated out of the Old Town onto the highway bridge over the Daugava River. She rubbed her tired eyes. Roberts was Turaida too. Like Ēriks. Maybe, this should be the end? Maybe it already was. How do American men react to being abandoned after lovemaking? Latvians didn't like it, Germans found it puzzling, but Americans, they were a mystery to her.

The pain was welling up again inside. Why had Ēriks said he'd loved her in that note? When he too wanted to end the affair . . .

Her phone rang.

She dug through her purse and found the cell. A glance at the display made her stomach twist. That same old Ukrainian number, one of the oldest contacts in her phone.

Agnese gathered her strength and answered the call.

"Yes," she said tersely. "I'm fine. No need to ask. Where? I spent the night fucking Roberts Vanags . . ."

10

"I don't wish to know your background, Mr. Vanags," said the old Russian clerk from under his shaggy hair, the thick white locks hanging down over a protruding nose and small, dark eyes. "If I may say so respectfully, I wish to know as little about you as possible."

Bob Vanags found these remarks very odd. In introducing himself to his new assistant, a Turaida-lifer named Evgeny Markov, he'd mentioned his reasons for coming to Latvia. To Bob's surprise, instead of feigning interest, Markov had bluntly said he'd no time for small talk.

"If I am frank, I don't think there is really any need of this meeting, Mr. Vanags." Markov glanced at the bronze clock in Bob's Turaida office, grimaced. "Richard Ash and I worked in the same capacity for nearly two years. I know my duties."

"That's all well and good," Bob said crossly, "but I may have a few progressive methods." Bob didn't really know if he *would* alter anything procedural, yet, but he was surprised at the resistance he was getting in a merely introductory meeting.

"Ēriks Helmanis changed little when I worked for him while Turaida was searching for Richard's replacement. I doubt you'll want anything done differently than those two poor fellows. Nor will your successors . . ." His voice trailed off here.

"I've a three-year contract and just received my residency permit, Mr. Markov. Rest assured, I'm not going anywhere."

"I would be surprised if you mark a quarter of that time."

"Why is that?"

"You've mentioned 'progress' twice in five minutes. Turaida does not progress. Latvia does not progress. You'll grow frustrated. Or they will of you. Accidents may happen."

Bob couldn't help but catch the reference.

"I don't scuba dive, Mr. Markov."

"Did the Ashes, sir? Not by any accounts I've ever heard of. And I went boating with them many times. Richard and Mindy became friends of mine. I won't make that mistake with you."

What game was this? "Mr. Markov, I have to tell you, maybe business in Latvia is different than America, but I've never heard such insolence. If your tone doesn't improve, you'll find yourself fired."

"Being fired is a blessing, sir. It's when you quit that things get uneasy."

Bob crossed his arms and sat on the edge of his desk. "Since you don't want to know my background, let's hear yours."

"What would like to know, sir?"

Something in the hostile tone of "sir" . . . Was this a nationality issue? A promotion or hierarchal issue? An age issue? Markov had to be north of seventy . . . maybe even seventy-five? "Give me a quick summary."

"I was born inside the gulag on the wrong side of the Arctic circle. I attended university in Leningrad—it was still Leningrad then—and came to Soviet Latvia in 1968. I worked in the foreign exchange, as much as it existed in Soviet times, until independence and Turaida." He paused here. "And I am a committed Marxist since age fifteen."

Bob couldn't help but be bemused. "A Marxist who works in a bank?"

"Marxists must eat too. Sandwiches, cat food, they are not free."

"So, you remember Soviet times fondly?"

"Why would I? I said I'm a Marxist. Not a Leninist, Stalinist or even a Putin-ist. Those ideologies are bastardizations of what should be beautiful, the bold lies of fascist monsters disguised in workers' clothes, or in Putin's case, draped in Russian pan-nationalism."

Good lord, his assistant was Noam Chomsky.

Well, Bob wanted a change from LaSalle Street.

"I could talk of revolution, but as an old man, why bother? I will not live to see it. I should hope you will, but that is up to you."

"Any family? Here or in Russia?"

"None above ground. Except Barsik."

"Barsik?"

"A cat. He is a stray. He found me. Now, I am more his than he is mine." He held up a finger. "When we travel for business, I must know a day in advance so I can find Barsik a sitter. He is old now and must take medicine."

What a bizarre conversation—from firing, to revolution, to pet sitting . . . "I think we can work with that, Evgeny."

"Good. Are we done?"

"Yes. For the moment."

"It is not working, Terēze!"

"Why is that, Roberts?"

Bob paced back and forth inside Terēze's spacious office. "They do not believe we are honest in Milan. The Perego Investment Group went on again and again about Turaida being corrupt. At the meeting, in the bar afterwards. Formally and informally. They won't do business with us."

She leaned back in her chair, regarded him with a slight distaste. "You told them we've clean audits from the Big Four?"

"Of course."

"Roberts, we brought you here—and are paying you handsomely—to overcome this stigma. It is the old stereotype against any Eastern European financial institution that harms even the most honest of us. A relic of the Cold War brought against us." She leaned forward, set her elbows on the desk. "You solve this. Come to me with solutions and I'll approve them. But with problems, I can only ask you to do your job."

He stopped his pacing, stood directly in front of her. "They say, repeatedly, that our loans to entities inside the former Soviet Union are going to thieves and gangsters."

"Who told them this?"

"They didn't say, but it was implied that it was Richard Ash. He met the Perego people in Brussels last January."

"I will take it upstairs," she said absently.

"The President is in? Finally?"

"No . . ."

"Then who?"

A shadow passed across her face. "It is a Latvian saying. Something lost in translation, I suppose. It means 'I'll think about it.'" She rose from the chair as if to emphasize her decision. "In the meantime, come up with a way to fight this, gather any information you need . . ."

"Well, the most obvious way is to go through the foreign loan history. Disprove what the Italians are saying."

"Then do it."

There came a rap on Terēze's office door, and Evgeny Markov stuck his head in, the old man's usually mop-ish hair combed and gelled into place for today's meeting.

"The IDB people are here, sir," said he.

"Showtime."

Bob excused himself from the office and followed Markov down the hall to Turaida's executive conference room. The butterflies grew in his stomach, more than they should for a "mere" hundred-million-euro Small to Medium Enterprise deal with the International Development Bank to build infrastructure in Moldova and Ukraine. He knew the reason, and the excitement and fear only rose as he stepped inside. At an ebony, brass-rimmed table sat six members of IDB led by Agnese Avena. In her gray suit dress, with a wide-collared orange blouse, and blonde hair pinned back, she looked formidable indeed.

They all stood to greet him. If Agnese smiled, he missed it.

Bob shoved away carnal desires and got to work.

It was talk of childhood pets, frankly, more than the alcohol that began to thaw Evgeny Markov. Bob, at his charming best, had worked on the banking world's most open Marxist whenever he'd the chance in the past week: when they'd taken smoke breaks with clients, or private lunch meetings while planning their strategy to fight stigma against Eastern banks, or even, when Bob had deliberately asked for advice on subjects he didn't really need: Rīga's museums, leftist lecturers, a cat show in Ogre. If they weren't friends or even friendly—Evgeny was clearly resistant because of some wound from the Richard Ash tragedy—then they'd become civil enough co-workers, with a growing casualness that spanned boss-employee or intergenerational relations. It'd been a short time really. He'd sway the old curmudgeon yet.

But Evgeny was sharper than Bob anticipated.

It was a late night, past two A.M., and they were still in his office, drinking whiskey, and going through the bank ledgers on loans to foreign entities. The number and amounts lent to Russian companies were staggering, yet Bob was having a hard time getting accounting details on the state of those loans or even any significant information on the borrowers. There was surprisingly little detail, Turaida's accounting department understandably resistant to revealing anything about their clients . . .

Evgeny, had been quiet most of the investigation, and when he did talk it was only to say something cryptic about Richard or Ēriks having "passed this way before." Given his seriousness, Bob was surprised when Evgeny tucked a pen behind his ear, leaned an elbow on the desk between them and said in a rather fatherly way:

"Call her, Roberts. Ask her to dinner."

"Who?"

"Agnese Avena at IDB."

"Oh her . . . why would I do that?"

"Because you find reasons to bring Agnese up twice an hour. On completely unrelated subjects. I have been in the meetings. It is obvious."

Bob shrugged, wondered what Evgeny knew. "I mean she's attractive. But that would be a conflict of interest."

"'Conflict of interest?'"

"Sure, I mean she and I are working for two separate financial institutions and engaged in a multimillion euro development deal, that can't be proper. And she lives in Frankfurt, too . . ."

He squinted at him in a way that made Bob feel young and naïve. "Let me tell you something, Roberts. My parents were in Arctic detainment camps eleven kilometers apart in 1941. They saw each other for the first time on a shared work detail in February, in negative twenty-degree weather, with armed guards watching and communication limited to hand signals. Their circumstance meant they could only meet once every two months for the first year. Despite that they courted, married, and conceived me and my late sister. We were a family even before we were freed. What then are your 'conflicts of interest'? If you want it, love conquers all."

"I suppose it does."

"Be a man, Roberts. Call her."

"Terēze might not like it."

"Overcome her. Terēze is not Stalin." Evgeny snorted. "No matter how much she might wish to be."

11

"She was on the boat," Jānis Šimkus said firmly.

Santa Ezeriņa stared at the man on the park bench next to her. How old was he? Sixty-five? Seventy? The leathery skin of his deeply tanned face, and the long, knotted gray beard beneath, made him look aged indeed. A primordial man, who seemed in Santa's imagination better suited to roam the ancient forests and lonely seashores of Latvia's pre-Christian past some eight-hundred years ago. Yet, here he was out of the mists of time, sitting casually in a blue and white checkered shirt, dusty black jeans, and thin, homemade sandals that revealed feet as sun browned as his face.

And this primordial man claimed he had breaking news.

"How do you know . . ." Santa flipped through her notepad for the dead girl's name, "that Maija Banga was aboard the *Leesma*?"

"I saw her swim out to it. The yacht was moored fifty meters offshore. A foreign man helped her in."

"Why 'foreign?' Did you hear him speak?"

"No. His manner, his movements. Definitely foreign. That's why Maija went I think."

Santa pretended to take notes but wrote little. She wondered about the reliability of his claims. That the *Leesma* was piloted that night by a British couple who later died in a diving accident was information available in the newspapers. This man could easily be some delusional crank, the *Baltic Beacon* surely attracted enough of those. If so, it was her own fault for letting out what she was working on around the office. When her colleague, Līva, heard that Santa was investigating Turaida Bank in the wake of Ēriks Helmanis's suicide, Līva had mentioned an old beachcomber who repeatedly told the other Vecāķi naturists—of which apparently Līva was a member—that one of their own had been on that doomed Turaida-owned yacht. Līva put Santa in touch with this witness, Jānis Šimkus. Now they sat on a canal edge bench, the green grassy slopes and red stone slabs of *Bastejkalns*—Bastion Hill—stretching up behind them. A beautiful early autumn scene, yet Santa was growing fearful this was all a waste of time.

Still, she pressed on. "Could it have been this man on the yacht?" Santa showed him a photo of the deceased Turaida executive Richard Ash, she'd gotten from the bank's website.

"That could be him. He was wearing a hat most the time."

"You can identify Ash fifty meters away at dusk?"

"I simply said it was possible."

Santa nodded. "As I'm sure you know, Maija Banga's body washed ashore on that very beach the next morning. The *Leesma* was found floating adrift one hundred-sixty kilometers away. It doesn't match up, Jānis. Maybe, Maija never climbed aboard but simply swam around the yacht? Or she jumped off before the boat left?"

"She boarded and did not get off." He said in the tone of one who did not accept disagreement. "I watched carefully until the boat was lost on the horizon."

"Anyone else see her go aboard?"

He frowned, compressing all the lines and wrinkles in that tan face. "No. Unfortunately none of the others on the beach were paying attention. There was a small fishing boat in the vicinity, but I did not get the boat's name. I'm not sure there was one."

"You saw all this in the glare of a sunset?"

"I have been gazing into sunsets since before your parents were born, Miss Ezeriņa."

Santa chuckled. "That'll only give you cataracts you know?"

Her mirth angered him. "If you won't take me seriously, I'll be going." He stood up from the bench. "Līva said you were responsible. I see no responsibility. Only another laughing face. They killed Maija Banga. She was a good girl. Better than you. And no one cares. Not the police. Not even her parents."

"Jānis . . ."

He marched away along the canal edge, beard blowing over his shoulder in the breeze. She watched him go towards the bridge and the tram stop to take him home.

She sighed. *Another triumph of your interpersonal skills, Santa.*

She closed her notebook. This was all a crock. Maija Banga had gone for a swim, drowned, and washed up on the beach. Nothing to connect her to the *Leesma* or the disappearance of Richard and Mindy Ash except this eccentric old man's sunset visions.

Yet, Richard Ash had been Ēriks Helmanis's boss. And now they were both dead under suspicious circumstances. Every thread must be followed to the end . . .

Better reel in old Jānis, soothe his ego, and get everything there is to get from him.

Then visit that ghost yacht.

Balancing two full bags of *Rimi* groceries in her hands, Santa stepped over the knee-high gate and walked as casually as she could along the pier to where the *Leesma* sat moored off the Daugava River. She knew the marina must have security cameras and she'd seen a guard post on the way in. Well, the groceries were her disguise, an excuse should someone stop her. *How could I unlock a gate with my hands full of produce and the keys buried somewhere down in my purse, Mr. Security Guard? Or . . . Turaida Bank ordered the yacht stocked with amenities. Is it my fault no one was here to meet me and take the delivery?*

Fortunately, no one challenged such a flimsy façade and now the elegant twenty-meter motor yacht floated before her—silent, dark, and apparently unmanned. Santa climbed over yet another small gate at the gangplank and walked up onto the ship's deck.

"Beautiful ship!" shouted a voice in Irish-accented English. Santa glanced towards the source. A man on a sailing schooner docked nearby gave a polite wave. "Love the new paint job."

"*Paldies,*" she said, thanking him in Latvian to forego any conversation. He made an overture for them to share a drink on his ship, but Santa walked around the deck until the cabin blocked her from his view. Here, relatively secluded on the riverside deck of the ship, she set the bags down and peered into the *Leesma*'s great darkened windows. As expected, the interior was appropriately opulent, though the thick glass and low morning light allowed little detail. She tried the door, found it locked, then leaned back on the sea rail thinking. She wasn't entirely sure what she expected to find. This whole thing was a high risk, no reward, endeavor.

Still, she was here . . .

Santa strolled along the sea rail, careful to keep the bulk of the ship's cabin between her and the pier. Near the bow, she noted several scratches over the decking, deep enough that the layer of new paint the schooner's skipper had mentioned failed to completely obscure the marks. Scratches on a deck were nothing unusual, but it occurred to her to refocus her sight. To look at every ridge, bump or depression in the paint, to see underneath, to see the *Leesma* as it looked on the night of the deaths.

It was perhaps five minutes later that she found the bullet slug lodged in the ship's exterior, high up in a corner beneath an overhang from the flybridge above; the paint had covered the entry hole, then caved in as it dried, leaving a slight pox-marked depression.

Santa photographed it with her new smartphone—one bought with Turaida's ineffective bribe money—then stood on her tip toes and used her index finger's nail to clear paint flecks away. She knew well enough not dig the slug out of the wall. Not yet.

Santa found her receipt among the groceries, rolled the bill into a tight cylinder, and pressed it into the bullet hole, leaving enough of the paper protruding to ascertain the direction of fire. Her eyes followed the angle down past the decking into sea; the gunman had been in the water, or much more likely, riding in a low boat that had come along the *Leesma's* side.

Was this shot a murder shot? The angle was possible, but unlikely, if a bullet had traveled through a body. A warning shot then? An accident? Santa thought fleetingly of the fishing boat Jānis had mentioned, but her consciousness took a jarring new path and she suddenly felt very cold. If she could find this bullet so quickly, a police crime scene investigation would never have missed it. Clearly, there had been no investigation despite what the papers said. Nothing more than a casual glance at the abandoned ship, if even that, by proper authorities. Which meant someone senior in law enforcement must have rubber-stamped the 'diving accident' story Turaida Bank was pushing and vetoed any further work on the case.

She couldn't deny what her instincts were telling her.

Richard Ash and his wife did not die by accident. Perhaps Maija Banga too.

And the crooks and law were working together.

12

On a warmish Sunday afternoon, Bob Vanags sat alone in his office catching up on his work. To his credit Evgeny Markov had spent most the morning assisting him, but seventy-plus year-old bodies need their rest, and after five hours Bob had insisted the old clerk go home to his cat. Markov tersely refused until Barsik's medicine time, and when he did go, the Russian went with a promise to return after dinner. For now, Bob was alone on the floor, possibly the whole building, except for a security guard on the ground floor, and one thin, muscular maintenance man washing his van in the parking courtyard below.

He found the silence of the Turaida offices on this off-day soothing, a balm well-needed as Bob made discoveries that upset him, indeed, caused him to regret having ever taken a position here. Chief among these was the precarious risk factor of the bank's Small to Medium Enterprise loan strategy. The Italians might have been right. Over the past year almost three hundred million euros in SME loans had been awarded to a mere twelve companies, mostly via cooperation with IDB. To have such a large amount of loan assets in the hands of so few was beyond dangerous, it was illegal. But, worse still, was to whom these loans were given. Twelve mysterious corporations in Russia and Ukraine, none of whom had websites, or appeared as anything more than simple text entries or addresses in any internet search engine Bob could find. No market presence outside of government registration, not even LinkedIn or Facebook. Calling them shell companies would be kind. They were closer to nonentities.

He assumed he was just reading these documents wrong, that Google Translate was not helping him properly through the Latvian ledgers. But Evgeny had confirmed these basic words and the correct column titles before he'd left, muttering things in Russian that sounded dark and foreboding even if Bob didn't quite know the words. Bob, frankly, hoped the records were incomplete. Emails to the Loan Department earlier in the week had resulted in "Ask Accounting" responses. Accounting, of course, said to contact the Loan Department. Terēze ignored his overtures, repeating that he needed to be able to handle his own problems without her "daily" interference.

And then there was this computer directory named *Roze* to which he had no access. Terēze claimed it was old data, yet he could see from the "last updated" and "total size" tabs information was being added to it hourly, though by whom he could not say. Evgeny had begrudgingly admitted Richard Ash had once had access to the directory, but like Terēze, he claimed it was no longer relevant.

Strange.

"*Roze*" was Latvian for "Rose," even Bob with his limited language skills knew that. When paired with the name Turaida, it brought to mind immediately the famous "Turaida Rose", the semi-legendary story of a Latvian maiden, a resident of Turaida Castle near Sigulda, who tricked her would-be rapist into murdering her, so she might keep her honor. A tale of deceit and murder-suicide long ago . . .

Even if Bob was somehow along the wrong path with *Roze*, it was an odd thing to name a locked folder in a financial institution.

Bob shut his laptop and leaned back in his chair, trying to comprehend his situation. Let's look at the present scenario. . . .

Three hundred million in fake loan assets, just at Turaida Group's bank in Latvia, didn't mean the bank was insolvent. However, it *did* mean that the bank's equity was substantially less than what the bank reported. More importantly, it meant that the management was dishonest and put into question the value of the rest of the assets. Especially the loan portfolio.

No visible effort was being made to recover the lost monies.

In effect, Turaida was giving away money to black box entities in the former Soviet Union.

He rubbed his temple, lit up a cigarette. He needed it.

Madness . . . it was like Turaida wanted to collapse.

He finished his cigarette, then another, silently looking out the window, contemplating . . .

He observed the man washing his van in the courtyard. It seemed to Bob that he occasionally glanced up to this very window, then would rush back to his work.

Good God, he was growing paranoid.

Bob put out his cigarette. Rallied his optimism. There was one hope. Turaida Group had a perfect audit record from all of the Big Four auditors over the past twenty years. The bank always reported profits and the auditors always signed clean opinions. Turaida Group had also issued bonds. The Group was continuing to issue more bonds to raise more funds and all bonds so far had received investment grade ratings from the rating agencies. It seemed impossible that the auditors and ratings agencies had missed the information he had found. They would find every impropriety. Or at least most of them. You might hide giving away a stray million in the financial wilds of Eastern Europe, but you couldn't do so with three hundred million. He *must* simply not have all the data. Perhaps, that's what *Roze* contained. . . .

What to do? There was a meeting with a ratings agency in less than three weeks. The agency would decide if Turaida bonds should still be rated investment grade. He would clear his schedule and attend. Come Hell or high-water, he'd have a seat at that table. See the numbers himself, ask questions. Learn beyond a shadow of a doubt that he worked for an honest institution.

Okay, he had a plan.

This calmed him.

Or at least he hoped it would.

It was well past one o'clock and Bob danced with Agnese Avena in his arms. Attraction—physical, emotional, intellectual—tugged with guilt over the professionally improperness of this embrace, and with old memories of her disappearance from his apartment after that first encounter. Still, Evgeny would surely be proud. He'd called her, they'd met, and clicked again, this their third night in row together. Love may indeed conquer all, sentimental cliché that it was.

As the last bars of an old Roxette tune faded, she took his hand and led him from the dance floor to their table by the full-wall, vista windows. If this disco bar was more than a bit touristy, packed with tipsy foreign businessmen and the Machiavellian evening ladies who sought such men, the magnificent view made up for it a hundredfold. Twenty-six stories up atop the Hotel Latvia, the Skyline Restaurant allowed a three-hundred-sixty-degree panorama of Rīga's center, the city aglow late on a Friday night. To dance above an endless sea of lights at the highest point in the country gave the feeling of floating on air, especially as the champagne took hold. And both Bob and Agnese had downed their shares of bubbly.

It was perhaps the alcohol, then, that caused Agnese to say a little too much.

"I'm jealous of you."

"Jealous?"

She lit a thin cigarette, then slid the lighter across the table to him. "Working at Turaida . . . If there's an opening there, I'd like you to let me know, Roberts."

This surprised him. Dissatisfaction after all her awards and recognition? Agnese was, as far as he knew, the rising star at the International Development

Bank. Why leave? She'd never struck him as overly ambitious. Still, some people always sought the greener grass.

"You don't like IDB?"

She sighed, shook her head a bit, as if the admission slightly pained her. "I'd like to move back to Latvia. Germany is nice but it's not home. . . . And IDB is not as efficient as it could be . . . I don't think the money always gets to where it's supposed to be. At least not in a timely way."

"I was thinking something similar about Turaida."

Her eyes widened, and she slipped from her seat across the table to join Bob on his side, as if the conversation were taking a more serious, personal turn. "Oh, no, Roberts . . . Turaida does so much good . . . The IDB would be nothing without the alliance with the Turaida Group."

They had grown close these past three nights, still Bob didn't quite have the resolve to mention his doubts about Turaida's asset quality. They were, after all, doing a project together.

"I'm having doubts," was all he had the nerve to finally say, "about how things are run at Turaida . . ."

Her voice took on an earnestness ill-suited for the disco surroundings. "In Moldova, in Ukraine, I've seen the businesses that have been started with Turaida money, Roberts. Seen how its changed communities. So much of Ukraine is still a dilapidated post-Soviet economy. And Moldova is worse; there are parts of the country that are truly medieval in character. For the most part, the education is already there. You start a few modern enterprises and the quality of life rises exponentially." She leaned against him, a hand on his knee. "There was a project Ēriks and I worked on in Western Moldova where the average income went from forty euros a month to nearly six hundred in less than two years . . ."

"I didn't say they weren't doing any good."

"Without Turaida, I'd fear for the standard of living in half-a-dozen post-Soviet countries. The whole region could implode into anarchy." She shoved him gently, as if his doubts were playful stupidity. "You should be proud to work there."

"I . . . I am."

"Good." Agnese took a long puff of her cigarette. "And promise me you'll let me know if something opens up at Turaida. I'd work under you, gladly."

"Sure," he answered softly.

They sat silently for a few minutes as a disco-mix of Joan Jett's "Do You Wanna Touch Me" drummed through the speakers. Finally, they talked of plans for next week, and the arrival of Bob's son from America. Agnese said she'd like to meet him. Bob, a bit reluctantly, replied that was possible.

A few minutes before two o'clock the lights came on, and the various parties and interlocked couples headed for the elevator exits. Bob and Agnese, among the last to leave anyway, were further delayed by her trip to the toilet. As Bob waited by the ladies' room door, watching the last crowds pack themselves into the elevators, his eyes descended to the rack of free tourist-orientated newspapers and promotional flyers nearby. Killing time, he plucked a copy of the English-language edition of the *Baltic Beacon* from the stand, began thumbing through it. The little paper's contents consisted of advertisements for clubs, tours, hotels, and spas, a few short articles on spots of local interest for the "first-time-in-Latvia" traveler; and near the back, a more serious piece, one that stood out amongst the fluff. The headline made Bob's stomach twist:

CAN THE EU REALLY AFFORD TURAIDA BANK?
An Editorial by Santa Ezeriņa

A little photo at the bottom of the piece revealed the author to be that journalist he'd met at the Helmanis funeral. The one who'd been dragged away unconscious.

Bob perused the article. *Investigations indicate individuals listed as major stockholders at Turadia Group, multimillionaires on paper, live in one-room apartments in Soviet-era tenement slums. Who really has the money and power at Turaida? Citizens of the European Union must demand to know . . .*

"Are you reading that Nazi paper?"

He looked up to see Agnese waiting for him. She'd reapplied her makeup, though the cross expression on her face clearly ruined that effect.

"I thought it was more of a tourist rag than anything political, Agnese." He folded the paper and slipped it back onto the rack. "Shall we go?"

"It's trash," she said and took his hand. The elevator came: empty, warm, its glass walls giving them one last grand view of nighttime Rīga as it descended.

Somewhere around the fifteenth floor, with Agnese snugly in his arms, he said:

"I want to fight corruption, Agnese."

"Say that again."

"I want to fight corruption."

"You're naïve. But not bad looking . . ."

13

Santa Ezeriņa knew the men were watching her. Of this she had no doubt. The only question was one of identity. She'd crossed many people during her years as a journalist and frequently stumbled upon old enemies in unexpected places. Latvia, after all, wasn't such a large country. Still, if Santa were to guess, she'd wager the men on the forested knoll with binoculars were agents of Turaida Bank. They'd been stalking her since the funeral of Ēriks Helmanis and the damning editorials she'd published in the *Baltic Beacon* after they'd assaulted her and tried to coerce her cooperation.

She'd seen their shadows on walls in Rīga and Liepāja, heard extra clicks on a dozen phone calls over the weeks since. Now, they'd tracked her to Sigulda, the wild, hilly area forty minutes out of Rīga known locally as the "Switzerland of Latvia." The designation was part Latvian sardonic humor and part tourist bait, as none of these tree-covered hills here could even approximate the Wagnerian ascents of the Alps.

Still, it was the most uneven terrain in the country and from her window secluded on a high vista above a valley of birches and oaks, she could easily see her spies. At least three of them, dressed as deer hunters, had been sitting idly on a knoll on her side of the vale since she'd arrived at the Vītols household. Another, pretending to walk a particularly vicious-looking Czech wolfdog, bid his time on the dirt road that wound itself up from the valley floor to the hilltop where this and several other nineteenth century wooden houses stood. Santa knew the man with the wolfdog was one of them. Occasionally the dog-walker made cellphone calls and the heaviest-looking of the knoll men would always raise his own phone at that very moment to answer.

Santa remained coldly confident in her perceptiveness, but she also knew her view was limited at the windowpane. If she saw four, she had to assume there was double or triple that number unseen in the forested hills. If they wanted to take her, as she suspected they had taken Ēriks Helmanis, Santa doubted she could make it down to her Toyota parked on the valley floor.

But that was a problem for another time . . .

She heard footsteps behind her. Santa turned from the window, back into the interior of the quaintly decorated, old-fashioned looking house. A thin, conservatively-dressed woman in her late sixties approached. In her hands, the woman juggled a steaming teapot and three large, glazed mugs decorated with floral designs and traditional Latvian folklore symbols.

"He's coming, Miss Ezeriņa. The arthritis slows Toms up a bit, but he's game for a chat with you," the woman said. She set the mugs and teapot down on a small table by the window. "He's been looking forward to it since your call yesterday."

"Thank you, Mrs. Vītola. I appreciate your husband seeing me at short notice."

She smiled. "No trouble at all, dear. Toms is flattered. We get so few professional visitors now." Mrs. Vītola motioned for her to be seated. Santa took a chair facing the window, an eye outside to maintain her vigilance.

They talked briefly of the turning of the seasons, how the gold, reds, and oranges made the Sigulda countryside impossibly beautiful. Mrs. Vītola, who never gave Santa her Christian name, remarked that she and her husband had lived six years on the valley ridge since his retirement from the Rīga police force and they'd never seen a more stunningly colorful autumn than this one. Santa politely agreed and sipped her tea, listening to wolfdogs barking in the distance.

They soon heard the creaking of small, un-oiled wheels. A man well past seventy, leaning on a wheeled walker, made his way slowly towards them, a fluffy orange tabby cat following at his feet. As plainly dressed as his wife, the man wore his silver hair parted at the ear in such an obvious comb-over that he might have looked spectacularly clownish had his appearance not been redeemed by the enthusiastic smile across his face and an impish gleam in his eyes. These eyes impressed Santa as wide and youthful for an old man and he radiated a genial grandfather-ness of the sort instinctively sought by children for stories, sugary treats, and surprise coins pulled from behind the ears. Though Santa had never met Toms Vītols, she immediately liked him. By all accounts, everyone did.

"I'm honored to meet you, Miss Ezeriņa," he said. "The late Dr. Pēteris Balodis was a dear friend of ours. Glad to know the woman who brought his killer to justice."

Toms set his walker aside, and with a grunt of effort, sat down at the table between his wife and Santa. The tabby immediately jumped up to settle on his lap.

"I heard you almost died during the Balodis Incident, Miss Ezeriņa. People out here in Sigulda appreciate that kind of perseverance in making our lives safer. You don't see it so much in later generations if I can be truthful. I'm glad to know it's still there, should the well need to be tapped again."

Santa smiled. She *had* nearly been killed along with Pēteris Balodis last January, surviving the bombing on a hill only a few kilometers away. It had taken a lot to get Santa to return to Sigulda. But she no longer trusted the privacy of her phone and emails, so she'd no choice but to meet Toms Vītols in person. Even the simple call to arrange their meeting had attracted those men on the knoll . . .

Toms sipped his tea, stroked the purring cat in his lap. "How may we assist you today, Miss Ezeriņa?"

"I'd like you to listen to two recordings and tell me if the speaker is the same person."

"We really should do this at the offices in Rīga. I've no equipment as a private citizen, but I can still pull a few strings at the police . . ."

"No police."

The enthusiasm faded from his face. Toms asked his wife to give them privacy. Without hesitation, she did so. When Mrs. Vītola was safely in the backrooms, he said:

"Please, go on, Miss Ezeriņa."

Santa placed her smartphone on the table, played a YouTube video of Ēriks Helmanis speaking English to an international crowd at a conference in Berlin. His accent was heavy, but the speech patterns clear enough. Of course, Santa was no voice analyst. But Toms Vītols was. The best any Baltic police force had ever seen. Trained by British counter-intelligence against the Soviets back in the day, when Latvia's independence came, he'd spurned the covert world and established a "Forensic Voice Analysis and Speech Biometrics" department within the Rīga police force in '96. By 2000 many argued the group was as good as any in Europe. He'd worked high profile cases in Belfast and Munich. He'd given lectures to the FBI, MI5, and surely many other groups that would never make the papers.

Then six years ago Toms Vītols had suddenly retired. Could be age, probably was health, but it might be something else too. We all had skeletons; a lot was happening behind the scenes these days. Santa didn't care as long as he helped and could keep secrets.

After about two or three minutes of listening to Ēriks Helmanis's Berlin speech Toms said: "That's enough for now."

"The second recording isn't quite as good." She withdrew headphones from her purse, plugged them into the phone, handed them to Toms. Then she pressed an app. The brief phone conversation she'd had with the anonymous Turaida source, the one from the payphone the night before Helmanis's suicide, played into the headphones. Turaida's thugs may have stolen her original phone, but she'd already had her recording stored in the Cloud.

Santa watched Toms's face, trying to read his reaction. After about ten seconds he removed the headphones. She paused the playback.

He looked at her sternly: "To record someone without informing them is a felony, Miss Ezeriņa."

"I never release such recordings. When people call me at three A.M., I don't want to miss any details. I'm a journalist."

"It's still illegal. I've sent men to prison for this very activity." A shadow passed across his face. "By assisting you, I become an accomplice. And a hypocrite."

"The police . . ."

"Show evidence and get the permission of a judge before making any recordings."

Santa scooted the mugs and teapot out of her way and leaned forward over the table. "Let's live in the real world. The police don't always have warrants . . ." She tried to dampen her sarcasm. "There are countless exceptions. I know *I've* been recorded!"

"When I worked on the force, Miss Ezeriņa, there were no exceptions! Do you presume to tell me my business?"

He was not quite the genial old man she'd thought. Santa changed the course of her argument.

"Mr. Vītols, the man on this recording failed to show. I think this is the same man who was found dead the next day. They say suicide. I believe he was murdered. Possibly by associates of Turaida Bank."

"Turaida Bank, you say?"

"Yes, another reason I can't go to the police. You know they have men on the force."

His voice turned to a whisper. "I've fought them ten years. Maybe more."

"You spoke of perseverance, *Izmeklētājs* Vītols. Maybe it's time to draw from that well again. Go to the end of that recording. He talks of billions to be stolen, of governments in jeopardy."

"Are you willing to risk prison to get the word out, Miss Ezeriņa?"

"I'm risking more than that by being here now."

He sighed, and for the first time Santa thought he truly looked old. Toms slipped on the headphones. She pressed PLAY.

For the next thirty minutes, he alternated between recordings, all the while making notes on a paper napkin on the table. The tabby grew bored and found another bed. Mrs. Vītola left the backrooms to putter about the kitchen.

Finally, he pulled off the headphones, stared up at the ceiling.

"Well?" asked Santa.

"You think too much of me, Miss Ezeriņa. Without equipment or software, listening to recordings made and played back on common devices," he shook his head, "and one voice is in English, the other in Latvian, to try and match them in half-an-hour is extremely difficult."

She thought of the men outside. "I may not have another half hour, *Inspector* Vītols. Give me your expert guess. Please. You're the best this side of the Danube."

"*Was* the best, Miss Ezeriņa. Now, I'm only a pensioner." He sighed. "If I were in court, I'd tell you that there is no way to be certain these are the same people. A judge would throw it out. As he should."

"I'm not a judge. I'm a *Baltic Beacon* journalist. Trust me our standards are much lower."

He smiled at this. "If you want a conjecture, I'd say, based strictly on the cadences and a rough pattern of the voices as determined by the speaker's anatomy, that there is a sixty to seventy percent chance this is the same individual. If the context you mention is accurate—a source from Turaida matched against an employee of the same bank in a relevant department—that number may even approach ninety percent."

"Ninety percent . . . Inspector, that's well beyond the gold standard at the *Beacon*."

"If he is the same man, then we have a very big problem."

"If we hypothesize Helmanis was murdered, then it is logical to assume his assertions of Turaida's intentions were correct or at least close enough to force his silencing. So, how does a bank steal billions? And how and why does it topple governments?"

"On the former, I can't say. You need an expert on financial crimes for that. On the later, I'd turn to history. Banks have toppled governments since there have been banks, Miss Ezeriņa. Time and time again. On every continent but Antarctica."

"How do they do it?"

"Their assets disappear. Then they collapse and take the country down with them."

After she left the Vītols house two hours later, Santa walked down the hillside road in the direction of her car. The deer hunters had abandoned the knoll for unknown positions, but the dog-walker still meandered along a bend in the road ahead and below. She had only descended a few steps in his direction when Santa realized the man had released his pet from its leash. The wolfdog, while still far away, was sprinting up the path towards her.

This, she thought, was not a good sign. Wishing to draw any conflict away from the home of the elderly couple who had hosted her, Santa changed her course, slipping through the garden alleyway between the Vītols house and its neighbor and crossing over the ridge-crest to the other side. Here was a mirroring valley with reddish rocky outcrops occasionally breaking the constant coverage of trees. A cable car line crossed the gorge from a point farther along the hillside, the suspended gondolas a favorite of tourists allowing spectacular views of the Gauja River and the orange-ish tower of the castle at valley's end. On the vale's far side, a host of buses lay waiting, bound for Sigulda's train station or routes directly into Rīga.

Santa moved to the edge of a stony precipice, considering whether to take the path down. She couldn't help but think of that journalist killed last year in Kyiv by a car bomb, the one who'd died for crossing the Russian mob. How long had her pursuers had access to her Toyota down in the shadows of the valley? It might be better to leave the car for now and find another path into Rīga.

She heard barking growing nearer. That Czech wolfdog burst from the gardens between the houses and charged towards her. The dog was a terrifying sight, white fangs, a bullish neck, and heavy jaws bred to crush bone. But Santa kept her head. A single attack dog wasn't insurmountable if you knew what you were doing. She pulled her pepper spray handgun from her purse and shoved it deep into her back pocket. Better to save the pepper gun for human opponents. As the animal rampaged closer, Santa folded her leather purse across her forearm, anchoring it there by twisting the shoulder strap and pulling it tight with her free hand. When the dog reached her, she shoved the protective arm forward. Breeding and training told it to bite, and its vice jaws clamped down on the front surface of the purse, tugging and tearing, refusing to let go. The purse slid from her arm, and still holding the strap, Santa engaged in a tug-of-war with the fierce animal, a game that would look like play if it weren't so deadly serious. Primitive impulse to grip its prey played against the beast. If it released the purse Santa had no other defense.

Santa counted on this instinct to keep her safe, and as the dog thrashed about, she slowly rotated their positions 180° until it was the animal, not she, who was at the edge of the cliff. Santa gave a strong tug in her direction, and when the snarling wolfdog responded by throwing its heavy head and shoulders back, she simply let go. The recoil sent the animal tumbling over the precipice and out of sight.

Santa heard a distant yelp as it hit the ground, then stillness.

A pity, she thought. I liked that purse.

It occurred to her then if the attack dog had Santa's scent that her Toyota, her apartment in Rīga, or both, were likely compromised. Not waiting for the wolfdog's handler to arrive, Santa descended the steep footpath nearby until it merged with the main road crossing the hill face. Ahead of her in the distance, a collection of a dozen or so tourists waited at the hillside station for the next cable car.

Santa joined the queue.

As she waited for the cable car to arrive, the dog's master appeared atop the cliff near the houses. His body language showed confusion, no doubt he was wondering at the fate of his attack dog. If this troubled him, it didn't last long. He spied Santa in the waiting crowd and navigated the footpath towards the station.

That cable car couldn't come fast enough.

When the car did arrive, the passengers flowed in slowly, feeding their money into an automated ticket booth and passing through a turnstile to board. Santa had just enough change in her pocket for the machine to dispense a ticket. She slipped the ticket into the turnstile's slot, waited for the light to turn green, and stepped inside the cable car gondola. Safe at last.

Or so she thought.

With remarkable agility, the assassin sprinted down the hill, arriving just in time to snatch a ticket from a slow-boarding passenger, fed the turnstile, and slipped inside as the doors closed.

A sign lighted that read: "Maximum Occupancy."

The cable car released from the station and began to move across the valley.

Packed inside, Santa stood nearly face to face with her hunter. A tall, muscular man of about forty, he had a strong masculine scent and a deep grayness in his eyes that hid his malice. If he was armed, as he surely must be, the location of the gun was not obvious. His jacket appeared too thin to disguise a shoulder holster, but you never know . . .

It was only a few seconds into their journey when he made a cellphone call, telling someone—the fat deer hunter most likely—where he was and when he expected to dock. Given the slow trajectory of the cable car, designed to give tourists maximum view time over the valley, his accomplices would likely be waiting for her on the opposite ridge. A virtual certainty if they had a car at the ready. They might even show up in her Toyota.

Santa gazed at the man, smugly biding his time. Well, she'd cut it short.

"Why are you trying to murder me?" Santa shouted.

A flicker of surprise appeared in the assassin's eyes. This amused her.

Yet, the crowd around Santa remained surprisingly unmoved.

They couldn't *all* be assassins? She shouted "murder" again. A few irritated glances came her way, but nothing more.

Were they foreigners? A tour group all ignorant of Latvian?

She shouted a third time, this time in English. Several faces grew stern, but by now she was just a crazy lady, screaming something every second. They moved away but did nothing else.

The assassin smiled.

No man is an island, but *she* apparently was. Santa plucked a pair of bird-watching binoculars from a hapless tourist and scooted over to the window. The cable car was now over the middle of the valley allowing a clear view of the vale-spanning bridge below. A flatbed truck sped across that bridge at breakneck speed, the now-familiar deer hunters in the back, the heavyset man at the wheel. When they reached the ridge ahead, two men armed with rifles sprang out. Indifferent to the panic they induced amongst those at the station, the riflemen jumped the turnstiles, awaiting her gondola as people scattered everywhere.

The tourist stole back his binoculars, spouting a profane Finnish insult in her direction.

"*Tämä on perseestä!*" she replied in his language.

Santa glanced around the interior of the car. The doors were electronically sealed until arrival. Yet, to keep *everything* locked would be an illegal fire hazard. There must be an exit that opened manually.

She looked to the ceiling.

There was one way out. Santa rose to her tiptoes and grabbed the bar set in the ceiling. A hatch descended giving her a handhold and it took all her strength in the swaying car to pull herself up onto the roof.

"A suicide," shouted the gray-eyed assassin. But no one listened.

How do you like it, mister? thought Santa. The Finns think you're as crazy as me. Guilt by association.

Santa reached the roof and slammed the hatch shut. Balancing on the vibrating car, she held onto the great steel arm that reached up to the heavy cables overhead. The heights were dizzying but also decreasing as land rose to meet the coming ridge.

The sound of a bullet off the steel arm above her. Then another. The hunters fired their rifles from her destination ahead.

I'm never coming to Sigulda again, she thought. *Never.*

Another shot ricocheted off the gondola roof at her feet. Desperate, Santa fixed her vision on the maintenance ladder of a cable-line pole rising above the tree-topped hillside and fast approaching. Santa had a chance if she had the nerve.

As the pole passed the front of the car, she jumped. An athlete in her prime, her timing strong, Santa cleared the distance easily. But her hand missed the ladder rung.

Not even close.

She cursed as her momentum took Santa into the trees beyond, her body accelerating as she fell through leaves of crimson and gold.

A beautiful death, she thought. So many colors . . .

But Santa didn't want to die. Not yet.

She clutched at the higher, more flexible branches. Santa caught one thick enough to survive her weight, but it bent under the motion and swung her against the trunk. She hit it hard, something cracking in her shoulder. Santa lost her grip and fell again. The lower branches whipped and spun her body as she plummeted. It was all she could do to protect her face until she landed prone on a long, shoulder-wide bough. Bones snapped, savage pain shooting like lightning through her body, but the massive limb stopped her fall.

For a moment. Half-in-shock and grievously injured, she had no strength to hold her position. Santa's broken body slid off the branch and fell the last four meters unimpeded to the ridge side. It was only the softness of the Sigulda earth that allowed her to survive. A steep gradient, she slid down through the underbrush, rocks and brush scraping at her flesh, until at last she came to a rest on some earthen outcropping on the forest hillside.

Santa lay stunned, unsure if she should move, unsure if she *could* move. Things were broken inside, her limbs dead, numerous scratches on her face and hands.

Time passed, impossible to tell how much. She tried to rise but shards of pain running along her neck, ribs, and both legs made that impossible. She vomited, blood in the mix, almost blacking out from the spasms.

Her mind slowly cleared, though. A car full of people had seen her fall. Even more witnessed the men with rifles. The police would be coming. A contest, who would find her first? The tree canopy hid her position from her enemies above for the moment. Somehow, she had to move, to seek a hiding place until the police and ambulance scattered her hunters away.

She could not walk, nor even stand for an instant. Her only choice was to crawl, to drag her useless body along the mud, over the dirt and fallen leaves of this thin outcropping. As she inched her way in agony, she came across her pepper gun, jarred free from her pocket in the last moments of the slide above. She clutched it in one hand, as Santa crawled towards the spot where the ledge met the cliff-side at its steepest point. Here were shallow caves, the walls made of the soft beach-like sand for which Sigulda is famous.

A strange taste seeped into her mouth. More than blood or vomit, it was a dark, iron grayish fluid. What organ had these broken ribs punctured? She'd need a doctor very soon if she were to survive this.

Santa reached the entrance to the nearest cave, dragging herself through the soft sand along its bottom. Her trail, her dark clothes and hair, all contrasted against the whiteness of the cavern's interior. The recess was shallow, reaching not three or four meters into the cliff's base. In this state, she'd be easily spotted.

In the heart of the cave, Santa removed the pepper cartridge from the damaged gun, and with the help of a jagged stone, pried out the pepper spray projectile, depositing it into the sands. Swiftness was paramount, before her pursuers passed within hearing distance. Santa set the projectile-less shell on a flat rock and struck the firing pin hard with another stone.

Nothing happened. She hit it again, the pains of the motion birthing a primal scream from her lips and sending black spots across her vision.

Yet, her shriek shook the sand looser on the walls above.

On the third strike, the shell went off. The sparking stone shot out of her hands, the discharge burning her fingertips. But the crack of a bursting shell was all she needed. The explosive sound dislodged a layer of the free sand from the cave walls, and it fell like snow over her, covering body and trail, stones and gun; a blanket as complete as it was thin.

Santa didn't dare move a muscle less the grains should slip away revealing some part of her. All she dared do was exhale lightly through her to nose to clear her nostrils, and open one eye to watch for enemies.

She waited to see who came earlier—her pursuers or rescuers.

The hunters arrived first.

She heard their distant shouts, husky Russian voices calling to each other somewhere below as they searched the lower hillside or valley.

Then another answered, his calls much closer. The man with gray eyes appeared out of the autumn haze, lingering just outside the cave entrance, a pistol in his hand.

Underneath the sand, Santa's hand slipped over a stone. It wouldn't make any difference to the final outcome, of course, but maybe she'd dislodge a few teeth or shatter a kneecap. Leave a fine scar for the bastard to remember her.

He probed the fine white sand with his boot tip. Paused. The man turned his head. He heard something outside.

Santa heard it too. The tone of the Russian voices had changed. No longer the calm calls of searching hunters, but the alarmed shouts of retreat, soon drowned out by police sirens echoing down the valley, the deafening alarms of multiple patrol cars, already near and growing nearer every heartbeat.

These sounds were no hallucinations. The assassin disappeared out the cave entrance. A welcome last sight as Santa's vision faded. She had just enough strength to roll over, to dislodge the sand covering so rescuers might spot her broken body.

Then merciful blackness took Santa's mind at last.

14

David Vanags wondered who the woman was next to his father. She was blonde, cute for her age, not quite his type, but whatever worked for Dad. She greeted him warmly, as if they were old friends, yet David found himself disappointed that his father had brought her to the Rīga airport to meet him on his arrival in Latvia.

Was jealousy the cause of his dislike? Maybe. But a jealousy for himself? Or his mother? Or was he just surprised? David juggled these emotions as they'd piled his luggage into the car, and his dad had rambled on about Turaida Bank and Latvia and the new school he'd be attending soon.

Time would sort his thoughts. It always did.

They climbed inside their rented Mercedes, and the car pulled away from the short-term parking with his father driving, this Agnese woman in the passenger seat, and David lounging across the back, elbow on a suitcase. The road outside the airport was straight and long, the land green and flat much like the American Midwest. Shiny new shopping malls and car dealerships whizzed by. They could still be in Illinois for all he knew . . .

Not such a big change so far. Other than the woman.

Dad had hinted on the phone of a romance, but to bring her to meet him implied importance. Was that a bad thing?

He sighed. He didn't know.

"Congratulations, on your court victory," said Agnese.

"Thank you." He could see she was trying to be kind. David fought off annoyance that she knew about his court appearance at all. Is this how Dad had described him to her? *My son, he has issues with road rage. But he's ok.*

"Elvis did a nice job actually as my rep, Dad."

"Elvis?" asked Agnese. "A Latvian friend?"

"My second cousin in Minneapolis," said his Dad. "We had him assist David with the case."

Like I'm a criminal, thought David. "Elvis wants a grand for the assistance, Dad."

"A grand? That's more than any fine."

"He said it was fair since he spent so much time in Park Ridge. He's clearly desperate for money."

"I'll talk to him."

David didn't say anything. Nor did he mention that the private dick hired by Patrick McMillan had still been shadowing their house as late as last week. Why alarm Agnese with more tales of Chicago crime. She'd think American life was something out of a noir novel.

He wondered if she wanted to live in America. Long term . . .

The road into the city finally had a bend, and as his father turned the wheel, David noticed for the first time he wasn't wearing his wedding ring.

This irked him. "I put flowers on Mom's grave before I left."

"Thanks, David."

"It's good to remember her."

His father looked at him quizzically through the rearview. "Yes, it is."

David drummed his fingers on the suitcase.

I'm being a prick.

A few days later, David, still trying to get used to his surroundings, slipped out of his father's Rīga apartment at two A.M. It was not an unusual habit. He'd taken late night walks regularly in Illinois, a favorite way of clearing his thoughts and getting a little exercise before bed. Nighttime sorties usually unmentioned the next morning. David didn't view it as "sneaking out" exactly, he'd keep his cell should Dad wake and discover him gone, and he'd never actually hidden or denied these ventures back home, though by the same token he seldom brought them up without prodding. Why add another worry to his widowed father's slumber?

Of course, those old walks were in American suburbia. Now, he was downtown in a foreign capital. But Rīga's Old Town streets seemed safe enough, full of late-season tourists, mostly Italians and Germans, headed to the taverns, discos, and various all-night restaurants. Medieval-looking towers, walls, and buildings were decorated with neon-lit signs for shawarma eateries, small casinos, and jazz bars, even a high-end strip joint in the base of a crumbling old church. Live rockabilly music pulsed through the night from the tents of an American-style burger restaurant dominating the center of a nearby square, the

Latvian greasers on stage doing remarkable imitations of Elvis Presley, Carl Perkins, and Eddie Cochran. There was so much activity David regretted not being here in the busier summer months. He'd heard the July streets were a fusion of European Renaissance-fair-clothing and carnival-in-Rio debauchery. Even out of season, the scene was quite the spectacle.

He stopped into an all-night music store, found the selection impressive—punk and Scandinavian metal dominated—but the prices daunting. Full of a wanderer's spirit, David exited through the back into a small, stony courtyard. Here Goth youths his age and younger, smoked cigarettes and drank a reddish beer from plastic cups, while music far heavier and more electronic than the tourist-friendly rockabilly blasted from the open door of an old brick building. Spray-painted sheets serving as signs called it the *"Vidusskola,"* the Latvian equivalent of a high school. A word he knew only because he'd be attending a *vidusskola* next Monday morning.

He doubted this was the same place.

Feeling self-conscious and feeding the need to *appear* as if he knew where he was going, David crossed through the courtyard, and entered the *Vidusskola.* He passed through a dingy, beer-scented passage without cashier or bouncer into a large, darkened hall that must have once been a theater judging by the bronze decorations and the balconies on three sides still adorned with faded bunting and tapestries. Now, it had been transformed into a rave hall engorged with throbbing teenage bodies, the room's sole light coming from a bar tucked beneath one balcony and the projection of enormous stylized animated cartoons that covered the wall above the stage. A fan of animation, David recognized the dystopian world, elongated characters, and leather-clad female assassin as Peter Chung's masterpiece, Æon Flux, and the combination of science fiction and aged Old-World theater, gave the whole scene a steam punk tint, if one more suited for the 1990s than the present day.

Still, it'd be more fun than watching middle-aged tourists dance to Latvian versions of "Wake Up Little Suzy."

David made his way into the crowd. He could count on the fingers of one hand the times he'd been to a club and never alone. David knew he wasn't a dancer, and though he secretly suspected *some* woman might find him handsome, he wasn't confident enough to act on that suspicion. Instead, he meekly passed through to the bar without a glance at any girl, bought himself a Coke, and stared intensely at the animations on the wall, feigning interest to mask his insecurity.

He sat there a while, wishing to socialize but unsure how to proceed. The bouncer at last appeared, a fortyish man, far too old for this scene, in a dark coat by the entrance. He surveyed the hall, more than once glancing David's way. He wondered if there was some cover he should have paid.

The bouncer soon disappeared down the entrance hall. David's eyes wandered to the dance floor where a particularly attractive girl, roughly his age, was dancing with two older boys. She was less Goth than most here and moved in time with the music in ways David found pleasing.

To his surprise she caught him staring and smiled. To his greater surprise the girl left her dance partners to go to the bar next to him. The bartender immediately handed her a shiny black purse from behind the bar. As she rifled through it, the girl said something in her language. It was only when she stopped and stared at him with a pierced, raised eyebrow that David realized she'd spoken to him.

"English only," he said. "Sorry."

"You want a drink?"

"I don't drink."

She looked him up and down with a smirk. "You must drink *something*."

"Well, another Coke." David felt he should pay. He pulled a crumpled five-euro bill from his pocket, shoved it towards her along the bar top.

She flipped the euros to the bartender. "You are a tourist?"

"I live here now."

"Why?"

"My dad's a banker."

"Boring?"

"A little."

She pulled a small bottle of what looked like Visine from her purse, began to put droplets in her eyes.

"Rich?" she asked, eyes rolled back to take the drops.

"Not really."

"I hate money."

"Who doesn't?"

She capped the bottle, threw it in her purse. "Dance with me."

"After the Coke."

"You don't like dancing?"

"I need to go to the toilet."

She nodded.

The bartender directed him to the toilets on the second floor. They smelled of urine more than most and in front of a scratched and graffiti-covered mirror, he washed his face, hoping the cool water would wake his courage.

Just act calm. Dance a little if she wants, but not too much. She won't be impressed with your dance. In fact, make some excuse about dancing. Get her *Viber* before dancing . . . *Don't* dance, just talk . . . You're American, they like Americans . . .

"*Vai varētu?*" said a guy waiting for the sink.

"Sorry."

David moved aside, looking at himself in the mirror over the other boy's shoulder.

All right, let's do this.

David went down the steps to the bar a little worried she'd be gone. But the girl remained, elbow leaning impatiently on the bar top. He drank the flat Coke with too much lemon waiting for him, made small talk about being from Chicago, asked her recommendations for good clubs in the Old Town. She said this place, no others.

The girl, he still did not know her name, got off the barstool.

"I'm going to dance. Coming?"

His stomach knotted in fear, contorted pains that remained as he joined her on the floor. She was a good dancer, moving in time to the music, but her skill only made him feel inadequate, un-sexy. He lost the rhythm, bumped into others, stopped dancing to apologize. His stomach twisted tighter.

She took his hand, pulled him to a clearer spot on the floor. But he was now growing dizzy and had a hard time keeping up with her.

This wasn't nerves. Something was wrong.

"Are you okay?" she shouted over the music.

"I'm . . . I'm not sure." His head was spinning, the pains so sharp he thought he might vomit. He bent over, hands on his knees.

"We'll get you some air," she said.

He was dimly aware of being helped from the dance floor by two larger bodies. He thought it might be those two she'd been dancing with earlier, the girl directing them all towards the door.

Then they were through the entrance hall, out into a reeking alley off the little courtyard. David found himself lying face down on the cold wet stones, breathing hard, trying not puke, some hand rifling through his pockets.

"Hey . . ." he said weakly trying to rise. Was this really happening?

Someone shoved him down, his chin bouncing off the alley stones, a knee on his back. The probing hands dug more aggressively into his pockets.

"No . . ."

"Shut up," said an accented voice. It was the girl.

The hands dug further, ripped his pocket away. His change fell out over the stones. They rummaged through the other pocket at his keys, his phone . . .

Then the hands were gone.

The largest assailant flew over him, thudded hard against the alley wall, shrieked, and gripped his shoulder where the arm had been wrenched from its socket. The next thief lost teeth from a blow that demolished his face. They screamed the hoarse, wet cries of the badly injured, the girl's screech healthier though no less fearful. The three of them scampered over each other as they fled the alley.

Strong, sure hands lifted David from the stones.

"We'll get you home," said a voice with an accent different than the others. It was the man he'd thought the bouncer. "Eye-drops in your drink, friend. Nothing you can't sleep off."

The Visine . . .

The man directed him towards the road, held David upright when he vomited, then set him in the back of a taxi.

He thanked the man. His benefactor had beautiful gray eyes. Angel's eyes.

And then those eyes were gone.

David didn't remember giving the taxi driver his address or payment, but somehow, he was back in front of his father's apartment. He pulled himself from the cab, stumbled inside the lobby to the elevator, slumped against the lift's walls until he reached his floor.

Inside the apartment, he shut the door gently, then fought his way to the kitchen to find some bread or saltines to absorb the acid in his stomach. Dad had nothing. Microwave popcorn was as close as he could get.

David heard a woman's voice speaking in Russian—at least he thought it was Russian, something Slavic, definitely not Latvian. He heard a quick "*Poka, poka*" and Agnese emerged from the backrooms, wrapped in his dad's bathrobe, a phone in her hands. Her eyes widened when she saw him.

"You look worse for wear."

"Yes."

"Drinking?" she cracked a smile that implied confidentiality.

"Not what I wanted to be drinking."

"I can make you some tea."

"No thanks." He tried to soften, to reflect her smile. "I need sleep."

She nodded briskly and he wondered if he'd hurt her. She sat down on the couch, pulled her robe tight, silently worked on some text message.

When the popcorn finished, David took it from the microwave, headed towards his bedroom. Paused.

"Popcorn, Agnese?"

"You need it more than I do."

"Those aren't words you hear about popcorn often."

She grinned and for the first time looked a bit young to him. "Have a rest, David. We'll keep each other's secrets."

"Yeah, all right. Good night."

"Good night."

On Monday, David entered the McCann-Kopans International Preparatory School of Rīga. Prestigious. Internationally recognized. Students native to fifty-six countries. Faculty from twenty-one. Instruction in English.

He should have assumed there was a school uniform or at least a dress code. His father or perhaps Agnese might have mentioned it. Or, frankly, David could have checked out the school's website as he'd been told to a thousand times. Reeboks, blue jeans, and an anime t-shirt were not sufficient, apparently, for an international private school. He was a public-school kid, so busy since he'd come to Latvia, it had never occurred to him to check. He'd wear jeans and a t-shirt every day of his life if he could. Clothes, frankly, never meant much to David.

But now they did.

"As this is your first day, David," said his Calculus teacher, Mrs. Murphy in a cool Johannesburg-via-London accent, "We won't send you home now. You can change at lunch. But today is the only exception. Take your seat."

He walked down the aisle toward the only empty seat, twenty eyes on him. The senior boys in suits, the girls in sweaters and skirts. The only differences found in the diverse ethnicity of the faces and the styles of their expensive accessories, individuality hinted through watches, pins, ties, scarves, and bows. No one was wearing anything close to him. Maybe, David hoped, they see him as "the rebel." More likely he was being viewed by his new classmates as a dope, an American clown who'd come unprepared. Nobody, at the McCann-Kopans School was poor. If you wore jeans it was by choice, not for lack of options.

He reached the open seat, and ashamed of the situation, sat as fast as possible, seeking to cover as much of his body by the desktop as he could. David sat so fast, he only caught a glimpse of the bright-eyed girl with curly red hair behind him, though he'd enjoyed the smile on her face. And he liked the words "Welcome" she said as he settled in.

Still, like the rest, she must surely think him an underdressed fool. What a first impression . . .

As everyone synchronized their laptops and iPad for the presentation, and Mrs. Murphy began her droning lectures on vector acceleration, this girl behind him whispered:

"*Dragon Ball Z*? Cool! I've a *Goku* shirt at home."

David smiled.

The rebel . . .

15

"Give me the info, Evgeny."

"After the meeting, sir."

Standing in the hall of the less-opulent third floor of the Turaida Building, Bob Vanags straightened his tie and stared quizzically at his assistant. The expression on the old man's face told him enough, confirmed Bob's worst fears.

Still, he wished to see the results himself. "I'll have that page now."

"Roberts . . . Even Richard didn't know all of this . . ."

"Now, Evgeny, please."

With the sort of sigh only a man born in the gulag can muster, Markov handed Bob the printout. He barely had time to glance at it to feel the frightening effects of what was on that paper before another interrupted their discussion.

Ingus Apinis, the Accounting Department's meteoric whiz kid, and newest executive, marched down the hall towards them. Trim, perfectly tailored, with black hair gelled back, he radiated order—and impatience with those not as capable as he.

"It's time, Roberts," he said with little-camouflaged disdain. "If you're coming in, now's the best. We want to get started."

Bob and Evgeny followed Ingus into the third-floor's conference room. Inside, at a long central table, sat the ratings agency team from prestigious Crenshaw and Larson, ready for Turaida's annual international assessment, the first long day of several meetings to determine if the bank's debt was still investment grade. Bob and Ingus took a seat at the table with the well-dressed men and women of Crenshaw and Larson, Evgeny sitting at the back on a chair against the wall.

Ingus made no overtures at introductions, but after remarking that everyone was "at last assembled and we could proceed," brought up presentation software on the screens of every tablet and laptop in the room. He began to address basic procedures.

Bob glanced down at the printout in his hands, made sure the words were indeed what he thought they were. There was still the possibility of an error . . .

He prayed.

"I'd like to ask a question, Mr. Apinis," said Bob.

"Later would be more appropriate."

"It's urgent."

Ingus looked at him sternly, his annoyance obvious. But what choice did he have? Conference room decorum . . .

"Go on, Mr. Vanags."

Bob stood up to get a clear look at all seated in the room, table and back chairs alike. He wanted to read faces, to search for complicity, maybe even for sympathy. "Three hundred million euros of Turaida loan assets are lent to only twelve companies." He glanced a last time at the paper Evgeny had given him, used the names printed there to gain courage. "And I have learned that those twelve companies are, in fact, owned by a mere five individuals. Tell me how this is legal? The risk is tremendous."

"Mr. Vanags . . ." said Ingus.

"As far as the borrowers, if I am recognizing these names correctly, these five men are all well-known Russian oligarchs. All part of the Kremlin's inner circle. All forbidden to receive loans from EU banks since the Russian occupation of the Crimea. That despite international sanctions, Turaida has loaned millions to these men through their shell companies."

"Mr. Vanags, that's enough." Ingus stood up, began to march around the perimeter of the table.

"Can anyone seated around this table, ethical men and women all, tell me that these loans are legal?" Bob continued. "Or, for that matter, show that these loans are being paid back?"

"Outside, Mr. Vanags!"

"Show me, conclusively, that one cent has been paid back by these Kremlin men? Please! I beg of you. Tell me I am mistaken in some other way?"

Ingus grabbed Bob's arm. "Outside!"

Bob relented and an instant later he—and Evgeny—were in the hall with Ingus Apinis.

"What the Hell are you doing, Roberts?" shouted Ingus.

"Asking questions."

"Then ask them in private. Not in front of outsiders . . ."

Bob moved closer to the younger man, eye-to-eye. "How can the Latvian people, or foreign investors for that matter, secure their money in this bank? When the money is being given away to a hostile regime over their borders? Well, Ingus? When our customers discover this, they'll withdraw their funds *enmasse*, empty their accounts, and this bank collapses!"

"Exactly. And so does the economy," spat the man, belly-to-belly with him. "So why are you telling an international ratings agency this? You work for Turaida. Remember?"

"Because it's the truth, damn it."

"We're safeguarding national interests, Roberts! Are you too stupid to understand that? Turaida is the one keeping Latvia afloat."

"By giving away its money?"

Ingus's face flushed with anger. "Yes. Do you really trust NATO? For the Americans to die for us? To risk World War III for little Latvia? We secure our borders another way, by paying . . ."

Paying whom? Bob felt his blood boiling. "You're a liar. And everyone who works here is a liar!" He pointed back towards the conference room. "And if Crenshaw and Larson approve, then they're liars too!"

Bob never saw it coming. Never expected it could. Ingus landed a sucker-punch, an uppercut to his jaw that sent him staggering back. The partition wall gave way and Bob collapsed back into the cubicle behind, flat on his back, tie over his face, feet in the air.

He lay there stunned for a moment; the action more shocking than the impact itself.

Ingus shook his hand, trying to ward off the sting from the blow. "If you want to survive in this company, Roberts, you'll learn to keep your mouth shut." He glared at Evgeny. "Richard Ash never went so far. And look at him!"

Ingus marched back into the conference room. Bob heard the click of a lock behind. Then, bizarrely, the sounds of a large, busy office slowly returned. The click-clack of keyboards, the bubbling noise of a coffee pot, and the distant, relaxed conversation of daily business. As if nothing had ever happened.

"Oh, now you've done it, Roberts" said Evgeny with a sigh as he helped Bob to his feet. "You've gone and angered Accounting."

"It's my dad, again," said David, clicking REJECT, on his phone.

"You can take it," replied Beatrise Liepa, the pretty redhead from his class, "I don't mind."

"Maybe, after the burger." He tried to take a bite, but the great bun, patty, and various flowing sauces slipped every which-way in his hands, covering his chin, and fingers, bits falling down to table and the floor beneath. Despite this, what food David *did* manage to intake was the most succulent treat he'd had since coming to Latvia and worth every bit the chaos. What could Beatrise say? Her burger mess was no better . . .

They sat in Fontaine Delisnack, a popular burger joint just off the center, known for the biggest and juiciest sandwiches in Rīga, 1/3- and 1/2-pound monsters that rivaled anything in Chicago. Not surprisingly, the place was filled with American soldiers in camouflaged fatigues, all stationed in the country to train Latvian defense forces against the growing threat of invasion on the eastern border. Of course, David couldn't hear a thing the soldiers were saying—the roaring Polish death metal of *Vader* drowning out all thought through restaurant speakers—but he imagined it had something to do with yet another close call between American and Russian fighters over the Baltic Sea. David thought the Russians were hoping for an accident as an excuse for action. Though he couldn't really prove this suspicion.

"Aren't you going to talk to your fellow Americans?" asked Beatrise, noticing his glances at the soldiers.

He'd already told a few he was proud of their presence here while she'd been in the restroom. But David thought he'd show Beatrise his focus was on her.

"Later. I'm talking to you now."

"Lucky you," she said with a smile. Beatrise's accent sat thick and husky in her throat, much thicker than his other classmates. The thickness required his constant concentration, but she could be forgiven for struggling with second-language cadences and spoken rhythms. Afflicted with degenerative hearing loss, Beatrise wore aids in both ears. Apparently new devices, she took them out repeatedly, adjusting volume, and complaining of chafing. On days she attended class without them, Beatrise would be in tears by lunch, frustrated at her inability to hear the lectures. David had twice accompanied her home to retrieve them.

Her condition, she claimed, was worsening. The doctors expected her to be completely deaf by thirty, thirty-five max. Despite that sad cloud hanging over her, he found Beatrise, already eighteen, a surprisingly kindred spirit given their different nationalities and short acquaintance. She, like him, was new to Rīga and the McCann-Kopans school, her family having emigrated from the Vidzeme town of Madona in August. She, also like him, had only one living parent and no siblings. They shared an outsider's perspective here, even if his was to a much greater degree than hers. The stiffness of their classmates at *McK* quickly became an in-joke between them and David and Beatrise mocked the posh sensibilities of the others from the back row seats in every class. Their interests were surprisingly close—anime, graphic novels, even, boating. Every activity, other than court appearances, he'd spent time engaged in during the weeks prior to leaving for Latvia. She was tailor-made for him.

His eyes dropped, subtly as possible, to her barstool. Beatrise wore black knee-high stockings and a plaid mini skirt that left her thighs bare. He liked this, much as he liked, in a very different way, the t-shirt with Miyazaki's "Spirited Away" characters on it just visible beneath her half-unzipped pink jacket. Frankly, he liked *everything* he saw. Forget getting laid . . . yet . . . His goal was a kiss. Seventeen years and five months was too long to wait.

"What are you looking at?" she asked, with an ambiguous smirk.

"I think I dropped some pickles on the floor."

"I'm deaf, not blind, David."

"You're neither, Beatrise."

"Not yet."

Someone turned the television station from Spanish league basketball to the news, the close-captioned BBC correspondent scrawl talking about the near collision this morning. The Nigerian cook left the grill, turned off *Vader* to hear the report.

Beatrise adjusted her hearing aids. After the pounding loudness of the metal music; she raised the volume for the television commentator.

The Russian and NATO aircrafts were a mere ten meters from colliding . . .

"Ten meters," whistled one of the soldiers. "Thirty feet. Less than the size of this room. Me to that refrigerator there."

"Those hit and it's all over," said another.

Beatrise leaned forward over the greasy table. "You think there really could be war over this country?"

"I doubt it," said David. "But you'd know better than I. You're Latvian."

"Americans make all the decisions in this world."

"That's not true."

"Isn't it?"

He grinned. "I let you pick the burgers, didn't I?"

"Well, thanks . . ."

"I'll let you pay for 'em too."

"Just like Donald Trump."

They laughed mutually.

"Want to see something interesting?" she asked.

"What's that?"

Beatrise pressed her thumb to a spot just beneath her right eye, began to rub vigorously, clearing away makeup David hadn't realized she wore. At last, she pulled her thumb away, revealing a small teardrop tattoo.

"Cool, eh?"

"Cool," he said, though that was a deliberate understatement. He thought it fabulous.

"No visible tattoos allowed at McCann-Kopans," she said. "It's my secret. I like secrets."

"I do too."

David's ringtone sounded once more. His dad yet again.

What was bugging *him* tonight? If Dad could have time alone with Agnese, so could he with Beatrise.

"You can get that."

"I don't want to."

David turned off the phone, went back to watching the news.

Finally, some peace.

16

"You have terminated the man who struck Roberts Vanags, Terēze?"

Terēze Ābele stood arms-crossed, face red in the fourth-floor security room of the Turaida Bank Headquarters in Rīga. It was too early, she'd had little sleep, and Terēze did not appreciate the tone of her colleague, if she could really call Kārlis Pagrabs that. The "Roberts Vanags Incident" yesterday played heavily on her mind. She did not want to be up here, in this barred, unheated office. But who could refuse the Scorpion's right-hand man and representative in Latvia?

"I told Roberts I had terminated Ingus Apinis for the violence, Kārlis. Instead, I transferred Apinis to Turaida Bank Ukraine, to their branch office in Kharkov. How can I completely discard one of our own for defending Turaida interests? If Roberts had kept talking it might have been worse. Apinis had the right instincts in silencing him, if not the right method."

Talks of 'methods' meant nothing to Kārlis. "I'd rather Apinis were gone. If Roberts discovers the transfer, he'll lose his trust in you, Terēze. That's more important than loyalty to Apinis."

"You don't make such decisions, Kārlis."

"I'll be sure to tell Moscow you think so."

"Please, do."

Terēze watched Kārlis lean back in his chair and rub the morning stubble on the top of his head. She never realized he shaved his scalp until this moment. Perhaps, Kārlis hadn't chosen the sunrise time of this meeting either. Perhaps, someone down along the Volga insisted he be here at dawn too. We all have our crosses to bear.

"It's not the end of the world," Kārlis said with a resolute sigh. "A leak that Turaida may capsize could actually accelerate the game ahead of us." He clicked a few messages on the largest of his monitors. "We will still get our needed rating. But thanks to Roberts's fit at the meeting yesterday afternoon, the cost has tripled. We may have to pay that ratings agency team simply for their silence." He looked up at her. "It will come out of your budget. Terēze."

"I'll put it under 'Yacht Sales,'" she answered sarcastically.

"Do so."

They stared at each other silently. Terēze counted the seconds until he'd buzz her out.

"Anything more, *Mrs. Ābele?*"

She tried to let her unease, annoyance, and revulsion at the security chief subside, at least momentarily, and concentrate on the issues at hand. "Roberts could go to the police, Kārlis. As Richard Ash did."

"And he'll be ignored as Ash was."

"And the press?"

"No one will talk to him. What's left of Santa Ezeriņa has slithered out of Latvia. Given her near-fatal accident at Sigulda, she should be less inclined to write editorials."

"Roberts may still contact the *foreign* press, the American media . . ."

"We have all his communications under surveillance. Just don't send him abroad until we know his intentions."

"He heads *International* Relations! You hamstring my department . . ."

"I remind you, Terēze, these are your employees we're covering for once again. I told you to wait before hiring Roberts. Now there must be punishment. Be happy you're not the one in front of the firing squad." His dark brow furled. "As you should be."

She ignored that remark. "What punishment?"

"That depends on Roberts. Moscow has given me a lenient option and a far harsher one. We'll see what our new feminine source has to say before taking action."

Terēze shook her head. "It will be impossible to replace yet another man."

Kārlis smirked at this. "Have no fear, Terēze. Roberts's fate remains in his own hands. As long as he doesn't do anything stupid . . ."

17

In his modest house on the shores of Lake Ķīšezers, member of the *Saeima* Dāvids Osis sat quietly by himself and watched television. In this home of twenty-two years, he need not be a politician, a living legend of his nation, or even the divorced head of a large and scattered family. On windy September afternoons like this, Dāvids could simply be an old man dressed in a robe and slippers cheering the soccer match on TV. And, for today, it was all he wished to be.

He smiled and pumped a fist as his team tied the game. Dāvids had not always loved *'futbols'*. He'd been a hockey man as a youth and most of his adulthood. But as he'd slowed in the sixth and seventh decades of life, he'd found himself often sitting in front of televisions with a match on. He'd grown to appreciate the strategy, the athleticism, the comradeship in the world's most popular sport. Now he was passionate about the game. More so, even than politics. Politics bored him. Perspectives change with age, Dāvids supposed. On many things.

So, with the score 1-1 and time running short, it irritated Dāvids when a knocking came on the front door. He lived alone. Dāvids didn't believe in the concept of servants nor did he wish for security guards. He was a man of the people and the people should have access to him if they wished. Even, alas, with the score tied.

Dāvids rose from the couch and made his way to the entrance. He knew the man he spied through the window. Even at his age, Dāvids had a gift for faces. Thousands met yearly, yet it was rare he forgot a visage.

Dāvids opened the door, and finding the breeze too strong for doorstep conversations, motioned into the house a handsome though very-tired looking American of about forty. Despite the winds, he reeked of cigarette smoke. His manner seemed twitchy and unsure.

"M.P. Osis, you may not remember me," said the visitor in English, "but we met a short time ago . . ."

"At the funeral. 'Roberts something' . . . the American executive at Turaida Bank . . ."

"Yes, Bob, Bob Vanags. I'm sorry to disturb you on a Saturday, sir . . ."

He waved the objection away. "Nonsense. Saturday is the best day for friends. I was only watching the *Virslīga* and my favorite team, *Skonto*, is not playing." This was a white lie, but why make his visitor uncomfortable? Every politician knows lies have their occasional uses. Dāvids closed the door behind and bid the American take a seat at a little table in the front sitting room.

"Sir, I'm sorry to intrude. I got your address from Agnese Avena."

"Please, call me 'Dāvids'." He sat at the table across from Roberts, pulling his robe tight, aware he couldn't look very officious or helpful in his present state of dress. "A friend of Agnese's is a friend of mine."

"I didn't know who else to turn to, Dāvids. I am concerned about the situation with Turaida Bank."

"And what situation would that be?"

"Are we alone?"

"Quite. It is only the television you hear."

Roberts then proceeded to explain his theories about Turaida. That there were too many loans out to too few companies, and that these, mostly shell companies, were owned by an even fewer number of Russian oligarchs, a handful of men who were on the books for nearly three hundred million euros. And Roberts could find no conclusive evidence they had paid a cent of it back. Turaida is being looted, claimed this visitor, and actively hiding the danger from the Latvian people.

"When I brought this up at a meeting," continued Roberts, "One of the employees became irate. He even struck me. That man has since been terminated. But there are other things as well . . . others, who might have known this have died, or disappeared, but I would be speculating . . ." He released a heavy sigh, as if sharing his knowledge was a great weight off his shoulders. "My greatest concern, Dāvids, is that should this bank implode . . . well, what it might mean to the country . . . I think Turaida needs to be shut down immediately and the government intervene to protect the people."

Dāvids nodded, the practiced, comforting nod of a professional politician. "The government is well aware of the risk with Turaida Bank."

The American's eyes widened. "Are they?"

"We in the *Saeima* have been conscious of improprieties for decades. However, it has only been in the past year that I personally came to realize the danger of collapse and the terrible things Turaida will do to hide that information."

"If that bank fails, Dāvids, Heaven help us. The Latvian economy may fare worse than Greece."

"*Will* fare worse than, Greece, Roberts. But modern Ukraine is a closer analogy, Roberts. Fortunately, I am spear-heading a permanent way of addressing this. Frankly, we cannot allow enemies of the Republic of Latvia to use Turaida as tool for our destruction. It must be saved."

The news seemed to dispirit the American. "This isn't why I came to Latvia, Dāvids. And I thought the Loop was corrupt. I'll quit Turaida, Monday."

"Oh, don't quit, my friend. Please don't. We need you." He reached out and put a hand on Roberts's shoulder, felt the tension in the muscles underneath his jacket. "Do you know why I insisted on speaking at the Ēriks Helmanis funeral?"

"No."

"He was working for me. Or, I should say, more correctly he was working for *his* government. Ēriks too wanted to quit, but we convinced him otherwise. In this very house not eight months ago. Ēriks was providing information. Valuable information now choked away. If you'd stay at Turaida for at least a month more, perhaps, you could assist us in preventing a collapse."

A shadow passed across the visitor's face and Dāvids wondered if he'd gone too far. "I'm not sure . . . An American, working for a foreign government . . ."

"The CIA is aware of the situation, Roberts. We can meet them together at your embassy if it will calm your loyalties." Dāvids scribbled his personal mobile number on a pad of paper, handed the sheet to Roberts. "Nothing is official and do nothing unethical. Just keep your eyes open. I expect the *Saeima* will make its move to secure the situation within a month's time. But, you know, I can only push it so quickly. Those who misuse Turaida have friends in the government too. Powerful ones . . ."

"I'm not sure, Dāvids . . ."

"We need you to be our eyes."

This seemed to touch something inside him. Roberts sighed again. "I've heard those words before. Can I talk this over with my family?"

"Of course."

Dāvids showed Roberts to the door, they parted with a handshake, and soon the American was lost from sight along the lake road. That last image gave Dāvids the impression of a man wrestling with some demon. Years of public service had given Dāvids an inkling about people. He suspected the American would choose to assist in the end. He genuinely hoped Roberts would live longer than Richard Ash, Ēriks Helmanis, and the other Turaida employees who had appeared on his doorstep. He imagined he wouldn't.

With a sigh, Dāvids Osis returned to the game.

PART II

18

Dressed in a baggy gray flannel suit, Elvis Gulbis walked through the sparsely attended convention hall, looking for a lead, a scoop, a contract, anything which might provide journalistic work for the desperate. It'd been . . . what? three months since he'd sold a paying story? The money his cousin, Bob Vanags, had given him to mind Bob's son during the teen's court hearing had long ago dried up. The financial wolves took the house and midnight appearances by collection men drove off Elvis's lovers. Only the narrowest escape prevented repossession of his sputtering Ford. He'd shed every phone number to avoid collection calls, but no good journalist could survive cut off from the world. Elvis still fancied himself one of the best "ambush" reporters in the States. Just with a bad turn of luck. As usual.

As Elvis wandered through the hall, the buzz of East Coast voices occasionally broken by Baltic accents, he felt very much on his own. None of his close family possessed money and Cousin Bob had disappeared into Latvia on his cushy finance job, ignoring repeated requests for loans. What was another ten grand to a bank executive like him? After he'd done that leg work for IRT in Chicago for nothing? Well, fuck Bob Vanags. Elvis could count on one stout middle finger the number of people he could trust in this world. Everyone else was out to screw him. And they usually succeeded.

Still, Elvis did his best to keep these dark thoughts hidden. People like winners and he couldn't afford to come away for the annual Baltic-American Journalists Conference without work. His Latvian heritage had never particularly meant much to Elvis, but he'd take any advantage he could, and the American Latvian community was small enough he could meet the players in a single convention day, keeping hotel costs low.

So far, though, he'd no success worth noting. It seemed this year the Lithuanians dominated attendance with endless presentations, floor shows, and kiosks; the Latvians, both American and Old World, were relatively sparse, numbering less than a hundred attendees. Slim pickings for opportunity.

His legs hurt, his back ached, and having circled the hall twice, Elvis decided to take a less arduous, more systematic approach. He saddled up to one of the registration desks, the elderly lady handing out badges and "Welcome" bags to those who paid to attend. While she was talking to a regal-looking rep from the Latvian American Association, Elvis picked up the attendee list, scanned it with an index finger.

He recognized name after name, crossing many off his mental list as unapproachable, and wincing at one publisher who'd paid him a handsome advance years ago only for Elvis to fail to deliver a story. He cursed under his breath. Not much left to hit up for work . . .

He found his own entry "Elviss Gulbis", with the proper Latvian extra "s" on the given name, a letter he usually dropped on business cards and bylines, but he was happy to include when it benefited him. A handwritten note next to it said "Card failed. Dues owed."

He sighed. Well, long ago he'd learned not to sweat debts under a c-note. Elvis furled his brow in concentration. The woman at the desk was requesting the list back, her polite enquiry ebbing towards a demand. Trying to ignore her, Elvis moved his finger down to foreign attendees. One familiar name stood out:

"Santa Ezeriņa, *Baltic Beacon*."

Well, well, he thought. What was *she* doing here? It'd been at least three years, as far as Elvis knew, since Santa crossed the Atlantic. They went way back, he and Santa, most of it bad.

No, come to think of it, all bad . . . .

Elvis returned the list to the lady, searched the convention hall for Santa's familiar and pleasing figure. The first time he'd met Santa, she was a journalism major from some American college—NYU? Columbia? He couldn't remember—working as an intern for the Latvian Press League in Washington D.C. He'd been on freelance assignment for the league, and as the older reporter, Elvis tried to show her the ropes. They spent a lot of time together. Frankly, he hoped she might put out . . .

Instead, she stole his story. Published it in three languages before he'd finished his draft. He proved later she hacked his email account and gotten her booted from the LPL. They in turn pushed for expulsion from her American college and sent Santa packing back to her native country in disgrace. She'd been working at lousy tourist rags in Rīga ever since. Served her right.

Of course, fair or not, the rumor that he'd been scooped by a nineteen-year-old foreign girl hadn't helped him any. First of an eight year downward spiral for them both.

Since then, they'd been sparring at their occasional meetings, usually a convention or Latvian-related function. Elvis kinda hoped it was sexual tension. Santa was a hot piece of ass when she wore makeup, which was almost never. Looked like she stepped out of a Nagel painting then. He'd love to screw her for screwin' him over. She was so . . . so . . .

. . . so crippled?

Elvis could hardly believe his eyes. But *there* she was . . . Santa Ezeriņa, sitting by herself in a wire-frame wheelchair parked at a table near the refreshments counter, her neck in a brace, casts on one leg and arm, her skin gray and ill-looking.

What the Hell had happened to her?

No wonder he'd missed her in earlier walkabouts over the convention floor. Shit, there had to be a story here.

Elvis stalked over towards her, taking a circuitous route that crept up behind Santa, then seated himself just outside of her peripheral vision. He coughed until he got her attention, made Santa wheel around to see who'd joined her.

Recognition. He enjoyed the disgust in her face.

"*Labvakar,*" Elvis said, with a wide smile.

"You pronounce it like an American," she answered without emotion.

"I *am* an American. Jealous, Santa?" He raised an eyebrow. "What happened to you?"

"I fell off a Sigulda sky gondola. Broke everything you can name. And undoubtedly a few things you can't."

He whistled, then remembered that many Old-World Latvians thought it bad luck indoors. "You gonna walk again?"

"Sure. Only reason I'm in the chair is I can't maneuver on crutches with a fractured arm."

He nodded, tried to hide his satisfaction at her predicament. He vaguely remembered some story on his news feed about gunfire in Sigulda a while ago and someone falling from a gondola. All names withheld . . .

Now, who in Latvia could silence the press so completely?

On their table, near Santa's coffee cup lay three business cards she'd obviously collected at the convention. Two Vilnius newspaper editors, and a financial executive from a banking group that was one of the most corrupt institutions in the Baltics.

There might be opportunity here.

"So, you workin' on a story?"

"Always."

"Anything to do with Turaida Group?"

She tried to hide it, but a flicker in her eyes told him he'd hit the mark. Score one for Elvis.

Now, Turaida could silence the press.

He scooted nearer her, set a hand on her chair, lowered his voice. He'd have to get this pitch in before whoever wheeled her around came back. "Maybe, we can help each other. I've got a source, a close relative inside Turaida."

"Roberts Vanags, I know."

"How could you . . . ?"

"He's Turaida's only current Latvian-American hire that I know of. Who else could it be?"

Elvis shrugged, tried to pat his shirt pocket as if looking for cigarettes. "No . . . no, it's not him."

"You don't lie well, Elviss. You never did." Some color returned to her skin. "Who is Roberts to you? A cousin? Yeah?" She smirked. "Well, your cousin's a great guy, stood idly by why some thugs beat me up at a funeral, you know?"

Who can blame him, lady?

"You've had it rough lately with Turaida, huh?"

"Nothing I can't handle."

"And they've got you scared so bad you're healing up on the wrong side of the Atlantic? This ain't the usual Turaida hardball on real estate deals. You're onto something bigger, Santa."

She leaned back stiffly in her chair. "'Hardball'? I don't know this term."

"You know, Santa. Now who's lying? Let me be your legs—literally—while you're in that chair. I can do it. We worked well together back on the LPL." He grabbed the wheelchair armrest and turned her towards him fully. "You owe me a story, Santa."

"I was a kid then. And I paid the price for my sins. Dearly." She smirked. "These aren't equal leads. No deal."

"Then, I'll do it on my own. I'll call Bob tonight." He stood up, towering over her.

"Elviss, your cousin is either corrupt or soon will be. And if he isn't, and you contact him looking for a story, you could put the both of you in danger. I know we've had our differences—but look at me! You want to end up like this?"

"You're trying to muffle my source. Admit it."

"I'm trying to save your life, Elviss. Or your cousin's. They read their employees' emails, listen in on their phones. You can't just go blundering in there. This requires delicacy. A potential whistleblower died because he tried to contact the press. They caught him on a payphone. At 3:00 A.M.!"

"If you could prove that you'd have it in print by now."

Santa tried to nod but the brace chafed her, she winced painfully.

"True," she said softly.

"Last chance. Partners?"

"Not a chance."

He felt his face tighten into a frown. "By the time you're out of that cast, I'll have the story broken."

"Elviss . . ."

He swiped her business cards from the table, turned, and walked away before she could do anything.

"May the best reporter win, baby."

19

As the sun reached its apex over the golden late autumn hills in western Moldova, a tuxedo-clad town mayor handed Agnese Avena an outlandishly large pair of scissors and said:

"Cut it, Ms. Avena. It is only right that you do this."

"I couldn't."

"We insist."

Polite claps and light cheers in the crowd grew until Agnese relented. She laughed, clearly embarrassed, and cut the ceremonial ribbon, officially opening the Sky Eagle Hotel and Spa. Bob Vanags playfully whistled, and Agnese flashed him a 'why me' glance, as she returned the scissors to the mayor. There was a round of handshakes and hugs within the assembly, then thirty or so officials, businessmen, and representatives from Turaida's Chişinău office left the little square of the rural Moldovan town and flooded into the lobby of the latest creation of Turaida-IDB money.

The community of Cuib de Vulturi, literally the "Nest of the Eagle," secluded in high hills of landlocked Moldova, just three kilometers east of the Romanian border, had been little more than a ghost town five years ago. It'd been rescued, frankly, by a single hundred-million-dollar loan by International Development Bank to Turaida who in turn broke up the money and distributed loans as low as ten thousand euros to the local Moldovan businesses to stimulate growth. These small medium enterprise investments had worked wonders, transforming Cuib de Vulturi into a budding resort town, offering Western facilities and professionalism with an attractive mix of Moldovan wine selections, health spas, and most importantly, Eastern-European prices that was quickly developing a buzz among budget-conscious foreigners. If not quite the jet set, plenty of university students and middle-class workers were finding their way to Moldova for the first time. There were plans to build a ski slope on the highest hills outside of town. This coming winter would see tourist-driven profits to justify those loans to the poorest country in Europe. It was the perfect model of what could happen when IDB, Turaida, and a national government worked together.

And, frankly, Bob Vanags needed to see it.

After the ugly incident in the office with Ingus Apinis, Bob had become skeptical of Turaida, its improprieties and intentions. Those indiscretions were no small thing and only Dāvids Osis's calming words had kept him from quitting. Still, for the first time, Bob was seeing the human side of what the relationship between IDB and Turaida could do. Spreadsheets and canned presentations only told so much. Bob felt the excitement in the handshakes of entrepreneurs given a chance to make something of themselves, the light in the eyes of people who would take that money and run with it to build a better society in a country that in rural places was almost medieval in character. He hoped they'd make it. And even if they didn't, the Moldovan government was guaranteeing all loans. There was little risk Turaida wouldn't get its money back or be unable to pay off its own loan from IDB.

He watched Agnese work the room, so elegant yet professional in a white suit-dress and pearls. Though all the local loans went through Turaida most knew the funding came from IDB. She had arranged this all through Turaida's Moldovan offices. They should build a statue to Agnese in Cuib de Vulturi. Hell, if the upcoming season proved successful, they just might.

He smiled. Bob couldn't deny an ache of arousal in him as he watched her. Agnese had insisted on proper business chastity on this trip. It was tough being with her, but not *with* her. He was falling in love, like a fool schoolboy, too fast.

But look at her? Who wouldn't?

When they got back to Latvia he just might propose.

In the backseat of the Mercedes, Bob slipped his hand out to lightly touch Agnese's. She let it linger there, the faintest of smiles on her face. He glanced to the front to see if their driver noticed. His eyes were locked on the twisting valley road.

Bob gave that hand the lightest caress. Her smile increased slightly.

He liked this game.

Soothed by the softness of her skin at his fingertips, Bob let his eyes wander out the window once more. They were descending through the Codri Forest from the so-called "Besarabian Switzerland", the highest extended lands in Moldova, a plateau cut deeply by river gorges and half-lost sylvan valleys. On the primitive paved road, evidence of fresh rockslides was plentiful, their driver swerving aggressively every few kilometers to avoid collisions with red-stone boulders fallen from the steep valley walls on either side. It'd been a harrowing trip, seat belts often tested, and Bob wondered why the Moldovan government, or the private investors back in Cuib de Vulturi, didn't do something about the road conditions. Surely, that would assist the tourism all parties desired.

"Mr. Vanags, Ms. Avena," said the driver. "You will notice the spire of the Hâncu Monastery on the left over the hill coming up. Seventeenth century, exceptionally beautiful interiors."

With his free hand, Bob brought up the GPS digital map on his smartphone, the monastery clearly marked as they approached. He noticed, for the first time, that the highway ahead branched near the towns of Bursuc and Nisporeni, two communities where Turaida Moldova had given out significant SME loans. He wondered how their businesses performed with the money. What did *those* towns look like? Were they as successful as Cuib de Vulturi?

"Excuse me," said Bob, wishing he could remember the driver's name. "We'll be passing Nisporeni shortly. Can we stop off there to have a look around? Briefly?"

"I'm afraid, I need to have you in Chişinău by six o'clock."

"It's only three now." His phone map said Chişinău was an hour away.

"There's no time, sir. I'm sorry. With these landslides, there could be unexpected delays. Roads are often blocked . . ."

He glanced at Agnese, back to the driver. "I mean we stay three days in Cuib de Vulturi, but we can't spend twenty minutes in any of the other towns we've invested in?"

"I have my orders, Mr. Vanags. My boss in Chişinău was very specific."

"Next trip, Bob," said Agnese. She subtly returned the hand caress. "They always maintain a tight itinerary in Moldova. The locals don't like unexpected guests. A cultural holdover from the Soviet days."

He watched the brilliant blue and white spire of the monastery pass, just visible over the forested ridgetop.

"Have you ever been to Nisporeni?"

She shook her head. "I've colleagues at IDB who've been there. We can't visit every town we've given a business loan. And we should be in Ukraine fresh and early tomorrow morning."

"How hard is it to swerve off for a five-minute detour?"

"Don't embarrass me, Bob."

"All right, all right."

* * *

Agnese and Bob skipped out of the Turaida Moldova party early that night, tired of exchanging overly formal pleasantries with strangers for hours on end. On the way to the hotel, they pulled aside on some little Chişinău side street, made love in the backseat of the rented Audi even as passersby walked by on the road outside. A breathless encounter that left them both spent, yet Bob feeling vibrantly alive as if he were sixteen again.

Come to think of it, sixteen was the last time he had sex in a car. Bob thought he lived too conservative an adult life. Well, now things were changing . . . Europe, a beautiful blonde for a lover . . .

Crime . . .

As Agnese snoozed in his arms, he thought of that town in the Carpathian hills, Nisporeni. He wondered if it was as well-developed as Cuib de Vulturi? Or was Turaida Moldova skimming off the top, as Turaida Latvia apparently was. That driver's refusal to go there today even for a moment aroused suspicion. The sex had enlivened his body. Now these thoughts set his mind racing.

Minutes later, Bob had the car on the highway out of Chişinău, Agnese still slumbering semi-nude in the backseat, a satisfied look on her face. He turned the heater on full to keep her warm. It was not yet late, only nine, but as soon as he was away from the capital the traffic fell away. A lonely drive over boulder-strewn roads along the bottom of forested valleys, the moon shining high above with only the hum of the engine and Agnese's intermittent snoring for company.

At last, the hills parted, the road opened before him, and Bob saw the outskirts of the town of Nisporeni. Or at least he thought it was Nisporeni, that's what the GPS said. But it appeared almost uninhabited, everything dark and silent. No illumination came from the low buildings that lined the narrow streets, no lighted lamps in the windows, nothing aglow outside. And not a person to be seen. Yet, even after the drive, the hour was not so late. His headlights revealed warped wooden houses, peeling paint, the winter-dead brambles of unkept yards and an encroaching wilderness.

A ghost town.

What the Hell?

Bob slowed, pulled over in front of some crumbling storefront, checked the address he'd given the auto-map. It seemed right . . .

Agnese stirred. He tilted the rearview mirror to observe, watched his lover resettle herself, turning to sleep on her side, eyes never opening. The moonlight caught the whiteness of her naked buttocks and he wanted her again.

But Nisporeni was calling his attention.

"Are we back at the hotel, yet?" Agnese asked in a dreamy voice.

"Nearly there."

"Good. Want a soft bed . . ."

"Me too."

Something sped across his headlight beams.

With Bob's eyes turned towards Agnese in the back, he'd missed exactly what it was. Some shadow quickly passing right to left through the light, then merging with the fabric of the night.

What was that? A dog?

He sat in the Audi waiting but nothing broke the stillness outside.

Well, this is a waste of time . . .

Had to be a dog . . .

With one last glance to confirm Agnese remained asleep, Bob exited the car to have a look around. Outside the air was colder than he imagined, a chill crawling over his skin even beneath his jacket. The gravel crunched beneath his shoes as he stepped away from the Audi to explore Nisporeni.

Three businesses registered to this town had been given collectively nearly sixty million dollars by Turaida Moldova. Sixty million dollars originating with IDB, funded by U.S. and EU taxpayers, and approved by Agnese herself.

Where had the money gone? This must be a mistake, the wrong town no matter what the GPS said. He was after all a foreigner here, likely confused . . .

Yet, that driver this morning had been so adamant about not coming here. Not even allowing a glimpse. The logical conclusion was the funds were all being stolen. That Cuib de Vulturi was the show village, that other developments were not in fact developments at all . . .

He wanted her to see this.

"Agnese!" he shouted, glancing back towards the car. Nothing stirred. She must be still asleep in the back.

His voice brought attention. Something growled in the dark.

Bob peered into the blackness, searching for the source of the sound. It *was* a dog . . .

He felt his skin crawl. No, *dogs*. Plural. Some mangy cur with its back up and teeth bared snarled about fifteen feet away, another six . . . *no seven . . . no eight . . .* more of its pack flowed into view from a littered alleyway behind the first.

Damn. Should have stayed in Chişinău.

The nearest dog snapped its jaws in the air, its fellows joined in barking, howling . . .

Bob backed away, turned, and fled. He made the Audi, had the door open, slipped inside . . .

One dog shoved its jaws inside before he could close the door. As a suddenly awakened Agnese screamed, he slammed the door on the dog's snarling, biting head until it withdrew, and he forced the door closed. They were all at the windows, scratching, biting, noses against the panes. One jumped up on the hood, snapping jaws in Bob's face.

"What is happening?" shouted Agnese.

Bob had no time for explanations. He ignited the engine, threw the car into reverse. He floored it, the dog on the hood thrown clear with a whimpering scream. The rest of the pack continued biting at the windows, chasing the car until he was out on the highway, and left them behind in the gloom of night.

"How can our banks invest sixty million in a town with no people?" said Bob, taking his eyes from the road to glance at Agnese.

"You've the wrong town, Roberts," she replied, now fully clothed and sitting in the passenger seat beside him.

"That's not what the GPS says."

Agnese did not glance at the GPS, her eyes on her smartphone, texting someone. Or maybe on Viber.

"It is Moldova, Roberts. Not everything works as in the West," she said tersely, eyes still on the phone. "We'll ask them tomorrow for the correct location."

"Location for another show village?"

She looked up at him at last. "What is a 'show village'?"

"Nothing," he said, exhausted. It seemed impossible he'd felt so young only hours before. "Tomorrow morning, Agnese, we'll be on a plane to Ukraine at six A.M., remember? You've meetings in Kyiv at nine."

"Then we'll see the correct town next time."

There'd be no 'next time.' He'd tell Osis everything as soon as he was back in Rīga. Then quit Turaida.

He hoped Agnese wouldn't quit him.

"It's just a mistake, Roberts. You have to trust me." She reached over and caressed his cheek, letting her fingers linger over the late-night stubble. "Become a more trusting person."

"I *am* a trusting person."

"Not yet, but you can get there." She leaned over, head on his shoulder. "I know you can."

* * *

In his Rīga office, Kārlis Pagrabs stared at his computer monitor with bleary eyes. On the left side of the screen hovered a feed from Agnese Avena's phone displaying all her communications since arriving in Moldova: calls, SMS, activity on social networks, on the right the identical feed of a man even Kārlis feared: Leonid Vovk, the oligarch of Kharkov and the Scorpion's right-hand man in Ukraine. An impossible man whose arrogance was exceeded only by his wealth. Passion, not logic, ruled Vovk. The very opposite of Kārlis himself. For that he detested the man.

Kārlis monitored their text message exchange. The GPS in Avena's phone said she was thirty-two kilometers outside of abandoned Nisporeni, same as Roberts Vanags, and traveling fast towards the Moldovan capital, likely as not in the Audi Vanags rented with his company credit card.

Kārlis smirked. So, they rode together while she communicated with the oligarch. Did Vanags know whom she texted? Their words were in Russian. They could text privately right under his nose.

AGNESE: I will be in Kyiv tomorrow.
VOVK: Meet me in Kharkov. Roses and diamonds, my girl.
AGNESE: I am with Vanags now.
VOVK: He will never know. Ēriks never knew.
AGNESE: No. Not this time.

It was all so dull to Kārlis. He had seen too much, watched too long, and their exchanges bored him. The practical side of his mind shouted there was nothing here of use. But the instincts and professional paranoia that kept him alive, that allowed Kārlis to flourish in the dark underbelly of international finance and security, now begged him to keep monitoring. He wished to be home in Ogre with his wife and son, but persevered. If the Scorpion asked tomorrow, Kārlis could say honestly, he knew what was said between Agnese and Leonid Vovk late at night.

Honesty was key. You could never lie to Moscow. Those who did met gray-eyed Ruslan at the most inopportune times and seldom, if ever, lived to tell the tale. There was a good chance the Scorpion had someone watching Kārlis as he watched Agnese, a chain of spies extending out from those deceptively plain offices three blocks from the Kremlin and covering most the world.

More texts came in:

AGNESE: Vanags is impatient. I need to go.

VOVK: What is he next to me?

She did not answer.

Ten minutes ticked by. Her phone turned off.

Kārlis popped amphetamines in his mouth, pushed back his chair, and thought about the situation. Was Agnese becoming attached to this American from Chicago?

That was a cause of concern. There'd been no further trouble from Roberts Vanags since the fistfight with Ingus Apinis three weeks ago. Other than an attempt at recruiting Dāvids Osis, as far as Kārlis knew, Roberts had done nothing with the revelation that Turaida had three hundred million out to five borrowers and was overtly hiding this fact from every ratings agency in the world. Perhaps, he'd thought it an anomaly. Perhaps, he'd decided it wasn't worth the destruction of his career. Who knew? Terēze was begging for Roberts's amnesty and maybe she was right. Maybe, Vanags would keep his mouth shut.

But then why had he gone to Nisporeni tonight?

Well, it was out of Kārlis's hands for now. This whistle-stop trip of Turaida's Potemkin "show" villages in Moldova and Ukraine, brought opportunity for others to play their hands. Tomorrow morning Roberts and Agnese would fly to Kyiv, where'd they'd separate. She'd meet with Ukrainian officials who were offering firmer government monetary guarantees in exchange for even larger loans. Loans totaling a half-billion U.S. dollars, facilitated from IDB to Turaida, and then from Turaida to Ukrainian businesses. All for the people.

In theory.

Meanwhile, Roberts would take the train to Kharkov, Ukraine's second largest city, a mere thirty kilometers from the Russian border. Terēze had given him some token work at Turaida's branch in Kharkov just as Moscow had requested. Of course, Terēze didn't know what the Scorpion planned for Roberts there. In fact, neither did Kārlis.

He rubbed his shaved head, deep in thought. Felt the clamminess of skin at this hour. He should really be home.

Kārlis sighed. If Moscow thought Roberts Vanags need disappear, it may happen in Kharkov. Away from Agnese, away from the eyes of the West, in a Russian-speaking city well within the range of the Scorpion's strongest allies. Less than three hours from the war-torn Donbass region, they could manufacture a hundred cover stories to explain the vanishing.

Still, there were reasons to stay Roberts's execution. Terēze's difficulty in finding a replacement was a factor, and more importantly, the mental stability of Agnese Avena. She was key to their long-term plans. She was our forty-billion-dollar babe. If Agnese suffered a breakdown after yet another lover died, things could take a turn for the worse.

He hoped Vovk remembered that.

A ping of his computer indicated the streams from the hotel in Chişinău were live. The hidden cameras waiting for Agnese and Vanags when they arrived. He wagered they'd be together. More grainy sex for the video archives . . .

He sighed, checked the clock. *Go home Kārlis.*

Yet, the Scorpion may ask . . .

Kārlis put on his headphones and waited for Agnese Avena and Roberts Vanags to return, to fuck for him one last time tonight.

20

Bob Vanags descended from the train onto the platform at Kharkov, the largest city of Eastern Ukraine and a sanctuary of stability in an increasingly war-torn region. A fusion of old Soviet manufacturing center with modern universities and Western-style technology startups six hours by rail from Kyiv, Kharkov did not appear at first glance to be in any more a perilous predicament than the Ukrainian capital. A few more soldiers about in combat fatigues, but truthfully there had been no shortage of those in Kyiv.

The normalcy was startling after all he'd read. People walked about calmly, families and young lovers saying tearful hellos or goodbyes at the entrances to every car. Vendors sold odd assortments of goods—chocolate, balloons, pencils, Star Wars figurines, sim cards—out of worn plastic shopping bags that read "Lido, Paris" or "MGM Las Vegas" on their sides. Life here appeared tranquil mere hours from the unending war with Russian-armed rebels that had killed thousands and displaced countless more. On a cool, November's day, one could be forgiven in thinking the dire situation for Ukraine almost forgotten.

Until he saw the tanks.

Two platforms over, a large engine was pulling away from the station, its chain of flatbed cars extending as far as the eye could see. On each car sat a pair of shiny new tanks, likely built in Kharkov's factories, and headed for the Donbass region to keep the insurgents and their Russian-backers at bay. That he'd seen heavy weapons wasn't surprising, but their sheer number seconds after arrival was bluntly shocking. Bob set down his bag and stood watching as the train rolled away. A full ten minutes passed before the last car carried a final tank out of sight.

Bob understood Ukraine's plight, had followed the war daily in the papers and on BBC News. But to see this tangible, physical sign of the war machine passing right in front of him? Well, this was a dose of cold reality. More such moments surely awaited him.

Leaving the platform, he entered Kharkov's central train station. Inside a high hall of yellowed marble, with angelic frescoes decorating the ceiling, and grim-faced police patrolling the floor, Bob found the taxi driver Turaida Ukraine had sent: a thin, old man in pleated cap, holding a cardboard sign that read "Robert Vanags—USA" in hand drawn letters.

Soon they were on the road towards Kharkov's center, darting through heavy late afternoon traffic. Every time Bob attempted to fasten his seat belt, the driver would reach over and deter him, as if the idea itself were an affront to his skills. A game they played until Bob relented, holding tight for the remainder of the drive.

While Agnese charmed government officials in Kyiv, Terēze had insisted he go out here to meet with Turaida's obscure, but staggeringly profitable, Kharkov office. They'd scheduled little more than introductions, something Bob felt could have been done with a video conference call from Kyiv or Rīga, if necessary.

Still, the visit allowed him to see new places. And if Turaida Rīga was proving mysterious, well, the Kharkov office was a complete black hole to him. A spirit of discovery in his soul, Bob looked forward to whatever he might encounter here.

They turned onto a long straight road fringed by dilapidated nineteenth century buildings, then crossed by bridge the low, muddy river that bisects the town. Near the river, stood a mammoth Orthodox cathedral, according to his guidebook, the largest in Eastern Europe. Kharkov's Annunciation Cathedral was beautiful, yes; impressive, certainly; but what struck Bob immediately was the structure's unusual coloring: alternating horizontal bands of red and white marble rose over the body of the building, the pattern extending up even to its towers and steeples. It looked rather like a peppermint house in a Christmas confectionery shop window, a magnificent "candy-stripe" church, a shot of glorious color perched in the middle of an old, gray, Soviet-style city. He smiled as they passed it.

Would wonders never cease . . .

"We are a little disappointed, Robert, that Agnese Avena didn't accompany you to our city," said Dmitry Syrhai, the sixtyish, olive-skinned and elegantly dressed manager of Turaida's Kharkov office. "We owe her so much."

Bob nodded, puffed on his cigarette as they sat at the Irish pub on the edge of Kharkov's *Maidan Konstytutsii* plaza, a small central square dominated by the statue of a heroic-looking winged woman holding a Ukrainian flag high in her hands. "Слава Україні!" or "Glory to Ukraine," the monument was called, the slogan of the Ukrainian War of Independence in 1917, and a popular greeting again since the revolution of 2014, when Putin puppet Yanukovych had been ousted.

Bob turned his eyes back to the branch manager. "Agnese may still get out to Kharkov, but her days in Kyiv are full of meetings, Dmitry. I just took this side excursion to—"

"Priorities, Robert. Those government ministers in Kyiv will be out of office at the next election. They are temporary. We've been in business twenty years and will stay twenty more. Agnese knows that," Syrhai said, censure in his practiced pleasantness. He put out his own cigarette, then raised a glass of coke and whiskey.

"Anyway, it's nice to meet new friends, Robert. To the Turaida Group worldwide!"

"Glory to Ukraine."

"Ha, yes!"

Bob downed his own glass, shook off the alcohol in it. He'd never drunk so much as doing business in Moldova and Ukraine . . .

In the lull that followed the toasts, Bob let his glance extend out around their little square. Behind the statue and across a narrow street, stood an old church and bell tower, its white towers and golden domes shining brilliant in the midday light. He liked the pairing with the statue.

Yet, despite these icons of nationalism and religion, the locals, Bob learned, still usually called this square *Sovietskaya*. Some conceptions were slow to fade . . .

These thoughts darkened his mood, brought his mind to foreboding places.

"I saw a train yesterday, Dmitry, with forty, maybe fifty tanks on it. Grim. How is the political situation these days in Kharkov?"

"Stable. Why do you ask?"

Bob shrugged. "Turaida has two hundred million dollars out in SME loans to businesses within the Kharkov oblast. And your office is asking for three hundred-fifty million more next year from IDB. That's a huge risk if the war extends north to here."

"The Ukrainian government is guaranteeing all loans. No need to worry, Robert."

"That government is teetering, itself, Dmitry."

"Well, our loan from IDB is Agnese's decision isn't it, Robert?" Syrhai's face grew into a dark frown. "Executives from the Rīga office have no say in our affairs, even if they are friends of Agnese Avena."

Friends of Agnese.

"It *is* Ms. Avena's loan to champion, others must approve it, of course."

He laughed. "We both know IDB opens its coffers whenever she says so, Robert." After a long pause, he said: "Still, have no worries. All is calm here. The pro-Moscow rallies you see on *Russia Today* are filmed from select angles to appear larger. There's never more than two dozen in attendance. And that man who put the Russian flag atop the Kharkov city hall? He turned out to be an FSB agent. I pass his prison nightly on my way home."

He shook his head. "'Glory to Ukraine' is right. You'll find no revolution here, Robert. This is a university city, thoughtful and connected to the world. Unlike Luhansk or Donetsk, steel towns teeming with low-level workers who fall for promises of renewed 'Soviet security' from the Kremlin's propaganda. There is no insurgent activity in Kharkov. I promise you."

"*Someone* tried to assassinate the mayor."

"The mayor lived, didn't he?"

"I'd say that's more of an execution problem, Dmitry. Pun intended."

That frown returned. "Yes, I suppose you could say it was." Syrhai looked at his watch. "I should be going. We will meet again tomorrow, I hope." He glanced across the square. "Ah . . . Here is your ride."

A white limousine pulled up alongside the *Sovietskaya* plaza.

"You sent a car?"

"Not us, Robert. A client. He appreciates the work we do in Kharkov. A perk of our friendly city."

"I really could walk."

"Don't insult him, Robert. It would hurt our reputation." Syrhai opened the limousine door. "It's a beautiful ride. I've taken it myself from time-to-time. Never will forget the experience."

"Robert Vanags?" asked a heavyset, uniformed driver.

Bob nodded, and despite feeling the whole thing excessive, sat in the rear seat. "You're not coming, Dmitry?"

"No, the wife is waiting at a jeweler. We'll see you—and Agnese—for dinner, Robert, tomorrow." Syrhai closed the door. "Enjoy Kharkov."

They pulled away from the plaza, onto wide *Sumskaya* street, the marbled buildings among the most beautiful he'd seen in Kharkov. The limo glided along, smooth as a ship on a sea of glass, classical music emanating from the speakers. Bob was just beginning to relax, to appreciate the scenery, when he glimpsed red and white stone through the window. They were passing the Annunciation Cathedral, heading back in the direction towards the train station.

That wasn't right.

"Excuse me." Bob leaned forward in the seat. "You're going the wrong way. My hotel is back near Freedom Square."

"*Ya ne ponumaya.*"

I don't understand. At least, that's what Bob thought he said . . . He'd lost his focus, during that flirty lesson with Agnese.

"This is the wrong direction. Go to the Kharkov Palace." He pointed backwards through the rear window. "The Kharkov Palace! A big hotel."

"*Ne ponumaya.*"

Bob typed up the hotel website on his smartphone, handed it through the window to the driver. "Here. Go here."

"Ah, *ponual,*" said the man with a nod of his head and broad smile.

"Thank you."

The driver shut off the phone. Closed the window between them.

"Hey!" Bob shouted, knocking on the glass. "What are you doing? Turn that on!"

The driver's only response was to press a button, locking all doors.

Bob tugged at the door handles, then pounded on the barrier between them until his fingers bloodied the glass. All to no avail. He was trapped.

They passed the train station, then countless city blocks afterwards, the buildings outside growing less frequent, smaller, and wooden until at last they left metropolitan Kharkov behind.

Headed for parts unknown in the war-torn Ukrainian countryside.

21

As the yacht *Leesma* cut through the cool waters of the Gulf of Rīga, David Vanags found himself at the helm.

It was a stimulating feeling being in control of such a large vessel. Something David never imagined would be possible so soon. Certainly, it wouldn't have been permitted back in the waters of Lake Michigan. But these were Latvian waters, and he was on a Turaida Bank ship. The rules were different.

With his father in Ukraine, Terēze Ābele had phoned and asked if David needed anything. When he'd half-jokingly said a boat to work towards his license he expected the Turaida brass would loan him, if anything, a little fishing launch or single-engine runabout. Instead, they gave him access to the company yacht and after the Russian-accented pilot steered it safely out of the harbor and down the Daugava River to the gulf, he'd handed the controls to David.

For the past forty minutes, he was master of the sea.

David was impressed with himself. And better still Beatrise was impressed. He could see her below, sitting on a deck chair at the front, wrapped in her coat, a bit cold, but smiling. When he accelerated, and sea spray came over the bow to sprinkle her, she turned that radiant smile up towards him. They both understood, it was no different than a playful splash in the pool.

He felt power. And a new sort of excitement.

Tonight would be the night. He knew it.

Good Lord, everything's on fire!

David lifted the pan with the flaming salmon and moved it towards the sink. A little too much oil . . .

The flames rose, fanned by his awkward movements. *No . . . no . . . no . . .* He was smart enough not to put water on an oil fire. Instead, he took a thick kitchen hand towel and patted it down, then turned the pan and dumped the fish into the sink basin. A ruined black husk tumbled out.

He sighed.

It'd be burgers or chicken and potatoes at *Lido* restaurant again he guessed. Beatrise would be *so* unimpressed.

The doorbell rang. Just past six.

Here she was.

He threw the towel over the ruined fish, quickly washed and dried his hands, and with a glance in the living room mirror, went to the door and opened it.

Beatrise stood in the doorway, a large bag over her shoulder. Besides happiness, arousal, and a bit of nerves, all he could think was: *What have I done to deserve a girl like this?*

She'd changed her appearance in the weeks since they started dating. When Beatrise discovered his semi-erotic doodles of fantasy girls in his sketch book, she'd adopted the style of his favorite just a few days later. This week, Beatrise wore her hair in beads, donned high-striped stockings, and on non-school days displayed a daringly open-midriff even as the weather was turning colder. She'd even gotten smaller, fully internal hearing aids, though the originals had never bothered him.

Wishes did come true.

"Are you just gonna stare at me all night, David or can I come in?" she asked with a smile.

"Oh, oh of course. . . . *Entre vous*, Bea."

As she stepped inside, her smile faded, a slight frown growing on her face. "Are you cooking something?"

"No . . . .no, why do you ask?"

"Uh . . . no reason." The smile returned and she pressed close to him. David put his arms around her, kissed her deeply for what seemed like heavenly hours. He heard the thump of her shoulder bag dropping on the floor.

It was a surprisingly heavy thud.

"Want a roommate?" she asked without quite unclasping their lips.

He pulled back, raised an eyebrow. "A roommate?"

"Mother's in Helsinki the next two weeks."

"Well done, Mother."

"Yes," she kicked off her shoes. "Who wants to carry so many things back and forth?"

"Not me."

"I want your energies for other things."

The doorbell rang. Again.

Beatrise's eyes widened in surprise. "Are you expecting anyone?"

David shook his head no and slipped away from her to open the door. It was an old man dressed in a faded Nehru jacket, gray sheepdog bangs obscuring his eyes, and a boxy leather bag hanging from each hand. He recognized him as his father's assistant from his visits to the Turaida offices.

"Mr. Markov?"

"Well, you remember me, David. I'm flattered," he said in a husky English and stepped inside. "I thought with your father traveling, it was about time someone made you a homecooked meal. A proper Russian meal!" Beneath those bangs, his old, small eyes focused on Beatrise.

"Who is this?"

"Beatrise," she said, crossing her arms and glancing from Markov to David.

"*Dobry vecher,*" he said, uncaring that young Latvians seldom appreciated the Russian language. "Call me, Evgeny," he continued changing the language back to English for David's sake. "Fortunately, I brought enough food for three. Where is the kitchen?"

"Really, it's not necessary Mr. Markov . . . Evgeny, I mean."

"The kitchen, David!"

David winced, glanced at Beatrise—she was silently laughing, thankfully—then looked backed to their elderly visitor.

"This way, Evgeny."

As they left the living room for the kitchen, the old fellow wrinkled his nose. "Why do I smell smoke?"

"I tried to whip up something . . ."

"'Whip up'?"

"Make a dinner."

"Well, my boy," he glanced at the trailing Beatrise, "if you want to impress this young woman you must be a better chef than that." He set one bag on the kitchen counter, another on the floor. "I'll come by every night while your papa is gone and give you a cooking lesson."

"Oh, that's not really necessary . . ."

"By the smell of this kitchen, I think it is."

"It's too generous," he gestured towards the counter, "I mean, two full bags of food . . . ."

Evgeny chuckled. "Only one for cooking, David." He unclasped the bag on the countertop revealing bottles, home-capped jars, and cellophane-wrapped meats and cheeses. "*This* is the food." He kneeled down to the floor and opened the top of the second bag. A pair of hairy, gray triangular ears popped out.

"And this is the cat."

Three hours later, the elevator doors opened on the ground floor and
Evgeny Markov carried his two bags through the lobby to the empty streets
deep in thought. They were nice kids, personable, particularly Roberts's son.
Beatrice appeared shy, despite her cavalier dress, talking so little through the
meal, but some girls were like that with older men. He knew he interrupted
their romance, but these things could not be helped. Evgeny had worked at
Turaida long enough to know their methods. The threat was real.

Since Roberts had started his digging into Turaida records and had those
confrontations with Ingus in and out of the conference room, the Vanags family was in grave danger. Evgeny had seen it with Richard Ash and others before
him. Whoever pulled Terēze Ābele's strings in that corner office on the ghost
floor, seldom wasted time. Roberts may very well have been sent on that trip to
Ukraine to be assassinated. If that were the unfortunate case, there was nothing
Evgeny could do to prevent it.

But Turaida might have alternative designs and Evgeny *could* watch over young
David. Kidnapping relatives of those who crossed them was an old Turaida play.
As were false arrests, blackmail, and corruption of the weak and innocent. It'd
frankly surprise him if the bank *didn't* send some agent to try something crooked.
Anything to get a hook into the loved ones of a troublemaker. Countless times
before, Evgeny had just stood by and let it happen. He always had his own family
to protect and by the time the family was gone, he'd been complicit in too many
crimes by his silence. But Evgeny was getting old now, positively ancient. With
age came a new bravery. There weren't so many years to lose.

They were good kids.

Maybe if Evgeny repeated those words enough it would calm the butterflies in his stomach. Or lessen this sense of dread that hung over him.

Before he reached his battered old car, he checked his watch. A quarter past
nine. Not so late. He had nothing to do. He could be vigilant an hour longer.

He crossed the street to a café called "The 25th Hour," and slipped inside,
balancing his bags as Barsik meowed in complaint. The café's interior was a
comfortable one, with deep plush chairs and red-wood shelves stuffed with
dog-eared books stretching back a century. The familiar aroma of the house
coffee alleviated his fears slightly. All could not be so bad with the world if
places like Meldra's café still existed.

"Hello stranger," said the forty-something redhead behind the bar. "I was
beginning to think you'd forgotten about us."

"Never, my love . . . ." He placed his bags at the foot of a stool near the window, unlatched Barsik's case, and set the cat free. "The new boss, the American, he keeps me busy."

"Americans don't understand life is for living."

"Yes," he said distractedly, watching Barisk jump up onto the counter near Meldra. "But Robert Vanags is a good man. The best we've had in a while."

As she looked at him curiously, Evgeny sat down and scooted his stool flush against the panel window, looking up at the apartment across the street.

"Not your usual seat?"

He didn't answer even when she repeated the question. Several silent minutes passed before Meldra moved the old chessboard table a bit closer to him at the window, then set a cup and two wafer cookies within the old man's reach.

"Would you like something to read with your coffee, handsome?"

"No, dear," Evgeny said absently, eyes still up at the Vanags apartment. "Tonight, I'm simply people watching."

"Creepy."

"I'll say."

David and Beatrise stared down from their apartment at the café across the street. There was the old man, sitting plain as day in the window, watching them.

"Why is he doing that?" asked Beatrise. "He never blinks."

"I'm . . . I'm not quite sure." David paused before saying more. "You know, my dad, thinks that Turaida watches their employees . . ."

"Oh, they do, it's well known in Latvia."

"I could never imagine kind old Evgeny a spy . . ."

"Well, he's certainly spying now." Standing behind him at the window, Beatrise gently put her hands around his waist. He felt the warmth of her soft body.

"You better tell your father next time he calls."

"Yeah." But that might be a day or two. David wasn't quite sure what to do *now*. He didn't exactly know what was going on. Something had greatly troubled his father at work in the last two weeks before he went to Ukraine. Something that had shut down their normal father-son communications. When David pressed him for answers, Dad promised to tell him when "the time came." That only scared him more.

Now this. He suddenly felt very far from home.

"I'll just pull the blinds, then we can . . ."

The doorbell rang once more, then quickly rang again, an insistent calling by an impatient hand.

David glanced at Beatrise, then the clock. 10:04 P.M.

"Now, who could *this* be?"

22

The buzzer would not cease and with a last glance at Beatrise, David answered the apartment door. The man outside was middle-aged, thin, in a baggy, disheveled white suit with a snap-on smile that failed to hide the impatience in his eyes. David recognized him instantly.

"Cousin Elvis!"

"Surprised to see me, Dave?"

'Surprise,' was the not the word. "What are you doing here? You should have told us you were coming to Europe . . . ."

"I sent your pop some emails, but he never replied." Elvis shrugged, stepped inside. "Is he home, Dave?"

"Dad's in Ukraine."

"Yeah? How long?"

"We're not sure."

That 'we' lingered between them until Elvis expanded his gaze to the room at large and found Beatrise sitting on the couch. His expression melted into something approaching a leer.

"How ya' doing, honey?"

Beatrise said nothing.

"Nice girl. She know English?"

"Perfectly," said David. "As for Dad, the bank sent him away at short notice. It could be weeks."

Elvis mumbled something deep down in his throat that David missed, then started digging through his coat pockets as if he needed a cigarette. "I need to speak to him for a story I'm doin', Dave. It's important."

"Did you mention that in your emails?"

"Yeah, but maybe he never got them. Hard to tell with your dad." Elvis found an empty pack, crumpled the cardboard, and shoved it back in his pocket. "Look, if he'll be gone for weeks, I'm gonna rack up quite a bill at the hotel, Dave. Can I ask a big favor? Can I bunk here?"

Ugh . . . "Where . . . where are you staying now?"

"A youth hostel two blocks over."

A hostel? Elvis must be pushing fifty. David didn't want him at the apartment, but what could he say to family? He knew Elvis had money problems.

"Well, I mean, all we could offer here would be the couch."

Beatrise made a sound somewhere between a sigh and hiss.

David felt trapped.

"What about your dad's room?" asked Elvis. "Wouldn't be a problem, would it? Seein' as he's not in."

David's stomach plummeted. He knew his dad's preferences well . . .

"No. I'm sorry. Dad's really particular about his things. That's not a good idea."

"You'd really leave me on a couch?"

"I mean . . . can't we just Skype him in the next day or two? He's pretty busy, but maybe you can do the interview . . ."

"Nah. It's gotta be face to face. Secure information exchange, you know?"

David didn't know really. He looked around, helplessly. "I mean, you can have my room. I could take the couch, I suppose . . ."

"Deal!"

That was meant more as a hypothetical . . . David rubbed his brow. "All right. I can help get your bags from the hostel if you want."

"After dinner."

"We've already had dinner. It's a bit late."

"Nothing left, Dave?"

David's reply was interrupted by sounds from the hallway. The front door still ajar, David heard the clear ping of an arriving elevator, then footfalls rushing closer. Evgeny Markov, still with his bags in hand, appeared in the doorframe.

"I think I left a jar of mayonnaise here, David." Markov smiled, something-like relief on his face. "Oh, look . . . you've a visitor . . ."

David sighed. "Come in, Mr. Markov. Let's all get acquainted. Looks like we're breaking out the leftovers."

Sometime after three A.M., with Evgeny long gone and Elvis, presumably, asleep in his new room, David sat on the couch trying to unwind. Beatrise's head rested in his lap, her auburn eyes staring up at the ceiling, that teardrop tattoo making her look eternally sad. He'd just finished giving her a vigorous neck and shoulder massage when she said off-handedly:

"I guess Latvian families are different."

"How so?" asked David softly.

"We would never have offered a visiting relative the couch if a bed was available."

This irked him. "I *did* give him my room."

"Not at first. He had to press you."

David sacrificed his room, might be sleeping on a couch for two weeks and had probably squandered a chance at sex—*his first sex!*—yet somehow, he was still being reprimanded. So much for being selfless.

David sighed. "That reminds me . . ." He gently sat Beatrise up, gave her shoulder one last affectionate rub, then rose from the couch and went to his father's bedroom door.

"What are you doing?" She asked, peering over her shoulder at him sleepily.

"Shh . . . Dad installed this right before he went." David withdrew a set of keys from his jeans, found the newest member, and locked his dad's door. Tried the knob to double-check.

"Just to be safe, Bea. You don't know Cousin Elvis like I do."

"I'm here to see Robert Vanags."

The receptionist in the lobby of Turaida Bank looked up at Elvis with stunning, almost turquoise eyes. A man could get lost in those eyes. He *wished* to get lost in them, but despite their rare beauty, he found no sympathy there.

"I'm afraid he's out of the office," she said curtly with only a hint of accent in her English.

Elvis feigned surprise. "When do you expect him back?"

She clicked her mouse, pulled up some record on her computer monitor. "Not this week."

"Not this week!?" He shouted with calculated outrage, making sure his outburst was loud enough that all eyes in the lobby turned his way. The brash, angry American who must be dealt with. He played the part perfectly.

"Look, Miss, I flew all the way from New York to interview Bob Vanags! We had a two o'clock interview scheduled today."

Trying to maintain decorum, the young woman picked up her telephone receiver. "There must be some mistake. I'll call Evgeny Markov, he's his . . ."

"No, no. Not Markov. I want Bob's bosses." Elvis pounded the desk in front of her until she scooted back a bit. "You get them down here, right now! Is this how you treat the *New York Times* in Rīga? I go through a transatlantic flight and two layovers and the guy skips town?"

"Excuse us, sir. We'll solve this as soon as we can." She waved away an approaching security guard. "Your name, mister . . . ?"

"Elvis Gulbis."

The receptionist nodded, waited for the line to pick up, then spoke quickly to someone on the other end. Elvis's fleeting knowledge of Latvian caught his own name, then 'New York Times' and a tone of respect in her voice. But that was enough.

She set the receiver down. "Someone will be with you shortly, Mr. Gulbis. Please be seated."

"Good. I'll be watching the clock."

"We'll do our best."

Precisely six minutes later, the elevator doors opened and a professionally dressed, statuesque redhead in her early fifties marched over to the desk. The receptionist motioned towards him.

Elvis stood up.

"Hello," said this woman, with a painted smile and puzzled expression. "I am Terēze Ābele, senior vice president and Robert's immediate superior. You are from the *New York Times?*"

"Actually, I'm a freelancer. But the *Times* is a possibility." He handed her a business card, pointed to the front. "Elvis Gulbis, journalist. And don't mind the handwritten number. I just got a Latvian sim card, yesterday. Oh, and I better put the extra 's' on Elvis . . ." He plucked the card from her hand, used a pen to correct his name.

Her smile faded. "How can I help you, exactly, Mr. Gulbis?"

"That's a good question," said Elvis confidently. "One I've been thinkin' about the whole plane ride over. But the better question, Terēze, is 'how can *I* help *you?*' You'll want to hear what I have to say. I'm Bob's family. Close family."

David steered the *Leesma* down the Daugava and out towards the open sea. The thrill of standing at the helm with the throttle in his hand had faded somewhat. Or perhaps it was just distraction. There were too many people on board today. In addition to Beatrise, Elvis and the almost ever-present Evgeny Markov, his Turaida pilot had brought an assistant. A tall, muscular gray-eyed assistant, who as far as David could see, did little but sit at the bow and watch.

There was something terribly familiar about this guy. He'd seen him somewhere before but couldn't quite place it. That this man had a tattoo on his arm, which Evgeny identified as a mark of "Russian Special Forces" only made him feel more ominous. He was long retired, according to Evgeny, but the fellow didn't look that old. Forty at most, probably younger.

His name was Ruslan and he spoke no English. Though David couldn't shake the feeling that he understood every word said. Elvis made a joke about Ruslan being an "advance scout" for Putin, and David swore he'd caught a flicker of anger in those gray eyes.

David wanted Ruslan off the boat. Frankly, he wanted them all off the boat and safely home. But he'd promised Elvis a tour. Well, it'd be a short one. Forty more minutes, tops.

After they'd left the mainland behind, David handed the controls to the pilot, then joined the others on the lower deck. Elvis had a Swiss-army knife key chain out, the blade extended, digging at something in the outer cabin wall.

"What are you doing?" asked David.

"They painted right over this Dave. But I think it's a bullet hole."

"A bullet hole?"

Elvis dug further with his knife, then pried out a very real bullet slug. "Look at that, Dave. What a beauty . . . You ever hear of this boat being shot at?"

"Uh, no."

"Hey big fella!" shouted Elvis at Ruslan, motioning him over. "What's this? What sort of bullet is this?"

The Russian took his time coming, and after Evgeny translated Elvis's question, he only gave a minimal glance at the bullet, then shrugged with obvious indifference. His answer was brief.

"He says he doesn't know," said Evgeny, standing behind Ruslan, and nearly eclipsed by his bulk.

Elvis didn't like this response. "Yeah? I mean can he at least guess? What caliber? Is it an automatic? Come on, he's 'special forces,' he should know this shit?"

Evgeny translated again, the big Russian's answer turning the old man's face white. It was several moments before Evgeny said:

"He thinks the American should stop asking questions."

23

It was growing dark for Bob Vanags.

After nearly two hours of driving through small wooden villages and lonely, empty fields, the limousine turned off its ancient road onto a dirt path worn into the late autumn grasslands by the tires of many vehicles. Ahead, half-hidden behind a screen of birch trees, Bob could just see in the nighttime gloom, the white-washed walls of an expansive estate, the reddish clay roof of the main house rising higher than anything he'd seen since Kharkov. Men in khaki uniforms and bearing machine guns guarded that roof, patrolled the surrounding walls, and when the limousine arrived at the towering iron gate in the front, similarly armed sentries approached the limo's windows. A military bearing to these guards, Bob could find no flag or insignia on any uniform. His glimpse was brief, though. They knew the driver, stepping away without a word exchanged, and slipped back into the shadows of the trees and walls. The gate opened, slow and majestic, and the limousine passed inside.

The compound within was extensive, paths of yellow gravel crisscrossing a blue-green grass that seemed alien to Ukraine and unnaturally resistant to the turn of season. Three smaller buildings fringed the manor, each with extensive Italian-style porticos, all lighted by electric lamps above and burning fires in wide stone cauldrons below. An opened garage in the nearest reveled the tails of two Lamborghinis, a 911 Porsche, a desert-camouflaged Hummer and another limousine too big for its space, the end stretching out into the yard where a bare-chested mechanic worked on a rear wheel well. Farther afield stood small greenhouses, an outdoor pool covered for the season, and a lighted tennis-court warmed by monolithic space heaters. Two attractive women in their thirties played doubles against young boys Bob suspected were their sons.

Bob heard a metallic "click" as the doors unlocked.

"We're here," said the limousine driver in suddenly clear English, a clarity Bob regarded very much as a taunt.

"Where is 'here,' exactly?" he asked. Bob briefly wondered if they were still in the Kharkov oblast. In fact, given the remoteness of the roads they travelled, he thought it not impossible they'd crossed over to Russia or even Belarus. Surely, there'd be border checkpoints but who knew? These last few kilometers were so broken, so wild and off the path, they could very well be clandestine routes used by smugglers or the secret Russian armies that flowed into beleaguered Ukraine. For the first time in his life, Bob wasn't entirely sure which country he was in.

"We're home, of course," said the driver.

"May I have my phone?"

"That's up to the boss-man, Robert."

"Who exactly is the 'boss-man?'"

The driver nodded to his left. "Him."

A muscular man, blond and balding, dressed in a black track suit and tennis shoes, approached up the gravel path from the main house. He might have been forty-five or fifty or even a well-preserved sixty. He had a deep-set brow that swallowed his eyes in shadow, wide Slavic cheekbones and was accessorized all in gold. Gold chains across his expansive chest, gold rings on every finger and through one earlobe, and a gaudy great gold watch, the expansive face of which covered his entire wrist.

The driver exited the limousine, and after a respectful nod to the approaching 'boss-man', came around to open Bob's door. He stepped out, unsure what else to do.

The man in the tracksuit shook Bob's hand briefly, then discarded it to embrace him in a great bear hug. Languishing in this stranger's constricting embrace, smothered in the smell of sweat and alcohol-scented cologne, Bob instinctively pulled away. But the man would not relent.

"Hello, hello, my friend," he said in a heavily accented English. Over this greeter's shoulder, Bob saw two of those armed guards, not twenty yards away, watching from the graveled path. One whispered something to the other. They both laughed. It sent chills up his spine.

"It is so good to finally meet you, Robert," said the man finally releasing him. "We have so much in common."

Bob doubted that assertion but under a cloud of confusion and fear he only stammered out:

"In common?"

"We both love Agnese Avena." He laughed, revealing a set of perfect capped, blazingly white teeth.

"You love Agnese . . . ?"

His laughter deepened. "Oh, have no fear, my friend. Mine is a platonic love." He slapped Bob on the back. "I love what she does for Ukraine. For Kharkov, Robert. We all do."

"I don't wish to be rude . . . but . . . who are you?"

"Dmitry Syrhai at Turaida didn't tell you?"

"He told me nothing." Bob's fear was ebbing slightly, replaced by a growing annoyance. "And your driver locked me in. Stole my phone. We've been driving for hours!"

"Oh, I am sorry, Robert. Let me enlighten you. We lock the doors because this is a most dangerous region. We are very near Ukraine's trouble. Car jackings by brigands are frequent. And common thieves use the chaos for their own nefarious purposes too. My driver, Denis, could not explain. He speaks poor English."

"His English seemed well-enough once we arrived."

"Not really. And the phone . . . well, I've many enemies jealous of my success, Robert." His host laughed. "They can track the GPS in a smartphone if it is on. For your own protection, I didn't wish the scoundrels to know you're here. You wouldn't want our talk interrupted by a shoot-out, would you?"

"What do we have to talk about?"

"Let us go inside. Did Denis offer you a cigarette? No? We've the best tobacco in my offices. American brands. You will feel as if home in Chicago. A lovely city. I visited in 2012."

"You still haven't said your name?"

"Leonid Vovk. I am a little wounded that you don't recognize me. If you were Ukrainian—or Russian—I'd be insulted. Might have to feed you to the dogs." He laughed as if this were a most harmless joke. "A man works hard for a reputation, Robert. I supposed I am not internationally famous. Yet. But here I am a king. No, I misuse the English article. Here I am *the* king."

That name Leonid Vovk struck a chord with Bob, but he couldn't quite place it. In the last week, he'd been overwhelmed with a thousand Slavic names to sort and memorize . . .

Yet, Vovk . . . Leonid Vovk . . . There was something to this 'king.'

With his arm around Bob's shoulder, Vovk directed him along the path and up the stone steps of the main house. Inside, beneath high ceilings with a nineteenth century spacing was an expensive but ill-fitting décor: plush couches and chairs, Art Deco table, and leopard-skin draperies. Two separate walls had enormous flat screen televisions one showing the London Stock Exchange, another some Russian-language soap opera. Here and there hung dusty bronze mirrors paired with frescoes of female nudes that were a little too new, a little too anatomically correct. All said money, none said taste. A hodge-podge of styles jumbled together.

They climbed a satin-carpeted stairway to a large, dark-wooded office with photographs of boxers, racehorses, and formula cars on the walls. A framed certificate in English announced that Leonid Pavelovich Vovk had owned the world record in military press in 1991 for men in the hundred-kilo weight class. Pictures surrounding it showed a much younger Leonid, red-faced and straining, involved in all sorts of weight-training activities.

As Bob took a seat in the deep, leather chair across from his host's desk, one of the women who'd been engaged in tennis followed them into the office, a racket still in her hands. Close-up her beauty disappointed, silicon in her lips and breasts, permanent makeup on her face, an orange-ish fake tint to her skin. She and Leonid exchanged words in Russian, the woman disappeared briefly, then returned, the racket replaced in her hands by a box of Cuban cigars. Though he knew he should refuse, Bob needed tobacco badly. The woman lighted their cigars and demurely exited. Leonid's eyes lingered on her ass as she left.

His host took a long puff on the cigar, then grinned broadly and said: "How are you enjoying Kharkov, Robert?"

"I'd seen very little before my abduction."

"Not abduction. Invitation, Robert." He laughed. "So many communication errors with foreigners . . . what can we do?"

The tobacco did little to steady Bob's nerves. It'd been a long, stressful journey to this gauche office. He wanted to get down to business. "Why am I here, Leonid? Are you a client of Turaida Bank's?"

The man across the desk shrugged, as if the questions were barely worth acknowledging. "I understand my name came up recently. In a discussion with Ingus Apinis in your Rīga offices."

There it was. Now, Bob placed the name. Leonid Vovk had been one of the shadowy oligarchs who'd taken out 300 million euros with dubious collateral, masking the exposure with various shell companies scattered around the globe. The same oligarch Ingus had used his fists to defend.

Bob's face betrayed his thoughts as Leonid said: "Ah . . . now you see." He grinned, clamping down on that cigar in his teeth. "I wanted to 'iron' out any problem, Robert. Make sure that the issue is behind us. Understand?"

"No."

"During your stay, here in this compound or after your return to Kharkov, anything is available to you. Women, cocaine, artwork from my personal collection. If the mind, soul or body wants, you've but to ask. We treat our friends well."

"What I want, frankly, is to go back to my hotel in Kharkov. And call my son in Rīga."

For the first time, some of the goodwill drained away from the man. "In good time. If you wish to leave, you wish to leave but the limo must be refueled."

The oligarch glanced up at photograph of a famous boxer violently pummeling an opponent into submission. The flesh of the loser's face splitting like a melon as blood poured out.

"I wonder if you understand, Robert, how Ukraine now functions. It is almost feudal since the CIA ousted the true national president, Viktor Yanukovych, in 2014. Kyiv has little power. The oligarchs each control their oblasts like dukes and kings. Some align with the West, some the East, some consider those only points of a compass. Do you know why this oblast has been spared the war that now consumes the Donbass? Why the fires that ravage Donetsk never touch Kharkov? Why we haven't been lost to the Russian Federation as has the Crimea?" He punched himself in the chest, with a concussive power that startled Bob.

"Me. My strength. I alone, Robert, keep millions safe."

Bob said nothing.

"Have some respect. Would you be in such a hurry to leave a nation's president? There are more people in the Kharkov oblast, Robert, than all of little Latvia. I do here what neither the Latvian government nor NATO can do there. I guard my people. I keep them safe. If a man like me has troubles, it endangers all. So, I must have no troubles. Again, I say, understand?"

Bob put out his cigar.

"Do you wish me any trouble, Robert?"

He did not answer.

Leonid watched him a long while. He set his own cigar down in the tray, folded his thick hands on the desk in front of him.

"I understand in that meeting Ingus struck you, Robert. I take responsibility for that."

This turn of the conversation startled him.

"Yes, he did." Bob said grimly.

"Would you like to strike him back? I promised you anything is available here. Hit Ingus with impunity. Bloody him, send him to the flood begging for mercy like a dog. Trust me, he'll do nothing in response."

"Ingus is here? In Ukraine?"

"He's now in my employ in Kharkov. I can have him at your mercy in mere hours. Others can deliver punishment while you watch if you prefer to keep your hands clean. Choose a boxer from the wall, they all owe their careers to me. You do like to watch boxing, Robert?"

"Mr. Vovk, do you offer acts of revenge . . . of violence . . . to buy my friendship?"

"If we are true friends, there is nothing to be purchased. I help you, you help me, together we help the Ukrainian people. I only offer—how, do you say in English—the 'perk' of revenge. Certainly, a masculine man, a man with testicles of brass, wouldn't allow an embarrassing act like this to go unpunished? What would Agnese Avena think?"

"She'd commend me for turning the other cheek."

"I wonder. Women have watched men duel since the dawn of time, Robert. How else does the female choose the best mate? Strength and money. Anything else is a lie to comfort those who have neither."

"Beauty. Love. Honesty. Common goals. Common interests."

"Illusions. Rationalizations."

"If you think so, I'm wealthier than you, Leonid."

The woman returned with two snifters of cognac. She set them on the desk between them. This time Leonid's eyes did not stray.

Neither man touched the alcohol.

"Robert, you do see that Agnese and I are helping the Ukrainian people? Our methods differ, but our goals are the same. I protect the oblast from the outside, from war, from death, as a man should. She nurtures growth from within as fit for a woman. She and I are one. Kharkov is our baby. No mere flesh-and-blood lover can come between us."

"Agnese, through proper and legal channels, funnels opportunity to those who need it," said Bob. "You, I suspect, are a thief and a despot, masquerading as a societal benefactor."

If this enraged him, he hid it well. "Such words cannot be allowed to corrupt Agnese. I'm sorry, Robert. She must believe those she works with are honest."

"Well, I love Agnese. I won't mislead her."

"Love another then." He said curtly. A beep on his mobile phone drew Leonid's attention. "Your limousine is refueled, Robert. Denis is waiting. If we are not friends, as your tone suggests, we can still do business. Think about a price."

"For what?"

"For silence. And to end your romance with Agnese Avena forever." The woman in the tennis attire reappeared in the doorway. Leonid stood up, the hospitality in his manner apparently gone.

"Darya, show our guest out."

The limousine dropped Bob Vanags off at the Kharkov Palace Hotel about ten that night. The return journey had been longer than the outgoing. He didn't know why. Perhaps to disguise Leonid Vovk's location. Denis, the driver, returned Bob's phone minus the battery. A clear stratagem to delay its use. Again, he wasn't sure why.

Exhausted, after the most stressful day imaginable, he entered through sliding doors into the preeminent hotel in eastern Ukraine. Inside, above a plush, elegant lobby filled with wealthy businessmen, an atrium ceiling rose eleven stories, glass-walled elevators silently gliding up and down the interior. More ostentatious than he needed, but Turaida Kharkov booked the room. He took the lift to the eighth floor, stumbled to his room, opened the door, entered his suite.

Laying naked on his bed was the most physically stunning woman Bob had ever seen. Blonde hair fanned out down her arched back, her pose one of pornographic dreams. Perfect curves. Perfect smile. Perfectly clear what she offered.

Bob thought of Agnese. Of Leonid Vovk. Of Donald Trump in Moscow.

Without comment, Bob exited, went to the lobby desk. Asked a bellhop to collect his things.

And found another room.

"He refused the prostitute?"

"Yes, Scorpion." It amused Leonid Vovk to call his boyhood friend by a code name over the phone. They'd known each other since school days in Stalingrad, as they both still called Volgograd, sown wild oats in the Afghan war and, later, the streets of Prague and Berlin. But even here, in a land Leonid thoroughly controlled, they could not be one hundred percent secure in their talks. MI6, the CIA, Interpol, rival oligarchs, all wished to listen in. So, Leonid called his lifelong *drook* the ridiculous name "Scorpion." Though Leonid had a code name of his own, his friend did not return the courtesy.

"You sent an attractive girl?" asked the Scorpion, as if Leonid were an idiot.

"The best. I've had her myself. She makes a man feel as a god. A night with Monika and Robert would have forgotten every thought of Agnese Avena."

There was a pause on the line from Moscow, a delay Leonid well knew. His friend spoke slowly, with deliberation, every word heavy and final.

"Then we must consider love, Leonid."

"Robert claims it is love."

"Kārlis in the Rīga office thinks their affair is infatuation. A widowed American's first exposure to a woman from his ancestral land. To him she is exotic. It will fade."

Leonid snorted with derision. "Kārlis is a dispassionate man, Scorpion. And Turaida, Rīga, well . . . Every time they plug a hole in that Latvian office, it springs three more leaks. That boat will sink us. Perhaps, you should consider replacing Kārlis?"

The silence again. Others might fear it, but Leonid feared nothing.

Or so he told himself.

"That's not for you to say, Leonid. Concentrate on your own case." A burst of static, as the security software switched to another encryption algorithm, all to keep their enemies at bay. "I leave it to you to solve this problem in your own way," continued the Scorpion. "After all, it was your dealings Robert discovered."

This irritated Leonid. Tycoons, members of parliaments, presidents of small countries, all spoke to him with respect. Yet, his old friend was open with his derision. "It was Terēze's man who blundered, who revealed the information before outsiders, Scorpion."

"I sent Agnese and Vanags to you. Now you hold both strands of this unraveling carpet in your hands. Mend it."

The line went dead.

Leonid Vovk sat in his darkened office for many minutes pondering the situation. He had half a mind to call the Scorpion back, tell him to hang himself. No one talks to him like that. Then it occurred to bring in Darya for a midnight blowjob to relieve the stress . . .

But his practical side was taking over, the instincts that made him master of Kharkov, one of the richest men in Ukraine, at least if all assets, visible and otherwise, were counted. A wealth he had no desire to risk by crossing his old friend from Stalingrad.

Leonid, frankly, didn't care about the Scorpion's politics. He'd give a percentage to Moscow as easily as Kyiv or London or Washington. But even he wasn't strong enough to keep the Russian tanks out when the time came. All he could do is count on the Scorpion's friendship, eliminate resistance in Kharkov, and increase his personal financial reserves for those days to come.

And to do that he needed Agnese Avena and her loans to keep coming. And no whistleblower boyfriend was going to upset that game. Had she learned nothing from Ēriks Helmanis? History was repeating itself.

Leonid felt stressed, tired, and old. He *did* need that blowjob from Darya. But first . . .

He picked up his mobile, a minute later a sleepy, masculine voice answered: "Hello."

"Ruslan, I have an errand for you regarding the Vanags situation. Yes, now is the time. I will be in Rīga shortly . . ."

24

"You are on the morning train to Kharkov?" said the text in Russian.

Agnese considered that simple message for more than an hour as the little Ukrainian villages and endless open fields passed by her cabin's window. Finally, she wrote: "Yes."

Two minutes later came the reply: "I will meet you at the Poltava station."

That was it then. Decision made.

Agnese sighed. It was a hard life. If she'd done this sooner, she might have saved Ēriks's life. Now there was Roberts. She always chose her lovers poorly.

When the train stopped at the city of Poltava—historic, elegant, and on the route from Kyiv to Kharkov—Agnese took her bag, descended from the train, and walked through the smallish station to the steps before the road beyond.

A black limousine waited. The hefty driver, Denis, she knew well. He leaned against the limo's body, smoking a cigarette. When he saw Agnese, he smiled, discarded his tobacco, and opened the rear door. Holding a thin bouquet of roses, Leonid Vovk stepped out.

"Agnese," he said in Russian. "It is good to see you."

She smiled softly and let the big man climb the granite steps to her. When Leonid arrived at Agnese's level, he made an overture to embrace her, but she took a step back, out of reach.

"Now, Agnese . . . you were so friendly in Frankfurt those many months ago. What has changed?"

"I always feel more comfortable in Germany."

He did not consider this long. Leonid prided himself on being a man of action. "Well, let these flowers comfort you on your way home." He offered her the roses. "I hope you will agree to take my small gift."

"I love roses." She took the bouquet, smelled their fresh scent in the crisp autumn air.

"A woman with a lover would not accept roses from another man. Especially seven red ones," he said.

"Not an honest one. Seven means love."

"And if I added an eighth it would not. The bouquet might be used for something else. Let us say a funeral. Or some other common occasion."

"Yes."

"You are too honest, Agnese. You break men's hearts." He smiled. "Don't break mine."

Her face noncommittal, Leonid kissed her on the cheek, descended the steps, ducked inside his limousine. Denis shut the door, went around to the front, took up his position behind the wheel.

Agnese watched the limousine pull away.

When it was out of sight, Agnese took the flowers into the station's water closet, found an empty stall, closed the door. There was no toilet to sit upon, only an old-style basin in the floor. She leaned on the wall, unwrapped the flowers, and found the bulky envelope adhered to the inside of the paper. Inside the envelope were numerous five-hundred-euro banknotes. Ten clips of thirty bills, one hundred-fifty thousand euros in total. The same sum as for Ēriks. A pity, she thought, that'd she'd never tell Roberts she was pregnant with his child. Life is cruel.

Agnese slipped the envelope into the interior pocket of her jacket, pressed it firm against her passport. She threw the flowers in the stall's toilet hole and left the water closet.

Agnese went to the ticket window and bought first-class passage back to Kyiv.

Bob Vanags stared at his phone's screen. The text from Agnese Avena said: "I'm not coming."

He found this profoundly disturbing. Not only that she wouldn't be meeting him at the Kharkov airport nor joining Bob on their scheduled flight to Rīga, but the curtness of the message, the lack of elaboration even on an SMS was unlike Agnese. He sensed something was wrong.

Bob called her mobile. It rang twice, then cut off.

He tried again, left a message.

Time passed.

Bob bought a latte from the *Koffein* counter, sat down on the long bench in the new departures lounge. The screen said check-in closed in fifteen minutes.

He called again. She picked up; Agnese's tone cold. For the first time, her voice sounded foreign to him.

"Roberts, I told you I'd not be coming."

"Where are you?"

"Kyiv."

"Kyiv?"

"I had some business come up."

More abruptness. "Our flight connects in Kyiv. I can meet you—"

"No, Roberts. I have no time."

She was like a different person.

"What's happened, Agnese?"

She paused. "Roberts, we cannot see each other anymore. Professionally or personally."

"I don't understand."

"There is nothing difficult to understand. It's over. When I have business with Turaida Bank, I'll deal directly with Terēze Ābele. She and I agreed to this by phone this morning."

Bob fought through the shock, sought answers. "Everything was going so well . . . There must be some reason, Agnese."

"My reasons are my own. Get another lover."

"But I love you."

"That is unfortunate. Goodbye Bob."

The phone went dead.

25

"Someone's been on dad's computer."

Beatrise looked over from the window. "Why do you think so, David?"

David sat down at the kitchen table, rubbing his temple in concentration. "When Dad called from Kharkov last night, he asked me to check something on his personal laptop in his room. Afterwards, I cleaned the screen and left it up to dry. Today, I found it shut."

She shrugged. "So? You shut it and forgot."

"I didn't forget. It's usually shut. Someone else forgot and closed it."

"You're certain?"

"One hundred percent."

Arms across her chest, Beatrise rubbed her shoulders as if she'd gotten a sudden chill. "You think your cousin might have . . . ?"

"Who else?"

Beatrise considered the question for several moments, pacing the room, fiddling with one of her hearing aids, a nervous habit she often performed when stressed. It was endearing under other circumstances.

At last, she said: "Evgeny. He's over nearly every night . . ." Beatrise stopped in front of David. "We know he's spying for Turaida Bank."

"It's a mystery." He sighed. "There's a fox in our henhouse."

"Is that an American expression?"

"I guess. It doesn't make me sound much like Sam Spade, does it?"

"No." She sat down on his lap, placed a supportive arm over his shoulder. "All will be okay when your father returns."

"Yeah."

They sat pensively for a long while, listening to the bustle of Rīga's Old Town down below. Finally, Beatrise asked:

"Who is Sam Spade?"

26

"Are you okay, Dad?"

Lost in his own thoughts, Bob hadn't even seen David. In his stunned state about Agnese and the termination of their relationship, Bob walked right past his own son at the airport exit gate, completely oblivious.

David came running up, that girlfriend Beatrise not far behind.

"Didn't you even hear me?"

"No . . . sorry, kiddo." He gave David a healthy hug. To his surprise, the usually reserved Beatrise embraced him too. Something about her perfume was familiar. In his addled state, he couldn't quite place it.

"Where's Agnese?" asked David.

"Taking a later flight." Bob didn't feel like elaborating now, even with David.

His son looked at him curiously. "We can wait for her."

"No, that's all right."

David nodded. Little more than pleasant generalities were said about his trip as they retrieved his luggage. Bob noticed a relaxed intimacy between his son and Beatrise now. A lover's closeness. He wondered if their relationship had turned physical. If so, good for David.

Yet, it somehow made him feel impossibly old.

When Bob's bags were collected, they went outside. Across the road, in the short-term parking, Evgeny waited, leaning against Bob's car.

Bob frowned "Why is he here?"

"He's always around, Dad. Been shadowing us since you left."

"Shadowing you?"

"Yeah, frankly, he's cramped our style a bit." He nodded over towards Beatrise, lowered his voice. "Know what I mean?"

Bob knew what he meant.

"Cousin Elvis is here too."

"Here? In Rīga? At the airport?"

"In Rīga but not the airport," said David. "We gotta talk to you about that . . ."

"Can you just pay the bail, Bobby?"

"Explain to me what happened. Succinctly."

Elvis leaned forward at the visitors' table in the *Brīvības iela* police station. "I told you. I found a bullet in the *Leesma*'s cabin wall. I took it to the cops. Asked them to tell me what kind of gun it came from. Next thing I know, I'm in here. If they've got a reason for it, nobody's explained it to me."

"They said you became irate, threatened an officer when they refused to help you."

"That's a bunch of bull crap. Me? Irate? Have you ever seen me irate, Bobby?"

"Many times."

"Not sober. And I haven't had a drop of spirits since I've been in Latvia. You think I'm stupid enough to threaten a cop while dry? A foreign cop where I don't even know my rights?" Elvis lowered his voice to a whisper. "Look, I'm in here because someone didn't like me asking questions about the *Lessma* yacht. That bullet doesn't fit with their diving accident story."

"You mean the deaths of the Ash couple?"

"Oh, yes. I know all about Mindy and Richard. I've been doing a lot of research." He looked over his shoulder at the guard. "Now, can you get me out of here, Bobby? It's too easy for them to whack me while I'm in the can."

"Who is going to 'whack' you?"

"The guys at your bank. You gotta give me the whole story."

"I'll get you out, Elvis. But this has been a long day and I'm not in the mood. You're paying me back."

"Sure, Bobby. I'll pay you back. By getting the word out about Turaida." He laughed. "Publish or perish, as they say. Except here it's literal."

Bob gave his cousin a sardonic glance, exited the visiting room, went to pay the bail. Elvis was crude, shifty, perennially broke. But behind all the bluster, lay a cunningness Bob envied. It *was* more than curious he'd been arrested when presenting evidence. If that bullet was genuine . . .

And Bob guessed he should be thankful that Elvis was here at all, especially with Evgeny acting odd.

Bob laid down the four hundred in euro bills and noticed the police officer put it in his pocket and didn't issue a receipt. Undeterred, Bob scribbled his signature across the forms needed for his cousin's release. He'd give Elvis his story, eventually. After he'd collected his facts and spoken with Dāvids Osis.

That trip to Ukraine had shown him too much.

"I need to speak with you, Roberts."

God, would this day end? "Can't it wait until work tomorrow, Evgeny?"

"Tomorrow may be too late."

"Too late?"

"Your family is being targeted."

"By whom?"

"There is a man. They call him 'Ruslan.' This is surely not his real name. He is connected to Turaida somehow. I suspect he works for one of their clients. Ruslan has been in the vicinity of your apartment since you objected to Ingus's way of doing things. He was watching David during your whole trip. He even posed as a pilot's hand on the *Lessma* when David took us out. I recognized him. He may have sensed I knew him."

"I'll alert the police."

"They'll do nothing."

"I'll call Terēze."

"She'll say you're seeing ghosts. I stood in the room when she told Richard Ash those very words. Ruslan stalked him too before he and his wife disappeared."

Bob felt a chill crawl up his spine. "David says you're the one hanging about too often, Evgeny."

The old man appeared wounded by these accusations. "I was doing my best, Roberts, to protect David, his girlfriend, and this cousin of yours. I could never stop an actual kidnapping or assassination, but at least my presence might make those less likely."

"'Kidnapping and assassination?'" He'd think the Russian mad if not for what happened in Ukraine. "Those are very serious accusations, Evgeny."

"This is a serious situation. No one marked by Ruslan lives long."

"Why? Why send him?"

"They fear you. Your reaction to the improprieties over a mere three hundred million in improperly booked loans. When the truth is infinitely greater . . . They will attempt to buy your silence . . ."

"They already have."

"And when that fails, they will isolate you—separate you from me, from Agnese Avena, from your son—then they'll take more drastic measures."

Bob felt his stomach tightening. *They had already stolen Agnese. What was more drastic than being separated from his son?*

"What is the truth, Evgeny?"

He took the question as a personal one. "The truth is I have been a very ignorant man. I thought it in my interest to ignore what Turaida has done, what they have stolen, whom they've bribed, threatened, and killed. A blind eye has kept me employed many years. But I am old, Roberts. Let us say, I've come to care for things more precious than employment. These thieves are vulnerable. Turaida Bank can be beaten if their history gets out. Their desperation to keep it hidden reveals their weakness."

"Where can I find this 'history?'"

"I'll show you, Roberts. But you must be prepared to act. That killer Ruslan has appeared again. The clock is ticking."

27

Late November. An appropriately stormy night took three weeks to arrive.

Bob Vanags worked in his Turaida office on that Saturday until nearly three A.M. Waiting. Praying *this* storm would be the one. Despite his best efforts to look busy for the security cameras, he could not stay seated. Electricity, physical and emotional, charged the air. Webs of white lightning stretched across the horizon, deep thunder rattled second floor windowpanes, imparting portentous feelings to all activities. Bob paced the halls to the restrooms or coffee station twice an hour, partly to be certain he remained alone, partly as an avenue to expend the nervous energy inside him. An anxiety that increased as the untamed tempest moved closer to the city center, the storm following the great river inland, the counted seconds between lightning and thunder growing ever fewer.

He wanted to be near the server room when it happened. But no such luck. Bob returned to his office, had just taken his chair, when a flash like an atomic bomb illuminated all the Rīga skyline, thunder shaking his soul to its primitive core, the sonic force igniting every car alarm in the parking lot below and for blocks beyond.

The lights went out at last. Just as Evgeny predicted.

These primordial Baltic storms crash the old Soviet-era electrical grids with surprising frequency. It was only a matter of time, staying late through every thunderous downpour until it happened. Now, half the city center was blacked out.

He had two minutes. Two minutes until the bank's private generators kicked-in and the security cameras functioned again. Two minutes to get what he wanted.

Now or never.

Bob sprung from his chair, out his office, down the hall to the server room. Its electromagnetic lock was a victim of the power outage. He ripped open the door and was inside in an instant. The room resembled a cold, deep, windowless storage closet, with ceiling high computers on each wall—black and gray, glass-faced cabinets, each with a vipers' nest of wires and board after board of switches.

It might have been confusing to a non-tech like Bob, but he knew what he sought. The Votec 2200—a box with blue metal casing, red wires—Evgeny had said. *The only one with red wires. You can't miss it, Roberts.*

But Bob did miss it. In the blackened room, using his phone's display as a flashlight, it took him a full minute to find the relatively small boxy device along the back wall, sandwiched between two black-cased Lenovos, the "Votec" label embossed in Russian: "Вотек – 2200."

Twenty-eight seconds left.

Bob opened the glass door, found the USB port, and pressed in his wireless connector. Shut the glass again.

He was out the server room with nine seconds to go, in his office at four, his chair at two . . . .

The lights went on, whirs of activity, a symphony of clicks and beeps as mechanical devices throughout the building came alive, a growing din until everything was again drowned by irresistible thunder outside.

Bob stared into his computer monitor, slowed his breathing, waited for the machine to boot. He was aware that the camera hidden in the ceiling tiles of his office must again be functioning. Bob frowned, pretended to be reading something on the screen. He knew himself a bad actor. *Jesus, why hadn't he taken some theater courses in high school or college . . .*

When a good five minutes had passed, Bob pivoted his chair slightly to the left and moved his hands to the keyboard of his personal laptop. He'd positioned it so the ceiling camera could not see the wireless receiver plugged into the laptop's side. A receiver once owned by Ēriks Helmanis and given to him by Evgeny. A recognized device on the Votec server.

Through the wireless, Bob had access. *Now, let's see what Turaida had to hide . . .*

He tried to login with Helmanis's old account, entering the password Evgeny had given him from memory. It failed. He tried again, failed again. *Damn, these Latvian words and their odd spellings.* Bob didn't dare risk a third attempt for fear of setting off some administrative security trigger. Instead, he tried to login via Richard Ash's account, the English-language password easier to remember. Of course, those British spellings were no cinch either, all those extra "l's" and "u's". . . .

But it worked. He was in.

Bless you Evgeny, you old Russian curmudgeon, bless you.

He clicked over to the drive, to the *Roze* folders. Suppressing his curiosity—*read later, just get the damn files now*—he copied them all to his laptop hard drive, watched the copying bar extend across his screen. It was finished in seconds.

They'd know he'd done this eventually. No going back now . . .

When the download was complete and doublechecked, Bob turned off both computers, folded up the laptop, and slipped it and its wireless receiver into his shoulder bag. Then he shut off all lights, exited the office, and headed towards the elevator. As he did, Bob passed the server room. With electricity restored the lock would be secure and the cameras watching. If he were lucky, really, lucky, there would be another power outage tomorrow night and he could retrieve the wireless transmitter unseen. More likely, he'd be unable to do so, and it would be waiting there to be discovered on Monday. Which would lead them to look for unusual activity, such as the deceased Richard Ash logging in from an unknown IP address at three A.M. on a stormy weekend night. With the cameras and security register showing only Bob in the building. There'd be Hell to pay, but by then the information would be out, David Osis spearheading an investigation and protecting Bob's family from Turaida, from men like that killer Evgeny claimed was shadowing them.

He sighed. *A lot of assumptions there.*

Bob adjusted the laptop bag's strap across his shoulder, pushed the button for the elevator. The lift lingered on the top floor before descending. When it at last arrived, the doors opened to reveal an occupant: a thin, casually dressed man with shaven head and five o'clock shadow on his chin. Perhaps he was in his late thirties, perhaps a little younger. Bob didn't know this man, but he knew the reputation of the floor from whence he came.

And that was enough.

He stepped in with a nod, the bleary-eyed man returned it, pushed the button to close the door. "Working late, Roberts?"

He knows my name. No, surprise there. Truthfully.

"*Was* working late. That short power outage cost me my work. Goin' home," he said with a tone that exaggerated his exhaustion.

"There's a complete file backup on all company computers every five minutes. It couldn't have cost you much."

"Yeah?"

"Yes."

They reached the ground floor. The doors opened.

"I can help you retrieve the backup files if you'd like, Roberts."

"You're a system administrator?"

He smiled. "Something like that. We can do it now if you wish. Let's go up to my office."

Bob stepped out of the elevator. "Monday. I'm beat, you know?"

"Certainly, Roberts."

"Thanks. 'Night." Bob walked as casually as could to his car, glanced back. The bald man was getting into a silver Bentley, one spot over from Terēze's empty space.

System admins don't drive cars like that . . . Not in Latvia, at least . . .

"I don't think I caught your name," Bob shouted before the man shut the car door.

"Kārlis." He smiled. "Until Monday, Roberts."

Yeah, until Monday . . .

Bob considered driving to that old Vidzeme beach shack Evgeny had mentioned, their safehouse should anything go wrong. But he was too antsy, and things had gone too well for a longer drive. Instead, he circled the city center until the power returned, then stopped by a 24-hour coffee house he often frequented in the Old Town. The tired teenage waiter seemed surprised to see anyone in this weather after an outage, but he knew Bob well, gave him a back booth and a dose of strong Cuban coffee. He ordered three more before daylight.

It wasn't the caffeine or the storm that made Bob jumpy or gave his hands a small tremor as he typed on the keyboard. The fear came from what he found onscreen, what he anticipated finding in the depth of these files. Sitting in that lonely café, Bob went through the information he'd downloaded onto the laptop. File by file, over the *Roze* directory's two-hundred thirty-two expanded loan files and fifteen related spreadsheets. These documents were more information dense then those given to auditors and regulators, with additional fields containing phone numbers, emails, IBAN codes, all of which appeared again and again on supposedly unrelated loans to supposedly unrelated borrowers. A macro search on one Russian phone number revealed it as an "alternate" contact on eleven different companies, none in Russia itself. Another email showed up linked to a sixty million loan to a real estate development company in Kyiv and five much smaller SME loans in Moldova. The more he typed, the more he realized the UBO's—the ultimate beneficial owners—were very few indeed and the cumulative loans given to them through shell companies and other nonentities, in total, must be staggeringly large. The nonentity loans weren't only 300 million euros as he originally thought. They were tens of billions of euros, most of the loan portfolio. Turaida was taking in money from depositors, bond investors, and the International Development Bank and giving out the money to oligarchs with these transfers booked as loans. However, these were uncollectable.

Leonid Vovk, whose name appeared less often than most, was just the tip of the iceberg. He was a small-fish UBO compared to the others—names Bob knew from the newspapers attached to every type of scandal—financial, political, and otherwise . . . Men famous in the tabloids, connected to the love-life of fashion models and pop starlets, owners of Crimea villas, formula race cars, works of great art leant to fine museums, and more infamously linked to the disappearance of enemies who criticized them . . . Journalists, politicians, business rivals . . .

This was a very nasty crew ultimately taking Turaida's money.

Bob glanced at the time. Nearly seven-thirty . . .

He must tell the world. Starting with the man he trusted most. The national hero.

Let Dāvids Osis rescue Latvia once more.

"How much has been stolen?" asked a bleary-eyed Osis, dressed in a bathrobe, standing in his own kitchen. "And by how many?"

Bob almost couldn't believe his own words. It sounded like something out of James Bond. "The equivalent of thirty-eight billion U.S. dollars. Thirty-eight billion in under-collateralized and fraudulently-booked loans that ultimately go to very, very few people, Dāvids."

He frowned. "How few?"

"Nine oligarchs. All part of the Moscow inner circle."

"Thirty-eight billion to nine! Just nine?! *Ak Dievs!*" He leaned back against the counter, rubbing his stubbly chin, stunned. "Are you certain?"

"They're working together, Dāvids. Using the same fake collateral, transferring monies through back channels. Under the guise of their front companies, a labyrinth snaking throughout the globe, Oligarch A pays off Oligarch B's debt to Turaida, then B uses the good credit to warrant a bigger loan the next year and pays A back. They both skim the margins. And on it goes the loans getting ever larger. It's a pyramid scheme, Dāvids, must be one of the largest in history. And Turaida knows who the UBO's really are, of course. If I can figure it out in two hours' time, they can't plausibly deny it." He patted the laptop bag, resting on the kitchen table. "We have them. It's all here in the *Roze* folders."

Osis was quiet a long while, considering what Bob had told him. Finally, he said: "Who else have you given this information?"

"No one. I came here directly from their offices. Nobody outside of Turaida has this . . . at least not from me."

"They must not be allowed to profit from these crimes."

"I hope profit, frankly, is the endgame. Half the monies are flowing through the Turaida Group from the IDB. Almost twenty billion worth of loans guaranteed by the respective governments of Ukraine, Latvia, Lithuania, Estonia, and Moldova. None of those countries, especially Ukraine, can survive if all those guarantees are called in at once . . . Maybe they are just thieves, but the Moscow connection could mean more . . . I can't work at Turaida a day longer, Dāvids."

"You shouldn't." He set a hand on Bob's shoulder. "Don't step a foot inside their offices again. Richard Ash, who knew a fraction of what you do, made that mistake when he gave notice. Send your resignation—two words "I quit"—by email. Or fax it from some cheap copy center. Don't telephone Terēze or take her calls." He grew momentarily silent, then added: "Leave your apartment for a hotel. Abandon your car, Roberts. Take only the tram and taxis now on. Are you solvent without work? Do you need some money?"

"I'm okay for a while."

"Good. If you need anything, just give the word." He turned his back, went to the kettle, and poured two cups of tea, handed one to Bob. "You have been our eyes, now you shall be our mouth. The time for stealth is over. On Monday, I'll call an emergency meeting with my most esteemed colleagues. Tuesday—or Wednesday at the latest—we'll have a press conference. I want you to be there, at my side. Turaida can't continue these criminal acts."

Fearful as he'd grown, Bob was slightly reassured to hear these words from the great man. "Do you want to see the files?"

"No. I trust you, Roberts." He sipped his tea. "Now, you must trust me. The government technicians, and law enforcement, will need your log files too to prove you were connected to Turaida's servers, that the source is genuine. Do you know, with hundred percent certainty, how to copy the log files?"

"No. I can't say I know one hundred percent . . ."

"Do you know which files exactly?"

"No . . ."

"What if we delete something we're trying to copy? The less we tamper the stronger our proof. I'll call the technicians. You can stay in my guestroom if you want until they arrive. You need sleep . . ."

"No. I should be home with my family. They don't know what is happening." Bob paused. "I can leave the laptop here, I guess."

"It would be best." He set another hand on Bob's shoulder. "I can see this worries you. Have no fear, Roberts. Thanks to you, justice will be done. Very soon, my friend."

28

"In summary," said Dāvids Osis, standing at the podium three days later. "The Latvian government takes these allegations seriously. Swift action is required to protect the millions who have entrusted their monies to Turaida Bank within Latvia and abroad."

Dressed in a perfectly tailored blue suit, Osis stood on a speaking plat-form before the Brīvības Monument, the very symbol of Latvia's strength and independence. The television cameras captured a growing crowd as his press conference entered its twentieth minute, a multitude of journalists, government officials, and interested private citizens in attendance.

Bob Vanags was generally impressed. Perhaps, Dāvids Osis spoke in more generalities than Bob would have liked, but he compensated for it with his usual eloquence. A man like Osis needn't say much. A few well-chosen words would be enough to ignite the fire. The hard facts would come out through press releases, a government information campaign driven by what Bob had found that stormy night in the Turaida offices.

Bob couldn't help but feel a little pride at what he was witnessing. Adrena-line and fear too, but also relief. That his suspicions would be proven true, at last.

Everything wasn't perfect though. It concerned him a little that Osis had changed his mind, called Bob near midnight last night and told him to skip the press conference, to watch it on television for his own safety, to remain in the country house he'd rented since leaving Turaida Bank.

Bob didn't need to be on camera, didn't need celebrity, what he needed was a better Latvia to live in. Still, he didn't wish to give the impression he feared Turaida reprisals. He was prideful enough for that . . . .

"You are the government's best source." Osis had said during that midnight phone call. *"Like any witness against organized criminals you must be protected. For now. Tomorrow I will take the baton, run the next leg of the race . . ."*

Osis was so convincing. Who could argue?

Protected or not, Bob had been far from anonymous or idle these past few days. He'd called or emailed at least forty media outlets in Latvia, America, Western Europe. Told them what he'd told Osis, that the Turaida Group was running a tens-of-billions euro pyramid scheme, a threat to the financial security of at least five nations, that Western taxpayers were unwittingly bankrolling much of the fraud, and he had the info to prove it—names, transaction ids, IBAN codes. If action was prompt, the regulatory authorities might freeze the suspect accounts, retrieve much of what had been stolen.

He wondered what kind of pained expression hung on Terēze's face as she watched this press conference from wherever she was. When he'd faxed in his resignation, Evgeny said she'd been enraged. Cursing as he put it "like a Bolshevik sailor." The next day Terēze was summoned to Moscow. By whom, Evgeny didn't know, but she hadn't appeared in the office since.

The only other change at Turaida? A thick padlock on the server room door.

Other than that, there'd been no response at all from the bank. No calls, no emails, no appearance by any company officials or its shadowy agents. This made Bob nervous. At Osis's recommendation he'd gotten out of Rīga, bunkering down with his son in a small rental house outside of Cēsis, a quaint, cobblestoned town known mostly for its medieval castle and little porcelain shops on every street.

Elvis joined them at this new abode, pestering Bob for a scoop, prying at him with the family angle again and again. But Bob had given Elvis exactly what he'd given every other reporter, no more, no less. Only provable allegations. No guesses on the fate of Richard Ash, no speculations that Turaida's scandal may be part of a greater agenda, no theories that the bad guys might be after more than money . . . He gave out only that which would be confirmed when Osis released his hard drive's contents to the world in a matter of days or even hours.

Elvis took this rejection poorly, viewed it as stonewalling. Even now, as Bob and his son watched the press conference on television, Elvis paced the room behind them, bitching that every revelation from Osis "should have been his." David finally told Elvis to "shut the Hell up."

Bob relinquished good parenting for once and let the remark stand.

Osis continued his speech:

"If some may accuse our government of being too hesitant to act, let none say those elected to safeguard the nation failed in their decisiveness when the time for action came." He glanced down at his note, the pages fluttering against the wind on his podium, then returned his eyes to the television camera, looking straight into the hearts of the nation. "Firstly, effectively immediately, there will be a freeze on all deposit withdrawals from Turaida Bank. This will prevent a possible bank run."

Not unexpected, thought Bob. *The right course.*

"Secondly, in conjunction with my office, the International Development Bank, long a friend to Latvia, will head-up a complete due diligence of Turaida Bank, after which they will make a public report and recommendations before the *Saeima* to determine if there were any wrongdoings and if further action is necessary."

Bob frowned. Why the International Development Bank? They're too wrapped up in this thing to be unbiased. Osis knows that surely.

"I have time for brief questions."

A thin reporter at the foot of platform raised his hand. "A former Turaida executive, Roberts Vanags in an email to me yesterday claimed that he was the informant who brought these transgressions to your attention? Is that correct?"

Osis never missed a beat. "Mr. Vanags appeared at my personal residence early Sunday morning to aid the government's ongoing investigation, yes. But we've been considering allegations against Turaida Bank for nearly five years. Singling out an individual as 'the informant' fails to do justice to those who so diligently worked to bring the truth to light."

Fair enough, thought Bob. *Good to know Osis had other sources into Turaida.*

"Only Roberts Vanags knows his true motives for asserting his prominence in the investigation."

Bob frowned.

What a curious thing to add?

Another journalist, Pēteris Baltkalns,—Bob knew his face from his website—pushed his way through the crowd to shout a question. "Vanags claimed in a message sent to me, and apparently to many others in attendance today, that Turaida's illegal loans amount to over thirty-eight billion U.S. dollars worldwide, with nearly six billion in Latvia alone. And that these monies were ultimately going to the benefit of seven Russian nationals and two Ukrainian nationals, he characterized as the "'Nasty Nine.'"

"I think it is too soon to speculate on the total monies or individuals involved. Though, I should say, those numbers exceed our early findings by an order of magnitude."

What was Osis doing? He had those exact numbers in the Roze files.

Baltkalns continued. "Vanags did provide the government a laptop hard dive containing Turaida Bank documents verifying his claims?"

Something like a shadow passed across Osis's face, his voice slipping an octave lower when he responded.

"There was no hard drive." Osis said bluntly. "Mr. Vanags allegations were strictly verbal. And I should say rather inconsistent with the findings of other sources." A mummer ran through the crowd. Baltkalns tried to ask a follow up question, but Osis interrupted him.

"All right. That's all I have time for. The International Development Bank will commence its examination immediately. We should have answers for you very soon. Good day, ladies and gentlemen."

Bob couldn't believe it. Why? Why deny the laptop? It cut the legs off every allegation, every email and call he'd made these past three days. He pressed a hand to his forehead, tried to reason what Osis was doing . . .

"He screwed you over," shouted Elvis, scrambling up from the back to cutoff Bob's view of the television. "He's gonna run off with those files, so he can take credit for them later."

"No . . . No, Osis . . . wouldn't do that . . . he knows I don't care about credit . . ."

"Bullshit. He's a politician. That's all they do. Take credit whenever they can."

"Elvis . . . let me think . . ."

Bob's cellphone rang—the new, cheap 'pay-as-you-go' one he'd bought just to talk with reporters without risk of Turaida listening in. It was the journalist, Pēteris Baltkalns.

"Roberts? Did you hear? Osis claims there was no hard drive. No files. What do you have to say to that?"

"I . . ." He wasn't sure what to say, it was hard to think with Elvis shouting in his ear. This must be some stratagem by Osis. Maybe he should go along with it?

But no, he'd do the right thing. Osis had promised him the information would be out. Let it be out.

"There *was* a hard drive. With more than 200 files, Mr. Baltkalns."

"You don't sound so certain, Roberts. Frankly, you sound confused. Why do you waste our time?"

"I'm just . . . just a little surprised at the moment."

"Well, you better become unsurprised quickly. There are a lot of pissed off people here, pissed off by what you've told them. People have already printed your allegations. If there are no files, no evidence, you've damaged a lot of people's reputations!"

"Mr. Baltkalns . . . you're right. There's more to tell . . ."

A hand seized the phone, cut off the call. Elvis shoved his face in Bob's. "That's right, Bob, a lot more to tell. And you tell it to family first!"

On the floor of a small apartment outside of Rockville, Maryland, dressed in wine-red leotards, Santa Ezeriņa leaned forward, legs out in a v, chest against the ground, and with a grimace of pain, touched her toes on either side. She inched further, in slow bouncing motions, until she gripped her feet at the heels, held her position to a count of sixty, dreadful tension running throughout her body, sweat dripping off her forehead to darken the carpeted floor. For the first time in her recovery, she successfully resisted screaming during this exercise. A triumph. A small one, but she'd take it.

Her flexibility was returning, Santa's range of motion eighty percent of what it had been before the Sigulda attack. She'd seized her rehab, as she seized everything in life, with a fierce two-fisted gusto. Santa walked without a cane or braces five weeks before they said she would. And even if the efforts were more awkward and painful than she'd admit to any therapist, even if it were something of a game to hide her agonies and force them to give her more challenging exercises each day, all admitted her progress was remarkable. Santa's insides may be slower to recover if they ever fully would. But she'd worry about things like spleens and liver damage later, all she wanted now was to be mobile enough to investigate, to defend herself.

To take Turaida Bank down.

This last thought dominated her mind during her three hours of rehab, pulling her focus from her stretches to the flowery words flowing through tiny speakers nearby. Propped against a pillow on the floor, her iPad streamed the news conference from Rīga and frankly Santa's emotions were mixed.

That the Latvian government was at last doing something about Turaida was welcome news, that legendary Dāvids Osis was heading it, even better.

Yet, some of his words and actions troubled her. Why hand the investigation over to the International Development Bank? An institution that shared too many projects with Turaida to be a legitimate impartial third party. And worse, why did none of the journalists in attendance ask that question? As she pressed her face to knee, her eyes caught the impression beneath her leotards, the long, thin scar on her thigh where they'd put in the screws to fuse the bone.

It seemed an answer.

Fear.

She grunted with effort of her stretches. And there were other troubling things. Roberts Vanags's claims that the illegal transactions were in the multiple billions squared more with what Ēriks Helmanis had said in that desperate last phone message, matched her own findings far better than Osis's discussions of transgressions that were "lesser orders in magnitude." Maybe Osis knew more than he was willing to say. Yet, that was unlike a man known for being bold.

If he still was bold. She'd followed Dāvids's public career all her adult life. Something had changed in him in recent years, a carefulness, a willingness to appease rather than punish wrongdoers. The great lion growing sleepy and toothless in his old age. It made Santa question his proclamation that Roberts Vanags had delivered no hard evidence.

Could it be fear again? Fear to show the world what Vanags found?

Of course, if Vanags *had* unearthed any smoking gun, surely Elviss Gulbis would have published it by now. But maybe not. Maybe Vanags knew what a screw-up his cousin was . . .

The broadcast view changed to a mobile camera, reporters following Osis to his car, peppering him with questions, all to no avail. Familiar faces all. Vanags's actions had brought many there. It was all over the Latvian journalist community, everyone she could name had gotten a call, email or tweet from Roberts.

Except her.

Who knows, maybe he'd tried to reach her? After all, that was nearly impossible since her injuries. She'd shut down all email accounts, social media, even her family couldn't contact her. All existing lines of communications were assumed compromised by Turaida's spies . . .

But she'd weathered the storm. Santa's health was improving and the days on her American visa dwindling. She'd have to return to Latvia, get back in the game, track down Roberts Vanags. Quickly.

Before Turaida silenced him forever.

29

"Where is Elvis?"

"I haven't seen him, Dad. No one's seen him for two days."

Bob nodded, trying to keep his anger, fear, and frustration from David. It was all he could do to retreat into the backroom of their rented Cēsis house, close the bedroom door and collapse onto the bare mattress. He lay there staring at the ceiling, rubbing his temples, and trying to comprehend the turn of events. Elvis's article was more than a disaster. It was betrayal. Slander. He'd been stabbed in the back by his own cousin. It was all over the internet, carried by a hundred outlets. Major newspapers, finance journals, every English-language tourist or expat rag except *The Baltic Beacon* had a version, abridged or unabridged. Elvis had too little clout to get published in so many avenues, no matter the subject. Someone was helping him . . . Turaida or Dāvids Osis or both.

Elvis had ignored the points he'd made about the bank and the way it operated. Instead, the article entitled "The Nature of Turaida Bank's Alleged Whistleblower by Those Who Know Him Best" was little more than a series of damning quotes.

"Robert Vanags was a disgruntled worker, emotionally unhinged, who once engaged in a fistfight with another Turaida employee after a meeting," the article said. *"As his cousin, one who has known Robert his whole life, I've seen the downward spiral within his professional career and within our close-knit family—the anger he can't control, the occasional violence, and the irrational and often dishonest actions he takes to vent his rage and frustration. Those who love Robert hope he seeks professional help soon, for his own sake and that of his son David."*

Bob closed his eyes. He couldn't believe this was happening . . . And the chorus of old "friends" Elvis had recruited to pile on . . .

"Mr. Vanags was the worst hire I've ever made," said Terēze Ābele, *Senior Vice President of the Capital Markets Department at Turaida. "We were planning to terminate him, and he knew it. Robert's answer was to spread falsehoods around the globe with little thought of how his words affect everyday clients who trust their savings to our bank.*

Let me be clear. Turaida has never failed any audit, never been convicted of any crime or transgression. We welcome the International Development Bank's investigation to clear these unfounded allegations."

"He was a tyrant, who treated his clients with contempt" said Patrick McMillan a Chicago area real estate developer who worked with Vanags in America. "Of course, they booted him out of Illinois. Good riddance to the bum."

Agnese Avena at International Development Bank in Frankfurt: "Robert often drank heavily during business functions and made unwanted sexual advances towards me on multiple occasions, including at the funeral of another employee. It was only a matter of time until this all came out."

Bob seethed, wondering how he'd reached such a desperate point. This article coupled with Dāvids Osis's statement that he had delivered "no laptop, with no proof" had destroyed his reputation with the media and policing institutions. Of the forty or so journalists and regulatory officials he'd contacted, few now answered his emails or calls, and those who *did* reply told him to never contact them again, threatened legal action, made public retractions on their websites. After all, how could they believe him? Osis was a national hero, and now Bob's own family called him unstable and delusional. An angry failure, a violent, borderline sexual predator, lying about those who stood up to him . . . .

He opened his eyes . . . unbelievable . . . Why? Why would Elvis do this?

Elvis Gulbis sat in the indoor pool of a private spa outside Cēsis, less than two kilometers from his distraught cousin. Yet he'd never felt more distant.

It wasn't easy torpedoing Bob's reputation, even if he sorta deserved it, not lending money, being so self-righteous, asking favors and never returning them. But it wouldn't have mattered if Bob were a saint, Elvis needed the money, wanted the money. It'd make a big difference in his life. More than a stingy cousin ever would . . .

He leaned back, felt the spa waters soothe his back and aching muscles. Who'd have thought three weeks ago he'd be relaxing in a medieval-looking village in Europe? The domed brick ceiling above appeared at least two centuries old. You don't get that sort of history in Minnesota, he thought.

Next to him in the pool, champagne glass in hand, was Leonid Vovk, a bigwig Turaida client from Ukraine who'd been financing the smear campaign against Bob. Or supposed to be funding it. Elvis had gotten an advance wire transfer of twenty thousand U.S. dollars via some Latvian company he'd never heard of. Now that his article was in every newspaper, on every website, and even Dāvids Osis, his cousin's childhood hero, was publicly punking Bob, Elvis expected the remaining forty thousand. No word when it was coming. He hoped for it tonight—in cash—but Leonid seemed only to want to party.

And even if they did finally pay up, Elvis wasn't sure it was quite enough for what he'd done to Bob.

"You know it wasn't easy screwing over family." He blurted out to Leonid, deciding he'd been diplomatic too long. "I should have gotten more."

Leonid looked over him, an almost sleepy expression on his wide, Slavic face. "This is a time for celebration. No talk of money. Relax, my friend."

Elvis frowned. "What are we celebrating exactly?"

"The International Development Bank's inquiry into Turaida."

"You want that?"

"Of course."

Elvis didn't know why Leonid would desire an inquiry. As far as he knew, the idea was to discredit Bob and make the allegations go away. Maybe there was something bigger afloat.

Elvis reached over and refilled his own glass of champagne. On a bench near the edge of the pool, sat thin, muscular Ruslan, fully dressed in a cheap-looking black track suit, towel over his lap, his boss's bag next to him.

Elvis nodded in Ruslan's direction. "How come he don't swim?"

"He's paid to watch, not relax," answered Leonid in a tone of disinterest. He finished his champagne.

Elvis too was bored. "We should really have some tail in here."

"There will be girls at the hotel in Rīga."

Yeah, probably prime Russian escorts that cost a fortune. Elvis hoped Leonid was flippin' the bill. The thought of expensive sex brought him back to his current situation.

"I'm gonna get my money, right, Leonid? Tonight?"

"All of it. And a bonus. We need your name for one last headline."

A bonus? Elvis grew excited but tried to hide his interest. "Yeah, well if the 'headline' is screwin' over Bob Vanags again, it's going to cost a lot more this time."

"Price wasn't a problem for you before."

"I'm developing a conscience. It'll take a lot—in cash—to overcome my guilt."

"I don't think it will be too expensive." Leonid rose from the waters. "One moment, Elvis, I must attend the toilet."

The big Ukrainian headed up the steps, set his champagne glass on the bench, took his towel from Ruslan, and disappeared down the tunnel to the changing rooms.

Time passed.

Elvis sat there drinking, stewing about money.

Leonid took too long. Elvis thought he heard a car engine outside, wondered if Leonid had left. But, no, his bag was still there on the bench near the bodyguard.

"Your boss is a tough negotiator," said Elvis as an aside in frustration.

To his surprise, Ruslan answered:

"Yes."

"I thought you didn't speak English?"

"Only a little." Ruslan unzipped the bag, turned his back, blocking Elvis's view. "A few words learned from school."

Something about the way he rummaged through that bag made Elvis nervous. "Looking for a suit now that Leonid's gone? Screw the boss, eh? The water's fine."

"I have to work. Unfortunately."

"Too bad." He downed the champagne. Elvis could just see Ruslan pulling on strange-looking gloves, thin latex with black disks covering the fingertips.

"What . . . what are you doing?"

"Making a headline." That gloved hand lifted a pistol fitted with a silencer from the bag's interior, turned it towards Elvis, fired three shots.

The spa waters turned a deep, wine red.

30

Bob Vanags sat in the darkened parlor. Waiting, listening to the voices in the lighted room beyond. Impatient shadows moved back and forth beneath the door, the snippets of hushed Latvian conversation occasionally rising to shriller pitches, giving away their alarm at his presence.

At last, the doorknob turned and Dāvids Osis entered, a look of deep concern—and something else—on his face.

"What are you doing here, Roberts?"

"Your granddaughter let me in. I guess she's used to seeing me in your house and is unaware you've betrayed me."

"Well, what do ten-year-olds know of politics and banking?" He shut the door behind him, flipped a light switch. "You're not angry, are you Roberts?"

"Angry? How could I not be?"

Osis lowered himself into a chair across from the couch where Bob sat. "I assumed you understood my actions. That by minimizing your input into the investigation, I've protected your life. Richard Ash, Ēriks Helmanis, did less than you and paid a higher price. The ultimate price." He reached over and patted Bob on the knee in a paternal fashion. "The fact that you're here and healthy—thank God—proves our ruse is working."

Did Osis think him stupid? "What about the article by Elvis?"

"I'm sympathetic, but the actions of your cousin are hardly my fault." He rubbed his bearded chin thoughtfully. "I can come out and back your words in the media, but then Turaida would surely strike at both of us, our families. You may be willing to risk your son, but I won't endanger that little girl on the other side of the door."

The man who had stood up to Soviet tanks on the Day of Barricades was now afraid of corrupt bankers. Bob felt disgust in the pit of his stomach.

"And the missing hard drive?"

"Those files were acquired illegally, Roberts. Stolen. Inadmissible in court. We work for the Latvian government, not WikiLeaks or One World Press. If

I confirmed their existence, both you and I would have broken the law." He smiled, held up a finger. "Now, if the IDB should find the same files, those same names, transactions, bank accounts . . . legally . . . ."

Bob sneered. The old politician had an answer for everything. "Why put IDB in charge? Half the suspect money flows from the IDB . . ."

"Which means they will be motivated to find the truth. You must learn to trust me, Roberts. I—"

Shouts in the hall interrupted his words. A quick pounding on the door followed and two burly men in trench coats burst into the room.

"Thank God," said Osis rising from his chair. "How much longer did you detectives expect me to stall a murderer?"

"Murderer?" shouted Bob.

Osis ignored the question. "I called the police before coming in here, Roberts. My granddaughter told me who waited for me. We are not so foolish as you believed."

"Murder? Who has been murdered?"

A detective answered in Latvian, but it was Osis who said the dreadful words in English:

"Your cousin was found dead, floating in a Cēsis spa three hours ago, Roberts." The police seized Bob's arms, handcuffed them behind, frog-marched him past Osis.

"You are under arrest for the killing of Elviss Gulbis."

31

The detectives escorted Bob Vanags out towards the road where a brown sedan awaited. They shoved him into the backseat, one of the officers sitting beside him while the other went around to the front and took the wheel. A moment later, the car pulled away from Osis's house, skirting the lakefront towards the main road to Rīga.

Something about the vibrations of the car, the motion itself shook Bob from his stupor, from the shock of arrest. This was really happening. He was being carted away, accused of murder, seized by policemen at the behest of Dāvids Osis.

And, yet, thought Bob as the cobwebs cleared, *Were they really policemen?* Bob noted there was nothing within the car to indicate association with law enforcement. No evidence at all . . .

"Can I see some identification?"

The man beside him struck Bob across the face, a stinging blow that sent his head hard against the window glass.

"Shut up," said the man in heavily accented English.

The pain brought understanding.

Brutality aside, this is not how cops act in an EU country.

He'd never reach any real police station. Bob knew his exact predicament. Do or die.

His head resting against the window, he noticed the door rattled with the sedan's acceleration. It was unlocked and barely shut. They'd erred. Handcuffing him . . . setting a man in the backseat to watch . . . they thought this would be enough.

Arrogant criminals.

Their road passed the edge of a steep embankment leading down to Lake Ķīšezers.

He saw opportunity, shifting his position so his back was to the door, staring at his watcher as his manacled hands found the handle behind him. No alarm appeared in his guard's dull face. When the driver slowed to take an incline up to the highway, Bob turned the lever, threw open the door, and hurled himself backwards into the black waters of the lake.

His ankle struck a rock, he tumbled over, then into the water. Disorientation came as he went below the surface. White bubbles. The shock of cold November waters. Gravity suspended. His manacled wrists prevented Bob taking any stroke, but he was calm in water, he did not fear drowning. He'd spent thousands of hours in the pool throughout his youth and college. Bob did not sink. A strong kick propelled him up. He gasped, head above the waterline, the prickly cool air on his face.

Then he heard another splash. Waves and white foam went over his head and shoulders as the other man jumped in beside him.

Bob tried to kick away. Thick hands grabbed one of his flailing legs, attempting to drag Bob towards the shore. But his assailant was no swimmer, his movements clumsy and inefficient.

A kick with his free leg to the enemy's jaw. He gagged, took in water, released Bob.

That was all the space he needed. Bob fluttered his legs as fast as he could, churning the waters, dolphin kicking away from the man. Even without effective use of his arms, he increased this distance. Bob had played this game as a child, beating his friends in swimming races without using his arms. The landlubber thug had no chance of catching him.

When he'd kicked forever it seemed, Bob gasped for air, raised his head to ascertain his distance from shore.

Not far enough.

He saw the water-soaked thug climb out of the lake. But Bob's victory was little enjoyed. The sound of gunfire split the night. Something passed into the water near him.

The other man, the driver, was firing from the shore.

Bob dove, plunging into the inky blackness of a nighttime lake. His heartbeat thundering in his ears, dolphin kicking through the depths, navigating as closely as possible towards the lake's far shore. When his lungs burned and he couldn't stave off the need to breathe a second longer, Bob at last surfaced. Dared a glance back.

He'd made good time below the surface and the distance startled him. The car was invisible in the night, the headlights reduced to thin beams of yellow along the shoreline. He heard the faint slam of a door and those searching beams moved forward, navigating the lake edge road, seeking him.

Bob took another hoarse, painful breath and dove down once more.

He lost all sense of time in the cold, blackness of the lake. When his legs were spent, numbed by frigid waters, Bob beached himself up on the muddy shore, inching up on his belly, arms still locked behind. His thighs and calves ached, his lungs on fire, and it was all he could do to push his exhausted body up the shallow embankment into the cover of the trees. He lay there, recovering his strength, shivering, gasping, pulling helplessly at the handcuffs.

He did not remain alone long.

The headlights of a fast-approaching car appeared on the road nearby. He scooted down in the mud, trying to remain hidden from view, manacled hands useless in defense. He coiled his muscles praying to have the strength to slip back into the lake. But that route too meant likely death . . . the waters were so cold . . .

Bob heard the car come to a stop close by. The opening of a door. He spied the shape of a woman silhouetted against the headlight beams.

"Roberts Vanags! I'm here to assist," the shadow woman shouted.

He stared up at the trim figure as she groped down the forested embankment towards him. She limped with every step, a brace around one leg. As the gloom receded, the stranger stepped into the starlight.

It was that journalist from the Helmanis funeral . . .

"Remember me, Roberts? Santa Ezeriņa, *Baltic Beacon*. You look like a man who needs a lift." She said, reaching him on the bank. "Or a handcuff file."

The engines of the journalist's little Toyota strained as they sped through seldom traveled, poorly paved roads. Bob was loosely aware that they were moving up into the forests of Vidzeme. More exact a location than that, he could not say. With the file she'd given him, he was a quarter way through one handcuff, a tough job on a rattling seat, the cuffs unseen behind him. But the journalist wouldn't stop to assist.

Santa talked *at* him more than *to* him, her eyes seldom wavering from the road. When she did speak, it was a little too fast. A fever growing in Bob's mind, he had difficulty keeping up.

"I was headed to Osis's house to pry an interview out of him, when I saw those goons escorting you out. Figured following you was the more immediate story," she said, her eyes glowing green in the dashboard lights. "I guessed right."

"They were going to kill me," he said softly.

She laughed as if this was expected. "You're lucky. Turaida's got better muscle than those keystone cops. Osis must not merit primo protection."

Bob shivered, still soaked from his unexpected swim. Santa turned up the heaters full blast, the car lurched, slowed by ten kilometers-per-hour, as if overtaxed.

She paid it no mind. "It's all over town that you killed your cousin."

"I'm innocent."

"I know. But it won't matter unless we can prove it. Rumor from my source in the police is they found the gun with your fingerprints all over the handle and trigger."

"My fingerprints?" It was all so impossible . . .

"They take electronic scans of fingerprints when you get a residency permit. The killers likely got ahold of them there, made duplicate casts out of latex or foam. More proof someone in the government is helping Turaida."

"It's crazy," he whispered.

"It's Latvia. The sort of thing no one mentions in those tourist photo-books." She glanced over at him. "Where can we take you?"

Bob said nothing.

"Hey, you with me?"

"My friend has a place on the beach not far from here. Near Lilaste Dunes. Isolated." Bob gave her Evgeny's emergency address.

Santa nodded, kept silent for a good ten minutes. Bob was aware they headed loosely in the direction of the dune beaches. He sawed away at the 'cuffs in silence.

Finally, the journalist spoke: "I want your story. Only me. Deal?"

So, that's why she aided him.

"Elvis said the same thing, you know?"

"Yeah, but he was a screw up. I'm chauffeuring you away from gun-toting gangsters."

"No one believes me. Osis made sure of that."

"I believe you. Trust me you got off easy."

He glanced down at the brace on her leg. *Yeah, maybe he did.*

She caught his glance. "I'm lucky to have a leg at all, Roberts. You don't know the . . . *Su'ds!*"

"What?"

"Your friends are back."

Bob forced himself around in the seat. Twin headlights shown through the rear window. He squinted into the growing glow, discerned the outline of a sedan closing quickly.

"Jesus, how did they find us?"

Santa muttered something profane in Latvian, flipped off the heat, and floored the accelerator. The engines whirred, the car lurching into highest gear.

The sedan dropped back. Bob saw the black figure of a man leaning out the passenger window. Gunfire.

A perfect hole appeared in the Toyota's rear window, the slug passing through the car in an instant to exit through the front window, leaving a shattered spider-web in the glass just over the dash.

"Ieva's not gonna be happy," said Santa, turning the wheel to take a hairpin curve.

"Who's Ieva?

"My aunt. I borrowed her car soon as I got back to Latvia. Promised her not a scratch."

Another bullet shattered the rear window, penetrating the seat beneath Bob, burst out of the chair with a flurry of stuffing, to lodge in the floor between his ankles.

He dropped the file. "You got any weapons, Santa?"

She didn't hear him, all attention on the road ahead.

"There we go," said she.

A break in the treeline revealed the open sea beyond.

"I know this beach well," she continued. "Sand dunes stretching for twenty kilometers, some fifteen, twenty meters deep. There's a soft embankment after the next curve. If we throw you out before they're around the bend, chances are they won't see you in the night. And they'll keep after me."

"Throw me out? Handcuffed?"

"I'll slow. A little."

Bob looked at the car's speedometer, then out the window at the trees whizzing by. "I've already jumped out of a moving car today, Santa."

"Then you should be good at it."

"What about you?"

They took the curve, the sedan lost in the trees behind momentarily.

"I'll be in touch." With one hand on the wheel, Santa reached across him and flung open the door. "Go!"

For the second time tonight, Bob threw himself out of a moving car. His body hit the sand hard, dust flying everywhere into his eyes, mouth, and nostrils, something snapping in his shoulder. As he rolled down the steep incline, sharp stones beneath the great sands gouged his back and stomach, tore at his clothes. At last, Bob came to a halt, far down the embankment, half covered in sand avalanches along the water's edge.

Up on the road, the Toyota sped away. A moment later the sedan appeared from around the corner, gunning its engines in pursuit. The cars raced along the highway, flashes of gunfire from the pursuers, terrible swerves by the pursued, then both sets of headlights disappeared behind the tree line. The sounds of engines grew distant, then vanished altogether.

They'll never catch her. She's tough, that one.

Bleeding, fevered, exhausted, and manacled, Bob lifted himself from the dirt and stumbled along the beach searching for shelter, for Evgeny's little shack among miles of sand dunes . . . A needle in a haystack . . . But then he had all night.

If he was lucky.

32

"It's all over television and the internet," said Evgeny, sitting at the bare table in his beachfront shack. "They accuse you of murdering your cousin. Revenge for the article he published about you. The campaign has started."

Bob grunted with effort as Evgeny's saw finally spilt the handcuff. He forced his raw, bruised wrist out, tossed the manacles contemptuously across the table. Evgeny's cat, Barsik, reaching up from an empty chair to bat them as they passed.

Bob looked at Evgeny, then over to David and Beatrise sitting on a worn couch against the wall. An atmosphere of exhausted tension filled the room. All eyes were on him.

"I'll go to the American embassy," Bob finally said.

"If you are wanted for a crime, there is no sanctuary. They'll just hand you over to the police," replied Evgeny. "And in jail, you hang yourself. It is the oldest KGB trick from Soviet times, Roberts."

"It happened to my grandfather," said Beatrise, her voice soft, eyes distant.

David caressed her hand. "We're not scared. Are we Bea?"

She said nothing.

Bob empathized with his son. Trying to be a man in this tragic, unfathomable trap Turaida had set. Bob certainly felt fear himself.

"Find a safe place outside Latvia for the time being," said Evgeny with unexpected energy in his voice. "I am no target yet. I will take all we know to this journalist." He paused. "You think we can trust her?"

"She saved my life."

"It may be a ruse to see what we have on Turaida."

"I don't think so."

He nodded, scratched his chin thoughtfully. "I will tell Santa Ezeriņa everything when you and David are safe." He glanced at Beatrise. "The girl goes with you too?"

"She goes," said David.

Bob started to object, but Evgeny read his thoughts.

"Better with you, Roberts, than held hostage by Turaida."

"Your parents . . ."

"I'm eighteen," said Beatrise. "I go."

Sadness and doubt overwhelmed Bob. That he was shepherding his son and Beatrise into danger. It gave him the greatest pause.

"Evil men count on good men doing what is easy and ineffective: staying home, reading their favorite papers, scoffing at misdeeds, and nothing more," Theodore Roosevelt had said.

"You're thinking of the Teddy Roosevelt quote, aren't you, Dad? The white hat always thinks of Teddy."

Impossibly, Bob smiled. His son knew him well.

"If we go. What route?"

"I'll get us out," said David.

Evgeny leaned forward across the table. "They'll watch the airports. The train stations."

"The bus stations too," added Beatrise. "And the cruise ships."

"I'll get us out," repeated David more assertively. "I can do it."

"How?" asked Bob.

"Easy. I've been practicing it the past two months, Dad. We take the *Leesma* . . ."

33

"This isn't going to work."

"It'll work, Dad."

A silent Monday morning at the marina, David pried at the *Leesma's* cabin door with a crowbar, father and son hidden on the riverside of the yacht, remaining invisible to any early wanderers on the landside dock.

"Let me have it."

"I've got it, Dad," said David with annoyance. He grunted, turned the bar again, digging hard into the space between doorframe and door. This time something snapped, chrome and plastic facing falling loose to the deck, the door rolling open six inches.

"See," said David with a smile.

"Well done," Bob briefly wondered if a parent should condone breaking into a yacht, but then these were desperate times. Bob shouldered the gym bag he and David had brought, and they slipped inside, shutting the door behind.

David rushed over to a keypad on the wall. Typed in "1-1-1-1."

"I noticed during my lessons the security alarm code was pathetically simple. Guess Turaida thought no one would dare touch their boat." David sighed as the alarm gave a simple accepting beep and lights dimmed on the keypad. "We should have all the time we need unless someone's scheduled to use the yacht."

"How often do they take out the ship?"

"No idea. But six-thirty A.M., on a Monday in November, has gotta be the least likely time. Turaida employees are on their way to work and its far too late in the season for most clients."

Bob grunted, a gnawing feeling still in the pit of his stomach. They ascended to the bridge with its countless dials, gauges, and buttons. He hoped David knew what he was doing.

"Fucking hell," said David.

"Language."

"We're committing an act of piracy and you're worried about profanity, Dad?"

"Always."

David gave his father a chagrined expression, nodded towards two small hooks on the wall. "The ignition keys are supposed to be hung right there. Have been every time I took the *Leesma* out." He sighed. "Guess it's 'Plan B'."

Plan B consisted of David prying apart the lower half of the control board with the crowbar, while Bob removed a car battery from his gym bag. Eventually, David extended two wires—black and white—to the battery feeds.

David sighed. "No clamps, and not enough bare wire to wrap it around. I'll have to hold them here." He glanced to his father. "Hit the ignition button, Dad. We'll jumpstart this sucker."

"If you've got those wires wrong, can that battery explode or spew out acid like when jumping a car?"

"If the charges are backwards, sure can."

"We're switching."

David resisted, but Bob allowed no argument. In a moment he held the wires, his son at the ignition.

"Go."

David hit the button, the *Leesma*'s engines roared to life.

Bob released a long sigh. "Well done."

"Who needs college? I can make a living as a boat thief."

"Not funny."

But it was apparently to David. He smiled triumphantly. Bob went out and untied the ropes from the cleats. Then David took the *Leesma* out, steering them through the calm waters of the marina into the Daugava. In thirty minutes, they'd be safely in the Gulf of Rīga.

"We'll take this thing as far out to sea as possible, Dad, disable every homing beacon, GPS, etc. on it. Then head back to the Vidzeme coast at nightfall for Beatrise and Evgeny." He checked the fuel gauges. "She's full up. We've enough for a long trip."

They passed a patrol boat on the river. And though the officers seemed to pay them no mind, cold fear ran up Bob's spine.

Yeah, "long trip,"

Let's hope, Son.

Evgeny Markov watched the sunset through the dusty window of his beach shack. Fear rested deep in his stomach. Not fear for himself, he was old, shackled with enough ailments that death was more a disagreeable concept, than truly horrific. But he worried for the others. For Roberts and David, too long delayed, and for young Beatrise, slumbering on the small bed in the backroom.

The electric teapot released a shrill hiss on the counter and Evgeny unplugged it before the noise woke the girl. He poured a cup of tea and continued to stare out the window.

Where is the boat? They should have been here by now.

Evgeny regretted letting the American father and son go alone. He should have never acquiesced to their arguments that an old man and a near-deaf girl would hinder their chances of success. There was too much pride in Roberts.

Yet, if that conceit spurred him to action, it was not such a bad thing.

He caught motion out of the corner of his eye. His cat, Barsik, batted something across the floor, the object rolling underneath the small rug he kept by the door. The animal's furious attempt to retrieve it amused him, a welcome reprieve from the worry and tension of the moment. Evgeny bent down and flipped up the rug to see what object Barsik had been toying with.

Beatrise's hearing aid.

She must have left it on the nightstand. Or it simply fell out as she slept. Barsik was always a boisterous animal. Nothing was safe from being batted away. At least, nothing so small.

He plucked it from the floor and took it over to examine in the dying light of the window. They were marvelous devices. He'd never seen a piece quite like this. White plastic, almost teardrop in shape, tiny embossed "+" and "-" buttons to raise or lower the volume. The filthy shack floor had left spots of dirt over the surface, and he dipped a rag in the warm teapot water to clean it. When it was spotless, his mind turned to a cat-proof place to store it until Beatrise awoke. Or Bob and his son arrived.

He heard a slight buzzing.

It took him only a moment to realize the sound came from the device in his fingertips. Had Barsik damaged it? Evgeny lifted it up and placed the aid in his own ear.

His face went white.

My God . . .

34

Anchored two-hundred yards offshore, the *Leesma* sat with her lights out in the night, the silence broken only by the sound of wind-driven waves thumping against the hull and the hushed argument of the two figures on deck.

"Stay on board, David," said Bob dressed in one of the yacht's thermal wet suits.

"Dad . . . I'm going with you . . ."

"If someone comes near, you're the only one that can steer the ship. Stay here. I'll get them."

"But . . ."

"That's an order."

As if to prevent further discussion, Bob dove into the freezing waters below the yacht. His old college swimming skills served him well. Even in the swelling sea, with a powerful kick and precise strokes, not four minutes passed until Bob reached the tree-lined shore. He rose to his feet, glanced up and down the beach to assure he was alone.

All looked good. Evgeny's little shack stood a hundred yards in, nestled back among the firs. The windowpanes dark, the glass reflected starlight, as if somehow the little house contained the heavens in the sky.

Alert, his pulse drumming in his ears, Bob made his way up the narrow path to the shack. Gusts of wind swayed the treetops, yet around the secluded house everything remained still. This serenity unwelcome. Evgeny should have seen him by now, come out to the beach . . .

Sand caking his wet bare feet, Bob was nearly at the door when sobbing caught his ear. In the blackness, under the tree canopy, he nearly stumbled right over her. Curled up against the base of a linden tree lay a woman, her hands in her face, crying uncontrollably.

"Beatrise?"

She did not respond. He called her again, but the young Latvian was lost in her tears. Bob kneeled, took her hands, pulled them away from her face. Gently at first, but harder, more firmly in control, as she resisted.

"Beatrise. It's me. Robert . . ."

She looked up at him. Despite the darkness, he could see her eyes were blood red from crying, her eyeliner running down her cheeks in thick caterpillar lines.

An air of recognition at last came over her.

"Roberts?" she asked weakly.

"What happened, Beatrise? Where's Evgeny?"

Emotions overwhelming her again, Beatrise said nothing but extended one hand towards the house.

That gnawing fear intensified. Bob released Beatrise, rushed to the shack, pounded on the door.

"Evgeny!" shouted Bob. "Are you in there? Evgeny!" The force of his blows sent the unlocked door swinging inwards. Bob hit the light switch.

"Oh Jesus . . . ."

On the floor lay a bloody, bullet-riddled Evgeny.

Bob stumbled back, nauseous, stunned, fighting to keep his reason. To fight off any flight instinct. This was no nightmare, horrific as it seemed . . .

His heart pounding in his chest, he stepped inside, prepared himself to take in details the shocking sight had pushed to the margins. The rear door to the shack's small bedroom was open, something swaying in the darkness. Bob's eyes adjusted to the gloom. A dead cat hung by a chord from the ceiling lamp. Other than poor Barsik, the backroom was empty.

Bob returned to the main room, kneeled close to Evgeny, shut his eyes, blood covering his fingertips as he did so.

He said a prayer for the old communist. Bob retreated to Beatrise.

"Who did this?"

Her emotional state remained tenuous, her voice a whisper, nearly lost under the winds. "I was in the outhouse. I heard gunshots. Many gunshots . . ."

"Did you see anyone?"

"I hid . . . there were three of them, I think. At least three."

"Beatrise, how long ago was this?"

"Minutes." Her face contorted in pain. "I don't know how long I've been out here." She was inconsolable.

He had to get her to the ship. Bob lifted Beatrise from the sand, urging her forward, down the beach towards the water. The *Leesma* remained waiting for them offshore, a black silhouette beneath the starry sky.

There was no time to swim out and get another thermal suit. "This is gonna be a bit cold, Bea." Bob eased the crying girl out into the sea, a hand on her shoulder as they doggy-paddled towards the yacht. The winds growing stronger, waves crashed over their shoulders and into their faces. Ahead Bob could see his son had lowered the stern's swimming platform to just above water level, and was leaning over the side, extending a hand.

"Easy does it," said David. "Almost there, Bea."

They reached the ship. She gripped David's hand, was onto the platform, when the *Leesma* lurched, jarred by a fearsome wave. Beatrise lost her footing, just caught herself as one hearing aid dislodged, plunging into the sea just beyond Bob' outstretched fingertips.

"No!" she shouted, reaching out into the darkness, leaning desperately over the platform's edge.

"It's gone Bea," said David, pulling her back in. "Let it go."

"I'm sorry," said Bob. He climbed aboard.

Beatrise turned pale, her hysterics quieting. She buried her face in David's chest, sobbing. He slowly put his arms around her.

As the two embraced, David looked over her shoulder to his father.

"Evgeny?"

Bob shook his head. "No."

It took seconds for full comprehension to ebb into David's face. And longer still for the horrible realization to pass. At last, he swallowed hard, and said:

"Okay. Where to now, Dad?"

That was the question.

35

Outside the *Saeima's* pressroom, the police security guard said: "You can't go in there."

Santa Ezeriņa held up a laminated card. "I have a press pass."

The guard glanced at the administrator across the doorway, a middle-aged woman with a clipboard in her hand. She shook her head.

"I'm sorry. Yours is on the 'No Admittance' list."

"This must be a mistake," Santa glanced between guard and administrator. "I've been to a hundred government press conferences over my career. This is routine . . ."

"A new admittance list was printed fresh this morning," said the administrator. "All *Baltic Beacon* press passes have been revoked."

"Why?"

"That information is unavailable."

Santa frowned. "You don't understand, I know M.P. Osis personally . . ."

"My dear girl, the directive came from the Osis office. Now please step aside, so journalists with proper credentials may enter."

Santa feigned retreat, then took two steps inside through the door. To call over someone reasonable to assist her. A journalistic colleague, a member of parliament opposed to Osis . . .

The guard caught Santa by the shoulder, pulled her back.

"You're out," said the administrator. "Don't make us arrest you. The Osis office has given strict special instructions for that contingency as well . . ."

"In conclusion," said Dāvids Osis to the assembled journalists in the *Saeima's* pressroom. "We are grateful for the work of the International Development Bank in this investigation." He glanced at Louis Stembridge, the energetic president of the IDB, a perfectly tailored, fair-haired fiftyish man standing at an arm's-length nearby.

"The Latvian government thanks you, Mr. Stembridge, the Latvian people thank you, and I personally thank you for your organization's exceptional efforts. It is a relief to the millions of depositors and clients worldwide that the allegations against Turaida Bank are proven to be false."

Mr. Stembridge gave a subtle nod, placed a hand on his heart as if greatly honored.

Osis turned his attention back to the crowd.

"As a gesture of assurance that their findings are accurate, International Development Bank has agreed to purchase twenty percent of Turaida Group stock at book value. A purchase Mr. Stembridge and his organization would never undertake if Turaida finances were not rock solid and pristinely in order. The world must know, Latvia's largest bank is in safe hands." He smiled. "I'll take a few questions now."

Pēteris Baltkalns raised a hand, stood to ask: "Can you tell us anything on the whereabouts of Roberts Vanags, the individual whose apparently-false allegations initiated this investigation?"

"We anticipated questions on Mr. Vanags. To elaborate on his pursuit, I'll hand the podium to Senior-Inspector Klikucs of the Rīga Homicide Department."

Osis stepped aside, and a small, hard-looking officer in his mid-forties took the podium. He stared at the crowd in an adversarial way as he bent the microphone to his height, a gold-and-diamond Swiss watch on his wrist. Finally, he said:

"Roberts Vanags remains at large. We've more than a few theories as to his location, but it would be irresponsible and counter-productive to comment on those now." His dark, probing eyes searched the room. "Let me remind any in the press who still give credence to the words of Mr. Vanags, that he is the prime suspect in the murders of his Turaida Bank co-worker Evgeny Markov, and his own relative, the American national, Elviss Gulbis. This is a desperate man, a fugitive who is likely armed and dangerous. There is evidence he may have kidnapped a young woman before or during his escape, presumably as a hostage. Citizens should use extreme caution if they encounter Vanags, alert the police as soon as possible but defend themselves first with necessary force."

He took a long, steady breath. "Which camera am I on?"

An aid pointed him to the correct one and the inspector looked straight into the lens: "I want to make one thing clear, to the people of our country and to the world watching. No matter where Vanags runs, no matter where he hides on this globe, he will be found and apprehended for these killings. Interpol, the American FBI, are all assisting the investigation. It is only a matter of time until Roberts Vanags is standing before you in handcuffs, awaiting Latvian justice for his crimes. This I promise you on the very souls of my children."

PART III

36

Hekla Stefánsdóttir believed in truth and transparency.

The forty-five-year-old director and editor-in-chief of One World Press was a controversial figure around the globe. Loved by many, reviled by others, especially in the former Soviet Union where her organization was well-known for exposing corruption. Even Hekla's most vehement enemies credited OWP's leaked "Tbilisi files" for aiding the miraculous turnaround in government accountability in the Republic of Georgia. It was when OWP turned its eyes Westward, exposing secret cables from MI6, MI5, and the American military establishment that Hekla was labeled a pariah, a thief, a bitch.

But in this moment, Hekla was none of those things. Nor was she a revealer of uncomfortable truths worldwide. Now, safe in her Oslo home, she was only a mother. And her eleven-year-old son Kristófer had played that violent computer game Grimdark Legions far too long.

"Enough, Kristófer. Turn it off."

"Three more minutes, mama."

"Now."

Hekla was not one to be opposed and her son well knew it. Though Kristófer had been born in Norway, and had never seen his mother's native Iceland, Hekla still spoke Icelandic to him in their house. There was a strong essence of nationalism to Hekla Stefánsdóttir, despite the wall-crumbling, borderless views of the organization she ran.

"Do your homework, now, Kristófer. Mama has a call to make."

The boy scampered away to obey. She had raised him well.

Hekla crossed the apartment's family space to her little office tucked away at the bottom of a small set of stairs. With her peripheral vision, she caught her reflection on a mirror near the office door. She was heavier than she wished to be, middle age beginning to find its footholds, though her prominent Nordic cheekbones at least gave her a strong frame to hang all this growing weight upon. Her hair had been prematurely gray since postgraduate days—an M. S.

at Brown University, a PhD at M.I.T. Her fellow students had called Hekla "The Professor" then, less from those gray hairs than from the way she carried herself. And somehow had all the answers.

Fifteen years later she wished she had all the answers now.

Hekla waited until she heard Kristófer's door shut upstairs, then sat in the leather chair at her office desk, waited for the Facetime meeting to begin on the screen on the wall. She glanced out the window at the snow-covered streets of Oslo's Frogner district. Deeply in love with a Norwegian man, she'd lived here too long. Kristófer and little Isabella didn't know what it meant to be an Icelander. The differences subtle to outsiders but very real to her.

The screen popped up, a thin bald man sitting in his Boston study. Her favorite lawyer, Charles Sutherland, from a prominent American civil liberties group. A good man, a blunt man, who always worked for OWP pro bono.

Hekla appreciated those qualities.

"Good evening, Hekla," said Charles in a Bostonian old money accent. "What time is it there? Eight-thirty?"

"Half six" she said smoothly. Charles never knew the Oslo time. Had mistaken it for years. It was almost a joke between them.

"I'm not interrupting dinner, am I, Hekla?"

"No." They talked regularly enough that chit-chat was unwarranted. She felt the responsibility to move the conversation along, so he could get back to paying clients. "What have you got for me, Charles? What should we do about the invitation from the Icelandic parliament?"

"Take it. Speaking before the *Althingi* could make One World Press bigger than Wikileaks, Publeaks, any of them."

"I'm not concerned about size. What I want is to show we are responsible, that OWP vets and confirms its information as well as any journalistic institution. And that I can prove it before the elected officials of my homeland."

"Then do it, Hekla. No one from OWP or a like organization has ever addressed a national assembly. Not Julian Assange, not Bradley Birkenfeld not Alexander Klöpping. It's a chance to legitimize what we do. As the next evolution in accountability. You'll talk about how everyone in the room is now held responsible by a global community. The government, the whistleblowers, and OWP itself as the conduit between source material and public judgement."

Of course, for some, 'legitimization' is a betrayal in itself. "If I go, what about the moratorium, Charles? OWP accepts nothing, publishes nothing until after the hearing?"

"It's the price their conservative *Althingi* members want, the price OWP pays for being on the world stage."

"I don't know . . ."

"You'll make the right call. You always do boss lady."

"I wish I had your confidence in me, Charles. I'll tell the *Althingi* we're coming, but still considering the moratorium. And get back to you . . ."

"Okay. Don't sweat it. As another bald man once said, 'Who loves you, baby?'"

She smiled. "Good night, Charles."

"Day here." He laughed. "Night."

She clicked off, reclined in her chair, rubbing her brow. Somewhere in the house she could hear Kristófer was playing that damn computer game again. She'd stop him in a moment. But first she just wanted to sit in this chair and think of the days to come.

37

Ruslan Kozlov's gray eyes watched the journalist, Santa Ezeriņa, walk up *Ģertrūdes iela* in Rīga. Under the shadows of late evening, he followed a block behind, as she made her way away over the lighted intersection with *Čaka iela* to darker roads beyond. By the time they reached the abandoned factory that dominated the right side of the street, the only remaining illumination was emanating from the ground floor windows of an internet club. With the boom of home internet and Wi-Fi in every café, this club was a relic from another age, now filled all hours with youths partaking in online gaming, fans of scandalous pornography they dare not stream at home, and gamblers betting on offshore accounts.

Ezeriņa entered through a door covered with papers announcing tournaments and sales on used computer parts. The club was too small for Ruslan to infiltrate unobserved, so he pulled his coat tighter and sat on the icy steps of the factory across the street. Through the wide-pane window, he saw Ezeriņa take a place in front of a bulky, old-looking computer monitor. From his angle he could not see her screen. This was little problem. He'd wait. There were ways to see what she did in there. He checked his watch. 22:56

Ruslan lit a cigarette, watched his breath rise in the winter air. He was tasked with killing Santa Ezeriņa. Something he'd enjoy after all her slander against Turaida Bank and his oligarch bosses. But he was forbidden to act until she led them to Roberts Vanags.

A pity. He was getting impatient. It'd been months since he killed a woman, Mindy Ash the last. Ruslan's own wife, also involved in the Vanags matter, would likely liquidate her target before he did.

He didn't want to lose their personal wager. Galina was insufferable when she won.

Ruslan checked his watch again.

And waited.

Sitting in an uncomfortable chair, with the springs and stuffing bursting out at every seam, Santa Ezeriņa searched through the desktop shortcuts on her screen, all adorned with fantastical logos and salacious names promising adventure and virtual-reality excitement. At last, she came upon the shortcut for "Grimdark Legions" the associated graphic depicting some sort of armored troll holding a blood-dripping mace, the logo's font aggressively large and typically gothic.

She clicked on it and opened the login screen, the background a *Tolkien-esque* map of a fantasy world. Santa never played an MMORPG—Massively Multiplayer Online Role-Playing Game—or, in fact, any type of computer games. But in the last two weeks she'd received very odd spam via an old social media account she'd seldom used since university in America, insisting she logon to Grimdark Legions "for an enlightening gaming experience that must be shared with players the world over." The use of "enlightening" and "must be shared with the world" coupled with the fact that she was not remotely the target market had caught her notice. Then the same spam repeated the next three days, now written in German with the appendix *"Hören Sie den Falken"* which translated to "Listen to the hawk."

The name "Vanags" meant "hawk" in Latvian.

She was sure her emails were being watched. But what spies monitored German gaming messages in her spam folder?

Clever.

She entered the code the spam message had given her.

Up popped a player screen window with the image of a premade character, some type of ridiculous bipedal golden dragon in wizard's robe which the name field revealed to be called "Cal Soothian."

What was she supposed to do with this *thing?*

She switched from the character window to the main gaming screen. A digital landscape of starling realism stretched out before her. It depicted a forested hillside crested with a bare sandy ridgetop; the summit honeycombed with octagonal openings.

Standing near her was a human figure in black chainmail armor. A message window popped up:

TALK REQUEST FROM TOTHELLO THE SLAUGHTERER.
ACCEPT? DECLINE?

She clicked "Accept" but nothing happened. Santa sat there several moments waiting, listening to the din of the busy club before she noticed the

low squawk of a voice coming from the headphones hung over the back of
the monitor.

She put them on.

A young male voice said in English: "Follow me."

"Who are you?"

"Don't talk, please." The armored character began to walk up the hillside.

It took a few moments for Santa to master the controls, to steer her dragon
character in the correct direction to follow. Soon, however, they were marching
up the virtual mountainside towards that sandy peak and the octagonal caves.
As they did so, they passed other fantastic characters—dwarves, elves, giants,
bizarre beings she could not name. There were players from throughout the
world on this sever, all mingling in a virtual fantasy land. Other talk requests
came in, but she ignored them. She noted as she passed pairs or groups of
characters locked in conversations the option to "Listen in" to their discussions appeared in a text box. She ignored the option and continued following
the armored warrior. Near the top they were ambushed by a kind of glowing
spider-like creature. Santa was ignorant of how combat worked in Grimdark
Legions, but her companion slew the monster in a short order, the spider flip-
ping over legs in the air before fading away.

The armored figure descended deep into the nearest octagonal cavern,
Santa's dragon following, until they were far into the depths of its darkness. A
blueish light appeared around them, either a spell cast by her companion, or
some illumination triggered by their arrival at the end of the passage. Ornate
columns propped up a domed ceiling above. Several oriental-looking mats
rested on the floor. The armored figure sat.

"Press 'Alt F6' to sit" said the voice from the headphones.

She did so. Her dragon-wizard settled on a mat in the foreground.

"These monk cells allow for unobserved conversation," said the young
voice. "The 'Listen in' option is disabled here."

"Who are you?" asked Santa.

"David Vanags."

The son of Roberts. Well, well, her instincts were right.

"I can't imagine you're going to tell me where you are?"

"I . . . I can't do that . . . yet . . . My dad wanted just to make contact for
now. There'll be more to come."

"Can your father hear us?"

"No."

"Is everyone safe?"

"Yes."

"Is that missing girl with you?"

"Yes . . . I mean, in general, yes. She's not in the room. Not now."

That girl had become a point of interest to Santa. The police and Turaida-controlled newspapers called her a kidnap victim, an innocent taken by the desperate and despicable Americans against her will, yet Santa could not find any record of an actual Beatrise Liepa that matched the appropriate age range. Even the documents given to that prestigious school in Rīga were clearly forgeries and full of lies. She had wondered if the girl were a complete work of fiction. A phantom kidnapping. Another crime to heap onto the allegations against Roberts and his son. But the boy's words proved some girl existed. One possibly living under an alias. And if an alias, who gave it to her? Santa could guess.

But now was not the time to probe the Vanags family. Not at first contact and not to the son.

"Okay. When will you tell me more?"

"Tomorrow. I'll be on sometime between nine and ten at night EEST. Meet near these caves."

"Will your father be here?"

"Probably just me. For now."

Every utterance told her something. Clearly David had to go somewhere outside their hiding place to login to this game, to make the contact. A place where he could sit and wait countless hours for Santa to discover the spam invitation, to at last logon. And the boy was less likely to be recognized than his father. Made sense.

"We'll use the same characters, David?"

"Same characters. I should go. They'll close . . . well, I gotta run."

The kid sounded nervous.

"Stay safe."

"Bye."

She discarded the headphones, logged off. Sat there thinking. After nearly a month she was in contact with Roberts Vanags, even if the most indirect of ways. That was a relief. And a responsibility. Wherever he was on this Earth, he'd be hunted as long as the murder and kidnapping allegations hung over him. The first step to combating Turaida was to legitimize Roberts by clearing him of those crimes. No easy task with the police in the bank's pocket.

Still, there were other organizations that might be open to the possibility of Roberts's innocence . . .

Her fingers tapped over the keyboard. She was no gamer, but as a news rag reporter, Santa had snooped around numerous computers in her day, been breaking the rules since long before she'd hacked Roberts's cousin Elviss Gulbis at age nineteen.

She brought up an old DOS command prompt window, typed in:

"RunDll32.exe InetCpl.cpl,ClearMyTracksByProcess 255"

That'll do.

Until tomorrow, Roberts . . .

When Santa Ezeriņa left the internet club, Ruslan waited until she was two blocks away before he crossed the street and went inside. The computer she used was now occupied, but it was little matter to chase off the teen who had taken the seat. Five euros got him moving, one glare kept him away.

The screen was full of shortcuts to games, sex chats, and assorted Dark Web torrents. He went to the browser history, to find where she'd been on the internet. It had been cleared. Curious.

He soon found all browser histories were cleared. As had the Recent Files, Device History, Search History, and Application History. All emptied. Even at the system level, nothing was to be found.

Santa Ezeriņa had wiped her computer use trail clean.

38

With his cap low and his face down to avoid the security cameras, David Vanags paid for his internet time at a kiosk very far from Rīga. He could barely contain his excitement at having finally reached Santa Ezeriņa, a tremor in his hand as he handed over the money. Fortunately, the Estonian teenager who ran the place barely glanced in David's direction. The boy's eyes remained on his own screen as he gripped the euro coins and cast them into a jar with countless others. Clearly, pesky financial transactions were an unwelcome interruption to his gaming. David had no complaints. The less he spoke, the less he stood out on this Estonian isle. He buttoned his heavy coat, slipped on his gloves, and hurried out the door into the freezing Baltic winter.

Outside, the late evening weather had cleared, the earlier snow flurries giving way to a crystal night with ten thousand stars overhead. The little village itself about him lay quiet and still, a sparse collection of dark wooden houses mostly brown in color, a few painted green or red. The place was nearly a ghost town in winter, a small indistinct community hidden on one of the more than two thousand islands off the Estonian coast.

A perfect spot to lose yourself. Especially during winter.

David stepped into a small grocery, bought bread, milk, and cigarettes for Dad. His father, so prideful, had fought him fiercely to be the one to come into town for supplies. David understood the emotions running through his father, the parental instinct, a need to protect his son, to assume the risk himself. But David was the only one who understood the mass emailing software, the only one who could have effectively and anonymously spammed Santa Ezeriņa until they got her attention. And David's face, plain and common, was less distinctive than his handsome father's. It made sense for David to go. An argument he'd won weeks ago, though it renewed every sortie into town. The waiting was clearly driving Dad mad.

David paid for the goods in cash, careful again to say not a word to the clerk, to divulge nothing that might indicate him a foreigner, much less an

American fugitive. Still, he sensed their suspicions. They knew him an outsider. In a town this tiny, on an island this small, during the wrong season . . . Yes, strangers by default were news.

He boarded a battered-looking ferry that made the rounds to several nearby islands, keenly aware of those who came aboard with him. Fortunately, at this hour there were few other travelers to call his attention; only an old man he suspected to be a fisherman and a middle-aged working-class couple who lived on some splinter island and always exited two dockings before his own. He let these three take their seats in the sparse, cold cabin. Then David sat in the back row, eyes on the sea, watching his breath fog the window.

The others disembarked at different docks. By the time the ferry reached his stop, David was alone. He exited the ship and walked gingerly over the icy pier to a wooded beach. Instead of following the paths inland or up the banks to any of the modest houses overlooking the water, he continued along the snowy seashore to where he'd chained his kayak to a stout fir tree hours ago. He cleared it of the new-fallen snow, unlocked the chain, and withdrew the paddle from the kayak's interior. Placing the groceries in the hold, he slid inside, cast off, gliding through the night waters of the Baltic Sea.

He watched his breath rise in the clear, cold evening air. As nervous as David felt on the islands, once out on the water, he passed into a state of welcome serenity. It was as if nothing could touch him here on the sea. The warmth of his thick downy jacket and hood contrasted with the chill on his face and the great cold rising off the water. All senses were wonderfully alive. Since their escape from Latvia, the open water was truly his only peace.

David passed tiny islands, some undeveloped, many with two or three small houses, and occasionally, the private isles of the wealthy. He felt safest near those lonely island mansions, even though he knew many were owned by the sort of oligarchs who now pursued his father. Yet, experience had taught him well. The bigger the house the less likely it was occupied, the rich seeking warmer climates in winter, leaving their island homes vacant for the season.

And vulnerable to invasion.

So many islands out here, some only a few hundred yards long. Along the starry horizon, David tried to pinpoint the place where'd they'd shut down all electronics aboard the *Leesma*, uncapped her floats, reversed the bilge pumps, and sent Turaida Bank's pride to the bottom of the sea. David, Beatrise, and his father had escaped that night on a rowboat they'd stolen from a pier on some nameless nearby island. Petty crimes like this were becoming too common in their exile, a challenge to keep the moral compass pointing due north.

His arms aching, the seeping cold cutting through his jacket, David pulled up his paddle, let the kayak glide forward as he recovered his strength. Fortunately, "home" was within sight, the black silhouette of a small, densely forested island rising up against the starry sky. They'd been squatters on this isle for nearly a month, a better, more comfortable hideout he could not have imagined. The perfect sanctuary as long as the owners remained absent. Judging by the printouts found in the study's wastepaper basket, they were spending the winter in Thailand, though there was no exact indication of when the family might return.

David set the oar in the water again, paddled around the isle's circumference to the entrance of a small cove, the trees along the waterline eclipsing view into the island's interior from most angles. A few paddles into this little bay, however, revealed an extensive two-story house of modern design. The expansive windows sat dark and frosted, except for two on the ground-floor which flickered with the jumping light of the great hearth inside. A feminine figure stood at the window nearest the door, a loved one who waited for him on every return.

Beatrise waved to him enthusiastically. He returned her greeting, rowed past the empty pier, and landed his kayak on the snowy lawn that crept down to the cove's edge. He dragged the craft behind a winter-dead hedge, so it, like the rowboat nearby, might be hidden from view by any who entered the harbor. By the time he'd pulled the groceries from the hold, Beatrise was down the stone path from the house, a cup of steaming coffee in her hands.

"Bea," he said without pause for kiss or java. "Where's Dad?"

"Downstairs."

"I found her, the journalist. Online."

Beatrise's eyes widened in surprise, a smile creeping across her face. "The journalist? Santa . . ."

"Santa Ezeriņa, I made contact. At last."

"What did she say?"

"She needs to speak to Dad. Directly. Very soon."

Leonid Vovk finished his glass of cognac while considering what Ruslan Kozlov's transmitted voice said, then leaned forward on the leopard-print couch in his Ukrainian home, and spoke clearly into the speakerphone's receiver, his tone exasperated.

"Ruslan, we pay you for information, not speculation. Has Santa Ezeriņa contacted Roberts Vanags? Yes, or no?"

The hard Russian would not be pushed into a definite answer. Even by Vovk. "Impossible to say. Attending an internet café in this WIFI age is unusual. Ezeriņa has no history of gambling. Why is she there? For computer games she could play from home? No . . ."

The voice of the third party on the call, Turaida's security man, Kārlis Pagrabs, broke in: "It could be a journalistic story she's working on. Pornography? Identity theft? Dark Web activities? The sort of things that people need seedy anonymous net access?"

Vovk laughed. "What has she worked on lately except slandering us? Arrest her, Kārlis. Have your people in the police see what's in her phone, her laptop."

"I'm sure she anticipated that. They'll be clean."

Vovk shrugged. "Couldn't hurt. What about the mole? Her silence is disturbing."

"Roberts is quite perceptive," continued Kārlis indelicately. "Maybe they found her out. She could be at the bottom of the sea next to Richard and Mindy Ash."

"No," interrupted Ruslan, pride and anger in his voice. "I've trained Galina well. She'll be in touch as soon as she's able. She'll give us the exact location of Vanags. Or his gravesite."

"I second, Ruslan," said Vovk with authority, and more than a little censure for Kārlis. "His wife is the best there is. Better even than her husband. Galina Kozlova won't let us down."

Under waning candlelight, Bob Vanags put pen to the page and wrote:

I leave this message for posterity. If I should be found dead, and God forbid, my son David is unable to relay events to the public, then I wish the world to know the truth. I returned to Europe to experience my roots, to live in the land of my parents, to drink the waters of the wellspring from which my ancestors sprang. Instead, I discovered the water tainted, poisoned. Corruption all around.

Here I failed. I realize that now. I proceeded against the evil I found; a modern Don Quixote ignorant of my actions, choosing to jeopardize what I thought was only employment to reveal the truth.

Little did I know how much I was risking. When I attempted to reveal the sins of Turaida Bank and criminal factions within the Latvian government led by MP Dāvids Osis, I thought the Latvian people would destroy this malignant institution within their nation and prosecute the guilty. Didn't Dr. King say the truth would set you free? But King was murdered for his words. Now, the shock has worn off and reality hardened me. I proceed forward only in the interests of my family. They have already suffered losses.

The world cannot be allowed to go to Hell, much as I'd like to tell it to, if only to make certain that David, and the other child dragged into this conflict, Beatrise Liepa, are able to continue their lives. Perhaps together.

So, let me enumerate the sins of the guilty.

1. *Turaida Bank, Riga Branch*

   a. *The murder and coverup of British citizens Richard and Mindy Ash.*

   b. *The murder of Latvian citizen Ēriks Hel—*

Footsteps on the stairs broke his concentration. Bob looked up to see David sprinting into the bedroom, Beatrise a few steps behind. The expression on his face told Bob it was good news.

"Dad," David shouted. "We've reached Santa Ezeriņa."

"Well done. Did anyone see you?"

"I don't . . . don't think so. I told her I'd be in touch again tomorrow."

"I'm not sure it's safe to go out too frequently. The islanders are bound to notice."

"No one has time to care about some Americans staying offseason." The boy sounded disappointed. "Isn't this what we've been waiting for?"

"Yes. Yes, it is, David." Bob softened his voice. "Many thanks, son."

"Listen," said Beatrise her nude warm body pressed against David's side beneath the covers of the bed they had claimed as their own. She adjusted her one remaining hearing aid. "He's at it again."

David sat up to one elbow, the comforter and quilt falling from his shoulders. Despite the working furnace they'd managed to resurrect, the cold on this island was nearly unbearable, even deep inside the house. If it weren't for recent romantic developments between them, David would be sleeping fully clothed.

"I don't hear anything, Bea."

They waited several moments. Then the familiar chopping sound rose up from below. "There," she said. "He's at the woodpile again with the ax. Splitting those logs into smaller and smaller sections. Pointless. Madness. At this hour?"

"Not madness. Just angry. It's cathartic." David collapsed back on the mattress, pulled the sheets over their shoulders. "There's been a lot pent up in Dad since Mom died."

"'Pent up?'"

"I don't think Dad came to Europe for his roots. That was a lie. He came to forget, to start again. Now, he's lost everything. It's a way to strike out at the world, I guess. Release tension, the helplessness . . . Just like that letter he's writing . . ."

Her answer was little more than a whisper. "I've lost everything too."

"Bea . . . we can't contact family. Turaida would use them . . . Dad forbade it."

He felt her slide away on the mattress. "Dāvids, it's been weeks. Mother doesn't know if I'm alive or dead. Think if your father had no clue if you still lived? How would he feel? Could he breathe? Eat? Sleep?"

"No."

Her eyes were so beautiful, so pained . . .

"What if *you* thought I lay at the bottom of the ocean somewhere, Dāvids? Could you just go about your life?"

"I . . . I wouldn't think of anything else. I wouldn't want to live . . ."

"Yes. Please. I need to reach Mother. Somehow." She moved closer again, kissed him. "Help me, darling. Let me make the call."

39

"What evidence, exactly, do you have that Robert Vanags is innocent, Ms. Ezeriņa?" asked the FBI legal attaché, Jonathan Simms, across his desk inside the United States embassy in Rīga. "And, more importantly, what evidence do you have that he is being framed by the Latvian authorities?"

Santa disliked the way Simms mispronounced her name as *Ezy-era-eena*. You would think an American official stationed this long in a foreign country would have a better understanding of local pronunciation. Still, he was the only person in the embassy who would meet with her about Vanags. She had to make the most of it . . .

"The fingerprints found on the weapons that killed Elviss Gulbis and Evgeny Markov both clearly match those Roberts gave to the Latvian authorities when he applied for his residency permit."

Simms looked bored. She was surprised he even bothered to ask: "And?"

"The problem isn't that they match Roberts's records. It's that the prints on the two guns match each other too well. In fact, exactly. Flaws and all."

"What do you mean?"

She withdrew her laptop from its bag, opened it on the desk between them, clicked on a desktop image. A photographic negative appeared, the image an extreme closeup of a gun handle, the white radial pattern of four clear fingerprints visible on the surface.

Santa continued. "These are the fingerprints found on the gun that killed Elviss Gulbis. A gun which was conveniently left at the scene. Ignoring how suspiciously clear the prints are, please note the positions of the little flaws in the prints. Here and here . . ." Santa targeted the little circular blemishes within the prints with her mouse pointer, "and there too, at the thumb print's inner radius . . ."

Simms frowned. "Normal enough. Those spots are where the prints failed to take due to dust or moisture on the hand or gun."

"Usually, yes." She clicked on a second image. Another gun-handle negative appeared, this one too decorated with fingerprints. "Now look here, Mr. Simms. These are the prints from the gun that killed Evgeny Markov. A gun, by the way, that was not discovered on the initial search of the victim's Saulkrasti beach hut but only found days later during a solitary investigation by Senior-Inspector Klikucs."

"Are you suggesting it was planted, Ms. Ezeriņa?" He didn't like her implication.

Too bad.

"I suspect it was indeed planted, Mr. Simms. Look how clear the prints are despite four days exposure to the environment. That is unlikely. Any forensic expert outside Latvia would tell you that. But here is the most damning evidence . . ." She highlighted the prints' blemishes with the pointer. "Look at the positions of those flaws in the prints, again, supposedly made by dust or moisture. They are at the exact same locations within these prints as those in the earlier marks left at the killing of Elviss Gulbis. Finger by finger. Not only do the prints match but so do the blemishes."

Simms turned the laptop towards him, at last seeming to consider what Santa said. "Yes. Rather startling. Go on . . ."

"Do you believe the same specs of dust or drops of moisture were by chance on Roberts Vanags's fingertips during both killings? Sitting on identical positions on his skin? With the same dimensions and volume? On every fingertip? I've done the mathematics. Mr. Simms, the odds of that happening are in the millions."

"What are you suggesting, Ms. Ezerina?"

"That these fingerprints were made with a silicon cast of Roberts's fingertips, and these spots are not the products of dirt, sweat or water, but flaws in the duplicate. Air bubbles. A common problem in silicon casting, especially when done by amateurs. I believe an individual or individuals wearing gloves affixed with a cast of Roberts's fingerprints committed both murders. Professional but lazy assassins, too casual about framing people knowing no one will dare look hard at the details in this country. And that very casualness tells me whom they are working for."

She'd gone too far. Simms shook his head. "You make a credible case for a frame up. What you should do is take this evidence to the Latvian police. Not here."

"As I said, I believe the police are the framers. Or at least in alliance with them."

"What do you want me to do? When an American citizen is accused of a crime in a foreign land, neither the FBI nor the embassy can interfere unless there is undeniable evidence of a willful misjustice against that American by a foreign power."

"As I said, the odds of those fingerprints being genuine are in the millions."

He snorted. "When they are in the billions come back to me."

"They will be, if these fingerprints appear again with the same dust spots in the same places. The odds of that happening three times are greater than seven billion to one."

Simms said nothing.

"Give Roberts sanctuary in this embassy, Mr. Simms."

He raised an eyebrow. "Are you saying you know where Robert Vanags is, Ms. Ezeriṇa?"

Santa's answer was slow in coming. "No. But I know how to get ahold of him. Should a sanctuary offer be made."

"You are becoming a person of interest, Ms. Ezeriṇa."

"Good. If the FBI is following me, I'll be safer." She nodded towards the window. From their office they could see through the embassy gate. Outside, across the street stood three plain-clothes Rīga policemen. Santa knew them all by name. They'd shadowed her here, tried to prevent her entry. She slipped inside just in time.

She could tell by his expression, Simms recognized them too. Understood their intent.

"Maybe you're right. But it is you who may need a sanctuary, Ms. Ezeriṇa." His voice had a hint of sympathy, the pronunciation of her surname a little closer to correct.

She closed the laptop, shoved it forward. "At least take the images."

He shook his head. "I'm sorry. If I accepted those, the implication would be we are considering action. We are not."

Santa stood, seized her laptop and tossed it with all her strength against the wall. The case shattered, the innards crashing in pieces to the floor.

Simms stared at her from behind that desk, eyes wide with surprise. She wondered if he thought her mad, if he'd considered drawing his gun or calling the guards. But the FBI man did nothing but sit and stare.

"Don't worry. The images are all in the Cloud, Mr. Simms. Several in fact." She nodded again towards the police outside. "Those officers will search me when I leave. I don't want them to catch me with the fingerprint photos. Unlike the FBI, they *will* take action. Unpleasant action." She shouldered her purse, turned to leave.

"It was an old laptop anyway. Never worth a damn . . ."

Senior-Inspector Klikucs emerged from the crowd of policemen outside, halted Santa as she stepped into the street.

"Who did you meet in there, Santa?"

"That's a private matter between me and the U.S. government." She almost enjoyed the consternation in her old adversary. If it weren't for the threat of yet another full body search, she might have laughed.

"You had a laptop bag when you entered the embassy, Santa? Where is it?"

"I left it with the Americans." This was not technically a lie.

Klikucs frowned. "What was on that computer? What did you give them?"

"Ask Dāvids Osis, Inspector. He knows all about missing laptops. The Americans found it all remarkably interesting. I'm sure your bosses, official and otherwise, will be hearing from them soon."

She smiled and stepped past him.

Let the bad guys worry for once . . .

40

Bob Vanags continued his writing:

11. Agnese Avena of International Development Bank, Frankfurt
   a. Financial fraud
   b. Gross lack of diligence in. . . .

He heard footsteps. Bob glanced up to see his son coming down the stairs attired in a heavy winter jacket and Wellington boots.

"Dad, if we're gonna go, now's the time. Santa will be waiting."

"How's the weather?"

David smiled cynically. "Worse. But we can't let that stop us . . ."

Bob folded up the paper, slid it between the pages of a Russian-language copy of Peter Drucker's *End of Economic Man* and set it on a shelf.

"Let's do this." Bob went to the door, donned his own thick jacket and the heaviest boots he'd found among the owners' things. The rubber boots were a size too small, and he grunted and winced as he forced his feet into them.

He'd just somehow gotten the second boot on, was trying to will himself to block out the pain, when Beatrise, also dressed for inclement weather, appeared before him.

"Please, let me go, Mr. Vanags."

"Beatrise, we've discussed this before . . . The authorities are looking for three people matching our descriptions. Two out and about is dangerous enough, but David needs to show me where to go, tell me what's what. I've never played that damn game before. A third person in the rowboat, on the ferry, at the café . . . especially a girl your age . . . It's unneeded risk."

"It's a risk I need, Roberts . . . My mother needs to know I'm okay. You must understand."

"I do understand. And we'll talk to the journalist about it. But you're memorable, Beatrise. You've that identifying tattoo at the eye. . . . A hearing aid over one ear . . . No . . . You're fairly unique . . . It's too much for you to be seen with us . . ."

She tried to step around him, break for the door. "I'll get in the boat myself, who can stop me."

He caught her arm. "Beatrise, listen . . . please . . ."

Beatrise's face reddened, "To Hell with you, Roberts Vanags. What am I? Your prisoner?"

"That's not how we look at it, Beatrise." She tried to pull away, but his grip tightened on her arm.

"Dad!" said David, stepping closer to them, clearly unsure what to do. "Don't hurt her."

"I'm not hurting anyone, David."

"I don't wish to do this, Beartise," continued Bob sternly. "I promise you, I never imagined I would have to. But I'll lock you in the basement if there's any more outbursts. We can't be exposed. There are more than our own lives at risk in this. Much more."

"But my mother . . . ."

David pressed hard against his father's shoulder, forced his parent's hand from Beatrise's arm. "Dad . . . don't you damn threaten her again."

Bob was unmoved by his son's efforts.

"You'll do what, I say. Both of you." He reached out and plucked the remaining hearing aid from Beatrise's ear, shoved it into his pocket.

"I'm sorry to have to do this, Bea. I am."

She stood quiet. Bob turned his gaze onto his son.

"Now, David, go put that rowboat in the water."

41

As the winds of a gathering Baltic storm rocked their rowboat, David Vanags said to his father:

"It's too rough, Dad. Maybe we should turn back."

"Let's go a little longer. It'll clear."

Silence.

That's all he would say? All he had said since they'd left their exiled home.

"What's happening to you, Dad?"

"I'm trying to keep us alive, David. This is not a time for weakness."

The waves broke over the bow, washed across David's boots. Even through all their insulation, he was freezing.

"I don't like how you spoke to Bea, Dad. She didn't ask to be here."

"Actually, she did."

"Because of us. Cause she didn't want to endanger her family."

"And we did?"

"No."

More silence under the storm. The boat felt exceedingly small. David balanced outrage and unwelcome guilt, but something had to be said. Much more remained unsaid.

They continued navigating the choppy waters. When Robert tired and David took his turn at the oars, he seized the opportunity to make amends, offer the olive branch.

"I'm sorry, Dad. Really, I am."

The answer was late, very late in coming. They had almost passed the nearest neighboring island before Robert half-whispered: "I'm sorry, too."

David barely heard the words over the winds. Perhaps he imagined them.

"She's a wonderful girl, Dad. I think I love her."

"I know, David. And when this is all over, I'll apologize to Bea. A hundred times. For now, the best we can do for her is to survive . . ."

* * *

Through an upstairs window, Galina Kozlova watched the Vanags's row-boat disappear into the sea mist. She weighed her options. If the men succeeded, overcame the itinerant weather, reached the island with the internet café, and made contact with the journalist, the roundtrip would be no less than three hours. It was the shortest time David was ever gone.

Yet, the coming storm may turn them back, Robert's determination aside.

What to do? She'd spent too long in this frigid mansion with these Americans, fucking a clumsy and inexperienced boy while enduring the suspicious glances and mistrust of his father. She wanted to be home with her husband, not on this tiny Estonian isle pretending to be a foolish Latvian girl named Beatrise Liepa, a spineless follower without initiative, five years younger than her real age.

But their family was being paid a lifetime's salary for this by Vovk, and potentially several times that by the Scorpion and his allies in Moscow. Despite these sums, Galina felt herself no mercenary. What she did was right. The Latvians treated the ethnic Russians in their country as dogs, insisting they learn their useless language and pass history exams that blamed their troubles on the Soviet Union, actions any patriotic pan-national-Russian would refuse. As she had refused as a girl in Daugavpils. Many ethnic Russians in Latvia were not allowed to vote, left at the mercy of ethnic Latvian politicians. A vicious game that kept her people powerless.

Soon that would change. Osis's change-of-heart was a harbinger of better days to come. So, what, if they bribed the MP to gain his allegiance? The ends justified the means. In a year's time, Latvian children once again would learn Russian, while their parents turned their eyes to Moscow for guidance. As would those of Russian blood in Ukraine, Moldova, Lithuania, these Estonian isles, and the mainland. Whether restoring the old ways was a step back to the Soviet Union or to its predecessor the Russian Empire, was a matter of preferred ideology and historical perspective. What was important to Galina was that they would be restored regardless. Families who had been marooned outside of Russia when the Soviet Union collapsed, would throw off the yoke of the American-backed oppression forever and be reunited with our own kind.

Ruslan knew that. It's why he told her to sleep with the boy, with both Americans, if necessary.

She'd lost her earpiece transmitter before further orders. But Galina knew their murder was an option as well. It'd be better, politically, if Robert were captured alive. David was expendable. The murders, the thefts, her own kidnapping pinned on them.

So, here she was. Alone on an isle with only her own wits to sustain her and aid her people. She must find some way of bringing the authorities here.

Though she had investigated the house many times before, this new solitude allowed her to move more freely than ever before. She rummaged through the bedrooms, the storage closets for some communication device. There was no landline to be found. The owners, like many these days, were cellphone only, and took their mobiles with them on their seasonal exodus to warmer climes. The internet too was turned off in their absence. As far as Galina could discover, she was cut off from the outside world.

From that high manor window her eyes came upon the kayak laying on the snowy banks, the white wind-driven waves rushing up against its bow.

How far was the nearest isle? They'd come here from the sinking *Leesma* in the depths of night weeks ago. She wasn't sure of the distance, even the direction really. And this weather . . . .

She took in a slow breath, calmed her nerves.

Would she get a better chance?

In fifteen minutes, in the warmest clothes she could scavenge from the back closets of the house, Galina had cast off in the kayak, paddling out of the tree-lined cove into the open sea. She was not an experienced kayaker, the waves unforgiving as they washed over her bow, the cold unbearable as she paddled onwards.

The struggle seemed to go on forever, yet when she looked back towards the island, she was barely fifty meters from shore. When Galina turned around a wave hit hard against her torso, seawater in her eyes. Instinctively, she lifted one hand from the oars to clear her vision. Another wave hit; the oars lost.

Galina reached out in the trough between two waves, vision still impaired, searching for the oars. Her body extended as she groped for them, a rise in the sea toppled the kayak, she found herself upside down, head and body in the sea.

She was not long stunned in these quiet cold depths. Galina threw her weight to one side, hoping the inertia would roll the kayak upright once more. But it didn't budge. Pulse drumming in her ears, adrenaline in her limbs she wiggled her hips and legs out of the kayak, broke the surface with a gasp. The frigid air somehow burned her lungs.

Galina clung to the capsized kayak, trying to comprehend her situation, to calm herself well enough to reach a course of action.

The water was impossibly cold. She felt the muscles contracting, tightening in her limbs. She'd drown if she stayed in much longer, lose her ability to hang onto the kayak.

At that moment, a gust cleared away the sea mist about her, and she saw the small, dark shape of a ship on the horizon. For an instant, she thought of rescue. But they were too far away, she too low in the sea to be seen. Another false hope, as so many in her life.

If she were to survive, Galina must depend on herself. As always.

With a prayer to Saint Eudoxia of Moscow, she let go of the kayak, swam towards shore. Only a hundred meters, maybe less. Her limbs were fading, but an eddy formed by an invisible current running close to the shoreline, carried Galina around close to the outer bank of the cove. She kicked with the last of her strength, crawled up onto land.

She fought the impulse to rest, to curl up for body warmth. That would be a fatal mistake. Instead, she pushed herself along the treelined shore, to the inner cove's bank, then up the lawn to the house. Inside, she tore off her soaked clothes, and collapsed naked before the great fire in the hearth.

42

It was more than two hours in her drive eastwards, well past the twin towns of Jēkabpils and Krustpils, when Santa Ezeriņa lost that persistent car that had been following her. Her instincts told her that her pursuers, likely undercover police or agents of Turaida Bank, would continue onto Daugavpils, the largest city of eastern Latvia. After all, that's usually the only reason to go this far east. So, she turned north instead through the frozen lake lands of Latgale, taking snowy sideroads that her Toyota struggled to navigate. Even with chains on the tires, Santa often had to gun the engine, and more than once exited the car to scout the clearest path forward. But these winter snowstorms were to her advantage, and by the time Santa arrived in the town of Rēzekne via a half-forgotten back route, she was certain that nobody was on her trail.

It'd been nearly two years since Santa was last in Rēzekne, but the little internet café she'd remembered was still in business. Unlike the seedy gambling and gaming café she'd visited in Rīga, this relic of the last decade was homey, comfortable and small, populated with only two customers and one remaining free computer station. The elderly woman who ran it professed no technical knowledge though she assured Santa her able nephew was only a phone call away if there was a problem. Instead, she served cakes, tea or *kakao* for those conservative customers who disliked the mobile internet or WIFI boom, and still surfed the web in a social café like this. Santa found her computer didn't have Grimdark Legions, and she silently sipped a tart cappuccino as it downloaded. When installed and operating, Santa logged in again as Cal Soothian, found her golden dragon-wizard character waiting. She set off for those digital mountain caves and private conversations.

Though she was early, Santa found David Vanags's chain-mailed warrior standing in the same cavern, in the very spot where they'd last met. Santa accepted the talk request and put on her headphones.

A male voice was already speaking:

". . . hear me, Santa?"

It was not the son, David, but Roberts Vanags himself. For some reason hearing his voice startled her, though it should be no surprise. David had promised his father for this meeting. That's why she'd come out all the way to the countryside to make sure they were undisturbed. But now . . . well, Roberts . . . a man sought by the Latvian police and Russian mob was on the line. And she was the one talking with him. His undeserved infamy brought a note of real celebrity. She'd tell him that personally someday.

"Yes, I'm here, Roberts."

"Where is here?" he asked, a clear tension in his tone.

"I'm not sure we should reveal that. Just in case we're not secure . . ."

He paused, and this hesitance brought a fleeting doubt in Santa's mind. Could this be someone else? An imposter imitating Roberts Vanags's voice.

"Is David with you, Roberts?"

"He's in the chair next to me."

"Put him on please."

Another pause. Then a series of rustles. Santa imagined the headphones exchanging hands.

Finally, a younger, higher-pitched male voice said: "Hello?"

"David?"

"Yes. Santa is that you?"

"Yes, David. Talk for a few minutes. Say anything. I want to listen."

"Like what?"

"Anything. A poem from childhood. I need to hear your voice."

"Uh . . . well, what? . . . The itsy-bity spider went up the waterspout. Umbrella-ella-ella. Umbrella-ella-ella. Will that do?"

Santa laughed. It was David. This was the voice she'd spoken to last time on Grimdark Legions. And Roberts seemed to be the one she'd heard in the car weeks ago. Santa's time in the USA had served her well. She knew American voices cold. Any doppelgangers would have to match both men's speech patterns.

Unlikely.

"That's good, David. Please put Roberts back on."

The boy mumbled something she didn't quite catch but his voice was soon replaced by his father's.

"Satisfied?"

"Yes. My apologies. One has to be careful."

"Understood."

"I'm not going ask where you are. Only that you are safe?"

"We are . . . for now, it seems."

"Is that girl, Beatrise Liepa with you?"

"No . . . we don't . . . we weren't sure we should all be together; you know . . ."

"I know." She tried to sound reassuring.

Santa heard David whisper something to his father.

"Yeah . . . yeah, David . . . Look, my son wants to know if it's safe for Beatrise to contact her mother."

"What's her mother's name?"

"Gunta."

"Gunta Liepa?"

Another pause. "Yes."

"I'll get the word to her."

If there is a Gunta Liepa. She needed to do more checking before alarming Roberts and his son. Or endangering this poor Beatrise if her identity was genuine.

Still . . .

"I'd keep her hidden, Roberts. The police photos show quite an attractive girl. Memorable. Men tend to remember pretty young things. And . . . her need to contact her parent might bring unnecessary risk. So, do keep an eye on her."

"David is doing that. Twenty-four by seven."

"I see." The man at the next computer stood and brushed by her as he left. Despite being way at the back with voice in a whisper, Santa was reminded how small this café' was, English so extremely unusual out here in the Latgale countryside.

But they had to communicate. "Roberts, I've met with fingerprint experts. Impartial fingerprints experts. They've fairly conclusive evidence that the marks on the guns that killed Markov and your cousin are silicon duplicates. Not yours. I presented them to the FBI at the embassy, but they won't do anything."

"My tax dollars at work."

"I think showing your assertions about Turaida Bank and the Latvian government are true would provide motivation to reexamine the evidence that they are framing you. An impartial review by international parties."

"No easy task. Osis probably ground that hard drive to smithereens at the nearest junkyard."

"Whose hard drive was that exactly? Yours?"

"Yes."

"Personal or from the bank?"

"Personal."

"And no sort of backup? Automatic? The information you collected in a Cloud somewhere?"

His voice turned positively savage. "Don't you think I'd have thought of that? The files are gone!"

"Hey, hey! I know these are tense times for all of us . . ."

"Tense times? The police are trying to arrest me, the Russian mob wants me dead, the economies of Eastern Europe are on the brink of collapse, the FBI doesn't care and I'm sitting talking on a video game in God knows where? Risking my son and another child . . ."

"I've had my troubles too, Roberts. You should see the bullet holes in the car."

A long pause. His voice returned. Softer. "Yes, I know. I'm grateful. We're grateful. Sorry."

"Did anyone else see that hard drive after you got the information from Turaida Bank, before it was lost to Osis?"

"No one."

"Not David? Not Markov?"

"No."

"Anyone ever on that laptop who shouldn't have been?"

Another inaudible whisper. She heard a rustling as if Roberts's hand covered the microphone.

After a moment, Roberts broke back in:

"David believed my cousin, Elvis, might have had access to it. But that was long before we stole the information from Turaida."

A light went on in Santa's mind. That old scoundrel . . . "Now think, Roberts. Did you run a full virus scan between then and the acquisition of the Turaida info?"

"I don't think so."

"So, if Elviss has copied a program onto the laptop, it could have still been there when you stole those files?"

"I don't see . . ."

"When I worked with Elviss a decade ago in D.C., he was quite adept at planting spyware on computers. That's how he got documents, inside information, etc. . . . . That's partly why we fell out."

"I didn't know you knew each other."

"We did. And I in turn stole some information from him as well. I was no saint in our parting either, Roberts." The wheels were turning now, and Santa had that antsy feeling she always got when discovering a lead. "Listen, who was the internet provider at your flat in Rīga, Roberts?"

"BaltiTech."

"Turaida pay that bill?"

"No. In fact, I switched providers when I started hearing unsavory things about Turaida spying on employees."

"Good boy, Roberts."

He laughed lightly, and for the first time a little of the tension in his voice evaporated. "You make me sound like a terrier."

"I prefer beagles. No offense meant. It was a compliment." She massaged her temple, tried to make a mental list of all the things she had to do. "Look give me a day or two to follow that up. I hacked Elviss once, maybe I can do it again, see what's got . . ."

"Santa, there are some people here taking a real interest in all the English."

"We can speak, Latvian."

"Mine isn't good enough. Look, we should go. How about, Friday?"

"Sunday. I'll need some time on the Elviss thing. And Beatrise's mother."

"Okay."

"Gotta go."

They logged off simultaneously.

After uninstalling Grimdark Legions and clearing the computer's digital trail, Santa went to her car. She drove all the way back to Rīga that night. Exhausted as she was, she wanted to sleep in her own bed before morning.

There'd be much to do come the 'morrow.

43

The U.S. Diplomatic Cable supplied by an anonymous source to the One World Press contained the following passage:

There is mounting evidence that the Latvian police directed by Pro-Russian elements inside the Latvian government are manufacturing evidence against American citizen Robert Vanags in the unsolved murder cases of American Elviss Gulbis (Vanags's second cousin) and Latvian citizen Evgeny Markov. Potential false evidence includes counterfeit fingerprints, and falsely attributed theft of information and property from Turaida Bank of Latvia. The Latvian police also allege a kidnapping charge of the Latvian woman, Beatrise Liepa against Vanags. No credible record of Ms. Liepa has been found outside her high school registration.

The whereabouts of Vanags, 41, and his son David, 17, are unknown. Both were last seen in Rīga on night of November 28th. We are continuing to monitor this situation.

Jonathan Simms, Legal Attaché, U.S. Embassy, Rīga.

Signe Novak, the assistant editor at One World Press, might have ignored this memo. It was one of nearly two hundred U.S. government communiques anonymously deposited into OWP's server drop box. To vet them would take days, if not weeks. But so much had come in about Latvia, especially related to their national hero, Dāvids Osis, that the little country across the Baltic Sea was on everyone's mind.

Signe needed an excuse to talk to Hekla anyways. So, she printed out the excerpt and crept down the long hall of OWP's Oslo offices, past the awards, framed headlines, and photograph of Hekla Stefánsdóttir with Andries Van Dam at Brown University in 2014 and slipped into the main conference room.

Hekla Stefánsdóttir stood at the end of the conference table, wearing a dark gray suit dress, equally gray hair pulled back into a tight bun. About the table were OWP's other editors whom Signe knew well, and the three technical leads who usually did their work from Stockholm, Paris or Reykjavík. There was another man, that Signe was fairly certain was a lawyer from New York. Body language said no one was happy with what Hekla was saying.

"We will close the drop box at 5 P.M. GMT tonight. And it will remain closed until after my Reykjavík conference."

"Our traffic has never been higher," said the Swedish technical lead. "Why close now?"

Hekla gave a heavy sigh, as if pooling her strength, then said:

"This is my olive branch to the Icelandic parliament. The *Althingi* have asked us to publish nothing and to take on no more anonymous submissions until I have detailed our position, our mission, and vetting process. I've agreed. A week from today I intend to leave Reykjavík having convinced my homeland, and the world, that transparency is the only way to proceed in the media age. That we, and organizations like OWP, are not terrorists or thieves, but the proper evolution of journalism in the twenty-first century."

Signe gauged the reaction around the table. This was not taken well. Many in OWP thought stooping to present the case before a national government was capitulation, felt this hearing and moratorium implied or even acknowledged that Iceland or any other nation might have the right to dam the free information released by OWP.

But Hekla had her reasons. Her olive branch as she said, her cease fire, that would allow OWP to make its case.

Signe thought Hekla Stefánsdóttir was gambling years of effort and strife on the judgement of her people. That Hekla's fierce nationalism was clouding her judgement.

Still, Signe said nothing.

As the meeting members went their separate ways, Signe approached her director and editor-and-chief.

"In those emails we got last night, Hekla, there's more that might connect back to Osis. You said you wanted to know."

Hekla's reaction surprised Signe. Instead of the usual spark from her director, there was only a weariness. Evidence that the current situation was weighing heavily on her mind.

She took the page from Signe without a glance at the words, slipped it into a briefcase on the conference room table. Locked it tight.

"I'll read it on the plane, Signe."

With the moratorium Signe wondered if she'd bother.

44

Standing in the office suite in Vilnius, Santa Ezeriņa rubbed her temple, felt the ache of all those Sigulda injuries, and prayed for good news. The young man sitting in front of her was too well-dressed for a Lithuanian hacker, attired in a nice Italian suit, an Armani tie loosely around his collar. But the best hackers could afford such clothes. And Benjaminas—anglicized to "Ben" for foreign clients—was the best she knew. She'd done a report exposing him last year, lobbing accusations and slander against his hacker circle. But while exposing him, she'd come away with one conclusion: Ben could get in anywhere with time.

Now, she'd switched sides. Promised him a full retraction of her article in the *Baltic Beacon,* numerous online apologies and fifty thousand dollars of Roberts Vanags's money when exonerated, all in exchange for a little help.

Whatever got her across the finish line.

While Ben worked, Santa paced the room, finally pausing at the office window. Outside, she could see *Maironio gatvė* running along the icy waters of the River Vilnelė and beyond the river, the Užupis neighborhood with its artist colony and fierce tradition of independence. Hidden among the colony's vibrant murals, creative graffiti, alley of abstract sculptures, cat-filled coffee houses, and the statue of Frank Zappa erected to replace a Soviet monument to Lenin, was a wall on *Paupio gatvė* inscribed with the Užupis thirty-eight-article constitution. Santa knew many of the articles by heart. Three touched her this moment.

> 28. *Everyone may share what they possess.*
> 29. *No one can share what they do not possess.*
> 38. *Everyone has the right not to be afraid.*

If Latvia ever threw her out, she could live here. Happily.

But Santa had more immediate tasks.

She turned from the window, glanced at one of the secondary monitors in this boiling hot office. A simple web browser was opened to the CNN homepage, the headline notable given she was in a hacker's office:

STEFÁNSDÓTTIR PREPARES FOR HER SPEECH BEFORE WORLD

"What do you think of that, Ben? The queen of One World Press having her day in court?"

"Ms. Hekla is as honest as they come." He shrugged. "If it means better pay and less persecution for hackers, I'm all for it."

"That's not very global thinking of you."

"It is. I've done work for OWP. Something you missed in your articles, Santa. They only let me hack public figures. You, what you're having me do is far less ethical than what they do."

"Thanks," she said sarcastically.

"Truth hurts," he hit a final key dramatically. "We're in."

Santa walked over to stand behind Ben. The contents of Elviss Gulbis's home Cloud account lay open before them. Files after files uploaded from spyware Elviss had put on computers across North America, and later, Latvia.

She shook her head. This was his journalism? Spying rather than reporting?

Then she realized the irony in that thought.

"Here's the password for future reference," said Ben. "'PinkPussy-Man1532FATONE.' The American is a bit sleazy?" he asked with a raised eyebrow.

Great minds think alike.

"*Was* a lot sleazy, Ben."

"'Was?' Now, don't tell me that. The less I know the better . . ."

Is there anything on Earth Ben couldn't know? If he really wanted it?

"I'll copy all files to your portable hard drive, Ms. Ezeriņa."

As the data copied over, the names flashed across the screen. One folder caused Santa's heart to skip, one Latvian word that Roberts Vanags had said must be there if there was any hope, one that could make all the difference.

A folder named "*Roze.*"

Santa smiled.

Everyone may share what they possess.

45

Hekla Stefánsdóttir hugged her son and daughter, said a tearful goodbye to her husband, and left their cozy Oslo apartment for the cold Norwegian night and the short walk to the waiting taxi.

The flight to Reykjavík was less than three hours and Hekla doubted she would sleep. The hearing with the *Althingi* was four days away. It would be precedent setting she feared, the freedom of those who wished to bring truth to the world in the balance. If history would remember her for anything, it would be this . . .

The taxi waited. So, did the world.

46

Santa was glad the little Rēzekne internet cafe was empty. Even the old lady who ran it had scampered off to buy supplies at the product store down the street, leaving Santa alone.

Trustful ole soul.

When Roberts Vanags's black knight appeared on the Grimdark Legions screen, Santa clicked the conversation requested button, and spoke into the headset's microphone as loud as she dared.

"We have it, Roberts. Names, transactions, amounts. Every bit you took from Turaida, Elviss took from you with spyware. He likely died before he knew what he had."

"Incredible," came that husky, American voice. "It could have only been uploaded by his software when I accessed WIFI at the café I stopped at the night I stole it from Turaida. It was the only time I had internet after getting the info."

"Your cousin just missed out on the story, once again . . . ."

"Will you give it to your newspaper?"

"I can't give it to the *Beacon*. When they'd try to confirm the data, their queries would be all over Rīga in minutes. Turaida or the police or both would shut them down. We need to go overseas."

"*The New York Times*?" His voice sounded hopeful. For the first time.

She hated to dash those hopes.

"By the time a traditional newspaper acted you could be dead. And the stolen money even harder to trace. I want to give it to Hekla Stefánsdóttir. None of the other 'leaks' organizations pursue the Russian oligarchy with the vigor of One World Press. Stefánsdóttir will be in Reykjavík in three days. She's addressing the Icelandic parliament. I want to give it to her personally before she speaks."

"No . . . I'd rather a traditional, reputable publisher. I'm accused of murder, Santa. I need maximum legitimacy to show there is a conspiracy against us.

OWP and the like . . . well, many believe they're thieves, indiscriminate publishers of anything." A few muffled sounds, he and David exchanging words that Santa was prevented from hearing, though she caught "Iceland" and "One World Press."

When his voice returned, there was a new strength in it. "I think we're safe in hiding for now, Santa. The place we're staying at should remain uninhabited through winter. Take your time to find the most authoritative publisher."

"No. We act today." Santa whispered, though she didn't know why. She couldn't tell him about her suspicions about Beatrise. If she were wrong, she'd endanger an innocent girl. The very fact that Turaida hadn't found Roberts and his son screamed Beatrise wasn't a mole.

But maybe she was a spy who simply couldn't contact her superiors? Who knew? Better to act immediately and let it all come out in the wash. The faster Santa acted the safer Roberts, and his son would be . . . .

"Look, I have my reasons. But the clock is ticking. I'll give the hard drive info to OWP."

"Well, I can't really stop you."

"We're on the same side, Roberts. Remember that. Tell no one anything more. Not even David. Not even Beatrise until you hear from me. What I'm doing, what we've found is between us. Ok?"

He didn't answer.

"Ok?"

"Ok."

"Roberts, one more thing, there was a file of emails in the *Roze* folder. They were mostly in Latvian, a few in Russian or Ukrainian. Did you have time to read them before Osis took the hard drive?"

"No . . . no, and I couldn't read them even if I'd been given the time . . ."

"Well, they're mostly innocuous. But there was one from someone at an International Development Bank address to an assistant of Dāvids Osis. It made an obscure reference to the Latvian government ensuring IDB's investment in Turaida was secure. Do you know what that would be about?"

"No . . . .Not unless it was referring to IDB's purchase of Turaida Group shares. After my failed whistleblowing."

"The reference sounds shifty to me. Sounds like the government guaranteed IDB's purchase. That was never public record. IDB bought those shares to assure the Latvian people and the world that Turaida Bank was solvent and your accusations were lies. However, if there is a secret guarantee, then it means the opposite. It means that the government and IDB know that Turaida isn't solvent and they are trying to trick people that it is. This is fraud and will hurt many people in Latvia and other countries. But the remark is too vague to do anything with. We have any allies at IDB who may shed light on this?"

"No. Not anymore."

"What about Agnese Avena? You two looked chummy at the Helmanis funeral."

"She and I parted ways." His voice cracked here, and Santa found herself feeling sorry for him. They had been more than chums clearly . . . .

What had Avena done to win a good man like Roberts?

"And after her involvement in all those fraudulent loans . . ." he continued. "I . . . hate to say it but Agnese can't have been fully innocent. It's impossible. The numbers are too great . . . I've named her in a sort of manifesto I'm writing."

"Never trust a blonde, Roberts."

"Yes."

"Avena is friends with Osis, isn't she? He gave her a parliamentary medal, right?"

"Yes. I saw photos of it . . . when we were seeing each other. It hangs in her Frankfurt apartment."

Instinctively, she drew a triangle on sticky-note pad on the desk before her, labeled the points of the triangle Osis-Avena-Roberts. Then realizing this was evidence someone might find; she tore the note off the pad and swallowed it.

Ick. Sticky and unhygienic.

"Look Roberts, I'm gonna go. There are a few things I've got to do, then I'm going to Reykjavík. Next time you hear from me, the world will know Turaida's sins. And they'll know you were telling the truth, Roberts. I promise."

"Thank you," he said softly.

Santa logged off. Cleared her digital trail.

Sighed.

Days that shook the world.

She'd break the biggest story of her lifetime in the next seventy-two hours. Or die trying.

47

Frankfurt

The message on Agnese Avena's office phone had been left at five A.M., two full hours before she arrived for work. This raised a slight concern in her, an apprehension that only increased when she heard the voice of the messenger.

Dāvids Osis.

Legendary heroes didn't make calls at that hour without reason. Agnese paused the playback, plugged in headphones to maintain privacy should anyone untrustworthy step into her International Development Bank office.

Fortunately, few were in at this hour. She skipped the message back to the beginning and listened carefully.

"Greetings, Agnese. I trust you are well this morning. A great friend of ours is coming. From Moscow. We must give her whatever she requests. No limitations. Her name is Alla Politukha. Thank you, old friend."

Now, what did Osis want? He was always sending emissaries to IDB at short notice. *Do that Agnese, do this Agnese.* While he had no official authority over her in Germany, his role in the *Roze* undertaking made Osis a voice that had to be obeyed. IDB president Louis Stembridge insisted upon it.

Speaking of Louis . . . She removed the headphones, pressed the intercom on her desk, buzzed Stembridge's assistant.

"Louis in yet, Tanya?"

The young woman's voice came through crystal clear on the phone speaker, much clearer than Osis's had been.

"He just arrived, Agnese."

"Good. Tell him I'll be in right away."

"Yes, ma'am."

Time to look out for yourself, Agnese. Time to provide for your unborn child. In other words . . . showtime.

"Louis, I want more."

"More?"

Agnese nodded, sat back in her chair, and gauged the reaction of the bank's president across the desk in his expansive office. Even at this early hour, Louis Stembridge's demeanor radiated controlled energy, as if the morning exhaustion others felt were simply impossible for an alpha male like him. It made Agnese instinctively dislike him.

Despite Stembridge's fifty years of age, his hair remained dark as his funeral-black suit. With a suntanned face and trim build, he could pass at most distances for a much younger man. But up close, over this desk, Agnese could see the lines in the Englishman's forehead and deep crow's-feet at his eyes. Agnese thought of him as all façade, a brittle shell, a man hollow and rotting from within.

Stembridge compressed those crow's-feet into a frown. Repeated himself. "More? What do you mean, Agnese?"

"The loans to the Baltics, Ukraine, Moldova. Everyone's taking their share. Everyone's getting rich over this—"

"As are you."

She looked beyond Stembridge, over his shoulders to the office's expansive window. The European Central Bank's tower was visible from here, rising over the Frankfurt skyline. What if the ECB knew what went on in these offices . . . ?

"I want to be richer, Louis. Rich as you. Rich as Leonid Vovk. Rich as MP Osis is going to be when we reach forty billion collected. I am the conduit, Louis, my fingerprints are all over half those fraudulent loans. Nineteen billion given out to Vovk and his oligarch cronies alone. And yet all I get are flowers, French Riviera holidays in three-star hotels and company bonuses. I want to be set for life."

Stembridge bit his lip, as he always did when assembling his thoughts. Another tendency that annoyed Agnese.

At last, he spoke:

"We can get a new conduit, my dear. If you are unhappy . . . And really, why should you be paid more? You haven't done such perfect work. Moscow, Kharkov, Rīga, are all concerned about your reliability. Need I remind you; you've been involved with two Turaida employees who tried to betray us? You've bad taste in lovers, Agnese."

Yes, but you wanted to be one as well. Remember, Louis? Proposition after proposition at every IDB function last year. She wondered if he bit his lip during sex too. God help her if she'd ever stoop to finding out.

"Neither Ēriks nor Roberts got anything of use from me, Louis. It's a Turaida problem, they've got leaks galore over there. Kārlis can't do his job . . ."

"Leave Kārlis to Moscow. You just keep championing those loans, you'll get what's coming to you."

"Yes, I will." She spoke firmly, as she had been practicing for days. "Before we reach forty billion stolen, I'll need a deposit of ten million U.S. dollars into my Ecuadorian account or I'll go to the press, Louis."

That tanned face turned to an expressionless mask. "Are you attempting to extort us, Agnese?"

"I've taken precautions that if I die or disappear, everything will come out. Everything. Not just financial. But politics, homicides, ties back to Moscow . . ."

"Roberts Vanags's influence, I see."

"Nothing to do with Roberts. This is about living well—and getting my share. Ten million is insignificant when we're talking billions. My needs are only a simple cost of doing business."

She stood, stepped away from the chair.

"Think about it, Louis."

Agnese marched out of the president's office.

She'd made her gambit. At last.

When Agnese Avena had been gone not two minutes, Stembridge roused himself from his silent thinking, pulled a key from his jacket pocket, and unlocked the desk's bottom drawer. He withdrew a battered cellphone, one with only three numbers in memory. He pressed the one for Leonid Vovk.

The call picked up instantly.

"Leonid," said Stembridge in a relaxed, overly-friendly voice, "Our little girl was in my office again. You were right. Vanags and his antics must have twisted her mind. Gotten her thinking about leverage . . . She might even be in league with him . . . Yes, more money. This time she threatened blackmail." He smirked. "I made no promises, Leonid . . . No, not yet. I have a better idea. Something I learned from Moscow."

At three P.M., Dāvids Osis's courier, Alla Politukha, appeared. She was a thin, radiant blonde woman in her late twenties or early thirties dressed in a white suit-dress with dark scarf, black thigh-high boots, and black lapel orchid. She reminded Agnese something of herself, though she was taller, wore glasses and had a masculinity to her movements that Agnese found rather unappealing.

Despite IDB's international status, Ms. Politukha made no attempt to converse in English or German but conducted their exchanges in Russian. Not really a surprise, Agnese thought, if she was an ally of Osis. His friends all spoke Russian these days in private. And Osis never quite trusted his country-men on *Roze* errands.

They made little small talk—Alla's plane had been delayed and she was anxious to get the exchange done and catch the evening flight. She made a big show of letting Agnese know she'd be continuing on to Moscow tonight.

Obviously, Osis's new masters were pulling the real strings here.

There were always procedures when Osis sent someone. Agnese left Alla waiting under pretense of getting the key to the locked walk-in closet in the back of her office, went down the hall to the first vacant desk, made a private call to Osis. His secretary said he was engaged for the next two hours at least. Agnese left word for him to call, adding that she'd received his message this morning regarding Alla Politukha. The secretary assured her she'd pass it on when the MP came out of his meeting.

On her smartphone, Agnese made a quick search of the Frankfurt airport arrivals. The morning flights from Moscow had both been delayed, one twenty minutes, another a full hour.

Good signs.

Agnese returned to her office, found Alla sitting patiently at a desk chair, purse across her lap.

"Sorry to keep you waiting, Alla. I know you've had enough of delays after being three hours late from Moscow."

"Actually, it was only twenty minutes. And I was lucky. The plane before was delayed almost an hour."

"What is the old line? 'Aeroflot barely floats?'" Agnese laughed.

Alla sat their patiently.

"Now, what exactly is it Dāvids Osis wishes you to retrieve?"

Before the Russian could respond, the phone on Agnese's desk beeped, and Louis Stembridge's voice came over the speaker.

"Agnese, I chatted with Leonid Vovk. I think when we get to forty billion, we can talk then about renegotiating your—"

"I have a guest in my office, Louis," said Agnese with more than a hint of censure.

Idiot.

"Oh," she heard the hesitance in his voice, the fear he'd made a grave mistake. She almost enjoyed it. "Oh, I see. Well, let me be clear, what I was referring to was simply—"

"My guest is an emissary from Dāvids Osis via Moscow."

"Indeed." His words brightened at this, relief in them. "From Moscow, you say. Should I pop in?"

Agnese looked at Alla. They exchanged faint smiles. Agnese felt some of the tension drain away.

"I believe she's in a hurry, Louis. Osis called this morning, said it was urgent. We should give her what she wants."

"Then we must assist promptly . . . I'm sorry . . . What was our friend's name? Miss . . . Ms?"

"Politukha," said Alla.

"Greetings to you, Ms. Politukha." That thick lacquered charm in his voice turned Agnese's stomach. "Give her everything she needs, Agnese. We'll finish up our conversation from this morning tomorrow at eight sharp. I'll think you'll be a happy girl afterwards."

"Sure, Louis."

The phone's speaker clicked off.

"Negotiating a raise?" asked Alla almost indifferently. To Agnese's relief, she'd turned the conversation to English.

"Of sorts. Now, what can I do for you, Ms. Politukha?"

"MP Osis needs a copy of the contents of the *Roze* files."

"Why not get that from Turaida Bank? Kārlis Pagrabs has everything on that top floor."

"That's just it. We want to make sure what Roberts Vanags stole matches what . . . other interested parties have in their possession. If the information ever leaks out, those difference may lead us to the source . . ."

Agnese frowned.

"May I see your passport?"

Alla produced a Russian passport. All looked proper.

"And I'm sorry to trouble you, Alla . . . .one last thing . . . can you show me Osis's direct dial on your phone?"

"Yes. One moment. You are most thorough." She withdrew an iPhone from her purse, pulled up a contact.

Dāvids Osis. The number was correct.

"Thank you. Sorry for this, but these are most important documents. I can't get you the *Roze* information immediately. It would take a day or two—"

"I see." The frostiness returned. "I'll have to change my flight. Unfortunate. What about the Latvian government's guarantee of IDB's purchase of the Turaida shares?"

"You mean the buyback agreement?"

"'Buyback'—yes, that's what I want. You know the English words . . . I'd have been clearer in Russian."

"Doesn't he have a copy? What does Osis need with ours?"

"He didn't say. Only that it was most important I bring a formal document. Perhaps, someone in the Moscow inner circle needs to know it exists . . ."

Agnese felt the slightest doubt. But the call this morning was clearly from Osis, she'd heard that voice personally a thousand times, and Alla's other credentials checked out . . .

She withdrew the key from her breast pocket, motioned Alla towards a door at the back of the office. "Only President Stembridge and I have access to this security cabinet. Not even the office guards . . . ."

"Wise," said Alla. "In this modern world of thieves and terrorists . . ."

Agnese unlocked the door, stepped inside a narrow, deep room lined with metal shelves. On each were combination lockboxes. Agnese went to a safe at the back, kneeled. Worked the combo.

She heard Alla's voice close by, behind and above her. "Osis tells me you were romantically involved with that fugitive traitor Roberts Vanags?"

Bizarre inquiry. Agnese didn't like Osis talking about her social life especially where Roberts was concerned. She briefly wondered how Osis knew . . . Louis or Vovk most likely . . . Did Vovk tell them all she was pregnant with a fugitive's child?

Assholes . . .

"Yes, Ms. Politukha, though of course I had no idea what he'd go on to do . . ."

"They say criminals make the best lovers. The unbridled passion and such. Did you find it so?"

Such odd questions . . . Agnese finished the combo, heard the final click of the tumblers, pulled open the safe door.

"I can't say. But Roberts was no slouch in bed."

"I imagine so. Maybe if they arrest him, you'll be allowed conjugal visits."

"They'll never find him alive."

Agnese pulled a sealed envelope from the safe's interior, then rose to her feet. To her surprise, she was nearly nose-to-nose with Alla Politukha, felt the heat of her body, the warmth of breath on her face. Agnese handed the envelope to Alla, stepped back but the proximity of the rear wall prevented further retreat.

"Why the interest in my sex life?"

Alla smiled. "To keep your mind off spatial relations and proximity." She produced a large, very sharp letter opener from her purse. Agnese recognize it instantly as her own, it had been sitting on her desk only moments before. At the time, she'd left the room to call Osis.

Alla slid open the envelope. Glanced at the page. Whistled.

Agnese felt her stomach knotting in growing concern. "That's what you wanted . . . isn't it?"

"Yes, it is. And more." Alla pushed the document back into the envelope, slid it inside her jacket pocket. Without a glance backwards, she kicked the security door closed behind them. "Now, stand flush against the wall. And stay away from that alarm trigger. Oh, yes, I saw it Agnese."

Concern turned to white-hot terror. "Who are you?"

"Your undertaker if you don't do what I say!" Alla set the point of the letter opener against Agnese's throat at the jaw, pressed upward so that Agnese had to stand on her tiptoes to keep from being cut.

"What is the forty billion Stembridge mentioned?"

"Just some money."

"'*Some* money?'"

"Yes."

"We know you've stolen thirty-eight billion dollars. At least. What's forty billion?"

"We?"

Alla pressed the blade in, a trickle of blood ran down to stain Agnese's blouse collar. "I'll ask the questions."

Agnese swallowed, tried to tame the tremors running through her body. Her limbs felt weak. "Forty billion is a goal."

"What happens when you reach that goal?"

"We all get rich."

Alla pushed harder, pressing a forearm across Agnese's chest, forcing her painfully against the cold wall. "Then why not keep on stealing, Agnese? Why renegotiate at forty billion?"

Agnese closed her eyes. *Give her what she wants. Just stay alive. Stay alive to be a mother.* "Currencies might be different then . . . Alla, you're hurting me."

"I'll do worse than that if you don't answer. Security can't get in here. Only you and Stembridge. And I'll cut him too if I get the chance."

Agnese felt she might faint.

"Well?"

"At forty billion—we make the losses public, the banks are discovered to be insolvent, the poor governments of Ukraine, Moldova, the Baltic Republics cannot meet their guarantees to cover the losses, and collapse. Economic chaos breeds internal strife, violence. Russian tanks roll in to protect ethnic Russians in those countries. The European borders of the Soviet Union are restored."

Alla's eyes widened in surprise. "You're a Latvian. Latvians have been fighting for freedom their entire history. How could you do this? What do you really want?" In Alla's surprise and anger, her fake Russian accent fell away. This assailant was Latvian too. Agnese knew it. And the face was somehow familiar . . .

Agnese changed their language, to confirm her suspicions.

"I want money. A better life. It's that simple," she said in Latvian. "Countries don't matter. The dollar is the only remaining nationality." Agnese spat in anger, the spittle running down Alla's cheek. "I don't know who you are. But I'll deny everything. You're a dead woman. You can't fight Moscow; our people have been trying for centuries and always failed."

Alla's brow furled, kept her response in Russian. "Maybe. But for now, all I want to fight is you."

Agnese saw the blur of Alla's fist flying towards her jaw.

Everything went dark as midnight.

Agnese Avena awoke to the pain of a throbbing jaw, the irate voice of Louis Stembridge and the incessant ringing of a telephone.

"Agnese! Agnese, can you hear me?" said Stembridge standing over her. She was on the floor in her office, Louis, his secretary, and two security guards huddled around her.

"What happened?" Agnese asked, trying to clear the cobwebs in her mind. "Was I unconscious?"

"You were locked in the security closet for two hours," spat Stembridge. "The safe has been emptied!"

It was coming back now. Agnese sat up, placed her face in the palm of her hands, felt the swell in her jaw.

"We were robbed?"

"Will someone answer that damn phone?" shouted Stembridge. Tanya scrambled to do so.

"Robbed?" Stembridge continued. "This doesn't have anything to do with the 'precautions' you mentioned this morning? I've seen staged events before, Agnese. Leonid Vovk's seen staged events before . . ."

"What? . . . No . . . No . . . I was attacked. Look at my jaw, my neck . . ."

"Ms. Avena," said Tanya calmly, handing down the phone's receiver. "It's the Latvian politician Dāvids Osis . . . He wants to know—excuse me—to use his words, 'Who the Hell is Alla Politukha?'"

48

As the last of her bleached blonde hair fell to the electric razor, Santa Ezeriņa examined her reflection in the dingy hotel room's mirror. Without her usual bangs, with only a stubbly naked scalp, her forehead looked high, her head too pointy, and the face somehow emaciated. The stress lines over her brows would be there regardless, she thought, locks or not. Yet, nothing hid them now.

She needed sleep. Or to get laid.

No time for either.

With the blonde hair went the persona of Alla Politukha, of course. Good riddance. *Never trust blondes, Agnese.* She'd known Avena would check her credentials, so she'd doctored an old Russian passport obtained from the black market on assignment in Ekaterinburg years ago, adding the Politukha name and her fake blonde image only hours before arriving in Frankfurt. The passport electronics remained untouched. Santa had no skill for such things. It would be unusable to travel by, but the document passed a quick glance from a banker like Agnese Avena who didn't know what to look for in a counterfeit passport. Santa's preparations weren't perfect though. She hadn't anticipated Agnese asking to see Osis's phone number. Blind luck, she still had it in her contacts from an old *Beacon* interview with the politician.

Truthfully, she'd been paranoid the whole time at the IDB offices, knew Agnese would detect a Latvian tint in her fake Russian accent eventually. It's never easy to fool a countrywoman. Santa had so Russified her speech, so overdone the "Natasha"-thing, she must have seemed a caricature. Yet, Agnese gave no hint of suspicion until Santa held that letter opener to her throat.

The message from "Dāvids Osis" was the key to everything, of course. A deception that suppressed any initial doubts in Agnese. All later success flowed from that call, made so early in the morning to ensure no one actually answered.

Digital magic.

That Sigulda sound maestro Toms Vītols had done an amazing job in only sixteen hours of work. It'd taken little to convince Vītols to help, not after the old police communications expert had witnessed Turaida assassins try to kill Santa in Sigulda, not after he and his wife had been threatened almost daily ever since, and twice had thugs barge into his house, turning the place upside down. Not everyone gave into Moscow's supposed invincibility as Agnese Avena did. Not everyone cowered.

With such a long public life, there had been countless Dāvids Osis sound bites for Vītols to draw from, collected from the *Baltic Beacon* archives, on *Youtube* and *SS.lv*, on Osis's own public website. Vītols had taken "Greetings, Agnese" from Osis's award presentation to Avena two years ago. "From Moscow" was captured when the doomed Russian oligarch Boris Berezovsky made a brief surprise visit to Latvia in 2005. Likewise, "We must give her whatever she requests" was plucked from press conference with the British monarch Queen Elizabeth II in 2009. On and on it went . . .

The formation of "Alla Politukha" was the most difficult, pairing up the given name of a Latvian physicist Osis had praised on many public occasions with the surname of an obscure Belorussian diplomat "Politukha" he'd referenced in a speech way back in 1994. Vītols had done a wonderful job splicing it all together, smoothing out the differences in tone and sound-quality, altering Osis's voice as needed, so the throaty old man's words of the present day flowed seamlessly with the fiery cadences of his younger self. The illusion would never have held up if played on a clear speaker in person, but over the phone, left on a voice mail? It had worked perfectly. Fooled the fool, Agnese Avena.

By now Agnese knew the game. Add IDB to the list of those hunting Santa. That she'd obtained these documents by force made them inadmissible in any court of law, made Santa herself a criminal. But what laws were broken to obtain information seldom mattered in the court of public opinion. Not when we're talking about hostile forces toppling five governments and stealing tens of billions.

As the last of her hair fell to the floor, Santa glanced away from the unpleasant realities of the mirror to her purse stuffed with documents she'd stolen from the IDB safe, documents she had only time to give the quickest glance.

Yet, two things were already evident.

Firstly, the so-called "buyback" document was a secret agreement for the Latvian government to purchase Turaida Group's shares from the IDB in three years' time. At a considerable profit for the later bank. The twenty-percent purchase of Turaida stock had been a sham meant to calm the public nerves after Roberts's whistleblowing in November. IDB looks like a savior, makes millions, maybe billions, and in the long run the Latvian people pay for the theft both banks have done.

Which led Santa to the second evident thing. Nowhere in the documents she'd stolen today, or in the *Roze* files Roberts had taken and Ben recovered from Elviss' Cloud account, was there any trace of the final destinations of the stolen monies. Those accounts were missing. Who knew where they were hidden? South America? Australia? Asia?

Announcing these crimes without a way to get back the money might trigger the very thing she was trying to prevent. Financial chaos and enough calamity that Moscow invades under pretense of preventing ethnic warfare.

Now, the clock was ticking. Not the three years the buy-back agreement promised. Every day that stolen money became harder to find. Especially after her offensive today. The bad guys would be covering their tracks, moving the money. And if the cash were not found, then sooner or later, Moscow would have what it needed to justify war.

She was now even more certain of the argument she'd used with Roberts. Traditional newspapers would vet, double check, and never accept how she'd gotten her information through a criminal act. Santa prayed One World Press would put it out without asking questions. Out fast enough that most of the thirty-eight billion stolen dollars may somehow be retrieved. And avert war.

This cheap hotel had no WIFI. It didn't matter, there was no reason to further risk exposing Roberts or his son. Or tipping off Beatrise Liepa, if Santa's suspicions were correct.

She changed into a fraying blue track suit she'd not worn since university, put a Yankees baseball cap on her bare head. Examined herself in the mirror.

Well, she looked nothing like the blade-wielding psychopath today at the International Development Bank. She prayed the disguise was enough of a difference to get out of Germany. Santa packed her things quickly and left the godforsaken fleabag hotel without checking out.

The young ticket officer at Frankfurt International Airport failed to flirt with Santa. It almost hurt her feelings. Men were seldom unimpressed with her.

The shaved scalp she thought.

"You've missed the last direct to flight to Iceland, Miss Ezeriņa. We can offer you a connecting flight through . . . ." He tapped a few keys. "through Moscow?"

"God no."

"Or Rīga?"

"No."

"Or London Heathrow or Edinburgh."

"Whichever leaves first."

"London it is."

She paid by credit card. Collected the ticket. As she was stepping away from the counter the clerk said:

"By the way, I love the shaved look on a woman." He pumped his fist with a laugh. "And 'Go Yankees!' That is right, isn't it? Never, quite sure about American sports teams . . ."

Santa smiled. Somehow it made her feel better. Free world in the balance, but she needed that . . .

"Exactly right, handsome. 'Go Yankees.'"

The little things in this life.

Santa left him smiling and boarded the plane.

49

Galina Kozlova stood on the highest ridge of the sea cliff trying to signal a passing sailboat. In her hands was a broom handle affixed with a red football jersey she'd found in a bedroom of the house. These Estonian isles were densely populated enough, even in winter, that it should be little trouble to hail for help. That is, if she had the time. Soon the men would detect her absence. She'd already been gone too long as it was.

Galina waved her make-shift signal flag furiously. The man on the distant boat took no notice of her, the triangular sails of his craft shrinking, their whiteness merging with the sea mist as the ship cruised away.

But there was the sound of a motorboat somewhere in the distance. She scanned the horizon, waved the flag in ovular paths above her. Where could it—

"What are you doing, Bea?"

The voice sent cold adrenaline through Galina's body.

She turned about.

David stood behind her, staring intently.

She kept her voice iron strong. "What does it look like, David? I'm signaling for rescue. I want to reach my mother . . ."

"Santa Ezeriņa is contacting her."

"You said only after she goes to Iceland. I don't trust a journalist. What if those bankers silence Ezeriņa? I want to hear my mother's voice. Confirm that *she* knows I'm alive!"

"Bea," he put a gloved hand on her shoulder. She shrugged him off.

"Look, I can't let you do this . . . ." David reached over her, grabbed the broom handle. "There are assassins out there. We'll find another way . . ."

"Another way? To keep me quiet? Like lock me in a closet? Steal my hearing aid again?"

"Don't see it that way, Bea." He held onto the pole, pulled it closer to him, tried to slip the jersey flag off the end.

She tugged the pole around. Unprepared for her strength, David's body lurched forward. He lost his footing, slipped down. For a moment, they both held the broomstick, as he slid farther down the cliff-face.

"Bea, help me . . ."

She placed her boot against his shoulder and kicked him away. His grip slipped. She watched the boy fall towards the rocks of the sea below.

The ink in his pen running low, Bob Vanags continued his listing of his enemies' crimes:

> *15. Dāvids Osis*
>> *a. Lying to the Latvian people*
>> *b. Destruction of property.*
>> *c. Conspiracy against the Latvian government*
>> *d. Obstruction of justice*
>> *e. Embezzlement*
>> *f. Treason*
>> *g. Accomplice to murder*
>> *h. Being a general ass*

"Roberts!" screamed a voice from downstairs. "Roberts, come quickly!"

Bob sprang from the table, thoughts of his work lost in an instant to cold fear.

Beatrise met him at the head of the stairs, her face red and twisted in anguish and pain.

"What happened?" he asked.

"It's David. He's hurt. Hurt very badly."

50

In the bottom of the rowboat, Galina Kozlova held the bloody towel against David Vanags's head, while his father rowed furiously towards the largest island in view.

"Almost there, David. Hang on," said Robert, grievous emotion in his voice. Of course, the boy couldn't hear him, thought Galina. David had been unconscious since they'd returned to the cliff. Galina knew the words were more for Robert to calm himself, to tell his conscience that all would be right soon. She understood it. And almost sympathized.

Almost.

Ahead was the coast of Saaremaa, the largest of the Estonian isles, and the only one certain to have a hospital. Robert did not slow in rowing or search the coastline for a pier. Instead, he steered right up into the shallows, dropped into the waist deep water, and dragged the boat towards the beach.

"Bea, help me . . ."

She left David for the moment, descended into the freezing waters of the shallows and helped him pull the rowboat ashore.

On the snowy path leading inland, two sturdy-looking men in their forties stood smoking pipes, a woman of about the same age with them. A boy in his mid-teens carried firewood. They gazed curiously at the scene.

The woman shouted something in Estonian.

Lifting David gingerly from the rowboat's bottom, Robert set him gently on the beach, then motioned for the strangers to come.

"Beatrise, call them over."

Unnecessary, Galina thought. The boy dropped the firewood, he and the two older males rushing down to them, the woman following a little more cautiously. The odds were strong that at least the youth knew some English, but Robert was too worried about his son to think straight. Russian, on the other hand, would certainly be known by the elders. It would allow Galina privacy from Robert's ears.

"This man is a fugitive," Galina shouted. "Robert Vanags! The American murderer. He kidnapped me and injured the boy!"

Even in Russian, Vanags caught his name.

"Beatrise, what did you say to them?"

Galina ignored him. "Robert Vanags! The banker! The American killer from Rīga. Surely, you've heard! Please, help us. Call the police."

There was a brief buzz of astonished Estonian voices, then the woman ran back towards the cabin, while the two men advanced, hesitant at first, but with growing speed and resolve. The Estonian boy stood still and unsure on the path.

"What are you saying?" asked Robert, real panic in his voice. He set a gloved hand on Galina's shoulder, tried to turn her around to face him.

She used his actions against him. Exaggerated the struggle, the intent, flopping back on the beach, kicking at Robert's shins.

"Get off me!" Galina sent a heel into his knee. He grimaced and backed away.

"Murderer!"

"Beatrise!?"

"Help!" she cried to the approaching men. One shoved Robert back with bullish force, he fell into the surf, shock on his face.

"Get away from them!" shouted the assaulter in English.

"Stay back," said the other man in Russian, fear and uncertainty in his voice.

Robert's horrified gaze moved from his attackers to her.

"Beatrise . . . why?"

"You can't harm us any longer!" she shouted in English to make the point. "No more murder, no more rape!"

The more aggressive man threw himself at Robert, but the American was surprisingly swift on the ground. He dodged the tackle, the man fell where he'd been a second before, splashing into the surf. Regaining his feet, Robert stalked towards Galina. But the other man stepped between them.

"Stop!" he repeated.

Outnumbered, Robert backed away. The first man gained his feet, a stone in his hand, and the two chased Robert along the coast. Two hundred meters along the seashore, he changed his course, rushing up into the island's interior. Behind the trees, the men were quickly lost from view.

The Estonian teenager descended to the beach; his mother having returned from the cabin with a mobile phone in her hand.

Galina kneeled by the prostrate David, lying so still in the slushy mixture of snow and sand. Gently as she could, she set his head in her lap, stroked his blood-matted hair from his eyes. She raised a real tear from her eyes, one that ran down her cheek to fall on David's face. Then she said as clearly as possible.

"Oh, I don't think the boy will survive . . . ."

51

When Agnese Avena stepped into the lift to her Frankfurt flat, her neighbor, an elderly silver-haired matron named Minna Kerr said, "I see you've been making repairs."

"Repairs?"

"A maintenance man was painting your door this morning. Though I must say the color looks the same now. All that effort for nothing. And why do you stay with green? A white or beige would be much more elegant."

"I didn't request any upkeep, Mrs. Kerr. It must be the superintendent's decision. And *all* the doors on my floor are green."

"Yes. So tacky. You'd think the owners would have better sense."

"I believe it's meant to feel sylvan." Agnese admired her own figure in the elevator's mirrored walls. Still, not showing . . .

They'd reached her floor. The doors opened; Agnese stepped off. "Goodnight, Mrs. Kerr."

"Goodnight, Agnese. Think again about a beige, it'll go—"

The elevator doors shut cutting her words short. Agnese laughed to herself. The old biddy was so concerned with the décor. It'd matter little to Agnese. She'd be living in far more opulent lodgings soon. As soon as Louis Stembridge realized she'd never wait for her money. Not with everyone else accruing wealth beyond their dreams.

Agnese Avena would get hers.

She walked down the thin carpeted hall, passing the doors of neighbors she barely knew, seldom saw with her frequent travels for IDB. So, rarely at home, she wouldn't notice changes to the furnishings. The wall lights were still retro sheik, meant to look like elegant nineteenth century gas lamps, and gave little better light than the originals. None of the doors, frames, or fixtures appeared to have new coats of paint.

And, yet, as she approached her own apartment at the end of the hall, there was a slight sheen to the surface of her own door, its frame, and especially the knob. In this poor light, Agnese might never have noticed if it weren't for Mrs. Kerr's words. The paint color was exactly as it had been when last she was home. Perhaps, they'd simply lacquered the door and frame.

Yet, it seemed thickest on the knob. Why lacquer an unpainted piece of metal?

She looked across the hall. None of the other doors had this shine, no thin paste on any other knobs.

Agnese felt herself paranoid. Still, she called the superintendent on her cell.

"Johan, Agnese Avena in apartment thirty-four. Have you had a man out today working on my door?"

He had not.

"You'd better get up here, Johan. There's something I want you to look at."

Five minutes later, Johan arrived. He thought the glaze on the knob unusual, but nothing to be too concerned about. Someone with oily hands, some electrician or plumber with remnants of a chemical on their hands likely touched the knob. Probably someone who went to the wrong apartment. He'd ask the day manager if any tenant had called for help . . .

Agnese begged him to go in with her. Just to make sure the apartment was empty. She batted her eyes, spoke of prowlers. It was never hard to convince men to come inside with her.

Johan took her key, unlocked the door, turned the knob. They went inside.

All appeared normal. She checked the bedrooms, the toilet, the closets, while Johan waited patiently in the kitchen.

By the time Agnese returned to him, Johan was on his knees, grimacing. He said his hand burned like Hell.

Thirty minutes later, he reached the hospital.

Two hours passed before Johan died.

52

Santa Ezeriņa sat uncomfortably in the economy class of her flight to Reykjavík, her seat at the window of the last row, allowing her to observe every passenger in the cabin ahead of her. She knew there was validity to her current paranoia. She'd been followed for weeks. Now that she was in possession of the smoking gun, the records that could bring down the Turaida Group and cripple its crooked backers from Frankfurt to Rīga and all the way to Moscow, Santa saw potential thieves and assassins in every face. The change of planes in London had given a little relief, but she wasn't naïve enough to think she was beyond the Kremlin's reach. Just ask the family of poor Sergei Skripal and his innocent daughter Yulia in London. Or Alexander Litvinenko more than a decade earlier . . .

She may never feel safe again.

Turbulence somewhere over Scotland rocked the plane, Santa's coffee spilling over her jeans and the seat. As she rummaged through her purse for something to mop the stain, a boy of nine or ten leaned over from his seat across the aisle and offered Santa a napkin.

"Please accept it," said a woman in the seat next to the boy, a hint of an unknown accent in her English. "Terribly bumpy. Makes us nervous."

"Yes. Thank you. Me too." Santa took the napkin from the boy's hand. His smile mirrored the woman's, the family resemblance too strong to be anything other than mother and son.

"Would you like something to relax you?" said the woman. "I've some Diazepam. Already downed two myself on the tarmac at Heathrow."

"No."

"Well, they're here if you need them."

"Thanks." Santa was surprised and a little embarrassed at the terseness in her own voice. The woman seemed nice enough and she was traveling with a child . . . what sort of assassin brings their son to a contract killing?

But that accent . . .

God, she was going mad with suspicion.

Santa sighed, leaned back in her chair, desired sleep . . .

But dared not close her eyes.

Keflavik International Airport is a good thirty-minute ride from Reykjavík, open tundra in between, endless white plains as far as Santa could see. Sleep deprived, her alertness compromised by exhaustion, she had no desire to take one of the frequent buses into the city, instead electing to hire a private taxi, expensive as it was. The woman from the plane offered to split the fare and share a cab. Santa declined. First politely, then more firmly. When she at last relented and they went their separate ways, Santa waited until the woman and her son had taken their own cab and were out of sight on the endless white horizon, before she climbed into her own taxi and said "Faxa Bay Hotel."

Standing in his hotel room Gunnar Ingolfsson looked the same to Santa as he had five years ago. Lank, handsome, overly dressed for a journalist, his platinum blond hair so light he appeared almost brow-less at a distance. Blessed with a boyish face, no stranger would have guessed Gunnar was approaching forty.

"It is good to see you again, Santa," said he, seemingly disappointed in a hug and kiss on the cheek for greeting. "Why do you limp, so?"

He was very perceptive. Santa thought she'd hid it well.

"It's a long story. For another time, Gunnar."

"And the shaved head?"

"I've adopted a rather punk attitude lately." She sat in a chair. He on the bed. This was not the first time in their lives they met in a hotel.

It would be their last. She was sure of it.

"What have you got for me, Santa?"

She patted the side pocket of her purse. "This. The files revealing the largest banking swindle in world history. Tens of billions stolen through pyramid schemes throughout five European countries. The trail connects politicians at the highest level in each nation to the scheme. And Moscow is behind it all."

Gunnar whistled. "So, why break the news here? Why not London? Or Brussels?"

"Because there's no European nation with less connection to Moscow presently than Iceland. And because Hekla Stefánsdóttir is or will soon be in Reykjavík. While the One World Press drop box is locked, it's the only way to get the information to her. I want to do it in person before her state hearing. Before the world puts handcuffs on OWP."

"Why not publish it traditionally? This could make your career."

"The information has to get out instantly to have affect. The double-checks of proper journalism work against us in this case."

He considered this a moment, crunched those faint eyebrows into a frown.

She did not give him a chance for more questions. "What I want from you, Gunnar, is the location of Hekla Stefánsdóttir before the hearing. Can you get it?"

"I can give you the place with eighty percent accuracy right now. What's in it for me?"

"I'll hand over a copy of information the day after Hekla Stefánsdóttir's hearing. If the government put the clamps on OWP, it becomes your scoop. You can publish any of it as you like, Gunnar. Let it make *your* career."

His eyes lighted at this.

"Is the stolen money retrievable?"

"I don't know, Gunnar. We know what was stolen, how it was moved, but not where it ultimately went. That remains to be discovered."

"How did you get this?"

Santa paused. She liked Gunnar. Had liked him too much at times in the past, until she found out about his wife and kids. She still more or less trusted him professionally, or at least as far as she did any other journalist. Still, as Gunnar omitted mentioning a wife all those years ago, she'd omit a few things of her own now. Turnabout was fair play.

"That's secret. For the present."

"But the evidence is solid?"

"Yeah." She leaned forward, elbows on her knees. "So, where is Hekla Stefánsdóttir?"

"The Daylight Press Corps and other similarly pro-OWP organizations have hired a private army of guards. Mums the word where they're stationed, but local eyes have seen several cars owned by security companies out at a private compound just beyond the Haukadalur geyser field. One hundred kilometers as a crow flies out of the capital, longer drive since the roads must avoid those geysers. They've been fiercely active since last year's tremors. When they go off, those steam clouds can make visibility too poor to drive for kilometers around."

"You think Stefánsdóttir's in residence? Already?"

"If she's in Iceland. I'd guess she's there. Too much traffic going in and out of the compound. But finding her isn't the problem, Santa. It'll be a major achievement if you can get them to admit that Stefánsdóttir is even present. They'll never let you actually see her."

Santa smiled wearily.

"Leave that to me, Gunnar."

He returned her smile. "When should we go?"

Go together? Why not? She could use an ally with poor Roberts Vanags off the radar. "Tomorrow morning. There's something I need to do today."

"I can save you a hotel bill. Bed's free here."

"Those days are over, Gunnar. Go home to the wife."

"Margret left me. Two years now. Sadly."

"I'm sorry. If not surprised."

"You won't believe it, Santa, but I did love her. Once. Such a pity."

She stepped towards the door. "Pity has little to do with it, Gunnar. But if it helps, I do believe you."

Hekla Stefánsdóttir did not feel comfortable at her compound one hundred kilometers outside of Reykjavík. The facilities were comfortable enough all right, with plush interiors rivaling the better hotels in the city. The windows, when she bothered to look out them, showed the same things in every direction: plains of ice that burned the vision on this sunny day. It was a beautiful, if repetitive vista, that brought serenity to many in her company. But Hekla was a woman of action, little used to delay. And her guards, a private army hired by sympathizers to One World Press, were unfamiliar in face and character to her. These mercenaries appeared appropriately deferential, of course, willing to do anything she asked. But their mere presence told of the dangers ahead.

Hekla had enemies of every political stripe worldwide. Those her organization had exposed. Those it might expose. Those opposed, on principle, to what she did. Even similar organizations to OWP which felt Hekla was a sell-out to whistleblower ideals for accepting any form of government regulation or felt her actions might set a precedent that would handcuff their own activities.

She was trying to legitimize OWP in the eyes of the world, to show what they did was the ultimate form of journalism, when nothing a public figure or political entity had done could be hidden from the righteous citizens of this planet. And for Hekla that most definitely included the former Soviet states which her rivals were always suspiciously hesitant to expose. Russia and its oligarchs would be under the same microscope as every other nation.

And it all started here at a hearing in a little country near the top of the world, a country that had already severed ties with Moscow for its position on gay rights, and for its aggression against Georgia and Ukraine. It was as good a place as any to make a stand.

These thoughts were interrupted by a lengthy, other-worldly hiss from outside. One glance outside told the story. The geysers of the Haukadalur Geothermal Field not far from the compound had erupted as they did regularly, steam clouds rolling over the plains, blotting out that bright sun, a white fog enveloping the world.

For a few moments, a pale darkness settled over everything. Hekla knew these clouds would soon dissipate. But while they lasted her little compound was truly cut off the world.

Surrounded by lawyers, advisors and armed guards, preparing for the world stage, Hekla felt impossibly alone.

Santa walked around the beautiful center of Reykjavík, following elegant Sklolavordustigur street up its slow slope to the majestic Hallgrímskirkja church. Though otherwise architecturally dissimilar, the seventy-meter tower that overlooked the city reminded her of St. Peters in Rīga. Both great churches after all were Lutheran. As were the peoples of their countries, generally. Maybe the Latvians and Icelanders weren't so different in their views and values . . .

Santa was not generally a religious woman, but even so, she wished to sit for a few hours in this great House of God. Whether from a desire to feel a genuine touch of the holy or simply the psychological security in this world, she hoped it might give her a serenity Santa could no longer find since they'd hacked Elviss Gulbis's Cloud account, raided IDB headquarters. She patted the pocket of her purse, as she did every few minutes to make sure that hard drive was still there.

Santa passed the great gray statue of Leif Erickson and entered Hallgrím-skirkja church through great bronze doors. The interior was a beautiful mini-malistic design, enormous, vaulted ceiling of tan basalt stone, the whole scene spartan yet undeniably powerful. Gabbing tourists walked about the margins of the church floor, looking at local art displays in the alcoves and antechambers, while the devout sat in the center on long wide pews, silent in prayer.

Santa took a seat on the first-row bench, and even here, in this holy place, she sat at an angle, so she could see the other pews and the entrance over her shoulder.

She felt that pocket again, reassured herself the hard drive was there.

If the information on this disk failed to get out, that great Ponzi scheme for Turaida Bank would bring about her homeland's destruction or, at the least, a loss of independence.

But what if she succeeded? There were risks then as well, nearly as dire. When this information was public, heads would roll in the Latvian government, people even more important than Dāvids Osis would fall. And the government may implode anyway. She may very well be risking her life for the same result either way. In fact, accelerating the chain of events that would lead to a third Russian occupation of her homeland. But at least this way *some* of the guilty would be punished.

Here in this Lutheran place, she said a prayer for Latvia.

When Gunnar Ingolfsson heard the knocking at his hotel door, he expected Santa Ezeriņa. He was dead wrong.

"Are you Mr. Ingolfsson?" said the tall, gray-eyed man in the doorway. He spoke English with a Russian accent, and tone of smoldering impatience. This visitor was dressed in a black ski jacket, dark tan pants, and mountain boots. He smelled of some sort of oily balsam that turned Gunnar's stomach.

"I am."

"Is Santa Ezeriņa present in this suite?" asked the stranger.

"No. Who are you? What do you want?"

"I want what she has given you."

"She's given me nothing. Good day." With considerable force, he began to shut the door . . .

The man shoved a booted foot into the crack, pulled a pistol fitted with a silencer from his pocket and shoved the muzzle between Gunnar's eyes.

"I'll confirm your words, Mr. Ingolfsson. If you don't mind. Now, on your knees . . . You may pray, if your gods have not abandoned you . . ."

53

Santa Ezeriņa drove her rented cherry-red Opel Mokka along the lonely highways of southern Iceland towards the compound where she hoped to find Hekla Stefánsdóttir in residence. Her mind, however, was not on that critically important meeting.

It was on the disappearance of Gunnar Ingolfsson. He'd simply vanished. Left the key in the room, checked out of his hotel by a remote app and gone missing. The editors at his paper hadn't heard from him, neither had his hostile-sounding ex-wife. Santa had been too long out of Gunnar's life to know whom else to contact. And twenty-four hours was not long enough to file a missing-persons report in Iceland.

She hoped he'd only gone on a bender as in the old days. And, if not, then maybe he was out here ahead of her trying to contact Stefánsdóttir, steal Santa's thunder and story. She could live with that possibility, much as it would annoy her.

But Santa couldn't help feeling certain something terrible had happened. Another disappearance on Turaida's watch. That they'd tracked her to this island country below the Arctic Circle, that despite her best efforts they'd found her, and that poor Gunnar may have paid the price for her appearance here.

The thought—and guilt—of it, made her dizzy, fed her desire to turn this rental car around and head back to Reykjavík, to find poor Gunnar or at least discover his fate.

But Hekla's address was two days away. And there was no time to be side-tracked. That's exactly what Turaida wished her to do . . .

So, she drove onwards, into the fading light of late afternoon.

Ahead, on her left, was the vast expanse of the Haukadalur Geothermal Field, its geysers, blowholes, and hot springs ignited by recent tremors, and releasing steam clouds that hovered over the landscape. The road took a detour around them, though even at this distance there was a slight haze in the air, obscuring full visibility.

Soon, through these mists a compound appeared before her, the low buildings and surrounding walls dark against the whiteness of the snow. On its margins stood a fenced-in car park, a mixture of expensive luxury cars and military-looking vehicles within.

It wasn't until she pulled up to the edge of that parking lot and exited her vehicle, that Santa saw other human beings. A small iron door in the compound wall opened, and two men in tan snow jackets and black trousers approached her. Both carried pistols at their hips, and corporate-looking insignias on their jacket breasts that Santa guessed were the marks of some-sort of private security firm.

They did not look friendly.

"Getum við hjálpað þér?" one asked, stopping about ten meters from her.

"Megum við tala ensku?" replied Santa, as she politely but firmly requested they turn the conversation to English.

"What do you want? This is private property. Please, leave the premises."

"I am here to see Hekla Stefánsdóttir."

The two men glanced at each other. Then the older guard shook his head. "No."

"I know she's here."

"Please, exit the premises. Or . . ."

"I'm a journalist," she interrupted. "Santa Ezeriņa of the *Baltic Beacon*. From Latvia. I'm carrying information that Ms. Stefánsdóttir will find of utmost interest."

"No. Let's go . . ."

"She'll require what I have before her speech at the *Althingi*."

"Go on." The guard pointed back towards her car.

"At least acknowledge Stefánsdóttir is here."

"Don't make us use force, Ms. Ezeriņa. Go!"

They walked her out to the Opel. Even when she was back inside her car, the two men did not relent. Santa hoped to sit in her driver's seat, gather her thoughts, make plans for a next step, but they would not allow her to tarry. The men stood at the windows, shooing her away, making more aggressive threats, until she ignited the engine and drove two hundred meters down the road. To the edge of those drifting mists . . .

What now?

Santa drummed her fingers on the dashboard. She'd break in, obviously. Little risk. No rent-a-cop would shoot her just for trespassing. If she somehow got to Hekla Stefánsdóttir, then she'd make her pitch. More likely she'd be captured and held until the police arrived. And while waiting for the cops out here someone was bound to tell Stefánsdóttir that a journalist had thought it worth being arrested just to talk to her. Knowing the reputation of the woman, she just might give Santa an audience.

Santa edged her Opel along a small, snow-covered path around the circumference of the compound, parked it near some sort of electrical transformer, this too, secured by a two-meter fence. She was scouting the perimeter, looking for a spot where she might surmount the wall, when another vehicle appeared from the gloom. It was a white, winterized Land Rover, engines gunning as it ploughed its way through the snow. She turned her field glasses towards this new arrival but could see little inside its darkly tinted windows.

Those guards at the compound had clearly called for backup.

Good. Come arrest me. Take me to Hekla . . .

Santa returned the field glasses back to the compound buildings. Was anyone watching from inside? Surely . . .

A light popping sound caught her ear. Then another. And another.

Gunfire.

Her first thought was that the Land Rover was shooting at her tires, Stefánsdóttir's security team trying to immobilize Santa's car in the snow.

Then the bullet came through the windshield. Centimeters from her head.

Through terror and shock, through clouding adrenaline, one thought remained in her brain, even as she threw the Opel into gear.

Who were these guys?

54

Santa gunned the engines, swung the car towards the path to the main road. But the Land Rover's driver was quicker, the bulky vehicle cutting off her route. Two more bullets flew through her windshield, the first throwing stuffing into the air as the passenger seat backrest erupted. The second shattered her windshield, glass flying everywhere, into her hair, cutting her face. The impossibly cold Icelandic air flowing in with it.

She floored the accelerator, wrestling with the wheel to turn sharply as possible. The Land Rover slid off to one side, her own car headed out into the open fields of tundra ahead.

Through her broken windshield she saw the mists hovering over the landscape. Could she somehow lose them in those geothermal fields? Wasn't there another road on the other side? A tourist information center for geyser watchers?

Another bullet entered somewhere in the rear of the Opel, passed through the cabin, to penetrate her dashboard. The engine's pitch changed in protest. The dashboard lights flickered, then went out.

As her car sped into the first tendrils of the drifting geyser fog, she became aware of a second car, a black Jeep, approaching over the ice. There was little doubt its intentions, by its reckless speed and closing path, it was headed directly for her. She veered, it veered.

And all the while the Rover closed from behind.

God, what'd she done in a past life to deserve this?

The gunfire stopped. Her pursuers not wasting their bullets as the mist thickened.

A geyser erupted directly ahead of her, a column of scolding steam straight up into the sky. She turned a hard right, the Land Rover re-opening fire as she passed across its field of fire. More bullets slammed into her hood, radiator steam shooting out of the fresh holes to mix with the natural vapors around her.

Santa just caught a glimpse of the Rover's gunman hanging out the window, some sort of automatic rifle in his hands.

Then that Jeep came flying by her, its driver firing a handgun out the window at her car. He should have kept both hands on the wheel on this icy field. Her car eclipsing the Jeep's view of the other pursuer, he was unable to avoid collision.

The Jeep slammed into the nose of the Land Rover, both cars spinning around on impact. The Rover's gunman thrown from the window, sliding across the ice. His body lay unmoving in the snow.

The two vehicles slid to a stop not far from each other. She heard Russian voices shouting.

Santa drove her little Opel away.

But she did not get far. The Jeep and Rover were barely out of sight in the mists behind, when her engine gave out, the Opel sputtering to a stop.

She too was marooned.

Santa sunk deep into the seat, tried to lose herself to reality. Just for a moment. But the cold flowing in through her broken windshield, the pain of the glass cuts on cheeks and forehead revived her. Forced away any respite for her situation.

She glanced at the mirror. Her pursuers were out of sight, though somewhere in these fogs, hunters were surely looking for her. She'd heard two Russian voices at the crash site, at least two enemies still out there.

Santa forced her freezing body out of the car, went around to the back, popped the trunk, cursed. This cheap rental didn't even have tire iron to use as a weapon.

She walked to the front, warmed herself by the billowing radiator. The car was dead. She was going nowhere in this thing. Her transport had become nothing but a bright cherry-red beacon to aid her enemies. Santa's instincts were to flee away from it as fast as she could.

But maybe there was another way.

Out somewhere in the fog she heard an engine stutter, stutter and start. One of those villains was moving again.

Santa stood in the snow a moment, solemnly closed her eyes, to block out the sounds of her pursuers' engine, to somehow focus . . .

Maybe the enemy would crash into one of these geysers, hot springs or mud pits.

Or maybe *she* could.

Her eyes opened. Santa returned to the car's interior, set the gear to neutral, then went around to push it from the rear. No easy task. She'd little solid footing on these icy plains, the wrong footwear for such a task. But the growing growls of those assassins' engines sent new shots of adrenaline through her. The Opel moved forward, slowly at first but quicker as the inertia grew. She could little steer it. But fortunately, the nearest depression was straight ahead.

Santa pushed quicker, harder, felt the wheels lose their traction, as the snow gave way to steaming mud. She barely kept her own footing. Then with a grunt that edged into a scream, she slammed her shoulder against the rear pushed it over until the car's end suddenly rose as the front fell forward. The whole vehicle plunged into the morass of a boiling, geothermal mud pit. Bubbles, steam spouts, and erupting air pockets spreading across its black-brown surface. The Opel sunk quickly, a hiss in the air as it went, before coming to a rest with only the rear window and bumper visible.

Maybe, her enemies would believe she'd crashed in there. Be too fearful of scalding water and its quicksand morass to go in to check for her body.

Maybe, she repeated the thought again to calm herself . . . Now to try and disappear into the mists. Make the roads or double-back to Hekla's compound . . . .

Santa backed away from the mud pit, trying to smooth out her tracks in the mud with her arms as she went, an undertaking with visibly mixed results. When back on solid ice, she turned her dark jacket inside out, the light lining a better exterior to camouflage her against the snow. Though it contrasted with the landscape, she had no choice but to keep her brown knit cap. A bare, shaven head would not last long in the Icelandic winter.

She pulled her phone from back pocket tried to Google the number for "Haukadalur police" but couldn't remember how to spell the damn field's name . . .

And people think Latvian has difficult spellings . . . .

The roar of an engine caught her ear. So focused had she been on camouflaging herself and the car, she hadn't noticed how loud that sound had become. But it was instantly obvious her enemies were near. The fog parted, and Santa saw the faintest silhouette of that black Jeep approaching. Hands trembling from fear more than cold she forced the phone into her back pocket and sprinted away at full speed.

But to where? Fatigue, emotional and physical, was taxing her strength. A despondency overwhelming thought. She could never outrun them, obviously.

And that engine was growing ever closer.

Sprinting blindly, Santa nearly tripped over a speed-bump sized ridge in the earth. She found herself on the lip of a great crater in the ice, the bottom of this bowl-shaped recess filled with more steaming, bubbling water. Easily, the largest geyser crater she'd ever seen. Likely the famous *Strokkur* or one on the same scale.

With nowhere else to go, Santa laid down within the inside lip of the crater, peered over its edge. Prayed this thing didn't erupt while she hid here.

That Jeep slowed to a stop forty meters from the mud pit containing her car. Two figures armed with what looked like Uzis exited. She heard Russian voices, too distant to understand. One pointed towards the Opel in the mud, the other with a posture of caution slowly approached the car in the quagmire.

Another distant geyser threw fresh steam into the air. The clouds around them grew thicker. It'd buy some time, obscure her tracks in mud and snow.

Maybe, just maybe. She'd get out of this . . .

The phone in Santa's back pocket began to buzz.

A beacon in the mist, the shadow men turned her way, readied their guns.

Fuck . . .

55

David Vanags lay in his hospital bed staring at the ceiling. His head wrapped in bandages, even under heavy medication there remained a perceptible ache where the Estonian doctors had stitched the pieces of his skull back together. He was lucky they told him; it could have been fatal. Should have been fatal. Even now he wasn't completely out of the woods, blood clots still a possibility . . .

What a lonely place to die. Kuressaare, Estonia. So far from home . . .

Without Dad. Without friends.

Without Beatrise . . .

He tried not think of her. It made his heart ache worse than any physical injury ever could. She'd tried to murder him, and all these Estonian and Latvian officials that attended his bedside during open hours claimed she was accusing David and his father of heinous crimes . . .

It seemed beyond belief. Made him almost wish he'd not survived that cliffside fall . . . Better to be dead . . .

He tried to roll over in his bed, the motion, the effort hurting him. On a table between the bed and the darkened windows, lay a cellphone. One given to him by a Latvian official who worked for his Christian namesake, Dāvids Osis. A direct line to and from the MP.

Osis had phoned him only an hour ago. Spoken in his usual overly elegant words:

Call me at any hour my boy. The sins of the father are not those of the son, David . . . We can assist you. Go home to America, just tell us what you know, where you've been . . . You're still a minor, yes? The argument you were coerced by an adult can still be used . . . If you help, it may reduce your father's penalty . . .

Screw him.

A tear in his eye, David tried to sink into the flimsy hospital. To disappear.

He missed his mother. She'd been gone too long.

David became aware of motion in the darkened room. A hospital orderly had pushed the door open just wide enough to slip in. As if he wished to enter the room as quickly and silently as possible. A step closer and the reason for the visitor's caution became obvious.

"Dad!"

His father pressed a finger to his own lips to hush David, moved to the side of his bed. This close, even in the dark, David could see his father's appearance had changed. He wore an orderly's coat, sported chin whiskers, had brushed his hair down in bangs over his eyes. He looked like a younger, careless man of thirty. Not the orderly banker of forty-one. His father reeked of sweat, his breath unpleasant.

But David was never happier to see anyone in his life. He'd take his dad in any state. Healthy. Alive.

"Son," he said in a whisper, gripping David's hand. "I'm sorry. They chased me away . . ." His father seemed at a loss for words. "What happened? A head injury, my God . . ." His voice cracked.

"I'll be fine, Dad." He tried to be strong, not to cry. "It'll just take a little longer . . . I can come with you if we need to go . . ."

"No. Stay . . . I'd need you to get healthy, listen to the doctors. Okay? Promise me . . ."

"Dad, Beatrise did this to me."

"I know. I'm sorry." He swallowed hard, turned silent, cocked an ear to the air. Someone walked past the door outside. When the passerby appeared gone, he said: "Beatrise tried to recruit others to do the same to me. She's a spy. For Turaida or someone that backs them . . ."

David pointed to the mobile. "Dad . . . Osis gave me that phone. He's been calling me."

"Unsurprising."

"I didn't tell them anything. About the island, about the journalist . . ."

"Have you heard from Santa?"

"No . . . not a word . . ." An old thought came to him then. "Dad . . . I may have made a big mistake . . ."

His father gripped his hand tighter. "David, you've done nothing wrong."

"I think I did. Bea . . . in bed, the night after we came back from the e-café . . . I told her that Santa would try again to reach her mother after she came back from Iceland . . . I heard you both talking about that at the café', Dad. Reykjavík, One World Press. I put two-and-two together, knew Santa was probably going to give the records to Hekla Stefánsdóttir. . . . I'm sorry . . . I told Bea everything, to assure her this would all be over in days, that she would see her family soon. I trusted her . . . I loved her . . ."

"Oh, David . . ."

"If Bea is a spy, they know, Dad. They know Santa's headed to Iceland."

His father glanced over to the Osis cellphone.

"Does that mobile have full coverage or only to Osis?"

"I don't know, Dad. I think it's just a regular cellphone. But it must be bugged . . ."

"I don't care." He seized the phone. "Turaida already knows she's there or going to be there. We need to alert her . . ."

"If it's a live bug, they'll hear your voice. Know you're in the hospital."

"It's my responsibility, David." He pulled his weathered wallet from his pocket, withdrew an old business card for Santa Ezeriņa, one he'd had since the Helmanis funeral, punched in her mobile number. "It's our fault she's in danger."

David sat up in bed, felt dizzy. "Then call from at least outside, give yourself a chance . . . ."

But the phone was already ringing, again and again without answer. David could hear the buzzing through the speaker at his father's ear, watch his face contort in frustration.

No response.

"Come on, Santa. Pick up," his dad said a desperation in his voice. "Where are you?"

56

Ruslan Kozlov turned his gray eyes away from the bullet-riddled Opel Mokka half-sunken in the mud pit before him and surveyed the mist clouds that surrounded them.

Out there, somewhere, a telephone was buzzing.

"It's coming from the geyser," said Ruslan's gunman, Vladimir. He gestured with his automatic, took a few cautious steps in the buzzing's direction.

Ruslan called him back.

"Stay near the Jeep, Vladi. The only way Ezeriņa can escape us is to steal our ride. I'll investigate this."

"As you say, Colonel."

She was *his* kill. Galina wouldn't win the wager yet. The Vanags boy had survived, and his father, her real target, was still at large.

Ruslan checked his weapon and advanced through the fog towards the geyser's crater, a huge convex divot in the earth, where the ice was replaced with steaming mud. At the center was a bubbling pool, here and there within the crater were smaller, relatively cool puddles left over from recent eruptions.

No sign of Ezeriņa.

That buzzing continued.

He stepped over the considerable lip at crater's edge, a ridge of mud built up by countless eruptions over eons, and headed down into the muddy center. Ruslan felt the warmth in the air and the pent-up geothermal power coursing through the earth below him. Even a man like Ruslan felt a touch of fear stalking these grounds. He avoided the steaming pools, circumnavigated the center to reach the other side. That buzzing grew louder with every step through the bubbling morass.

The Icelandic winds shifted; the eclipsing tendrils of steam momentarily parting. On the inside lip of the geyser crater he spied a smartphone lying flat atop the mud, the screen brightening with every buzz.

He looked about him cautiously, wary of a trap. Nothing triggered his instincts. Most likely Ezeriņa had dropped the phone in her flight and was now running over the tundra for the nearest road.

He'd run her down in their Jeep. Watch her skull pop under his wheels.

But the phone was useful evidence. It may help them find Vanags.

He picked it up. Clicked it on.

"Santa!" shouted an urgent American voice. "It's Robert Vanags."

"Vanags?!" seethed Ruslan.

"Who . . . who is this? Where's Santa Ezeriņa?"

That answer came suddenly. Ruslan felt the pain of impact, his body jostled forward, Uzi jarred loose as someone tackled him from behind. They fell, his torso plunging deep into the warm mud, his face submerged into one of those countless shallow pools. Her weight atop his spine instantly, her knees and hands forcing him down. He gasped, choked as the muddy water rushed into his lungs . . .

The bitch did everything right, pressing his elbows nearly together behind his back, pushing them upwards in a police hold, the motion forcing Ruslan's face deeper into the pool's muddy bottom, his chin scraping across the hard stone below. She had him locked, none of his strength, his masculine mass mattered now.

She'd been hiding behind the crest at geyser's edge. Or buried herself in the ridge's mud to lunge out when his back turned. That phone bait . . .

He kept his head. Went back to his training.

Yes, he was a fool but also lucky. This pool, a remnant of previous eruptions, was merely hot, not blistering. The only danger drowning. She couldn't move without releasing him. Vladimir must have heard the commotion, be rushing to his aid . . . The clock ticking for her too . . .

Flee, Ezeriņa. Run. It's your only chance . . .

He went limp. Played dead. Tempted her to let go.

When at last she moved, he was up in a minute, trying to clear his throat, gasping for breath in the steamy air.

Ezeriņa's back was to him as she plucked up his Uzi and sprinted away across the floor of the geyser pit.

He spied Vladimir running across the tundra towards them.

Ruslan tried to shout, to warn Vladi, but coughed up muddy water, only a gurgle from his lungs.

Ezeriņa flopped to her belly, took aim.

Fired.

Vladimir screamed. Collapsed.

Blood on the snow.

Though his limbs were weakened from his near drowning, Ruslan did not hesitate. Even as Ezeriņa murdered Vladi, he was darting across the pit and atop her not a quarter second after his comrade fell.

A savage kick to her back should have broken her spine, but somehow, she only screamed, maintained her grip on the gun. He seized the Uzi, his gloved hands over hers, pulled it up to him. Ezeriņa did not let go, rising with it.

They fought over the gun, standing in the geyser crater, the Uzi firing in the air, the heat of the muzzle burning each through thick, Arctic gloves.

The earth was shaking, steam blasts rising around both combatants now, scalding him, her. Ruslan risked pulling one hand away from the gun to pummel Ezeriņa across the face. But she would not let go, would not fall . . .

Why won't you die?

Instead, she rallied. Clamped her teeth down on his exposed ear below his cap, tore off part of the lobe, blood over his shoulder and neck.

He recoiled. She kicked him away.

Ruslan fell to the steaming earth.

But the gun landed near.

He was the faster warrior, his hand on the Uzi's handle. He had it up, aimed as Ezeriņa dove over the pit's edge to the tundra beyond.

The geyser erupted.

Fifteen thousand liters of scalding water eviscerated Ruslan Kozlov.

Hekla Stefánsdóttir stood just inside her compound's main gate, locked in conversation with her guard captain, demanding an explanation on the gunfire she'd heard outside not thirty minutes ago.

The captain said they'd sent men out to investigate. Found a Land Rover, bodies in the snow. The details just coming in . . .

Bodies . . . now . . . ? Hekla felt her stomach knot, insisted the captain call his men for an immediate update. He was scrambling to get a man on the horn when motion outside the compound caught everyone's attention.

A black Jeep was headed their way, speeding over the tundra to the edge of the car park. It showed no signs of slowing. Men on the roof readied their rifles. The guard captain told Hekla it'd be safest if she went inside.

Hekla ignored him, moved closer to the gate for a better view.

The Jeep at last came to a stop on the road thirty meters from them. Without pause, the door flew open and from the vehicle's interior emerged a muddy . . .

burnt,

bloody,

bald woman with a pronounced limp and hellfire in her eyes.

It was an otherworldly apparition. Some bizarre creature between a zombie and Valkyrie came to Hekla's mind. Only a murmur of recognition from two of her guards told her this *thing* was fully human.

The visitor shuffled closer to the edge of the gate. Then she silently unzipped her filthy jacket's pocket, reached inside . . .

The guards at the gate raised their guns, the men on the roof scrambled to the best angles for clearest shots.

Hekla ordered all weapons lowered. They obeyed. Reluctantly.

From her pocket the woman revealed a USB portable hard drive secured in a protective snow-proof casing and locked inside several clear plastic baggies. Through the gate's bars she offered it to Hekla.

"Ms. Stefánsdóttir," said the woman, hanging on the bars to keep herself up. "This is from Roberts Vanags, the American fugitive, the whistleblower, the so-called 'KGB Banker' of Rīga. It is the key to thirty-eight billion stolen dollars and Europe's future. I have killed and nearly been killed to deliver this information, Hekla," the woman groaned, pushing her offering deeper through the gate and into Hekla's gloved hands.

"And you damn well better publish every word . . ."

57

Somewhere past three A.M., Santa Ezeriņa sat on a pullout couch in that Icelandic compound waiting for someone, anyone, to tell her what was going on. Despite complete physical exhaustion, she could not sleep, her burns, bruises, and cuts making it agony to lie down. She could only sit and hold an ice bag to her swollen jaw, possibly broken when that last Russian thug had punched her. In her other hand, resting at her bent knee, she held a lighted cigarette between two fingers, letting the vapors rise to her nose, to breathe them. It frankly hurt too much even to lift the hand, to open her tortured lips and take a puff . . .

Santa laughed internally. Getting her tobacco fix off secondhand smoke, how pathetic. The glamorous world of international journalism, folks . . . beats the tabloids, right?

She needed to be in a hospital, this was obvious, but Santa refused to go anywhere outside this compound without an audience with Hekla Stefánsdóttir. Hekla and her guards had carried Santa in here from the gate, locked her inside with barely a word. Every hour someone came in with medical supplies, food, water, cigarettes . . . but no one said anything. Were they going to hand her over to the police? To someone worse? To Turaida? To the Russians?

Stefánsdóttir's reputation said 'no.' But time will tell.

Until then, the ice was getting low and only two cigarettes left . . . hard times . . .

A door opened.

The great Hekla Stefánsdóttir herself entered, a thick selection of print-outs in her hands. Santa inched painfully forward on the couch-bed, tried to rouse her strength, loosen up that jaw for talking.

She was without guards. A good sign, right?

"We expected you would be resting, but I saw the light on," said the older woman flatly. Santa couldn't quite read her expression. Adversarial? Sympathetic? Hekla must be an excellent poker player.

"As long as you didn't expect I'd died . . ." Santa smiled.

Hekla didn't. "The guards said your injuries looked superficial, not life threatening. But you should sleep . . ."

"We don't have much time for sleep, do we, Hekla?" She used the given name to show they were equals and potential friends. Santa wondered if the Icelandic woman understood the significance of such seemingly minor things . . .

"No, perhaps we don't." Hekla pulled up a wooden chair across from the couch-bed. Sat down. Her tone remained neutral. "There are two dead bodies out in the geothermal fields . . ."

"Three. Unless the geyser shot the third assassin into orbit."

Hekla didn't like this joke.

Santa pressed on. "Those killers were trying to prevent delivery of what I've given you, the Vanags hard drive, the International Devel—"

Hekla interrupted her. "We know what you've given us. We've been examining and verifying since the moment we obtained it. OWP wastes no time."

She sighed, her glare turning reproachful. "Violence seems to be a regular feature of your reporting, Ms. Ezeriņa. As we examined the materials, our own detectives found traces of blood on the envelope and agreement between the Latvian government and the International Development Bank. The protective packages you carried today were machine sealed airtight. Nothing can get in. This wasn't blood from your wounds. And it wasn't the blood of the men who assaulted you out in the geothermal fields. So, I ask you Ms. Ezeriņa, whose blood, was it?"

Santa's initial instinct, honed from all those years in the tabloids, was to lie. To claim she didn't know where the blood came from. Or that it was her own, from some paper cut made since obtaining the document. But she wanted to start anew with Hekla Stefánsdóttir. Santa respected her. Told the truth.

"To obtain those documents, I had to defend myself with a sharp letter-opener. Almost a knife, really. One of the IDB sources might have been cut slightly, but no harm done. She is uninjured."

"Will you reveal this source?"

"I can't."

Hekla set the envelope in her lap atop the printouts, crossed her arms. An aura of skepticism radiated from her that Santa didn't appreciate. "What's this all about, Ms. Ezeriņa?"

"To tell the short version this stolen money we're reporting is the first domino that will lead to the collapse of five former Soviet countries, invasion by Russia and war."

"Can you prove these assertions?"

"The money theft, yes. The war-related information was obtained strictly verbally. But I believe it."

"Then we can't use it. The whole reason I am standing in front of the *Althingi* is to show OWP a responsible organization. This is not your tabloid *The Baltic Beacon*. I cannot publish unsubstantiated hearsay. Whispers and possible lies have nothing to do with OWP. Especially now."

"At forty billion dollars stolen, the war starts, Hekla. Surely, this is worth passing on. An emergency alarm to Europe."

"You were told this too? By the same person you held at knife point?"

So much for truth.

"No."

Her lie was transparent. If the roles were reversed Santa herself would have walked out.

But Hekla was the calmer woman. "I'm sorry, I don't believe you. A confession under threat is coercion. It is inadmissible to the *Althingi*. We proceed with only what was obtained without violence, the evidence of the Vanags hard drive data." She shuffled through her printouts. "All this Latvian language . . . how many billions exactly have been stolen? Thirty-eight?"

"That may no longer be current. The losses grow daily."

The older woman frowned. Santa feared she'd reject this data too for some reason. The info too old. Too stolen. Some excuse to make it all for naught. Santa's stomach knotted.

They'd come so far.

Santa silently prayed. Pressed her point.

"You say One World Press is responsible, Hekla. Okay. You say they always verify. Fair enough. But you also claim it keeps the bad guys accountable. That to this policing end all actions are justifiable. And—"

"Not all actions, Ms. Ezeriņa. You think us monsters? We are not Big Brother. We are not Stalin. We are in principle the very opposite. We are libertarian to the core."

"The world needs to know. My people need to know. They've had enough invasions in their history."

Hekla said nothing, stared at the wall.

"What will you do?"

Her gaze returned to Santa. "Do? We do what must be done, Ms. Ezeriņa. We investigate. More quickly than anyone else is able. We have two days and a legion of the world's best hackers in our employ. We are well-armed. And your friend Vanags has shown us where to look."

Hekla smiled, and Santa saw a flash of the old anarchist who had shaken the globe's journalistic establishment to its foundations. The tension between them drained away. "Ben in Vilnius speaks highly of you. I trust *my* sources."

Thank God . . .

"These 'bad guys' won't know what hit them, Santa."

58

The young woman on the television with the teardrop tattoo spoke of kidnapping, rape, and attempted murder. The media was eating it up, hanging on every word. The story was all over the Baltics, by end of the day it'd been all over the world.

Yet, FBI attaché Jonathan Simms did not believe her.

"Beatrise Liepa is not who she says she is," whispered his assistant Suzannah Dublin, as she thumbed through the latest wires in a cramped meeting room at the FBI's regional sub-office within the U.S. Consulate at Tallinn. "I'd wager she's not even Latvian. At least not ethnically."

"Tell that to the Latvian government. They've a ceremony planned Thursday to give her the 'Three Star Award' and reunite her with her family."

"What family?"

"Exactly. Maybe actors, Suzannah. Though Dāvids Osis will be there to facilitate the reunion. He's real."

"Is he?" She snorted. "I'm beginning to have my doubts. . . ." Suzannah glanced down at her smartphone. "Roger's got the Kuressaare hospital film transferred."

"Put it on screen two."

The desktop screen on the wall's smart television was replaced with a black and white video of a hospital corridor. A timestamp read 18:54 yesterday. A fortyish male in boots, jeans, and a medical worker's coat walked briskly along the hall, stopping before a room labeled 112. He listened briefly against the pane before going inside.

"Well, there's our man himself. Bob Vanags," said Simms. "That his son's room?"

"Yep. Roger says he spent a little over twelve minutes in there, then scurried off through the South exit. Not seen since." She fast forwarded to Vanags's exit from the room, then paused it as he turned to retreat down the hall.

"How'd he get past the guard?"

"Let's say Estonian security is lax to say the least."

"Have Roger put a man of our own in that hallway." Simms rubbed his brow, leaned forward in the chair, stared pensively at the frozen image on the screen. "What's the boy say?"

"Estonian police are keeping mum on that as a courtesy to Latvian authorities. Someone gotta a call this morning from Member of Parliament Osis, we know that."

"No surprise there. The Vanags kid still conscious?"

"Yep."

Simms closed his eyes, let out a slow breath as if gathering his strength. At last, he stood, pulled his jacket from the back of the chair.

"Get down to Rīga, Suzannah. Try and beg the ambassador to tell the Latvian government to layoff the Estonian police."

"That'll never work."

"Just try. I'm going to the Kuressaare hospital. Let's see what David Vanags has to say in person."

"Think they'll let you see him?"

"Suzannah, you know what persuasive guy I am." He pulled on his jacket. "David's still an American citizen, fugitive or not. They'll let me see him. At least as long as he's in Estonia."

"So, you're a cop?" asked the boy from his hospital bed. Despite the bandages, the pale skin, and exhausted expression, David Vanags's voice was exceedingly strong. Simms could hear the skepticism in it. Well-earned, no doubt.

"I'm Jonathan Simms, FBI embassy legat for the Baltic Republics. I'm an American. Like you and your father. And I want to help."

"Go away."

Simms did not go away. Instead, he took a seat in a chair near the bed. "Look, David, we know your father was here. We've seen him on the hospital cameras." He paused and tried to take some of the edge off his voice. "We'd like you to help us find him."

"So, you can help the Latvian police arrest him? Like Osis?"

"Nothing like Osis. I want to protect him, David. And you."

"How so?"

Simms sighed. "There's a theory among some in my group that certain parties in the Latvian government are framing your father for things he didn't do. If you or he can help produce evidence to support that theory—conclusive evidence—then the American government may possibly intercede. Otherwise, we have to leave you in the hands of the foreign state that claims you broke its laws."

For the first time Simms saw a change in David's expression, the smallest spark in tired eyes. "What do you need to intercede?"

"I'll know it when I see it or hear it, David. But the best chance of getting that information is to talk to your father."

The spark died; David's countenance turned hard. "Bullshit. You're trying to trick me. Just like Osis." He tried to turn away from him in the bed, the effort clearly pained him. "I don't know where he is. Get lost."

Simms sat silent for several moments, then picked up the television remote from the beside stand. He turned on the signal, flipped channels until he found what he wanted.

A despondent-looking Beatrise Liepa was giving an interview on her ordeal, the closed captioning set to English.

He let David watch. Sadness, but no surprise, radiated from him. He felt for the boy.

Finally, Simms said: "You were seeing her?"

"Yeah."

"How long?"

"Awhile."

"Did you ever meet Beatrise's family? Or close friends? Did she ever give or show you something from her past?"

"Why?"

"She's accusing you and your father of terrible things."

Simms could see the rage building in the boy. First love betrayed? It seemed a fair guess.

"She pushed me off a cliff. I told the Estonian cops that. And the Latvian officials too. Why do I have to repeat it to you?"

"She claims it was necessary to escape the captivity you and her father held her in." He turned off the television. "I could be convinced to believe you instead of her, David. You up for helping me make that step? The more you tell me about Beatrise, the better."

The anger inside him broke. Like a dam giving way, tears rolled down his face. Poor kid.

"You'd be surprised how little I know."

"Actually, I wouldn't. If I had to guess, I'd say she's a Russian spy."

"A spy?"

"Being duped by a Russian agent. Kinda cool. Kinda James Bondish, David. How many boys your age back home can say that?"

The slightest of smile broke under those tears.

"Yeah."

Galina Kozlova sat in the passenger seat of the black Mercedes, her body and mind exhausted. She wanted only sleep. But Kārlis Pagrabs had wanted to meet. And one did not say 'no' to Kārlis. Not these days at least . . . .

"It was a good performance, Galina," said Pagrabs from the driver's seat." Every station in the Baltic is carrying your story. It'll be on Russia Today tomorrow."

"I shouldn't be here.

"You're not a criminal. You're an innocent victim of the Americans. You can leave the hotel to get spirits or cigarettes. Nothing amiss at that . . ." As Kārlis spoke, he fiddled with a leather kit bag in his lap, searching through it for something.

"They'll miss me. Someone might call the room."

"At two A.M.?"

She sighed. He was right. She was becoming paranoid. When would this ordeal be over?

Pagrabs found what he was apparently looking for in the bag. Opened a candy wrapper, popped a mint in his mouth.

"Mentos?"

"No."

He shrugged, went back to his rummaging. "As you wish."

"Did you give the message to my husband?"

"We have not heard from Ruslan since he arrived in Iceland. We have theories on why that might be, but I'm not at liberty to discuss them now."

"Even with his wife?" she asked tersely.

"Vovk's rules . . . But you will be reunited with your husband very soon."

"Good," she said softly. "What's our next step?"

He pulled a pair of gloves from the bag. They looked familiar, latex with odd fingertips affixed, like ones Ruslan had packed for a trip the last time she saw him . . .

"We must continue the media war, Galina," continued Pagrabs slipping on the gloves. "Locally, some parties are beginning to soften their position on Roberts's guilt. Fortunately, the hospital cameras prove he was on the island. We'll have him commit another crime. Something to horrify the public, yet again. To remind them what a monster the American is. To get the Estonian police fully on our side."

"What sort of a crime?"

"Another murder. Of a poor kidnapped girl who told the world her tragic story only today . . ."

59

The police found Beatrise Liepa's body stuffed into a dumpster in a carpark two hundred meters from her hotel. The cameras in the convenience store nearby indicated she was still alive at 1:49 A.M., purchasing cigarettes and whiskey. Cause of death, the Estonian authorities said, appeared to be strangulation.

Jonathan Simms used every ounce of American leverage, every personal favor owed to have his fingerprint man there with the Estonian forensics team.

The gamble paid off.

"It's a match, David."

The boy looked up from his hospital bed, eyes red, face puffy from crying, from living through agonies no one could possibly expect from a first love. He loved her, or at least thought he did, then she betrayed him, tried to murder him. Now she was dead. It was too much to process.

Simms admired David for even responding.

"What's a match?"

Simms waited until the nurse who had been changing David's bandages left the room. Then he leaned close to the boy and whispered: "Your father's fingerprints were found on both Beatrise's body and the dumpster."

"You say that like it's good news. He would never—"

"He didn't." Simms lifted his smartphone. On the screen was an image of prints sent directly from the lab.

"Do you see these, David? The imperfections in the prints?"

His frown deepened. "I don't understand . . ."

"Those spots occur in nature from dust, moisture, or just a place where the print didn't take." He swiped the phone's screen to another set of prints. "These were found on the gun that killed your cousin, Elvis Gulbis. The imperfections are in the same place."

"I . . . I see."

"Here are the prints taken at the Evgeny Markov murder. Another perfect match." He looked into David's eyes. "The odds of that occurring three times in the exact locations within the print is in the billions. It can't happen, David. Can't happen unless you have a silicon copy of someone's fingerprints. Little bubbles in the silicon cast would leave identical blank spots every time a print was left."

"A glove?"

"Exactly. Worn by an individual, or maybe individuals, at the murders of Gulbis, Markov, and now Beatrise Liepa . . . Someone trying to pin it on your father. Someone who didn't expect the authorities to look too closely. Possibly because they were in close with those authorities."

"You're a good detective."

"I can't take much credit for this."

Simms put his free hand on David's shoulder. "David this is reasonable enough for the FBI, the embassy, to take action. If we can find your father, we'll try and protect him. What do you say?"

He was silent for an exceedingly long time, eyes starting at the wall, through it to places unknown.

"David?"

"Is this a trick?"

Simms felt his stomach twist into knots. "What?"

"A trick. Maybe, you're faking all this to get me to speak? To find my dad and arrest him?"

"David . . . no . . ."

"How do I know? Everyone's been lying to us since I came to Europe. Turaida Bank, the government, Elvis, Bea, even Dad. How do I know?"

Simms stared at David a moment, then desperate, he glanced about the room. Seized the Estonian-language Bible, *Piibel,* from a corner shelf. He couldn't read a word, but it would do.

He held it out in front on him. "I'll swear on this. Would it satisfy you?"

David frowned. "I'm not . . . not really religious . . ."

"Then what, David? What can I swear on to convince you? To make you understand? My passport? The American flag? Photos of my children? What?"

"Give me a minute . . . I need to think . . ."

"We don't have a minute, David. Every minute forces that have killed three people—at least—are getting closer to your dad. I'm your only chance of seeing him alive again. And that is the absolute truth. I promise you."

60

The speech had gone well for Hekla Stefánsdóttir. For nearly forty minutes she outlined to the Icelandic parliament and beyond through the television cameras and live online feeds, to the entire planet, how One World Press was a benefit to mankind. The next evolution in journalism, a responsible entity that ensured fairness and accountability to all. While applause was rare, there had been few protests outside the *Alþingishúsið* hall, and fewer interruptions inside, even the most conservative of the sixty-three members of the *Althingi* listening respectfully.

She had made her case for legitimacy.

Now it was time to close the deal.

Hekla glanced at the hall's clock. Noted the hour.

"Speaker Sigfússon, esteemed members of the *Althingi*, ladies and gentle-men in the gallery, watchers around the globe, some of you will remember the case of the American Robert Vanags, who attempted to expose corruption in Rīga last November. He claimed a staggering thirty-eight billion dollars had been stolen by the Turaida Group throughout Eastern Europe. He implicated the International Development Bank of Frankfurt, at times a friend of Iceland's, in the scandal as well. It made headlines worldwide. But his evidence, handed over to the Latvian government, never materialized. Then the man vanished." Hekla paused, glanced at the clock one final time. "One World Press has retrieved that evidence in its entirety. Proving Mr. Vanags's assertion unequivocally true and the Latvian government's claims utterly false. We will release all this evidence on the One World Press website at the top of the hour."

A growing buzz filled the chamber.

She continued. "Given the Latvian government's denial that this evidence existed, we must seriously call into question the crimes alleged by that same government against Mr. Vanags and his family. One World Press insists upon an impartial multinational investigation into the accusations against Mr. Vanags and beseeches the United States government to protect its citizen from harm until that investigation is complete."

Hekla paused. Surveyed the crowd before continuing.

"What's more, One World Press, at its own expense, has employed the best computer experts in the world to retrieve updated information. Since late November when Mr. Vanags reported the thirty-eight billion stolen, another eight hundred million dollars has been embezzled from these corrupt banks. This too will be published on our website within the hour. The most up-to-date journalism in the world."

"We can make a difference together, ladies and gentlemen. This is a new world, with new technology and new rules. Transparency, accountability and swift action are our hallmarks. One World Press has spent the last two days in an information exchange with the European Central Bank. Their agents are acting as we speak to retrieve the billions stolen before it can be moved. It is happening, my friends. OWP will ensure the corrupt have nowhere to hide . . . We ask for no thanks; it is our job. It is our calling . . ."

61

Suzannah Dublin, the assistant FBI legat to the Baltic region sat in an office at the U.S. embassy in Rīga, listening to the ringing of an outgoing call on the speaker phone on the table beside her. While waiting for Jonathan Simms to pick up, Suzannah's eyes wandered to the glass partition that bisected the room. Against the opposite wall sat a very distressed, very well-dressed woman, clutching her purse like it was a life buoy. In some ways, Suzannah thought, it might have been.

The call picked up at last.

"Simms," said Suzannah, "There's another Latvian beauty here who wants to see you. What'd you do to be so popular with the ladies?"

"Is it Santa Ezeriņa?"

"No. This is a blonde named Agnese Avena. Says she needs to speak to you."

Suzannah heard the annoyance in his voice. She was only doing her job.

"Did you tell her I'm busy in Estonia, Suzannah?"

"She said it concerns the Turaida Bank scandal."

Simms sighed. "Do you think she's credible?"

"Can't say. You're the expert on that these days. But, if I were your Effie Perine, you'd see her, Bogie. Trust me."

"Get her in here. Let's give her five minutes."

Suzannah motioned for the guard to show Agnese Avena in. She walked slowly inside, carrying that bag pressed against her breast, then took a seat at the table across from Suzannah.

"He's on speaker phone, Ms. Avena," Suzannah said flatly.

The Latvian woman sneered. "Doesn't the U.S. government have Facetime?"

Simms voice rose through the speaker. Terse and impatient.

"What do you need Ms. Avena?"

The woman released a slow breath and some of her composure seemed to return.

"I am a senior executive for the International Development Bank of Frankfurt, Mr. Simms. And I am a criminal."

She paused, apparently to let that sink in. "One of many criminals at my organization. Not the chief, but the . . . catalyst, I'd say. We have used the Turaida Group as a conduit to steal billions for ourselves and our friends. Now, that the Vanags info has come to light, heads will roll including mine. I offer full disclosure of what I've done and what I know in exchange for leniency and protection."

"Why go to us?" asked Simms through the speaker. "Have you broken any U.S. laws?"

"The International Development Bank is funded by U.S. and EU taxpayers. We have defrauded them too. Take me to America, arrest me there, hide me in your witness protection program . . ."

"It is not that simple, Ms. Avena," said Suzannah. "And we don't have the authority to make deals for the Witness Security Program."

The desperation returned in the visitor's demeanor. "Well, then at least imprison me in the U.S.A. Or put me before Congress. In America, I have a chance. If I stay in Europe, I'll be murdered. They have already tried once." Her eyes were turning puffy, tearful. "I have everything you need. Starting with these . . ." She plucked a thick folder from the purse in her lap. "These are the documents One World Press will not publish, Mr. Simms, likely because their source seized them by force. Well, I give them to you, to the FBI, to the European Central Bank regulators, to the world, by my own free choice. These and much, much more. Everything I know. Embezzlement. Influence peddling. Murder. Extortion."

She tossed the folder on the table, the contents spilling across the table-face. Document after document on International Development Bank letterhead.

"Now, God damn you, just protect me and the child I'm carrying."

62

In the late dawn of winter, Bob Vanags walked through the car park outside the Kuressaare hospital. He'd wanted to visit David again while it was still dark, arriving near the end of the hospital night shift when all inside were sleepy, exhausted, less alert. But it had taken Bob longer than expected to slip from the woods he now haunted into the town of Kuressaare. Police were everywhere, and more than once he'd been forced to hide, to sit in the shadows and wait for the threat to pass and the comparative safety to return. His anxiousness growing with every delay to see his injured son.

Torture.

As he neared the hospital's entrance, Bob buttoned the orderly coat he'd stolen on a previous visit. Wrinkles covered its exterior, a small coffee stain at one cuff, but it had more-or-less stayed clean tucked inside his winter jacket for three days living in the woods. As long as no hospital staff did a double take at a slightly slovenly, unshaven orderly, he had a good chance of reaching David's room.

Ahead of Bob, just outside the hospital entrance, a security guard stood. This was a new development. The previous guard was an old man, stationed in the interior, one easily avoided if you were dressed as hospital staff.

Bob paused, unsure if he should seek another option.

A green Nissan SUV drove up, cutting Bob off from the entrance, another white SUV right behind it. Out of the first vehicle sprung two figures, a muscular black man and a petite fierce-looking woman, both dressed in gray jumpsuits and black caps.

The man seized Bob in an instant, the woman handcuffing him before he could even resist.

"Inside, Mr. Vanags," said the man in an American accent, forcing him up into the door of the green SUV. Another man, well-dressed and in his late thirties, waited inside the vehicle.

"Easy does it, Robert," he said.

Bob resisted but was pushed inside. The doors closed behind. His assail-
ants climbed into the SUV behind, leaving Bob alone with the man in the suit,
and a driver up front.

The SUV peeled out of the car park and onto the road.

"I must see, David," said Bob. "Let me talk to him before you incarcerate
me."

The man gave a wry smile. "David told us you were coming, Robert."

"What?" *He would never* . . . "What did you do to him? If you hurt my
boy—"

"David is fine. We've done nothing. You will see him in a matter of hours,
Robert. We moved your son to Rīga last night by special car. Stay calm. All will
be explained."

He withdrew a key from his breast pocket, unlocked Bob's handcuffs. "I'm
Jonathan Simms, the FBI legat within the Baltic Republics. These cuffs were
just a show for any Estonian witnesses. Politics, you see."

He threw the handcuffs to the floor.

"We have much to talk about, Robert."

63

As their car sped across the Väinatamm Causeway connecting the Estonian islands of Saaremaa and Muhu and then over the winter ice road to the European mainland, FBI Attaché' Jonathan Simms explained to Roberts Vanags about fake fingerprints, the billion-to-one odds he was guilty, and America's prerogative to interfere under such circumstances.

Vanags, Simms thought, displayed appropriate relief at the welcome news but also parental concern.

Simms appreciated that. He had two kids of his own, back home in Raleigh.

"Beatrise is dead?" asked Vanags, stunned. "Does David know?"

"Yes. The boy's torn up," answered Simms softly. "He needs his father."

"I haven't been there for him."

"Where exactly *have* you been?"

"Some sort of park at first, near the Kaali meteor lake, then huddled with hobos for warmth under a bridge outside Kuressaare. Trying to survive the winter yet stay within reach of David." He sighed, looked through the window at the icy landscape whizzing by. "Not my finest moment . . ."

"Not so quick . . . your finest moment may have happened without your knowledge, Robert. Did you have internet access, see the papers, television, yesterday?"

Vanags shook his head no.

"One World Press released hundreds of Turaida Bank records they say they got from you. The data matches exactly what you alleged in November, what MP Osis claimed was fake, what he said were lies on a phantom hard drive that never existed."

"It's all out . . . Santa succeeded?"

Santa Ezeriņa, it made sense she was involved in the delivery.

"Those lies are another reason not to trust Osis and his cronies in the Latvian government, Robert. And another point in your favor. Covering up the theft of billions is a good reason to frame a potential whistleblower with murder. Now, you've got physical evidence *and* a genuine enemy motive on your side of the ledger. It's why the ambassador gave me permission to do what I'm doing. You and David will have sanctuary in the embassy, on American territory where no one can touch you until this is all sorted out."

"Can't you just fly us home?"

"The government would seize you in customs. And we need you here for the moment. It's all I can do to keep you secure on embassy grounds."

"I'm grateful," he said softly.

"Don't be. It's my job. And we're both Americans over here . . . There is more, Robert . . . or Bob. Can I call you, Bob?"

"Bob's, okay."

"Well, Bob, I'm told Agnese Avena of International Development Bank is handing over additional documents on the scandal. She's after a plea, protection, something's got her scared. Avena wants a first-class ticket to anonymity. Deal's likely not gonna happen, but what she's given us already is filling in the gaps from what you and One World Press brought to light. Osis, Turaida, her bank, Ukrainian oligarchs, Moscow elite, factions of the Latvian government, all involved."

"It seems impossible . . ."

"Bob . . ." Simms put a hand on Vanags shoulder. "You've done more than you know and suffered more than anyone should. I'm gonna ask one more favor. If you say 'no' we'll head straight to the embassy in Rīga. You've my word. But I need a little more . . . I want us to make a pit stop first."

"Where?"

"The European Central Bank is making a raid on Turaida headquarters right now, seizing evidence—those billions are still missing, and a lot of economies are gonna fail if they're not found. Washington and Brussels are threatening to expel Latvia from NATO and the EU if they don't back off and let the ECB's special agents do their job. The order of magnitude is unprecedented. The ECB asked for me to take you to Turaida Rīga if we apprehended you today. Can you show their agents, step-by-step, computer-by computer where you got your evidence originally?"

"Into the devil's den. They won't like me there."

"It's all about strengthening the ECB case. Can you handle a few hostile glares from old co-workers?"

"So, then, take me to Turaida Bank. Can I bring a wrecking ball?"

"Bob, you *are* the wrecking ball . . ."

* * *

Bob Vanags never thought he'd walk through those doors again. Never ascend to that second floor where he'd discovered Turaida's crimes nearly two months ago. Yet here he was. Walking down the familiar hallways, passing Evgeny Markov's old desk . . .

Emotions welled up inside. It was for people like poor Evgeny that he endured the hostile glances, terse remarks from the moment he'd walked through Turaida's lobby. After trying to kill him and his son, to frame them, to slander him, what were a few more insults? Bob had become a harder man, immune to anything they might say or do.

He was done with fear.

Everywhere, Turaida employees were standing back from their desks, told by the agents of the European Central Bank to move away from their computers, to touch not a file or drawer. Not even pick up a phone. In groups Turaida employees were being marched down to the lobby, where they waited for ECB permission to retrieve their things. Bob hadn't seen a policeman inside—a lucky thing as he may still be a public fugitive. Simms hadn't made that distinction perfectly clear.

Maybe, the ECB knew to keep the authorities at bay, to let them do their work, and collect their things. The corrupt local police force barred by Brussels, Frankfurt, and covertly Washington, from entering the building. Operations seemed to be going smoothly. Bob showed the ECB agents his old office, the computer room where he'd first obtained the *Roze* files. It took less than five minutes, seemed little worth the effort. He sat in his old office, while Jonathan Simms stood nearby locked in conversation with two agents dressed in black suits wearing dark shades. Like two *Matrix* 'Agent Smiths" with German accents. Agent Schmidts, really . . .

A statuesque redhead appeared in the office doorway. Terēze Ābele. Their eyes locked and she marched into the room with a look of one prepared to go to war.

"That's not your chair any longer, Roberts. Get up and get out. These agents can't stop me from calling the police."

Bob glanced at Simms. He shrugged, didn't look overly worried.

Bob remained in his seat.

"Have you been sleeping outdoors?" Terēze tried her old intimidating stare. "You're filthy, Roberts."

"And you're a criminal, Terēze. But unlike you, I can wash myself clean."

Judging by her reddening face Terēze was about to say something truly terrible when one of the agents interrupted.

"Mrs. Ābele," he said in thick English. "We would like access to the top floor."

"There's nothing up there but empty offices. The floors relevant to your slanderous assertions are on the second and third levels."

"We're told, security is up there . . . Please, Mrs. Ābele. Comply."

Terēze's face was nearly as red as her hair. "Security is on the ground floor. They've been cooperating with you since the moment you arrived this morning. I've made sure of it."

Bob laughed. "The ground floor security is a sham. Everyone knows the real security is on the fourth floor, gentlemen. Make her take you up there. Especially to the secret room on the south-west corner where all the exterior wires run. The one with a private satellite dish."

"Comply, Mrs. Ābele," said the agent.

She was silent a very long time but at last relented. It was an odd sort of surrender for a normally steely woman. Bob noticed tears welling in her eyes.

"Then, let's go," Terēze whispered. Bob read her lips more than heard the sounds.

"You as well, Mr. Vanags, said the more senior agent. "We'd like you to identify the room you mean."

"Happy to," answered Bob.

"I'd better go too," said Simms. "You're technically still in my charge."

"The more the merrier."

Terēze lead them to the elevator, stood outside the door, allowing the two agents, Simms, and finally Bob to enter first. As they passed, she slipped a key from her chain, tried to hand it to an occupant of the elevator.

It seemed to Bob anyone would do.

"This will take you to the fourth floor," she said tersely.

"Aren't you going" asked Simms.

"You must go," insisted one of the agents taking her key and activating the button for the top of Turaida headquarters. "Board now, Mrs. Ābele. We've been given full emergency authority by your government to arrest—"

"I've something to do in the town," interrupted Terēze stepping back. "I—"

"Get in here," shouted Bob. He grabbed her around the waist and pulled Terēze inside. The doors closed.

Her eyes went wide as the moon.

"Stop it. Stop this elevator." Terēze pounded on the doors, kicked them, tried to hit the emergency stop but Bob prevented her. The elevator rose.

"What is going on, Terēze?" he asked.

No clear answers came from her lips. Only sobs. Terēze was in hysterics and by the third floor she shouted "Wires Roberts. You think all those wires are for communications?"

"Tell me!"

As an agent reached to press the stop. But it was too late. The lift was nearly at the top. Terēze sank to her knees, mumbled softly in a child's voice as if resigned to her fate:

"Pagrabs is up here, Roberts. One step off the elevator and he'll blow the whole building . . ."

64

As the elevator rose, Kārlis Pagrabs awaited his own self-inflicted destruction.

He did not view it as suicide. He was a happy man, generally, but the ECB's appearance meant the fourth story was off limits. Their regulators could not be allowed to seize records, carry off computers as on other floors. The crimes of Terēze Ābele and her staff were insignificant compared to his. Clever investigator software could still trace account numbers on wiped hard drives. When billions were missing, every program on Earth would be used to retrieve the data. It *would* be found. The only way to be secure was destruction. He'd obliterate this level, and likely by collateral damage, the whole building.

Too bad for Turaida's employees. But the fewer left alive the better . . .

Kārlis's family would be well-compensated, have choice lives when the old borders were restored. When Rīga was again the best port in Russia, he might have a statue erected in Esplanāde park, be remembered as a hero. A modern Jēkabs Peterss . . .

Such thoughts were fleeting. Kārlis was always a man of the moment even last moments. He savored these final breaths as his monitor showed the elevator rising past the third floor. Their defenses were really quite clever once he'd turned off the fail-safes. The key inserted and turned by the ECB agent was the primer, metal extenders atop the elevator would complete the circuit when it reached this floor. A circuit that would set off the five tons of explosives housed in the roofing.

He glanced to the other monitor, a camera image of the interior of the elevator car. Terēze was on her knees sobbing. She knew her fate. But the men did not believe her. Why would they when they all knew her a liar?

Not two seconds more . . . .

Goodbye, Ita. Tell Pavels of his father . . .

Vanags pressed 'stop.' The car congested, Kārlis wasn't quite sure what he'd seen. Had Vanags really . . . He glanced to the second monitor. The car sat unmoving between floors three and four.

They'd believed Terēze? What was she telling them? The electric doomsday charge interfered with lift microphones; he could barely hear anything . . .

Kārlis cursed. It was merely a reprieve. When the elevator restarted, the car would automatically complete its route, rise and trigger the bombs . . . No matter how many times the passengers pressed buttons for lower floors, it was all in vain . . .

The four men forced the elevators doors open. The floor of the fourth story at their shoulders, the ECB agents climbed out onto this level. Terēze fought to climb down to the lower floor, but Vanags dragged her up with him to join the ECB men. Only the FBI legat tarried, drawing a pistol from inside his jacket, he fired the gun into the elevator panel, shot-after-shot until it was unusable, shattered metal in smoking ruins.

Then he climbed up to join the others on Kārlis's floor.

Shit.

Kārlis kept his head, knew he had only seconds to react. They were headed down his hall, no easy way to get past them and ignite the explosives manually. He was trapped like a rat in this corner office, only an electromagnetically locked steel door to keep his enemies at bay.

But there were alternatives . . .

Kārlis flipped the switch for his door's defenses, set the pulse box to disrupt all WIFI and cellphones. Then he rummaged through a box on a nearby shelf, found what he needed: a pair of cables with metal clamps on each end, like two-meter-long automobile jumper cables. Hardly high tech but they'd suffice to take us all to oblivion . . .

Wrapping the twin cables around his shoulder, Kārlis checked that his Beretta pistol was secure in his pocket, opened the gate in the barred window and stepped onto the narrow ledge outside. Carefully, hands against the cold roofing, and feet slowly shuffling forward, he made his way around the corner of the building.

Below on the street, protestors screamed, chanted against Turaida, their masses held back by military-police barricades around the bank.

Let them shout, they'll all be running for cover when I blow this building to Hell . . .

Kārlis inched along the route, his body trembling in the cold of the season. Ahead was the only other unbarred window at this level, the window of nominal president Baiba Lāce, a figurehead seldom here.

Trying not to topple backwards to his death, Kārlis withdrew his Beretta, smashed the gun's butt against the window glass, watched spiderweb cracks spread across the pane . . .

***

Bob Vanags and the others approached the door to the corner office. It was an imposing green steel panel that looked like it belonged on a battleship somewhere . . .

"Is that it?" He shook Terēze. "Is this the door?"

"Yes," she spat.

"Only one way in or out?"

"I think so."

"Don't think, know Terēze!"

"This is Jonathan Simms of the American embassy," said Simms into his cell. "Send a bomb squad to Turaida Bank headquarters immediately . . . A credible bomb threat . . . I said a credible threat . . . damn, I don't think they can hear me . . . Hello? Hello?" He looked to Bob. "Jesus, 'Top of the world, ma.' We're on our own."

The older ECB agent touched the lever on the iron door. He screamed. Collapsed. A whiff of ozone in the air.

"The lever's electrified," said Bob. "Whole damn door, probably."

The poor man trembled in fits at the base of the door. By the time they pulled him back, a yellow foam was rising up over his lips.

"Fuck, a seizure . . ." said Simms, kneeling to the man's side. "Gimme space, I know CPR." He motioned to the ECB agent. "Come on, fella . . . We gotta keep his throat clear."

Under the distraction of a dying man, it was seconds before Bob noticed Terēze Ābele was gone. He turned, caught a glimpse of her fleeing body, before she disappeared around the corner, down the hall towards the elevator.

Unable to help the others, Bob chased after her.

In high heels, Terēze was a slow, easy target. Bob tackled her midway through the hallway, their bodies crashing hard to the floor. In hysterics, she kicked at him . . . He took her blows, fought to subdue her . . .

"God, I'm trying to save you, Terēze—"

The crash of breaking glass somewhere. Bob raised his eyes.

From one of the presidential offices, Kārlis Pagrabs came rushing into the hallway, gun in hand . . .

65

Bob Vanags was lucky.

Lucky that Kārlis Pagrabs was brushing glass from his face.

Lucky that the man's inertia had taken him into the hallway with his back to them.

Lucky that Terēze seemed to fear this man intensely, becoming instantly silent at his appearance.

But enough of luck . . .

Bob watched Pagrabs sprint down the hallway towards the elevator without a glance in their direction. Bob released Terēze, followed the man stealthily, ducking into doorways, moving as quickly as he could without sound.

Pagrabs reached the elevator, climbed onto its roof. Bob couldn't quite see what he was doing in the shaft's darkness, unwinding something coiled about his shoulders . . . .

Gun or not, that didn't look like something he wanted to allow . . .

Bob said a prayer for David. Then quickened his pace, charged down the hall, leaped to the elevator's top. Slammed his shoulder into Pagrabs's back, the bald man grunting, falling forward to a knee, turning his hateful gaze towards Bob.

Bob was lucky again, Pagrabs had tucked his gun into his trousers to do his work, something resembling a short jumper cable now in his hand. Another such cable ran from the cab's roof to an electrical nub on the shaft's ceiling.

A free nub nearby waited. Bob put two-and-two together.

Yeah, that ain't happening.

He socked Pagrabs in the face. Stunned him. Closed their distance, kept Pagrabs from drawing the gun. Bob shoved Pagrabs, tried to force him off the top, back between the car and shaft wall, send him falling . . .

But his opponent had some sort of military training, used his weight against him, slipped aside, sent Bob to the edge of the abyss . . .

Terēze was on the car roof now, pounding on Pagrabs's shoulder blades, screaming "I don't want to die!" An elbow from Pagrabs sent her toppling back down to the hallway floor.

The shouts of Simms and the ECB agent approaching. The cavalry on its way.

In that instant, Pagrabs threw his weight against Bob.

Bob fell. Slipping down the shaft wall, past the car into the free air below. Doom.

But Bob refused to die. Caught the trailing chain line from the elevator's bottom, wrapped about his arm, hanging free in the darkness below the car.

My God, why did I take this job?

When he realized he was not dead, that for the moment he would not plummet further, Bob willed his galloping heartbeat to slow, tried to push the thundering pulse from his temple, let his mind clear, his senses return . . .

In his free hand was the jumper cable torn from Pagrabs's grip at the last moment. Somehow.

He set it between his teeth, put the other hand on the line to secure his position.

"Give me that cable," came a voice from above. Pagrabs had forced himself down the gap too, pressing his back against the car, boots against the shaft wall. Descending towards him like a chimney sweep in days of old.

One hand free, another pointing his gun at Bob.

Bob did nothing. Let Pagrabs descend precariously to the very bottom of the car, as close as he dared.

The security man extended his free hand, kept the gun two feet above Bob's head.

"Give me the cable or you're dead, Vanags."

Bob laughed internally. The irony . . .

He was dead either way.

Bob curled his lips into a smile of contempt and spat out the jumper cable. Let it fall. Enjoyed the horror on Pagrabs's face.

Instinctively, his opponent reached out. In that instant, Bob risked all. He took a hand from the line, grabbed Pagrabs's arm, tugged.

They both plummeted into darkness.

Yet Bob knew the line beside him, regained his grip, the chain swinging his body hard against the shaft wall.

Pagrabs was not so lucky. He fell, gun firing. The bullets whizzed by Bob to lodge in the elevator's bottom, into the wall, kept coming until a heavy thud at shaft's bottom turned everything silent.

Bob hung in the darkness,

Swaying.

Slowing.

Still.

It seemed like eons.

At last, a door opened on the second floor. Somehow Simms had gotten back down to that level. A mass of Turaida employees stood behind him, staring.

"Jesus, you bankers live exciting lives," said Simms. "Puts the FBI to shame . . ."

He extended a hand to Bob, pulled him inside.

66

Leonid Vovk shut off his phone, glared forward from the back of his limousine at his chauffer.

"They've arrested Terēze Ābele. Kārlis Pagrabs is dead, Denis."

"I'm sorry to hear that, sir. But some deaths were expected if things went sour? Weren't they?"

Vovk seethed. He didn't appreciate the patronizing tone in a servant, even one as old as Denis. He was a bit too familiar these days.

"Ābele, yes, but I thought Pagrabs would be smarter. He let them have everything . . ."

"You will think of something, sir. What does Moscow say?"

He glared at his driver. "That's private, Denis."

"Of course, sir. Excuse me."

Vovk glanced out the window, tried to think of the next course of action. The authorities worldwide were seizing bank accounts, retrieving billions given out by Turaida through that bitch Avena. He'd personally lost hundreds of millions, several of his oligarch friends lost more . . .

One wonders what the Scorpion himself had lost. If he'd answered Denis's question honestly, the fact is Moscow had said nothing. His old Stalingrad friend failing to take Vovk's calls. He'd have to go to Russia himself, make amends. After all, it was he who'd been tasked with solving the problem of Robert Vanags. Avena too. Instead, they'd revealed the game to the world.

The former Soviet republics that had been absorbed by the West were stabilizing, those authorities sympathetic to Moscow being toppled one-by-one as word of the scandal got out. That fool Osis was trying to save his own skin, naming names as Avena had before him.

The Scorpion would have to terminate those loose tongues. He wondered who'd be first . . . .

The limousine slowed.

"There's an obstruction ahead, sir."

Vovk leaned forward, gazing from the back, over his driver's shoulder, through the front window. A barrier of burning logs blocked the road.

It frankly looked like the sort of thing the Kremlin-backed rebels did . . . but they were far from here . . .

"Can't you go around it, Denis?"

"I'll check, sir."

Denis exited the limousine. Vovk, sat back in his seat. Well, no pro-Russian militants would harm him, the vehicle was well-marked. All allies in the big picture . . .

Still, mistakes could be made. He didn't feel safe.

Cursing, Vovk stepped out of the limousine. Found his driver standing off to the side engaged in conversation with two men in camouflaged, insignia-less combat fatigues. Three more stood in the weeds, machine guns raised.

Denis pointed at him.

The men fired.

It was the last sight of Leonid Vovk's life.

Santa Ezeriņa sat in One World Press's Oslo office, across from Hekla Stefánsdóttir. Near them sat three lawyers. One German, two American. The conversation was not going well.

"It is your choice, of course, Santa," said Hekla with that familiar poker face. "OWP can acknowledge you as a source, as you desire. Or we can completely attribute the whistleblowing to Roberts Vanags, as he was the original procurer of the Turaida hard drive. The IDB information you personally obtained—by force—has by-in-large come to light through Agnese Avena anyway. Avena is also claiming she was robbed and assaulted by a Latvian woman who may possibly match your description." Hekla glanced at one of the lawyers. "We believe she's even named you as a suspect. If you admit yourself the source of the International Development Bank documents, it is tantamount to a confession. You may face prison time, good intentions aside."

Santa sat forward, elbows on her knees. It still hurt to physically speak, but she forced herself through: "The biggest story of my lifetime and I can't make a public claim to breaking it? I'm a journalist . . ."

"*Were* a journalist," interrupted the American lawyer, "have you not been terminated from the *Baltic Beacon*?"

While true, Santa did not dignify this with an answer. "I need some recognition, Hekla . . ."

"Your assistance is being acknowledged by the FBI in dismissing the charges against Roberts Vanags. Isn't that enough?"

"No . . . it's not. That'll never pay the bills."

Hekla's expression saddened. "Then we would recommend you procure new work."

"I risked my life for my country, for the truth, and this is how the world repays me . . . unemployment, anonymity!" The muscles in her jaw were cramping again. Santa put her head in her hands trying to take it all in. So much for doing the right thing . . .

Hekla sighed, looked at the men. "Gentlemen, would you excuse us?"

When the lawyers had shuffled out, Hekla came around her desk, kneeled on her haunches in front of Santa. Gently, raised Santa's head up.

"How about you work for OWP? For me? We could use a few traditional journalists on our team. Especially ones as fearless as you . . ."

Santa stifled tears. Such rollercoaster emotions . . . She smiled. "What's the assignment?"

"Get everything you can on Roberts Vanags. The world wants to know about him." She grinned. "Just don't rob him, okay? No knives . . ."

Santa brightened, took the older woman's hand.

"With pleasure, Hekla."

67

The driver honked and swore as the Mercedes-Benz forced its way through the crowd clogging the streets of Rīga's Old Town. In the car's backseat, MP Dāvids Osis remained attentive to the situation, if not quite alarmed. It was chaos outside the car's walls. Not the sort of anarchy that Moscow had wanted, not one of defeat, of a crumbling society that would accept Russian intervention as rescue and relief, one willing to swap independence for stability. Instead, the prevailing sentiment was outrage, resistance, and anger at those the populace felt had swindled them. A dicey situation. A lesser man might have been intimidated by the enraged faces at the car windows, the fists pounding at the glass. But his oratory would sway them, as it always had. Osis knew himself a master speaker. Hadn't he always moved the populace to calm when needed? Hadn't he done so on the Day of Barricades all those years ago?

He would do so again. Accept the people's pain, absorb it, and turn it to his own ends. In a perverse way he looked forward to the challenge. If an amateur like Hekla Stefánsdóttir could move the world, well, Osis knew he could certainly regain sway over his own kind.

Their car had finally reached the corner where Turaida Bank's offices stood. Here the mob's density thickened, and despite the fearsome curses of Osis's driver, they could proceed no further. Not without running someone down. And Osis wasn't quite ready to do that. Not yet.

It was a terrible scene, and even Osis felt the first tremors of fear in the pit of his stomach. After the Turaida computers were seized by the authorities under the direction of the European Central Bank it all went down. The ECB immediately revoked Turaida's banking license, and all depositor accounts were frozen, as were the correspondent accounts at other banks worldwide.

Nobody, criminal or innocent, could get a penny out of this disgraced national institution while the ECB and world authorities tracked down the missing funds. Those loyal to Osis within the Latvian government ran for cover, and the ECB's watchmen were making it impossible for his party to cover it up. Heads would roll next election.

But Osis was a hero . . . His reputation unassailable.

With the car unable to advance, Osis would not stand idly by. He forced his door open, slipped out to stand among the mob. Their shouts and violent animation increased when they saw him, the swelling crowd surged forward.

Osis remained steadfast. His words would carry him through. They always had.

"People. Citizens. This is not the answer. Rage will not return your money to you." He raised a hand solemnly in the air, as if his words were an oath sworn before them. "Have faith in your government. It is only a matter of time until your accounts are opened. I am working tirelessly on your behalf. All of yours, all of Latvia's . . ."

The crowd surged closer. His driver exited the Mercedes, hand on his holster, worry on his face.

"No, Fricis. I have this . . ." said Osis confidently. He radiated assurance, raised his voice to its most magnificent, beguiling cadences.

"For nearly three decades, friends, you have entrusted me to steer you through difficult times. From leaving the Soviet Union to privatization and joining the European Union, I have dedicated my life—"

"Liar! He's a thief!" shouted one in the crowd. "A thief for Moscow!"

"Those are untrue allegations, my friend. Allegations that ultimately will be—"

"You'd enslave us again. To fatten your wallet," said another, closer to the limo.

A tin can, thrown by some anonymous agitator among the people, hit Osis flatly in the face. Though the can was empty, and did no physical damage to the old man, it robbed him of his invincible demeanor, triggered something primitive and ugly inside the crowd. They rushed forward, hands grabbing at Osis and his driver.

Fricis was overwhelmed in an instant, dragged down into a sea of bodies before he could unholster his pistol.

"Let him go!" shouted Osis. But no one paused. They came for *him* now, his people. Osis turned and fled, forcing his way out of the congested street before his most aggressive pursuers had fully subjugated the screaming, bleeding driver. For a moment, he gained distance from the crowd.

Ahead was freedom.

The street before Osis let out into the open space of Cathedral Square, the spot where he'd stood against the Russian tanks three decades ago, where the world had first seen what Dāvids Osis could do, what he meant to the Latvian people.

It promised a new kind of freedom for him now. Freedom to maneuver, freedom to be seen by the police and the cameras of the world that were all now turned on Latvia . . .

But Osis was an old man, slow afoot. Despite adrenaline pulsing through his body, his limbs grew weak after only a few steps. And the mob remained relentless. Tidal. Savage.

He could not outrun them. Osis turned to speak, but found himself out of breath, unable to summon a single atom from his aged lungs. For the first time in his public life, Dāvids Osis stood speechless.

They caught him there, the former national hero, overcome on the plaza where he'd made his reputation so long ago. Pulled down before the cameras of the world . . .

A fitting bookend to his career.

68

Bob Vanags lay on his bed in the second story suite at the U.S. embassy, dreaming of his release. A few more days Simms had promised. Only one more hearing to clear things with the Latvian authorities. The records seized on Kārlis Pagrabs's computers, coupled with the evidence from those falsified fingerprints, had exonerated Bob of every crime. The Latvian government, desperate to atone for the sins of Dāvids Osis and their decades-long tolerance of the "KGB Bank", had been startlingly cooperative. They'd little choice if Latvia wanted to stay in the EU and the world banking system.

He'd be free. Back in Chicago within days. A week at most.

The only problem is Simms had recommended absolute silence with the outside world until the process was done. Nothing could be leaked or said that might embarrass the Latvians further. Prudence meant no emails, calls, anything until that last hearing.

David, his head free of bandages, came in from their small common room.

"Dad, there's someone at the window. On the road outside."

"There's always someone at the window these days." Reporters, supporters, protestors . . . "You'd think at this hour they'd go home. I told them I've a gag order from the FBI."

David smiled, something knowing in the grin.

"You'll want to see her, Dad."

"Her?"

David nodded.

Puzzled, Bob pulled his sore body from the bed, followed his son out to the main room and to the window overlooking *Samnera Velsa iela*. Outside the embassy gates stood a short-haired Santa Ezeriņa, a large cardboard sign in her gloved hands. On it was written:

ROBERTS,
COME TO THE WINDOW!

He laughed. *Well, well. Am I glad to see her . . .*

"Hey, Santa! Don't you people have a curfew in this city? This is a government building, you know . . ."

She held up another sign.

MEET IN CHICAGO?
YOU BRING WINE, I BRING CIGARETTES!

David nudged his father. "It sounds like a date, doesn't it?"

"I . . . I think she only wants an interview?"

"With wine?"

"Alcohol relaxes the conversation, David."

Santa flipped over the sign.

YOU TALK NOW!
I TALK WHEN JAW HEALS
NO KNIVES (I PROMISE)

"'No knives?' What can—"

"Dad . . . sounds like you'll be seeing a lot of her."

Bob smiled and despite his age, he felt himself flushing. "Just her job, David . . . And you know . . . our last two relationships didn't work out so well here . . ."

His son's reply was almost parental in tone. "Third's a charm, Dad. I'll dig up some cardboard, so you can answer properly for God's sake . . . You're hopeless . . ."

Yes, thought Bob. *When will I learn?*

He sighed. Smiled.

Good to be alive . . .

EPILOGUE

Frankfurt

In a plush office, on the top level of the International Development Bank headquarters, Louis Stembridge sat and rubbed his temple. He craved alcohol but dared not impair his senses. He might miss something . . . footsteps in the hall, a bomb beneath his Porsche, the old friendly face who'd come to assassinate him.

He'd won, for now, even as everything crumbled around him. Louis was a capable shifter of blame. He prided himself on his Machiavellian skills, his cunning and survival instincts that threw the scandal on his underlings, especially the naïve Agnese Avena. He'd sidestepped the scandal, made it appear the crimes, the connections to Moscow were all hers. Proclaimed that she'd gotten cold feet when the scheme grew too large, told her Russian masters she wanted out, and when they tried to kill her, falsified documents to support her failed plea deal. It would never hold to even short-term scrutiny but did succeed in delaying the investigation a few days. For the moment, he managed to retain the IDB presidency. Something of a miracle given that so many here were being taken down by the financial watchdogs of the world. Play dumb, share the outrage, ax anyone the authorities looked twice at.

But he could hold his position forever, he knew that. The "buyback" agreement with the Latvian government had been deemed illegal. IDB had lost the entire billion it'd spent to purchase Turaida shares. And that was just the tip of the iceberg. Very little of the twenty billion dollars leant to Turaida was going to come back. The stolen money was nearly all found thanks to what Vanags and Avena showed the world, and more specifically, the records the late Kārlis Pagrabs failed to destroy during his last stand atop Turaida Bank headquarters in Rīga. The government guarantees from Ukraine, Lithuania, Estonia, and Moldova were all voided. A move that allowed those governments to survive, prevented economic collapse and invasion, but meant the IDB had lost tens of billions on his watch. Billions that came ultimately from the support of the U.S. and EU taxpayers. And those great powers were frothing at the mouth for his head.

Stembridge's presidency would not survive. The clock was ticking.

He only hoped he'd literally survive.

A fifty-fifty chance, he thought. The Scorpion was punishing so many others. More important cogs than Stembridge were turning up dead.

He thought of suicide. Stembridge pulled his Luger from the desk, made sure it was loaded. Did he have the nerve? To stick this under his jaw and pull the trigger? It was the only way to ensure little suffering in death. The agents of the Kremlin would have far more painful ways of ending his life.

The cellphone he kept locked in the bottom drawer of his desk began to sound. He'd set the ringtone as *Back in the USSR* long ago for self-amusing irony. Now, that familiar tune sent chills up his spine, seemed all too appropriate.

He unlocked the drawer. Pulled out the phone.

It was Moscow.

Time to pay the Piper. He clicked it on.

"Hello."

The familiar, electronically altered voice said:

"Greetings, Louis. How do you spend your day?"

He tried to sound calm yet failed. . . . "I was reading about the unfortunate death of Leonid Vovk. Ukrainian militants are so rare in the Kharkov region . . . It seems we aren't safe anywhere."

"You've maintained your bank presidency, Louis. To this point. Do you know why?"

"Because of your assistance?"

"Because you are important to *us*. To those even I answer to. We have taken steps to ensure you'll be spared criminal prosecution, though you will have to step down, of course. The costs will be withdrawn from your Arabian accounts. I believe there won't be a penny left when all is said and done."

Anything, anything. "I'm grateful, Scorpion."

"Gratitude isn't required. What we need is action before your resignation. Put down the Luger and find a pen."

He set the gun on the desktop. His hands still shaking, Louis seized a bronze fountain pen, scrambled to withdraw a notepad from his drawer.

The voice did not wait. It waited for no one. Never again.

"Please take careful notes, Louis. Whom to buy, whom to kill. The West has won only a reprieve. We start the long road back today . . ."

Four months later . . .
New York, New York

Agnese Avena sat in a stuffy late Spring office, dressed in unstylish maternity garb, and surrounded by lawyers, and representatives of the INS and FBI, including Jonathan Simms.

She did not wish to be here. But she had no choice. It was her last day as "Agnese Avena." She'd be given a new identity, a new life, and U.S. passport that expired in 2024 with possibility of renewal if she continued to cooperate with authorities. Foreign nationals, especially those who testified against the Russian mob here and abroad, were not unknown in the Witness Security Program. That her testimony went beyond the mob to political entities in six countries made her a special case. The ECB, the CIA, and others often *used* Agnese for their purposes . . .

But still WITSEC called the shots.

"You will be living in Tonopah, Nevada," said an FBI man Agnese did not know.

"Nevada? Isn't that desert? I'm not used to desert. My skin will burn . . ."

"It's nice," assured Simms. "Been there myself."

"You have no choice," said the first FBI man, and he set the contract down in front of her. She'd already read it, been over it with native-speaker attorneys to make sure she understood every nuance of American legal language.

She thought of the fate of Ēriks and so many others. Agnese picked up a pen, noticed the contract was thicker than the one she'd reviewed.

They'd added an addendum. A list of names she was expressly forbidden to contact else breach of contract.

She scanned the list, pages after pages. So many names from childhood to adulthood, professional, personal, political. All alphabetized by surname, the final page ending in "Roberts Vanags."

Agnese felt the baby kick.

She signed.

And "Agnese Avena" was no more.

ABOUT THE AUTHORS

WILLIAM BURTON MCCORMICK is a Shamus, Derringer, and Claymore awards finalist whose fiction appears in *Ellery Queen's Mystery Magazine*, *Alfred Hitchcock's Mystery Magazine*, *The Saturday Evening Post*, and elsewhere. He is a graduate of Brown University, earned an MA in Novel Writing from the University of Manchester, and was elected a Hawthornden Writing Fellow in Scotland. His historical novel of the Baltic Republics, *Lenin's Harem*, was the first work of fiction added to the permanent library at the Latvian War Museum in Rīga. He is the author of the suspense novella *A Stranger from the Storm*. A native of Nevada, William lived more than a decade in Latvia, Estonia and Ukraine, the key settings of *KGB Banker*.

JOHN CHRISTMAS is a former banker whose banking career ended when his whistleblowing against his employer was covered up by the European Bank for Reconstruction and Development. He earned a BA at Dartmouth College and an MBA at Cornell University. He has lived in the United States, Latvia, Spain, United Kingdom, and Malta. He wrote the dystopian novel *Democracy Society* which was released in 2011. Now he enjoys time reading, writing, and boating in Europe. His experiences as a whistleblower inspired *KGB Banker*.

CPSIA information can be obtained
at www.ICGtesting.com
Printed in the USA
BVHW040308290623
666504BV00001B/5